PRAISE FOR THE ROMA NOVA SERIES

INCEPTIO
"Brilliantly plotted original story, grippingly told and cleverly combining the historical with the futuristic. It's a real edge-of-the-seat read, genuinely hard to put down." – Sue Cook

CARINA
"This is a fabulous thriller that cracks along at a great pace and just doesn't let up from start to finish." – Discovering Diamonds Reviews

PERFIDITAS
"Alison Morton has built a fascinating, exotic world! Carina's a bright, sassy detective with a winning dry sense of humour. The plot is pretty snappy too!" – Simon Scarrow

SUCCESSIO
"I thoroughly enjoyed this classy thriller, the third in Morton's epic series set in Roma Nova." – Caroline Sanderson in The Bookseller

AURELIA
"AURELIA explores a 1960s that is at once familiar and utterly different – a brilliant page turner that will keep you gripped from first page to last. Highly recommended." – Russell Whitfield

INSURRECTIO
"INSURRECTIO – a taut, fast-paced thriller. I enjoyed it enormously. Rome, guns and rebellion. Darkly gripping stuff." – Conn Iggulden

RETALIO
"RETALIO is a terrific concept engendering passion, love and loyalty. I actually cheered aloud." – J J Marsh

ROMA NOVA EXTRA
"One of the reasons I am enthralled with the Roma Nova series is the concept of the whole thing." – Helen Hollick, Vine Voice

THE ROMA NOVA THRILLERS

The Carina Mitela adventures
INCEPTIO
CARINA (novella)
PERFIDITAS
SUCCESSIO

The Aurelia Mitela adventures
AURELIA
NEXUS (novella)
INSURRECTIO
RETALIO

ROMA NOVA EXTRA (Short stories)

ABOUT THE AUTHOR

A 'Roman nut' since age 11, Alison Morton has clambered over much of Roman Europe; she continues to be fascinated by that complex, powerful and value driven civilisation.

Armed with an MA in history, six years' military service and a love of thrillers, she explores via her Roma Nova novels the 'what if' idea of a modern Roman society run by strong women.

Alison lives in France with her husband, cultivates a Roman herb garden and drinks wine.

Find out more at alison-morton.com, follow her on Twitter @alison_morton and Facebook (AlisonMortonAuthor)

·INSURRECTIO·

ALISON MORTON

PULCHERIA
PRESS

Published in 2018 by Pulcheria Press
Copyright © 2018 by Alison Morton
All rights reserved Tous droits réservés

This is a work of fiction. Names, characters, places, incidents are either products of the author's imagination or used fictitiously. Any resemblance to actual events, locales or persons living or dead is entirely coincidental.

ISBN 9791097310127

DRAMATIS PERSONAE

Mitela family
Aurelia Mitela – Government minister and imperial councillor
Marina Mitela – Aurelia's daughter
Miklós Farkas – Aurelia's companion

Mitela Household
Milo – Comptroller/steward of Domus Mitelarum
Callixtus – Head of security

Tella family
Domitia Tella – Head of the Tella family
Caius Tellus – Domitia's great-nephew
Quintus Tellus – Domitia's great-nephew, brother of Caius
Constantia Tella – Domitia's granddaughter
Conradus Tellus – Constantia's young son with Richard Berger
Richard Berger – Constantia's companion

Military
Volusenia – Colonel, Praetorian Guard Special Forces
Fabia – Major, PGSF
Numerus – Ex-senior centurion, PGSF
Pia Calavia – Lieutenant, PGSF
Atrius – Guard, PGSF

Palace
Severina Apulia – Imperatrix
Silvia Apulia – Severina's daughter
Julianus Apulius – 'Julian', Severina's son
Fabianus Apulius (ex Mitelus) – Severina's husband, father of Silvia and Julian
Drusilla – Housekeeper

Government
Tertullius Plico – Senior imperial secretary, External Security Affairs
Claudia Cornelia – Aurelia's assistant
Quirinia – Budget minister and Aurelia's friend

Castra Lucilla (Mitela home farm)
Priscilla – Farm manager
Gavinus – Technical manager
Sentia – Farmworker
Albina – Farmworker

Other
William Brown – EUS defence electronics contractor
Senator Calavia – Pia's grandmother
Paula Atria – Atrius's sister
Phobius – Caius Tellus's henchman

PART I

AURELIA

1

———

Early 1980s Roma Nova

'Anything else, Claudia?'

At my office in the Foreign Ministry, I'd just finished a briefing meeting for our new *nuncia* appointed to head up the Roma Nova legation in Louisiane. She'd returned the previous day from an intensive refresher course in New World French. Her success as political officer in Québec three years ago made her ideal for this promotion. I'd handed her the letters patent to present to the *gouverneur général*, wished her luck and shaken her hand. Claudia Cornelia, my assistant, escorted her out while I took a few moments. It was past seven-thirty and thank the gods, my last meeting. I'd flown back from Berlin early this morning; now I had a headache and wanted to go home.

Claudia diverted to the side table and poured me a glass of water. Shorter than me, a graceful figure in a navy suit, her serious dark brown eyes and tightly drawn back hair gave her an air of maturity. She was only twenty-one but she'd achieved two promotions since starting with the foreign service at eighteen. And now she was an assistant minister's assistant.

'Nothing scheduled, *consiliaria*, but Tertullius Plico is waiting in the side room.'

I'd only seen Plico four days ago for our regular fortnightly briefing. What could he want so urgently that he'd come to see me at this time of night?

I swallowed some water to relieve my parched throat. The only things disrupting the surface at the moment were minor trade disputes, diplomatic mumblings which were more about hurt feelings and ego than anything else, and the failed attempt by an overseas corporation to bribe one of my ministerial colleagues. All were relatively low-key and being handled by more junior functionaries; none fell within the remit of the intelligence service.

On my nod, Claudia opened the door to usher Plico in. His plain face had fleshed out in the thirteen years since I'd first met him; jowls now disguised what had been an angular jawline. His hair was greyer, but it emphasised his deep brown eyes. I knew how he worked from when he'd been my supervisor. I might have shot up the promotion scale to assistant foreign minister, and he might now be a senior secretary, but he remained the same crafty bastard running foreign intelligence as he had been all those years ago.

'Assistant Minister.' He held out his hand as he advanced across the room.

'Cut it, Plico, it's just us.' I shook his hand.

'Humph. Well, at least you haven't gone all high and mighty on me like some people.' He sat down without invitation and pulled a folder out of his briefcase – a red one.

Hades.

Red files usually contained a maximum of half a dozen sheets, often only one. Each sheet had a unique log number. The penalty for copying anything from a red file was a minimum of two years' imprisonment.

'I thought long and hard about showing you this,' he said, 'but it does affect you directly. I'll sit here while you read it,' he prompted. Not a sign of any emotion on his face. He crossed his pinstripe-suited legs, unbuttoned his creased suit jacket and waited.

I didn't want to open it, although I'd handled two similar cases over the past five years. It always meant deep trouble. But Plico wouldn't have brought it to me without cause, so I took a long breath, and flipped open the cover.

Two sheets of double-spaced typescript on the right-hand side and a photocopied form in Germanic were held at the top left corner by a stationery tag with a page at the left containing a scrawled note with yesterday's date. Unusual that it had been originated on a Sunday. More unusual that it was signed 'Severina Apulia Imperatrix'. I was cleared to red level, so that wasn't the problem. I froze when I read the name typed above the first line.

Just over twenty minutes later, I set the file back on the table and breathed out. The three sheets of paper, so pristine with the neat black typing, looked innocent but the memory of my desperate escape from being terminated that evening thirteen years ago in Berlin slammed into my mind. Even now I could recall the pain shooting through my bleeding and broken foot as I hobbled away, attempting to run from two killers. I smelt the stale prison air again, the despair of the courtroom where I was being framed for murder and the fear of losing my daughter's childhood. A sour taste rose up through my throat; it was all because of the man whose name was on this file. I swallowed hard.

'See what I mean?' Plico interrupted.

'I thought the Prussians weren't due to let Caius Tellus out of prison for another two years,' I said, pulling my wits out of my emotions. 'But according to this file he's out in two weeks. Why?'

'Apparently, he's been a model prisoner.'

'He would be.' I snorted. 'I never understood why the sentence wasn't longer. Here, he'd be in Truscium for twenty-five years – if he survived that long.'

'Bit too soft, the Prussians,' Plico said. 'They're into rehabilitation and re-education up there. They say Caius is quite the reformed character; their psychologist reports conclude he's genuinely contrite about killing Grosschenk and trying to frame you for it. He's followed several educational and self-development courses.'

'But?'

'This stinks. In my bones, I know he's a danger, but we have nothing here to put him away for – not even his part in the silver smuggling.'

'Why can't you arrest him for that?'

'We'll detain him, of course. He's being deported from Prussia, so that's automatic. The *accusatrix*'s department is not optimistic. There's a strong case that he's already served his sentence for it. After all, the Prussian sentence for smuggling ran alongside the murder one.'

'Surely that doesn't count here?'

'No, not strictly, but he'll get some fancy lawyer to plead it out.'

'Give me strength. You know something? We need some serious legal reform in this country.' I flicked over to the second page. My fingers trembled, but it was anger now. 'I accept the threat to me and my daughter is real. In a funny way, I'm pleased to have it recognised officially. But what can we do about it?'

'That sharp lawyer, Galba, who defended you in Berlin, wrote a full report after the trial.' A few flakes of dandruff were liberated as he scratched the top of his head. 'She grumbled when I went to see her in her plush office the other day. I asked her to update the report. She gave me all kinds of reasons why she hadn't got time – she's such a big cheese in her law firm now – but she filed it a day before my deadline. Anyway, she recommends maximum protection to you and your property.' He lowered his eyes. 'I'll talk to the Praetorian Guard legate and the local *vigiles* chief, but I can't promise anything. I think the Praetorians will be better – they always look after their own.'

I wasn't sure of that. I was forty-three and I'd left the Guard when I was twenty-nine. Times had changed.

Caius Tellus, safely contained for twelve years in a Prussian prison, was about to be set loose again. I'd never forget how he'd threatened to corrupt my daughter. Nor that he caused me to miscarry my second child. Caius had undermined me constantly when we were children, tried to rape me when I was sixteen, and nearly succeeded in having me falsely imprisoned for murder in Prussia. I would never stop loathing him – we had too much history between us – but when I'd fought and defeated him in Berlin, I thought I'd overcome my fear of him. So why were my nerves jumping around? I stood and walked over to the coffee maker. Plico shook his head when I raised an empty mug in his direction. As the machine bubbled away, neither of us spoke.

'Look, Plico,' I said as I came back to my desk with a steaming mug, 'I'm always driven about in a radio car and escorted everywhere on official business. This building is secure. We'll take additional precautions at the house,' I smoothed my skirt as I settled back behind my desk. 'Marina has her companion with her and is always chauffeured.' My daughter hadn't shown any interest in learning to drive herself – a blessing. 'And Miklós is there with us – he'd need only the slimmest excuse to beat the living daylights out of Caius. Or go further.' I picked up my silver fountain pen and twisted it between my fingers. 'When Caius sees trying to touch us is too difficult, he'll think again,' I lied to both of us.

'Are you being naive or just stupid?'

'Neither, just objective.'

'I know you have good security, but Caius Tellus is not an idiot. He got into your house twice when he was on the run. And not being rude, your companion tends to take off every now and again. I've seen the intelligence reports on him.'

'Are you tracking Miklós?'

'Not actively, but his name comes up now and again.'

'Well, keep your nose out.'

'Miklós Farkas has done nothing wrong as far as we're concerned. As a Hungarian national, he has no obligations to Roma Nova and we have none to him. As far as I know, he's broken none of our trading laws with his activities, so we're not interested. However, the Prussians still want to talk to him about a few things.' He glanced at me. 'I've told them he's off limits.'

'Thank you so much.' I tried to keep the sarcasm out of my voice. Plico knew I would use every *solidus* I possessed and every drop of influence I could squeeze out from anybody to protect Miklós. We'd been lovers – no, heart and soul companions – since I'd been on that mission in Berlin, but Miklós was a free spirit and became restless after a few months in one place. It pulled us both to pieces when he felt compelled to go wandering again, but he always came back to me.

'Going back to Caius,' I said. 'Perhaps he *did* reform in prison.' I hoped I didn't sound desperate.

Plico replied with a very rude word.

A hard, dark silence hung between us. Plico was right, Jupiter blast him. I knew in my heart that Caius would be satisfied with nothing but my death and Marina's destruction. He'd sworn to do it when I'd visited him in the maximum security prison in Prussia following his conviction. I trembled for my daughter, but I would not let him or his presence in Roma Nova pollute or constrain our lives.

'Very well,' I said. 'Putting aside the threat to my family, I recommend he should not be allowed near the imperatrix or her family. Not just her children but also her cousins to at least the first degree. Nor must he attend any of the Twelve Families events.'

'Do you have the ability to stop him? Since old Countess Tella's sister died, he's the next heir after Constantia Tella.'

'I wouldn't be the least bit worried if it was Quintus,' I said.

Caius's younger brother, now a senator and deputy city prefect at only thirty-seven, was his complete opposite. How they were children of the same mother baffled me. After serving in one of the better legions, Quintus had rocketed up the administrative and political career path – the *cursus honorum*.

'Well, having a murderous half-brother in a Prussian prison doesn't seem to have put a brake on his progress so far.' Plico shrugged. 'Quintus Tellus is reckoned to be a possible for chief secretary one day.'

'Perhaps, but he's running in the election for one of the deputy praetorships next year. Ambitious, surely, but he told me he'd be home and dry before Caius got out.'

'He's stuffed, then.'

'Juno, that's so unfair.'

Plico shrugged. 'You need to judge how much you take to your minister, if anything. After all, monitoring Caius is really the interior minister's problem. But if you want my two *solidi*'s worth, it would be fortunate if Caius Tellus suffered a fatal accident before he got back here.'

2

'I'll do it.' Miklós shrugged. 'That way, none of you Roma Novans will have the moral dilemma and Caius Tellus will no longer exist as a problem.' It was nearly midnight as we sat in the easy chairs in the atrium. He put his glass, empty of brandy, back on the low table and glanced up at me. 'And you'll be able to sleep at night. You were tossing and turning in bed last night as if witches were chasing round in your head.'

'I can't let you do it, Miklós. It's murder. We'd be as bad as him.'

'*Let* me?' He raised an eyebrow and his eyes glinted.

'You know I didn't mean it like that.' I put my hand out and rested it on his shoulder, my fingers just touching the black curls at his shirt collar. He still wore his hair long like an unruly teenager's even though he was thirty-seven, but now fashion had caught up with him. He took my hand and pressed it to his lips. A warm flow passed down my arm. His eyes lost the sharp look and brightened as he kept hold of my hand.

'I know, *drágám*.'

'Let's forget Caius,' I said. 'We have better things to do tonight than wasting our time worrying about him. And I've been away for three days.'

He laughed – a rich, sexy sound that I'd first heard on a freezing mountain top when I'd been chasing smugglers on our border. It had stayed imprinted in my memory ever since. I stood, holding my hand out, inviting him. But he didn't follow.

He leant forward on the sofa, his whole frame tense. He became completely still, uncannily so. His eyes narrowed, almost closed, and the skin stretched over his face as he stuck his chin out. It reminded me of a rapacious hunting bird, reflecting something stretching back to his Hun ancestors.

'I will be watching him,' he said, looking straight ahead. 'The first step he takes towards you or Marina, whatever you say, he will be a dead man.'

I waited airside behind the smoked glass of the service vehicle as the Prussian aircraft landed at Portus Airport. Two green-uniformed Royal Prussian Police officers escorted Caius Tellus down the steps. He ambled across the tarmac with his escorts as if he were on a Sunday afternoon stroll. Two of our *vigiles* were waiting for him. He held out his handcuffed hands and raised one eyebrow, obviously expecting them to remove the restraints, but they ignored him. One *vigilis* grabbed him by the upper arm and pulled him to the waiting truck. They shoved him in the back and slammed the doors.

They held him for the statutory twenty-eight days. I sat in the court hearing when the public *accusatrix* led the state's case against Caius for silver smuggling. An old law giving automatic protection against double-jeopardy stood in the way of a conviction. Without glancing at Caius, I gave my evidence and repelled questions from his shifty lawyer. But even Galba's detailed report citing every possible precedent and circumstance didn't secure our case. As Plico predicted, Caius was acquitted. As I listened to the judgement, a wave of anger rolled through me. The law, the damned outmoded law.

I filed a private action for his assault on me here in Roma Nova thirteen years earlier. He'd stolen a small boat from the main river and rowed up the tributary that ran along the far edge of the home park behind my house. I'd been jogging in the park, safe on my own land, I'd thought, but he'd attacked and badly injured me. He'd beaten me so badly I'd miscarried my child and finished any hopes I had of carrying another. I sat on the hard bench in the draughty civil court with iron in my heart listening to his lawyer pleading it out.

My lawyer argued that *audiatur et altera pars*, that the other side
had to be heard on an equal basis, couldn't apply in this case. Caius
had been incarcerated in Prussia so I hadn't been able to summon him
into open court to face the charge. Fluent and experienced, my lawyer
used every drop of his oratorical talent to push the extenuating
circumstances argument, but I knew it was hopeless; there was no
such thing as a court hearing *in absentia* in Roma Novan law. The
magistrate looked down at me with a sympathetic expression, but
ruled in a dry voice that it was outside the ten-year statute of
limitations for assault; I was out of time by two years. Despite the
statements by my retired steward, Milo, and my ex-comrade-in-arms,
Numerus, who had been instrumental in sending Caius back to
Prussia to face trial, the case was dismissed.

Nor could it be linked to the public case against Caius that had
failed. As I listened to the judge cite an eighteenth-century law
dismissing my right to private redress of a public case, I resolved to
bring a proposal to the imperial council to cut the automatic tie
between public and private actions – it was ridiculous in the twentieth
century. And when Caius stopped by my bench, tilted his head and
smirked at me, I swore to start drafting it that very evening.

The Praetorians tracked Caius for a couple of months, I was sure as a
favour to me as a former comrade, and then the *vigiles* took over. At
Domus Mitelarum, we doubled the security. Marina was
accompanied everywhere overtly by the assistant steward's daughter,
a sensible girl a year older than Marina in age, but many years
advanced in maturity, and covertly by one of our security team. And
the steward's daughter carried an emergency transmitter. I was taking
no chances.

But the monthly reports forwarded from the *vigiles'* prefect's office
contained nothing. Caius lived quietly at Domus Tellarum, visited the
family villa outside the city for a few days at a time, drank and ate in
city restaurants and went to a few dubious parties and the games.

I'd seen him there once when I'd stood in for Severina. As
imperatrix she should have opened the big games, but she shirked it.
It wasn't as if they were still the old killing-fests; now it was a mix of
sports with weapons demonstrations plus, of course, the touristy

chariot race at the end. Caius had looked up at the imperial box and bowed to me in an exaggerated way; to mock me, I was sure.

Otherwise, he kept below the *vigiles'* radar; he didn't even get a parking fine. Miklós followed him sometimes through the less attractive parts of the city nightlife and asked his trading contacts in the city to report any news of Caius.

One morning, I found Miklós dozing on the sofa in the atrium, still wearing the casual suit and shirt he'd gone out in the evening before. His upturned loafers had been deposited at the side. His face was tight, his lips straight, slightly turned down at each end; he was almost frowning. My heart clenched. I'd seen that look many times before in the past twelve years. I couldn't bear to wake him and hear him confirm it.

I was sipping my coffee when he appeared in the dining room an hour later dressed in his leathers. His black curls were still damp which made him look like a cherub who'd been river-bathing. But his expression was far from heavenly as he plonked himself down opposite me and helped himself to bread and cheese. He said nothing until he'd munched his way through two slices and drunk a whole mug of coffee.

'Aurelia, I—'

'Yes?' I interrupted.

'I have to go.'

'I know.' I couldn't stop the tears squeezing out from the corners of my eyes.

'I haven't found out a single thing about Caius. I've followed him nearly every night this last month. It'd be rash to say he's given up, but I think you're safe.' He glanced at me. 'I know you don't need me to protect you with all your Praetorians and security, but my scouts will tell me if anything looks out of the ordinary.' He stood up. 'It's so stifling here,' he said looking past me at the wall. 'It's not the city and you know it's not you. I need to stretch myself, somewhere I can ride for days, weeks, not hours. And I have some business to conduct.'

I knew the almost deserted high alp in the west of Roma Nova wasn't wide enough for somebody born on the Magyar Plains. Nor was the regulated city a place he could thrive indefinitely. But I felt sick and empty.

In the courtyard, he grabbed me around the waist and almost

crushed me. He nuzzled my neck. His curls brushed the skin on my face. I gasped at the tingle that raced through me. He whispered in my ear. 'You know I will never stop loving you, my heart and soul.'

'Don't go. Please,' I whispered back.

'It's only for a few weeks.'

I shook my head.

He stared at me, bent and kissed my lips almost chastely, then turned and climbed on his new Bayerischer motorbike. He revved the engine and roared out of the gate. I watched the blue and silver vanish to a speck before I went back inside and threw myself on the bed. He'd be back, but I kept him by letting him go.

Miklós returned one afternoon five weeks later; laughing, his skin tanned and eyes full of love. His 'business' had turned out well, he said. He never explained exactly what he did and I never asked. But he had connections in informal trading throughout Europe. The following morning, his hand stroking mine, he said none of his people had seen or heard anything suspicious about Caius. It was only when Marina and I went for a social visit to Imperatrix Severina three weeks later that I heard news of him.

Strange, but in my head, the word 'imperatrix' always conjured up her mother, Justina Apulia, a strong ruler who had passed into the shades not long after I became an assistant minister. Her daughter, Severina, was hesitant rather than decisive, often taking the last person's advice instead of the best. I tried to make sure I was that last person. Justina had grasped my hand as she lay dying and commanded, then begged, me to guide Severina to do the right thing for Roma Nova. Her chief secretary had handed me the appointment of *consiliaria in perpetuum* signed with a shaky hand by Justina shortly before she took her last breath. It was a duty I accepted, and dreaded.

Severina Apulia had a habit of looking to anybody else but me; she resented, firstly, that Justina had foisted me on her and secondly, that I sometimes called on the privilege of being the head of the senior of the Twelve Families to sway her decision. Gritting my teeth, I stood back when the issue wasn't important, but sometimes I had to intervene to stop Severina making a serious error of judgement. The gods knew I hated doing that, but once she nearly repealed the land redistribution law in an imperial council meeting after the head of the agricultural chamber had lobbied her hard. I almost broke into a sweat thinking of it again. That memory retreated as her husband approached us. Severina had married one of my cousins in the junior branch, Fabianus Mitelus, now Apulius, and it was he who greeted Marina and me.

'Aurelia, come in and hear the latest gossip.'

I admired him for his patient and steadfast loyalty to Severina. She would have driven me spare within a week. They had two delightful children in Silvia, just fourteen, and eighteen-year-old Julian, about to join the legion. Personally, I thought it was because of Fabianus's steady nature and devotion to them that the children were as balanced and well-educated as they were.

Severina gave me a brief nod and Marina a full smile. Silvia, a little solemn, exchanged kisses with Marina. I clasped arms with Julian in the military way. He flushed, but smiled in a proud way as he drew himself up straight. Being the imperatrix's son in the military would be an advantage in one way, but not in so many others; the least little failure would be thrown in his face. But he was fit, intelligent and willing to learn. I was confident he would weather it. And if he were inclined, I would welcome him as a son-in-law. I pushed that away. He and Marina were far too young. But still…

'Tea, or something stronger, Aurelia?'

Fabianus's voice penetrated my daydreaming. He held a tumbler lined with ice, rivulets of amber liquid percolating through to the thick base, and smiled at me, understanding.

'A glass of white wine would be perfect, thanks.'

I listened to my light-minded daughter chatter with our light-minded ruler about fashion, films and gossip. I had never been interested and when they laughed at some in-joke, I felt awkward and excluded. They would have been a better mother and daughter combination. In contrast, Severina's daughter, Silvia, stood quietly with her brother and me, and watched the two of them. I gave her a sympathetic look, which she returned.

'Did you hear the latest, Aurelia?' Severina raised her head as she spoke and half twisted round in her seat to face me. 'About Caius Tellus?' Her eyes gleamed.

I tensed, my glass halfway to my lips. Julian had been telling me about how the legion had worked him hard during his cadet assessment week. I was commiserating, but laughing, with him until I heard that name. Severina had all my attention now.

'He's only gone and married Constantia Tella. Quite the whirlwind romance, I gather.' She almost, but not quite, smirked.

'What?' I stared at Severina.

'Oh, didn't you know? How unlike you, dear Aurelia. I thought you knew everything.'

Constantia Tella was a bright woman, a professor at the Central University and the fearsome Domitia Tella's granddaughter and heir. She'd met Richard Berger halfway up a mountain in New Austria when she was on a walking holiday. Three weeks later, they were installed in a charming house off the Cardo Max and a baby boy appeared nine months afterwards. They hadn't married; they didn't need to. Under Roma Novan law all the children belonged to their mother whether or not the parents contracted formally. Perhaps Richard Berger wanted to maintain his independence.

'What in Hades is Constantia doing dumping her handsome Austrian for a piece of shit like Caius?' The words were out of my mouth before my brain could stop them.

Severina winced.

'Richard Berger is all very well but he's a foreigner,' she said. 'Caius might have had problems in the past, but at least he's a Roman.'

I couldn't believe she'd said something so xenophobic. I hoped my mouth wasn't gaping. Most Roma Novans had overseas relatives or ancestors, including her. Everybody else stopped speaking and stared at her. A pink flush crept up her neck into her face.

'But they're inseparable,' I said. People had joked behind Constantia and Richard's backs about how they couldn't keep their hands off each other even after more than six years together.

'Evidently not,' Severina retorted.

'But they have little Conradus,' I said. 'Richard dotes on him.' I'd seen them at a Families' children's day, two bleach blond heads together, Richard chuckling as he made the boy giggle, and chasing each other; other times the man carrying the child on his shoulders, both laughing and singing.

Now Constantia had married another man in the traditional way, she would keep the child in her household and Richard would be condemned to occasional access visits. And Caius would ensure they were as difficult as possible.

'Well, it's up to them,' Severina said, huffily.

'Did you know they were going to marry?' I shot at her.

'No.' She looked down and picked at her skirt. 'And don't glare at me like that, Aurelia. As they were contracting within their own family, they didn't need to tell me,' she added in a resentful tone. 'But I think it's a bit much, not inviting me. I shall be quite cross when I see either of them next. But it all sounds so romantic. And little Conradus will have a proper Roman father. Maybe Caius can persuade Constantia to change the boy's name to a proper Roman name as well.'

I closed my eyes for a second. I opened them and glanced at Fabianus who shook his head. That poor child, having Caius Tellus as stepfather. Worse, much worse, was that by marrying Constantia, Caius had taken a significant step nearer heading the richest family in Roma Nova. Old Countess Tella was still with us but if Constantia and Caius had a daughter, he'd be the father of the next Tella family heir.

3

Richard Berger spent the following few months trying to make Constantia see reason. The Tella family lawyer served him an eviction notice from the couple's former house – at Caius's instruction, I'd bet – so I invited him to stay with us. He was distraught, poor man; he'd lost his love, his child and his home. As head of the Twelve Families, I intervened twice on his behalf but the third time, Caius threw me out of Domus Tellarum. Constantia had stood at his side, smiling and supporting her new husband. Without a complaint from her, I could do nothing.

Eventually, Richard gave up and left Roma Nova to return to New Austria. When I dropped him off at the interrail station, he still seemed dazed, unable to speak beyond 'yes' and 'no'. He wouldn't or couldn't give me a forwarding address. A week after his departure, I flew to Vienna on official business and added some private time to my trip to try to find him.

I swept into the VIP arrivals lounge at Wien-Maria-Theresia Airport, my gold-eagle-monogrammed briefcase in hand and foreign ministry assistant in tow but stopped in my tracks when I saw the tall, slim figure of Miklós waving at me from the other side of the roped barrier. He'd gone to a horse fair in Bavaria and wasn't due back yet. How had he known I'd be on this flight? The purple-suited Praetorian who met us looked Miklós up and down, her eyes measuring him up for any possible threat to me. He returned her stare second for second.

I'd given up trying to explain to him how they felt it their duty to protect me at all times.

I was caught up in official dinners and meetings until the Thursday, but reassuring the protection detail that Miklós was sufficient escort, I started my search for Richard Berger early that morning. I had to find him; he'd been in such distress.

Despite our traipsing from housing offices to hostels, searching bars, dragging through public records and pressuring the local police, we found no trace of Richard. Even Miklós's connections in the informal trading networks, which I shut my mind to, couldn't locate him. Before I left, I bent the rules and instructed the Vienna legation to carry on looking for Richard. Livilla Vara, the *nuncia* I'd appointed two years ago, sniffed and said that as he wasn't a Roma Novan citizen, she wasn't obliged to. I let my temper out and suggested she consider her position now and in her future professional career. She sniffed again, but grudgingly agreed.

A year later, it was one of Miklós's contacts who discovered Richard had been found in a doss house in Graz and had died an alcoholic.

Now, a year after Richard's death, Constantia herself followed him into the shades. The medical certificate stated the cause was pneumonia, but I suspected the main cause of her death was living with Caius and the heartache of being deceived by a brief infatuation and losing her true love.

Listening to Caius give the *laudatio* to the crowd in the forum for her funeral, I was nearly sick. He dressed it up, vowing to honour the deep love and esteem he would hold for his beloved wife until the day he died – the hypocrite. Severina seemed genuinely moved at Caius's performance as we sat together on the rostra in the front row behind him and the lectern.

'Poor man. So tragic,' she said, dabbing a fine lawn square at her eyes. 'And not even a child left to console him.'

'For goodness' sake, Severina, he's faking it,' I whispered in a stagey voice hoping Caius would hear. His broad shoulders tensed. Good. I would have hated there to have been any misunderstanding.

'How can you be so harsh?' Severina whispered back, her eyes round and horrified.

'Because I know him. Believe me, he's taking the opportunity to work the crowd.'

'Nonsense!' She turned her shoulder to me.

I was several metres away from Caius and sitting with other Twelve Families' heads; the Praetorians surrounded us, Severina's husband, Fabianus, was behind me and the imperatrix next to me, but I still felt threatened being so near to Caius. I shivered and pulled the fold of my woollen *palla* into my neck. Not just at Severina's inability to see past the surface of everything; the fresh spring breeze was blowing straight across the vast open space. Thank Juno, there was no child from the marriage. I wouldn't trust Caius within a hundred metres of one. As for Constantia's little boy, Conradus, although he looked tall and strong for a six year old, how safe would he be now with Caius? I'd never been certain Caius hadn't touched Marina during that time I was away when my mother was alive. Severina had queried Marina's absence today as my heir, but I'd invented a bad head cold for her, allowing her to stay safe at home.

I glanced over at Quintus Tellus. On his right, old Countess Tella looked blankly in front of her; on his left, Conradus clung on to Quintus for dear life. The child's blond head was bowed, and his shoulders spasmed as he sobbed. Quintus had his arm round the boy, but was watching Caius with an intensity I'd never seen before. I knew the brothers didn't get on, but I'd never seen such a hard look on Quintus's face.

Several hours later at the burning ground, the priest sprinkled water and wine to douse the last embers of Constantia's pyre. Caius turned to the trembling Conradus, still clinging on to Quintus's hand.

'Come, boy. Home,' Caius beckoned imperiously. The child shrank against Quintus.

'Caius, leave him with me for at least a few days,' Quintus said. 'Can't you see he's beside himself?'

'All the better to be in his home.'

'There is nobody there to care for him. Great-Aunt Domitia is an invalid who can't even look after herself.'

Caius raised an eyebrow. 'My house is full of caring women.'

Quintus flushed with anger. 'Your whores, you mean.'

'Language, brother, and in front of the child. I couldn't possibly think of consigning the boy to you if you use such words.' His eyes both mocked and challenged his brother.

Quintus curled his hands into fists, tensed his arms and drew his right arm up. I thought he was going to smash the sneer off Caius's face, but he became aware of people watching. Severina put her hand on Quintus's forearm.

'Now, Quintus, let's not quarrel, especially today. I'm sure Caius will look after the dear little boy.' She almost simpered at Caius, who smiled at her and tilted his head in a minimal bow.

'*Domina*, I—'

'Now hush, Quintus, let them go home.'

I stepped forward. 'I'll take Conradus into my household until his care is clarified. I'll call a meeting of the Twelve Families Council and we can settle the whole matter there.'

'There really is no need, my dear Aurelia,' Caius said. He studied my face for a few moments, making me feel uncomfortable by the intensity in his strange greeny-brown eyes. Whatever the Germanic prison psychologist had said, I saw no softening. His lips formed into a wide smile. What was coming next? 'Constantia named me as the child's guardian. He will come with me.'

Quintus took a step towards Caius, but before he could say anything, a slight, brown-haired figure stepped in between them.

Silvia took Conradus's other hand and looked squarely at Caius. 'I'm inviting Conradus to stay at the palace with Mama and me. He knows us and I can look after him until the Twelve Families have met.'

'Good gracious, Silvia, come back here this instant.' Severina reached out, grasped Silvia's arm then pushed her towards Fabianus. 'Don't interfere in adult business.'

'Imperatrix, your daughter may have the solution.' I glanced at Silvia. Her face was tight and her eyes glistened, but she stood confident for a fifteen-year-old and looked steadily at her mother's face. Fabianus rested his hands on his daughter's shoulders as if protecting her from the adult squabbling.

'Don't be silly, Aurelia,' Severina said, 'she's just a pert child interfering in something she knows nothing about.'

'No, she's nearly of age and she's—'

'I've had enough of this nonsense,' Caius snapped. 'Keep your nose out, Aurelia. I have the right and there's nothing you or anybody else can do about it.' Caius gave Severina the most minimal bow I had seen that day and wrenched Conradus away from Quintus. The child struggled in Caius's grip, but the bastard yanked him to his side, causing the boy to yelp in pain and throw a desperate look at Quintus. Caius turned in the direction of the gate of the burning ground, tugging the boy behind him. Conradus glanced back, his hand imprisoned and tears shining on his face.

'You can't defy the Twelve Families code,' I called after him but he strode on. I hitched up the excess material of my formal *stola* in my left hand and went to run after them, but Severina gripped my other arm. Her fingers were surprisingly strong.

'No, Aurelia. Stay where you are.' Severina beckoned with her other hand. A hard-faced centurion and another Praetorian stepped forward, blocking my path to the car park.

'But, *domina*,' I said, 'you can't let that, that piece of—'

'Leave him alone. He's entitled.'

'We don't know that. We only have his word. That's not worth the breath he took to say it. But it's clear – the child's care is openly disputed and that's a matter for the Twelve Families.'

She glared at me. 'You're just prejudiced. Do as I tell you, for once.'

'*Domina*, I'm duty-bound to protect Conradus. You must know that. He's a child of the Families and that's our responsibility.'

In the car park, Caius had reached his car and wrenched open the back door and pushed the child in. I prised Severina's fingers off my arm and hitched up my *stola* ready to go after Caius, but before I could take the first step, she nodded and the two Praetorians seized my arms.

'Get your hands off me, you oafs,' I shouted in their faces. 'How dare you lay your hands on the head of the Twelve Families!' They released me as if they were touching a scorching pillar of flame.

Quintus and I ran towards the car park, but we were too late. Quintus swore softly and obscenely. I let out words of anger and frustration that would have made a centurion blush as we watched Caius drive away, the grit skittering up from his car tyres.

Back at the palace, Quintus and I followed Severina in silence across the smooth marble floor of the magnificent colonnaded atrium.

Despite the low temperature, my anger hadn't cooled one degree. At the back, down some steps, we passed into a narrower, much older stone hallway with several doors off. Severina nodded to the Praetorian standing at the oak door set back in an archway at the far end and led us into her private drawing room.

She ordered the guard who had accompanied us to remain outside with the other guard, but within call. Ridiculous really, as the stone walls were a metre thick and the massive oak door hundreds of years old; they wouldn't hear a thing from outside. Inside, Severina paused by the sofa and fiddled with the fabric covering the top, but didn't invite us to sit. Fabianus, Quintus and I waited.

'Your behaviour at the funeral was inexcusable, Aurelia.' Her voice was brittle and she glanced at me. Fabianus stepped forward but she waved him away. I didn't say anything; there was no point and I was too angry. 'Well?' she continued. 'Have you nothing to say, cousin?' She glared at me.

I took a deep breath to steady my nerves and recruit my patience.

'Imperatrix, I was merely offering the protection of my household to a small child in distress, the subject of a family dispute. I will convene the Families Council to settle the matter.'

'You tried to interfere with the *pro tem* Tella heir and a child from that house over whom he has full jurisdiction.'

Jupiter save us. I exchanged a glance with Quintus, who kept a neutral face like the good civil servant he was.

'If we are citing legalities,' I said, 'then you may well remember that as head of the Twelve Families, not only am I perfectly entitled to intervene where there is a conflict, it is my duty.' I tried, I sincerely tried, to keep the sarcasm out of my voice. 'Or perhaps you are not familiar with one of the most basic of our founding laws?'

Quintus gasped. I kept my eyes on Severina's face. She flinched, strode towards me and raised her hand.

'I wouldn't, Severina,' I said. 'Really, I wouldn't.' I stood my ground, unmoving, and stared at her. My heart beat faster. She was so unpredictable, she might do it. I braced myself for the blow.

Her skin reddened. The next instant, her lower lip trembled. She dropped her hand. Fabianus moved to her side, darted an angry glance at me. Severina's face crumpled. She burst into tears and allowed Fabianus to draw her down onto the sofa. He put his arm round her and hugged her to him.

I stayed where I was. For once, I wasn't going to give in to her emotional blackmail. She used this learned helplessness to muddle through awkward situations, getting others to solve problems and sort out messes for her. If only she'd been more diligent, learned at least the rudiments of governing from shadowing her mother. If only she could see beyond the surface of things. If only she had a gram of political common sense. Normally, I'd go to her, comfort her, apologise and say I'd take care of everything. Well, she'd crossed the line in the sand. No more.

Quintus glanced at me, but I shook my head. And waited.

Severina finished sniffling, wiped her nose and looked up at me. 'Well, why don't you say something, Aurelia?'

'For myself, I have nothing to say, but as Mitela whose family has supported Apulia across the centuries and led the Twelve Families in your cause, I have a great deal to say. You know there is no question of the Families wavering in their loyalty. They swore their allegiance to the first Apulius at the river crossing with hands and oaths. Despite war, conquest and death, nothing has changed that. The Families have willingly served to the limit of their abilities, often facing ruin and death to preserve Apulia, and ultimately Roma Nova. But you Apulians, in this case *you*, have to fulfil your side by respecting and accepting our counsel. You have the right to rule, Severina, but the obligation to listen. You do *not* have first right to adjudicate in Families disputes. It is you who acted unlawfully in preventing me from intervening at Constantia's funeral.'

'You… you cannot speak to me like that!'

'I am merely telling you the truth.'

'You quote grand principles, but this is just part of your grudge against Caius.' She looked like a sulky adolescent caught with her fingers in the honeypot instead of a ruler commanding a tough people. Her mother would have given her a first-class dressing-down for being such a simpleton.

'My "grudge", as you call it, with Caius is a personal matter, but we are discussing something much more important – the relationship between ruler and counsellors, something that very few rulers have failed to realise is essential to the survival of Roma Nova. Without the

Families to guide and advise, the ruler could become a tyrant. Without a leader who rises above factions and individual interests, and commands their loyalty, the Families would be ungovernable. You have threatened to destroy that fine balance. Without it, Roma Nova will self-destruct.'

Only the fire crackling interrupted the stone-dead silence that followed.

'What are you going to do?' Severina said in a tremulous voice after a few minutes.

'I shall request Caius to come to the Families Council and discuss his situation with the heads of the Twelve Families. We will call witnesses as appropriate.' I looked down at her. 'In the meantime, the Families will withdraw from the imperial council and all government functions to consider this development. I will, of course, resign my own ministerial position, effective immediately.'

'You don't think you were rather harsh on her?' Quintus asked as we walked across the palace atrium to the vestibule. A servant placed my formal cloak around my shoulders and I smiled my thanks. When she was out of earshot, I glanced around the vast cavern. Rebuilt in the 1500s in the style of that time, the atrium had plenty of alcoves and recessed seating where others could loiter and listen.

'Look, Severina's had a free ride on our backs for years. She can't hold a thought for more than a minute and when she does, she becomes pig-headed about it. Justina was always worried about her daughter's lack of interest in learning to govern which was why she appointed me *in perpetuum.*' I took a deep breath. 'Juno, Severina's a mature woman in her forties, but she acts like an airheaded teenager.' I rubbed my forehead. 'I try my damnedest to keep my personal feelings out of anything to do with Caius, but it seeps in. I'm sorry, Quintus, you know it's nothing to do with you or the other Tellae.'

'Gods, I'm behind you all the way on this, Aurelia. I'm very concerned about Constantia's son.' He looked up at the painted ceiling, then back at me. 'If Caius has hurt Conradus, I'll beat the shit out of him so hard he won't forget it for the rest of his life. In the meantime, let's get this Families meeting organised and force the bastard to release Conradus.'

4

————

I snatched a few hours' sleep and got up at six to draft a personal note to the head of each family explaining the background to the suspension of support. As I lifted the nth cup of coffee to my lips, I realised I didn't want it. My hand trembled as I placed it back on the saucer. The words on the last letter – to Quirinia – were almost exactly the same as the previous ten had been, but I added, *I'm sorry, my friend, to take this measure, and trust you will forgive me if it means you lose your post. It wasn't an easy decision, believe me.* Quirinia was the deputy *quaestor* responsible for the entire government budget and would very likely become the finance minister when the current one retired. Or she would have. Was I destroying everybody's career?

My business manager sat on the far side of the desk in my study as I signed and sealed the paperwork to organise the extraordinary Families Council for two days' time. Normally poker-faced, his expression looked tight this morning as he waited. As I was signing the last one, Milo, my steward, interrupted to say Secretary Plico was on the line and wished to speak to me urgently. I lifted the extension handset.

'I hear you've flounced off and called a strike,' he said.

'Hardly.' I glanced up at my business manager. 'Can you give me a minute, Plico?'

'Sure, all the time in the world to stave off a constitutional crisis.'

'Just hold on.' I laid the handset down on the table.

I wax-sealed the last convocation order. My manager nodded, gathered up the eleven orders, bowed and left. I blew out the flame, laid the wax stick on the little tray and picked up the handset.

'Is this line scrambled?' I asked.

'Of course. Want to let me into the little secret of what's going on?'

'I'm not sure.'

'Oh, come on.'

'No, I don't want to put a strain on your loyalty to the imperium.'

'Come to that, has it?' Plico snorted. 'Surprised it's taken so long.'

'What do you mean?'

'Let's just call it a clash of personalities any fool could see coming for a good year.'

'Juno knows, Plico, I've done my best, but I will not see the Families system of balances change on my watch. A pause for reflection will calm things down. And it's not without precedent.'

'You mean that business in the 1700s?'

'Yes, and significant legal reform came out of that,' I said.

'But only after your great-great-whatever sulked for four months.'

'She didn't, and you know it.'

'That imperatrix was being stubborn beyond reason, just like her current descendant, eh?'

'I didn't say that – you did.'

The line went silent for a few moments.

'So what are you going to do now?' His voice sounded very matter-of-fact.

'I've summoned Caius to a meeting with the Families Council in two days' time.'

'Do you really think he'll turn up?'

'No, but let's hope for the best,' I said. 'It's not only the constitutional position, a child's welfare is at stake.'

Two days later, the heads of the Twelve Families of Roma Nova sat round the oval oak table that Milo's staff had set up in the atrium at Domus Mitelarum. As speaker for the Families, Mitela was charged with convoking the council when required. Of course, we met socially and in our jobs, but this was the formal *caucus*, named after the ancient silver cup in front of me on the table.

In the month after he'd led the four hundred or so north out of Italy in the fourth century, Apulius had set up a council consisting of the heads of each family to discuss problems and propose ideas. Its existence was later written into the Twelve Tables; its influence reached far and deep.

Legend had it that Apulius confided in his friend and fellow senator Mitelus that he'd rather know what the rest of them were plotting and grumbling about than finding it out the hard way. Apulius accepted his election by his fellow exiles as imperator and had led them with courage and fairness through hard times, but scholars considered he would not have succeeded without the solidarity of the Twelve Families firmly behind him. My mother had put it neatly; Mitela was to Apulia as Agrippa was to Augustus in ancient Rome.

Spring had retreated today and light rain fell outside. It was so dull the glazed *oculus* in the roof didn't let enough light in to forego artificial lighting. Even Milo had conceded we needed the heating on again. I sat at the head of the table in my mother's antique carved oak chair and faced my peers. Calavia and Quirinia smiled in a friendly way; Volusenia the Elder, the sister of the Praetorian officer who'd guarded Marina years ago at the palace, nodded; Cornelia, the Senate president, sniffed; the remainder – Livia, Vara, Sella, Aquilia, Branca, Aemelia – merely stared.

One seat was conspicuously empty, but I didn't expect it to be filled. The buzz of conversation died as I took the cup, sipped the wine and passed it on. When everybody had taken some and the *caucus* came back to me, I placed it in front of me again. Sharing wine symbolised sharing counsel and in the past had diminished the risk of serious dispute. Somehow, few wanted to break the ancient code of hospitality.

'I welcome you, Families, and wish you well.'

'I have to say, Aurelia, this move of yours is extremely inconvenient,' Florina Vara's strident voice travelled the length of the table without losing a decibel. She was the mother of Livilla Vara, the Vienna *nuncia*, and no more likeable than her daughter.

'It's uncomfortable for all of us, Vara, so hold your tongue,' Calavia shot back at her. She was one of my grandmother's contemporaries, and at ninety, still fiery.

I glanced at my watch. We had five minutes to go before the official starting time. As an advisory body, we reported direct to the imperatrix and what we said to her was nobody else's affair. No written records, or these days, recordings, were ever made of what the council discussed. Historians reproached us that it made their task difficult when documenting the official history of Roma Nova; their only sources were the notes the family heads had made in their own journals and they were embargoed for a hundred years.

I took a breath to begin when there was a tap on the door. I glanced at Quirinia and passed her the key. Traditionally, we locked ourselves in until all business had been concluded. Private meant private.

Domitia Tella tottered into the room, her hand curled round the top of a silver decorated walking stick. A long dark *palla* wrapped tightly around her figure swamped her. She'd been a formidable orator in the Senate in her time. Now, she was a wisp of her own ghost. Poor soul – she could do without a predator like Caius hanging around her. She waved Quirinia's offered arm away with an abrupt gesture and grasped the back of each chair as she made her way slowly to the empty seat to my left. She sank into the chair and gave me a brusque nod. Her eyes shone, but they were sunken in sockets above cheekbones that stood out under wrinkled skin. Her nose and chin jutted out at harsh angles; she seemed to have lost even more flesh than when I'd seen her at Constantia's funeral. Her hand trembled as she brought the *caucus* to her lips and took a sip.

'Now we are all present,' I began, 'there are two topics to discuss: a Families dispute and a constitutional matter. As they are directly linked, we'll handle them together. Some of you may have heard accounts of the incident at Constantia Tella's funeral.' I bowed my head towards Domitia Tella who frowned. 'Here are the facts.'

After I'd finished my account Vara looked away, Branca, the youngest, studied the table, Cornelia shrugged and Tella's face reflected nothing. The remaining seven stared back at me, disbelieving, stunned or incredulous.

'Although I think you are allowing your, er, differences with Caius Tellus to colour your views, Aurelia, I must back you on this.' Calavia looked at the other family leaders around the table, most of whom nodded in agreement. Her age commanded respect, but so did her long legal career. 'Severina was indeed *ultra vires*. Surely, Justina must have dinned some basics into her? The imperatrix stands away from Families disputes unless it becomes a matter of a criminal act and even then, the courts decide.'

'Well, I think it's a lot of fuss about nothing,' Vara said. 'My daughter has a prestigious post heading the Vienna legation and I won't have any falling out with the imperatrix that will endanger her career.' She screwed her eyes up and stared at me, too vain to wear her spectacles.

'You may remember, Vara,' I replied, in my driest voice, 'that I was the assistant foreign minister who had the confidence to appoint her.'

'Exactly! I won't—'

'She's a state servant, Vara. Unless she steals a bag of imperial gold or starts a war, her position is secure and unaffected by our dispute.' I looked around. 'Anybody else?'

'How long will this withdrawal last, Aurelia?' Cornelia asked. She looked down her nose at Vara. 'I'm not asking for personal reasons, just so I can make a formal statement in the Senate.'

'I think it would be safest to say "for a short period", if you feel you have to make an announcement at this point.'

'Of course I do. Proper procedure is very important.'

I cursed Cornelia silently, and her stiff neck.

'Very well,' I continued. 'Now, the child, Conradus Tellus. With his mother dead, his natural and legal carer would be his nearest female relative.' I glanced at Domitia Tella, who had closed her eyes. 'However, as Countess Tella is in poor health, I suggest the child would be better fostered with one of the other Families which has children of a similar age.' I smiled at Branca whose children were five, eight and twelve.

'What does Quintus Tellus say? He's very fond of the child,' Calavia said.

'He's in the anteroom. Let's have him in.' I nodded at Quirinia to open the door.

Elegant and restrained in his light grey suit, Quintus bowed to the heads of families, keeping a solemn expression on his face. He bent and kissed his great-aunt's cheek and rested his hand on her shoulder. She brought hers up to cover it. He smiled back, but didn't say anything.

'Please sit, Quintus.' I stood and pulled a spare dining chair from the side of the room. 'Now outline your concerns for us.'

He fidgeted for a moment, and looked down at the table. When he looked up, his face was set.

'I had a speech prepared full of fine words and logic, but instead I'm going to be brutally honest.'

A chair creaked as somebody shifted, but all eyes were on him.

'I despise my brother for his lack of morality, his hypocrisy and unprincipled and selfish attitudes. More than that, he cares absolutely nothing for the welfare of Roma Nova, its institutions or its people.'

'Don't hold back, Quintus,' Vara snorted.

'Shut up, Vara,' said Calavia. 'Carry on, young Tellus.' She nodded at Quintus.

'He made Constantia's life a misery. She turned from a confident academic into a cowed semi-servant.' He looked around the room. 'The death certificate may state pneumonia as the cause, but I have no doubt at all that it was living with my brother.'

'We don't know the ins and outs of the marriage. He had a bad time in Prussia – in prison for all those years,' said Vara. 'Perhaps that made him harder than he would have been.' She glared in my direction.

I was about to remind her exactly why he had served thirteen years in a Germanic prison but Quintus was faster.

'Florina Vara, my brother murdered a Prussian citizen, smuggled silver, tried to murder Aurelia Mitela and conspired to frame her for that Prussian's murder. He got what he deserved. In my opinion, he is extremely lucky not to have been charged with illegal silver trading here, but all the Roma Nova transactions were found to be legal.' He rubbed the back of his hand with the palm of the other. 'Going back to the case of my nephew, Conradus—'

'Actually, he's your second cousin, Quintus, if truth be told,' Cornelia interrupted.

'I regard him as my nephew and always have,' Quintus shot back so ferociously that Cornelia recoiled. 'Constantia was like a sister to me when I was growing up in Domus Tellarum before I went to live with my father. And I stood as supporter when Conradus was formally named as a baby. Caius terrifies Conradus, mocking him as a foreigner for his light colouring, his hair, and humiliating him whenever he can. I've seen bruises on the boy more than once. And that was while Constantia was alive and could protect him. Mostly. You all saw at the funeral how scared the child was of Caius. I tremble for his safety if he stays with Caius.' He sighed. 'I think Caius wants to hold on to the child just to show he controls him. He doesn't see him as a human being, but as a source of power. I would love Conradus to come and live with my father and me – we'd help him to recover from the shock of losing both his parents. He's a sensitive child and I fear for him. However, if the Families consider he should be fostered with other children, then I will acquiesce.' He struck the table with the flat of his hand. 'Anything to keep him out of Caius's reach.'

I went to touch his hand in empathy, but he'd turned to Domitia Tella and put his arm around her shoulder. She looked up at him, moisture in her eyes. He smiled at her.

'Well,' I said, 'as Caius Tellus hasn't deigned to present himself to us this afternoon to pursue the matter of young Conradus Tellus's custody,' I continued. 'I propose we—'

Heavy pounding at the door. Who was knocking as if it was the exit from Tartarus? Domitia Tella wheezed and broke into a fit of coughing. Quintus's figure stiffened. Of course, it could be only one person. As the noise continued, I signalled Branca to fetch some water for Tella. Her hand, barely more than skin-covered bones, shook as she raised it to her lips.

I nodded to Quirinia. She unlocked the door and Caius Tellus strode in, brushing against her, causing her to take an involuntary step backwards. He wore a shirt, no tie, casual jacket and slacks. He stopped a few paces into the atrium, took in the thirteen of us and gave a half smile, half sneer. He sauntered along the table nodding at each of the family heads as if he was their superior. He reached his great-aunt's chair and placed his hand on her shoulder. She flinched.

The bastard.

'What a cosy gathering you have here, Aurelia. Is it time for tea?' He looked around. 'Aren't you going to invite me to sit?'

'No.'

He shrugged and folded his arms. The scars running down in white lines from under his nose, through his lips and to the edge of his chin stood out prominently, much more so than at Constantia's funeral. Was he anxious about this appearance today? He looked down at me, his eyes hard as agates, but a tight smile pasted on his uneven lips. Every time I looked at his face, I remembered fighting him for my daughter's life. I had no regret for ruining his film star looks before sending him back north to prison.

'Well? What do you want me here for, Aurelia? I have other, more important things to do than this.' He tipped his head slightly and made a big show of studying his watch.

'As you know perfectly well from the summons served on you, Caius, we're deciding on the custody of Constantia Tella's child. Under the rules when there is a dispute, the Families Council or, if necessary, the Families Court decides. Quintus Tellus disputes your claim to custody. As the child prefers his company and Quintus and his father offer a stable family environment, we are inclined to grant his claim. The alternative, if there is an equal vote for and against, is to foster him with a family where there are other young children in the household.'

'All very elegant and no doubt you've gossiped with the others here to stitch up the decision, but you've forgotten one vital fact.'

'Really? And what is that?'

'Constantia's testament naming me the child's guardian.' He threw two ribbon-bound sheets down onto the table in front of me. 'It's legal and binding. No argument.'

I studied it. The date was a week before Constantia had died.

'Quintus, is this Constantia's signature?'

He picked up the stiff papers as if they carried the plague. He read the document through, then returned it to me and nodded. He looked as if he was going to be sick. Caius smirked at his brother.

'I would like Cornelia's view on this testament's validity,' I said.

She studied it for a full five minutes, flipping back from one page to another. The rain was hammering down on the glazed centre of the roof directly above me as if Jupiter himself was trying to burst through. I longed to get up and walk over to the French windows to break the tension. Eventually, Cornelia looked up.

'It's legal.' She looked up at Caius. 'Has it been read to the family?' Until it was read aloud to the assembly of the Tella family it wasn't proven.

'The lawyer has been trying to assemble them, but they won't answer the summons,' Caius replied, and kicked Quintus's chair.

'I haven't had any call or letter from the lawyer.' Quintus turned round to face Caius. 'When did he send out the summons?'

Caius waved his hand. 'I don't waste my time checking every letter my employees dispatch.'

Quintus leapt up. 'He's not your employee – he's Aunt Domitia's. Don't even try to read the testament without her present. Or me.'

'Do calm down, brother,' Caius said, 'or these ladies will think you're hysterical.'

Quintus clenched his fists and I thought he was going to hit Caius.

'Enough,' I shouted. 'Sit down, Quintus. Caius, if you say one more provocative word, I'll sanction you. One thousand *solidi*, and don't think I won't enforce it.'

He narrowed his eyes and sent me a look of pure hate. After a moment he shrugged.

'Cornelia, give us the legal position, please.'

'Normally, we would decide the child's status as he is an orphan and his head of house is in frail health with no female responsible adult to care for him. However, Constantia's testament is very specifically worded and even cites a legal precedent. Whoever drew this document up knows their law. The Families could attempt to contest it, but it would be a difficult litigation.'

Caius looked triumphant and thrust his hand out for the document.

'However,' she continued, not conceding it and giving Caius a cool look, 'there is provision under the fiduciary regulations where a minor child inherits from a dead mother for supervision by the Families of that child's welfare and inheritance. I propose we stipulate a supervisory order in this case and nominate Quintus Tellus to execute it.'

Juno, she was a clever woman. Caius looked as furious as Pluto himself. He slammed his hands down on the table, leaned forward and thrust his face in Cornelia's.

'Don't be ridiculous, woman. You're making it up,' he bellowed.

'Not at all. It's all set out in the Families Code, Table Seven. Would you like me to send you a copy?' she asked in a pseudo-agreeable tone.

'Don't think I'll forget this, Cornelia.'

'The law is the law, Caius Tellus, and you are as subject to it as the imperatrix or the poorest labourer.'

'Give me the testament.' He curved his fingers and flexed them, beckoning imperiously.

'No, I will take a copy and attach the supervisory order to it when I return it to you,' Cornelia said. 'Don't worry. I'll take good care of it.'

Caius spun round and jabbed a finger at me.

'This is your fault, you and this crowd of witches.'

'I believe it is time you left, Caius,' I said in a neutral voice. 'Thank you for your attendance.' Quirinia jumped up and opened the door. At that moment a clap of thunder exploded outside. Caius shot a last angry look at Quintus and stormed out.

5

———

'Juno Moneta, Caius *is* a nasty piece of work!' Quirinia said and took a gulp of water. She'd stayed on after the council had broken up. Her hand trembled as she placed the glass back on the table. 'I've never quite taken on board what you said about him, Aurelia.' She looked down at the empty glass. 'I know there was that business in Prussia and the attack on you here at home. But that was years and years ago. Being honest, I wondered if you'd been exaggerating about him in the pre-meeting briefing. I always think back to that business at Aquilia's party—'

'Yes, well,' I interrupted. 'Let's not go over all that again.' Even as I said it, a warm flush spread through me at the memory. Then it had been shame; now it was anger. That was when my childish unease and desire not to be near Caius had turned to loathing and real fear. We were at Aquilia's emancipation party, all of us a bit tight and the dance music turned up to blast level.

I was outside, grabbing some breaths of air – it was stifling in there and my toes were bruised from some idiot treading on them. I rested my forearms on the terrace balustrade and watched nothing in particular in the formal garden of box hedges, gravel paths and tall cypresses stretching out into the darkness.

An arm round my waist and lips on the back of my neck.

I spun round, but he gripped harder. In one swift movement, he dragged me up against the house wall and grabbed my breast. My head thudded against the hard sandstone and for a second, everything swam in front of me. Then I felt his hand up between my legs. I twisted, trying to pull away and batted his face with my hands.

'Don't struggle, Aurelia. You know you want it.'

Caius. How bloody dared he? I managed to push his hand away from my chest, but he laid his forearm across my throat and grinned. My heart thumped with fright.

As he leant in with his smirking mouth, something red seemed to burst in my head. Mars gave me strength and I brought my knee up hard into his groin. His face crumpled with pain and as he doubled over, I smacked him in the eye with my fist. Listening to him groaning and swearing like a centurion, I slumped against the wall, dragging breath into my lungs and trying to stop shuddering. It was stupid but I closed my eyes to block out what had just happened.

Gods, I must get up or he'll try again.

'Aurelia? Are you out here? Come on, they're drawing the prize.' Quirinia's voice. 'Hey, are you all right?'

I opened my eyes and just caught sight of Caius stumbling away and a couple of his cronies laughing at him. Blast him to Tartarus.

'Yes, just catching my breath. Thanks.'

Even in the poor light, I saw her pitying smile.

'One too many, eh? Have you thrown up?'

'For Juno's sake, Quirinia,' I snapped back. 'I just wanted some air.'

'Yeah, right.'

'I'm fine. Let's go in.'

I couldn't bring myself to tell her – I wasn't quite sixteen and too embarrassed. I wanted to forget it. Not in an eon would I tell my mother, but the memory of Caius pinning me against the wall, his hand shoving up between my legs and touching me had made me feel sick for days. When Quirinia came round to see me the following week, I'd burst into tears and sobbed it all out to her. She'd said I should report him, but I knew it was useless. It was always my word against his and he'd wriggle out of it as he always did with his charm and convincing tongue.

I shook off the fear and mortification that had swamped my teenaged self as Quirinia's anxious voice dragged me back into the present.

'He *will* be able to contain Caius, won't he, though? Quintus, I mean. He'll have Cornelia's supervision order.'

'Don't hold your breath.'

'So how did it go?'

'Come off it, Plico, I can't tell you that.' I was in the *tablinum*, my office, which unlike ancient times had a door which I went and closed. I picked up the extension handset again. 'The Families discussion is entirely private and the council maintains its withdrawal from public life.'

'Oh, that's very helpful.' His sarcastic tone cut through. 'How in Hades are we supposed to run a country with half its ministers missing?'

'You're always telling me the imperial secretariat could manage very well without the patricians. Now's your chance to prove it.'

'What will it take to get you back?'

'Gods on Olympus! Are you offering terms already?' I said. 'I thought you'd hold out a lot longer.'

Silence.

'Plico?'

'I'm still here. I'm trying to work out how to get across to you what a dangerous thing you're doing. Just for some tiff over a kid.'

'No, it wasn't that and you know it. Severina was in the wrong. She was the one who—'

'Yes, I know. I have a recording of the whole thing.'

My turn to be shocked into silence.

'Tell me, Plico,' I said after a minute, 'do you spy on the imperatrix *all* the time?

'Of course not. Only when some potential threat like that bastard Caius Tellus is likely to be in her vicinity.'

I didn't know whether to be pleased or outraged. I took a sip of the brandy I'd brought into the office with me. 'How is she?'

'Lost.'

Severina had never worked without the circle of the Families to support her, poor woman. She'd been my friend when we were younger, but she'd never grown up. She relied on others to rescue her.

I'd sworn to her mother to stay with her and guide her. Was I failing in that now?

'Look, Plico, all she has to do is acknowledge that she overstepped her position in respect to the Families and everything will slot back into place. She'll have her support circle again and we'll fall over ourselves to help her.'

'I rather think she's expecting your apology,' he said in his driest voice.

'You're joking.'

'Unfortunately not.'

'I can't believe she can't see what she's done.'

'No, she doesn't grasp it at all.'

'Well, until somebody explains it to her letter by letter, she can go and suck a lemon.'

Three days later, Plico burst into my house and slammed three tabloids down on my desk. His face looked like Jupiter's on a bad afternoon.

'I know, I saw it on the wire service,' I replied. The headlines screamed, '*Twelve Versus One*' and '*Historic Breach Wrecks Government*'. I pulled the thickest one out from the bottom and groaned. The *Sol Populi* was running with '*The Fall of Roma Nova*'. Gods.

'One of your crew has blabbed,' Plico accused.

'Very unlikely. Some sharp-witted journalist could have noticed the absence of several family heads from government and worked it out for themselves. I wonder if anybody has been helping them along?'

'Never mind that. The imperatrix is flapping like a goose and has cancelled the Senate session for this afternoon. The palace comptroller has a whole team fending off the press and the Praetorians have already chucked one reporter in the cooler for climbing over the palace gates.' He frowned. 'And there's a crowd gathering in the forum, a few hundred and growing. They're waving placards, mostly about jobs.'

With the increase in unemployment sparked by companies going through a spurt of modernising it was hardly surprising. Of course, nobody demonstrated in support of increased benefits and free retraining financed by the state. Why anybody *wanted* to toil in old industrial jobs in hot, noisy factories, I'd never know. But it was fear of change, fear of the unknown, something we had to spend more time and budget on. I'd make sure it went at the top of the agenda for the next imperial council meeting. If we had a next meeting.

'There's the odd placard with "Where's Severina" in amongst them,' Plico said.

'Well, she hasn't appeared in public for weeks,' I replied. I knew she didn't like crowds and wondered if she was frightened of them, but it was her job.

The *vigiles* say they've got it under control,' Plico continued, 'but—'

'How did all those people get there so quickly?'

'At this precise moment, I don't really care – we need to stamp on this.'

'How did you get out?'

He shuffled his feet and glanced at the closed door.

'It's safe here, Plico. No flapping ears.'

'Well, in times of stress and danger—'

'You used the tunnels,' I said flatly.

'You know about them?' His jaw didn't quite drop open.

'Oh, do come on! Of course the Mitelae know.' I glared at him. 'Something to do with Mitelus and Apulius being inseparable friends?'

The tunnels connected the palace, Senate and various strategic points like the Praetorian barracks. The first ones had been hacked out of the solid rock under the hill on which the castle and then the palace stood following the nearly fatal siege of Roma Nova in the fifth century. Gradually developed through the ages, they now included some unremarkable exit points which acted as safe houses, bought discreetly by the government. Apart from a very few sworn to secrecy, most people thought they were derelict and abandoned. My mother had told me about them just after my twentieth birthday.

Things must be serious if Plico didn't feel confident to have come openly by car. Or perhaps he didn't want to confirm any kind of wild rumour circulating out there by looking if he were acting as go-between. He wandered over to the bookcase, grabbed a book in the middle of the top shelf and flipped it open. He frowned at it, without looking at it properly. After a few moments, he snapped the book shut and jammed it back into the bookcase upside down. He opened his mouth to speak, but I held my hand up.

'Very well,' I said, 'I'll go to the palace now. I'll gather some of the others on the way. We'll walk out together onto the balcony, all smiles for the people and the press. And then we'll start the straight talking.'

Severina flopped down into the chair and smiled nervously at the rest of us. I nodded to Branca to help Calavia to an armchair; the older woman was tough in her mind, but standing out on the balcony for half an hour would have been fatiguing. I didn't care if Severina thought it was impolite or not. Quirinia, Branca and I were not invited to sit.

'Well, Aurelia, I suppose I have to thank you for coming to support me. You seem to have remembered your duty.' In that moment, I glimpsed something of her mother, Justina, in her. At last. Perhaps this experience had been a turning point for Severina. A little truculence from her would be a small thing to put up with, if she'd learnt to become confident and decisive enough to provide Roma Nova with true leadership.

'The Families have never forgotten their duty to Roma Nova, Imperatrix. It was with the deepest regret that we withdrew for consultation.'

'Consultation? You ran off and left me with nobody to look after me,' she shrieked, her face becoming blotchy and red. 'What in Hades do you think you were doing? I should throw you all in the Transulium.'

Quirinia gasped, but I ignored her. Calavia stared at Severina as if she were a child having a tantrum. The room stewards were trying their best not to look interested; the Praetorians by the door resembled marble statues, but they hadn't suddenly become deaf.

'I think that would not be a wise step, Imperatrix,' I said. 'And it would be *ultra vires*.'

'You think you can bully me because of that commission my mother gave you.'

'Not at all. I and the others are your and Roma Nova's loyal servants.' I lowered my voice to try to calm her. 'If we could talk privately amongst the five of us, I think we should be able to resolve any differences.'

She screwed her mouth up, but gave a brief nod. The senior steward clicked her fingers at the other two and withdrew, taking the Praetorians in her wake. I glanced at Quirinia and Branca who fetched chairs and positioned them so we were in an arc around Severina.

'Imperatrix – no, Severina – I am going to talk very straight. My peers will be witnesses and contribute as necessary.' She shot me a resentful look, but I continued. 'The matter of the child Conradus Tellus's welfare has now been settled where it should be – in the Twelve Families Council. That is a closed matter. I am more disturbed that the news of the difference between the Families and yourself has appeared so quickly and in such detail in the public domain. This interferes with the delicate balance mechanism instituted by the founders. However, if we agree tonight and resolve it, then there is nothing further to be talked about.'

'Diplomatic words, Aurelia,' Calavia said, 'but the fault lies squarely with Severina.' She turned to the imperatrix. 'I sponsored you at your emancipation when you were sixteen and promised your mother to care for your welfare, but you've acted like a prize idiot.'

I winced at Calavia's words. Severina's eyes bulged and she shrank back into her chair as if Calavia had struck her in the face. The older woman took Severina's hand and gave it a little shake.

'My dear, you treated Aurelia dishonourably in public and you owe her an equally public apology.' Calavia glanced at me. 'I'm sure she'll forego the public one but you have to understand something. You cannot rule without us and we must be ruled by you. This cuts both ways. You have a duty to respect the responsibilities that belong to the Families and to keep above the disputes and governance between them. Aurelia had no choice but to withdraw when you interfered at Constantia's funeral. Look at it from a practical point of view. Do you really want to become mixed up in hundreds of petty squabbles and grievances, the endless charity committees, children's affairs, organising contracted marriages, negotiating financial settlements between them, the land swaps, and hours of policy committees? The reason the government burden is so light is because of the work the Twelve carry out. Don't jeopardise it.'

•   •   •

The next imperial council meeting was formal in tone, bordering on the chilly in contrast to the early April sunshine piercing the diamond panes of the council chamber windows. Severina glanced at me once just before she delivered a short speech about the guidelines clarifying the relationship between the Twelve Families and the ruler. She nearly choked when she had to say 'apologise'. Nobody moved as she spoke, not even to write a note. Even the secretariat staff were still. She finished, laid the single sheet of paper on the table and stared down at it as if it were the most repulsive text she had ever read. But we'd never in fifteen hundred years had to put into written words how the balance worked. History had been broken.

I spotted a tiny movement to Severina's left. Plico raised one eyebrow. I nodded and he waved his fingers at his senior assistant who started writing as fast as a gods' messenger flew. The soft scrape woke us all from our stasis and we passed on to the agenda proper.

'Will she ever talk to you again?' Quirinia whispered as we shuffled our papers together at the end. I smiled and nodded at the others as they filed out, then turned back to Quirinia. 'I give it two or three days,' I murmured. 'She'll want something and then she'll pick up the phone. Or, more likely, make Plico do it. If she ever does anything like this again, I won't be responsible for my next action.' Quirinia said nothing, but nodded, her expression grave. 'In the meantime,' I continued, 'we'd better get back to our offices. The gods know what's been happening while we've been away.'

Quirinia laughed, in relief, I thought. I was about to make a joke about rusty abacuses, when I felt a light touch on my arm. Silvia, Severina's daughter, stood there, a serious look on her face.

'Aunt Aurelia, may I have a word, if you have a moment?'

'Of course. *Consiliaria* Quirinia will excuse us, I'm sure.' Quirinia said nothing, but shot a questioning look at me. I shook my head, so she waved her hand as a farewell and hurried off.

'Did you find it interesting, your first council meeting?' I asked.

'It all seemed such a muddle at first and everybody spoke quickly about things I'd never heard of. And all that paper!'

Poor child, she was only fifteen; her emancipation wouldn't be until her sixteenth birthday in the summer. But she had to learn. We didn't want a second ruler who knew nothing about the business of government.

'Mama was very embarrassed. I was so sorry for her. I wanted to hug her.' She looked away for a few moments. 'But I suppose she *was* wrong, wasn't she?'

Her brown eyes pleaded for me to contradict her.

'I'm sorry, Silvia, but yes, she was. You were at Constantia's funeral. You saw what happened.'

She looked so dejected that I placed my hand on her shoulder and pressed it. She looked up and searched my face.

'I don't ever want to be humiliated like that so I'd better make sure I never make a mistake like that.' She pinched her dress skirt between her fingers and twisted the material. Her face was a picture of misery and doubt.

'Darling, you don't have to worry about that for many years, decades even,' I said. 'Your mother's only just into her forties. You'll have plenty of time to learn the ropes.'

'Perhaps.' She released her skirt, patted the crumpled material smooth and drew herself up. 'I'm going to see Mama now. She'll need me.' Dignity had replaced misery, but as she walked off, her shoulders drooped and by the time she reached the other end of the council room, she was trudging as if she were carrying the world like Atlas himself.

PART II
MARINA

6

───────

Four months later, late July

'Mama! Where are you, Mama?'

Marina's high voice pierced my concentration. I closed my eyes, drawing my thumb and forefinger across my eyelids to meet at the bridge of my nose. So much for working at home this morning. I swivelled my office chair round and smiled brightly at the figure of my nineteen-year-old daughter scampering through the *tablinum* door. Still too thin for my liking, she *had* outgrown many of her health problems, but was still childlike in so many ways. And I feared for her.

'I've met someone,' she said, her voice and breath catching up with her. 'Will you invite him here?' Her cheeks flushed almost scarlet in the pale shiny face, making her look like a wax doll from Cathay.

'Slow down, child,' I said and pulled her over to sit on the sofa with me. Her fine hair was dishevelled, falling forward over her face, and her summer tunic was twisted at the waist.

'He's here on business. He's an electronics engineer. He has his own business. He—'

'Marina.' I squeezed her hands. 'Swallow. Collect your thoughts and start at the beginning.'

She made a moue, but paused long enough to take a few breaths.

'He's from the Eastern United States, New Hampshire, and is

called William Brown. Mama, he's tall and gentle and safe and so kind. And I love him.' She looked straight at me, her face set. I was taken aback at how her expression mirrored my late mother's when she was in her most domineering mood.

'Of course, he can come here,' I said. 'Shall we say tomorrow, for lunch? Miklós will be here as well, so Mr Brown can meet both of us.'

She flung her arms around me, nestling her head into my collarbone. 'Oh thank you, thank you.'

I stroked her hair, held her close and smiled down at her. After a few moments, she jumped up and sprinted off, giving me a second's wave of her delicate hand. I waited five minutes then reached out for the handset on my desk, set it to scramble and dialled. After some clicks and beeps, a gruff voice answered.

'Plico.'

'Mitela here. Tertullius, could you run a check for me? Personal, so charge it back.' I gave him the details and added, 'And I need it by eleven tomorrow morning.'

Claudia Cornelia coughed.

I looked up, straight into the late afternoon sunlight. And my stomach rumbled. All I'd had to eat was a quick sandwich as soon as I'd reached my desk at the Foreign Ministry just after midday. I'd forgotten how late it was. Poor Claudia must have been itching to get home.

'Tertullius Plico is waiting in the side room, *consiliaria*.'

I glanced at my desk clock. He'd got back to me in under six hours. That meant he had a full file on this Brown, or nothing.

After Claudia ushered him in, Plico studied the dark wood panelling that lined the walls until she closed the door behind her. Odd, she was cleared almost to my level, and I was now the foreign minister.

'What have you got for me?'

'Before I answer that, why do you want to know about Brown?'

'It's personal,' I stalled.

'How personal? You're not sleeping with him, are you?'

'Diana's tits, Plico, that's outrageous!'

'Nice language for Imperatrix Severina's chief advisor.' He grinned at me. 'You're a similar age. He looks strong enough to cope.'

'Just hand over the file.'

'Keep it to yourself, will you? Don't copy it. I'll come and collect it myself.'

'Why? Are you running him?'

'No, of course not. He's a foreigner.'

Plico didn't glance away – that would have been too obvious – but I knew he wasn't playing it straight.

'When did that make any difference?'

'You know the rules – Romans only and *in situ*.' He shrugged. 'He's a person of interest, let's say.'

'In what way?'

'Just read the file.'

Plico stood up, glanced back at the file as if he was leaving a baby with a poorly qualified minder, nodded at me and left.

'Welcome, Mr Brown,' I said, extending my hand.

A tall man, sturdy as a farmer, crossed the atrium. He smiled pleasantly, held his hand out and gave mine a firm handshake. The smile passed up to his eyes, producing small sunbursts of lines at the outside edges of his eyes – light eyes, hazel. Strange, they were almost the same colour as Caius Tellus's eyes. Pure coincidence. William Brown had been born in the United Kingdom where a large proportion of inhabitants had light eyes, hazel or otherwise. A lack of sun, perhaps. I introduced him to Miklós and the two men shook hands. All smiles, but I watched them measure each other up in that instant way that clever people did.

'Please.' I indicated he should sit in one of the easy chairs by the large glass doors opening to the courtyard garden. I manoeuvred Marina to perch on the leather sofa beside me.

'I understand you're visiting Roma Nova on business,' Miklós said.

'Yes, Brown Industries is expanding and the Roma Novan Defence Ministry is very interested in our communications products.' His bland smile was for us both, but I saw in his eyes he was watching me for my reactions as much as I was watching him.

'Tell me a little about your family, Mr Brown,' I said.

'William, please. My people come from Kent, in the south of the United Kingdom, but I emigrated to the EUS when I was eighteen. I won an offer from the Cambridge Institute of Technology in Massachusetts to pursue my studies and stayed there for five years. It was a wonderful life.'

He smiled at Marina who responded immediately. They held each other's gaze, eyes only moving to flicker over the other's face. It wasn't the hunger of lust, it was more; a gentle knowing. Miklós and I could have been pieces of sculpture. I undoubtedly had more sexual experience than my daughter, but I had never seen such a tangible display of bonded affection.

I raised my hand. A servant brought drinks and the moment broke.

Once we'd finished eating our lunch, Marina jumped up. She took William Brown by the hand and pulled him towards the garden doors. Miklós and I watched as she half danced alongside his tall figure. Once on the terrace at the back of the house, he gazed down at her, smiled, extended his arm around her waist and pulled her in. His other arm settled on her shoulder and he bent down to kiss her mouth, firstly with a light touch, then as she brought her arm up around his neck, a deep, passionate world-ending kiss. I sighed as we watched them progress down the garden.

'Why the sigh, Aurelia?' Miklós asked. 'They seem perfectly matched. Better than us, in a way.' He laughed and slid his arm round my waist, but his remark stung. I loved Miklós unconditionally; he was exciting in his mind and his love-making. He made me laugh. So far, I had coped with his urge to go wandering, but in my heart I wished he would settle here with me permanently. William Brown was the steadfast type, I was sure. He would marry Marina, cherish her, give her a white clapboard house in New England and a steady home life.

Of course, it was impossible. Apart from the twenty years between them, Plico's file had made that decision for me.

I should have been more careful, but William Brown was due to leave Roma Nova on the first flight out two days after our lunch. He would go back to the Eastern United States and become absorbed with his expanding business. I decided to keep Marina busy elsewhere. I nudged Severina to invite Marina for the weekend; the daughters were friends as well as cousins and they hadn't seen each other since Silvia's birthday and emancipation ceremony three weeks earlier. My plan was going well until Silvia phoned early Saturday evening to ask if Marina was ill.

'I hope I'm not disturbing you, Aunt Aurelia. I know Marina can get distracted, but she still hasn't arrived.' I glanced at my watch. It was five o'clock.

'What had she arranged with you?'

'She should have been here for lunch.'

'My apologies to you, Silvia, and your mother and thanks for calling me.'

She rang off and I leapt up and started pacing the floor. I didn't know how to be more furious.

'Calm down.' Miklós grabbed me as I returned from the other side of the room.

'Marina's lied to me, defied me. I bet she's gone off with William Brown.'

I checked with the chauffeur; she'd dropped Marina at the palace side entrance, and then returned here. I called Brown's hotel, but he'd checked out that morning.

'You can't set the *vigiles* on him,' Miklós said. 'He hasn't done anything wrong. She's of age. So what if they've spent the day together?'

'You don't understand.'

'No, I don't,' he said. 'Suppose you explain exactly why you don't want Marina to pair off with him. He looks so... so respectable.' Miklós didn't quite sneer.

'I can't. It's a security matter.'

He looked long and hard at me.

Plico's file had been explicit. Brown Industries was about to become the premier supplier of our most advanced communications and information systems. As such, we would give William Brown long-range protection and monitoring, and a Roma Novan technical intelligence officer would be employed in his company as a liaison officer.

'How can I put this?' I said. 'Our government will be working closer with Brown Industries than before. There are implications.'

'How is that bad for Marina? Surely it will make things easier for everybody? What aren't you telling me, Aurelia?' He frowned and released me.

'Don't push me, please.'

'You're being unreasonable. This is your daughter. Don't you care about her happiness? Brown will look after her and give her everything. She couldn't be safer.'

Juno, I hated this. I looked up at him. He must see my misery. I couldn't tell him the EUS government, which was a significant customer of Brown Industries, would be wary of our involvement. Their administration would try to obtain a controlling interest or at the least exert pressure on the company or on William Brown or his family. They'd watch Marina, monitor her activities and even have an operative befriend and manipulate her. They could even honey-trap her. One day, they'd give her the choice of working for them or being the cause of Brown having some misfortune such as an accident, or threatening his company, his life's work. And she'd comply. Gods, she'd be torn apart.

William Brown must return home to manage Brown Industries. I was sure he wouldn't come here to live and work. Marina was scarcely able to fend for herself now, let alone survive in the harsh patriarchal society of the Eastern United States with sharks circulating waiting for an opening.

'Marina would be so lost there,' I said, 'and William would be fully occupied with his growing business. He would try to look after her, but she'd become homesick, fade away, or worse.'

'Don't be ridiculous. Perhaps you haven't given her the opportunity to stand on her own two feet. She may be stronger than you think. When I've talked to her, she's always seemed to know what she wants.' He shrugged. 'She's a gentle soul, but you should give her a chance.'

'I can't. There are other factors to consider.'

He stared long and hard at me. I had to look away in the end.

'Sometimes, Aurelia, I don't know you.' He went over to the atrium windows and stared out at the rose garden. He crossed his arms and bowed his head as if in deep thought. The blazing summer light highlighted the curves in his face, emphasising his cheekbones. Last night, I'd kissed the skin and flesh just below them as we'd made passionate love. Now they were like ramparts of a fortress guarding his inner thoughts.

'You Romans are a strange people, almost mechanical sometimes.'

'We've had to harden up to get through—'

'Don't give me a damned history lesson.'

'Then don't lump me together with a million and a half other people.'

He frowned.

'I know you're an important functionary and you take it all seriously,' he said, still looking to the outside, 'but how can you put your political machinations ahead of your daughter's happiness?'

'It's Marina I'm thinking of. I know I said there were other things to take into consideration, but she'd wilt in a country like the EUS.'

'You won't even let her try.' He turned to face me, but he didn't budge from the windows. 'Sometimes I don't know what I'm doing here.' After a few moments, he said, 'I was wondering how to broach this, but now is as good a good time as any. I had a letter this morning from my aunt. My father is very ill and she's urging me to go home and make my peace with him. I broke off with him years ago when he thrashed me for the very last time. I was fifteen. I left and swore I'd never go back. I didn't know what to do this morning, but now I think I *will* go.'

An hour later, he was standing in the courtyard, a hiker's rucksack on his back and a large suitcase on the ground.

'I've called a taxi,' he said, not looking at me.

'Miklós, you can't go like this. I'm very sorry about your father. Of course, you must stay there as long as you need to. But please don't go believing I'm doing this for ego reasons.'

He looked at me with a sardonic expression on his face. 'Aren't you?'

A harsh sound from a car horn interrupted us and he picked up his case.

'Goodbye, Aurelia. I'll let you know when I decide to come back.'

'Don't count on the door being open when you do, then.'

I almost bit my tongue off the second the words were out of my mouth. The rage and hurt in his eyes were almost palpable. Gods, what had I done? I was numb with misery and couldn't move. After a moment, I roused myself enough to run out to the front gate, but only in time to watch the passenger door slam and the taxi roar off.

When Marina eventually came home at nearly midnight, I was waiting for her. Nursing a glass of brandy, I sat in the dark; only the garden lights glowing through the French windows relieved the gloom. I'd grabbed the decanter and glass and flopped down in a seat in the atrium after Miklós left and had been too stunned to move since then.

Marina removed her shoes and was creeping across the marble floor without making a sound. I watched from behind the long leaves of the palm stretching over the wooden planters in the middle of the atrium.

'Marina.'

Her hand flew up to her chest, her shoulders jerked up and she stumbled. Her mouth dropped open and she froze on the spot like a nervous cat.

'Mama, I—' She clamped her hand over her mouth.

I said nothing. I stood up and flicked on a standard lamp by the planter, and kept my gaze on her.

A dull flush crept up her neck into her cheeks, but she lifted her face and looked back at me, defiant.

'Why are you waiting up for me? I'm not a schoolgirl.'

'No, you're not. You're a grown woman who has responsibilities. The imperatrix and her daughter were expecting you today at the palace. And you ignored their invitation.'

'I'm sorry. Truly. I'll write and apologise, but I know why you wanted me to go there. You fixed it so I couldn't see William before he went back.' Her voice was shrill. 'Well, we spent the day together and I'll never regret it.'

'I hope you don't. Did you take precautions?'

'Why do you have to ruin everything? We are in love. But you wouldn't know the meaning of the word,' she taunted.

I caught my breath. 'My private life is not under discussion.'

'Miklós can't love you or he'd stay with you all the time.'

'How dare you!' I strode over to her and slapped her face.

She burst into tears.

I was appalled at myself. 'Gods, Marina, I'm so sorry.' I stretched my arms out to embrace her, but she writhed out of my reach and ran off. I dropped my head into my hands, gulped and wept. For her, for myself and for my shattered love.

7

———

'Any use?' Tertullius Plico asked Monday morning.

'Oh, yes, very thorough. Thank you.' I handed the file back to him. William Brown was safely on his flight. Marina was sulking at home. She refused to speak a word to me. I didn't know how to claw my way back to her. A heavy stone lay in the pit of my stomach and I couldn't shift it. And the telegram I'd received last night from Miklós, tersely announcing his safe arrival and giving me his father's farm address 'if I was interested', hadn't relieved it.

'What's the matter?' asked Plico. 'You look like you're eating funeral ash.'

'Nothing,' I lied. I glanced away, not wanting to meet his cynical expression.

He didn't say anything. I reached for my glass of water and took a couple of mouthfuls.

'Very well, *consiliaria*, if you're ready to continue, I have a report I want to discuss with you before it goes to the imperial council tomorrow. It's not strictly your remit, but I'd welcome your views.' He paused, as if weighing something up.

'Gods, Plico, when you go this formal I worry.' He looked as if he was holding Pandora's jar in his hand.

Juno alone knew we had enough to be concerned about with the recent demonstrations. They'd sprung out of small group protests on the street and local meetings with a lot of declamations and heckling.

Nothing to worry about, Interior said at the previous council, just some nostalgic ranting about noble toil and lost traditional jobs. The *vigiles* would monitor them, he said, and maintain public order; they would soon fizzle out. Unfortunately, the demonstrations were *growing* in number, size and frequency.

Facing change was frightening and not everybody wanted to adapt. After the disturbances a few months ago, I'd pushed through the formation of a joint task force with government, social and industry leaders to re-examine the benefits and retraining structures, education opportunities and job creation. The group reported to the imperial council three weeks ago that the employment rate had started to rise again; Quirinia had given us encouraging figures that inflation was stable.

My department monitored continuously for any foreign influence and Plico's intelligence service ran regular checks. It wouldn't be the first time we'd been attacked from outside. During the barbarian invasions in the centuries after Roma Nova's foundation, families had almost died out in the mountains. The European religious wars in the seventeenth century had threatened our destruction but we'd secured recognition of our political independence in a footnote during the Peace of Westphalia. These days it was more likely to be economic. I'd had direct experience of that with the silver smuggling operation I'd broken when I was younger.

'You know I report to Interior as well as you,' he continued, 'but you'll take more notice.'

'What do you mean?' I shot a look at him.

'The minister's not an idiot, but he's not very well and I don't think he's kept his eye on the ball.'

'Explain.'

Plico outlined how the *vigiles* and the Urban Cohorts hadn't been well coordinated to keep law and order over the past few months. I sighed. I'd pushed Severina to consider a full reform of all the police services and amalgamate these two leftovers from ancient times. They were top-heavy and arthritic as organisations; ordinary people didn't know which to rely on, who to call and who to trust and it was getting worse. The *vigiles*, who knew the people in the neighbourhoods where they lived, resented the UC interfering and often sided with the locals for a quiet life. The smaller, tougher UC who acted on occasion as riot police despised the *vigiles* dealing pragmatically with the day-to-day. Severina had told me to keep my nose out. Her face had screwed up into a stubborn mask and her voice risen several tones. I'd politely pointed out I was there to give her advice on any topic, but she'd dismissed me with a wave of her hand. It was only my loyalty to her dead mother that kept me from sending her my letter of resignation.

'You remember that demo out at Aquae Caesaris last month? Where that boy got killed?'

'Juno, yes. Hasn't that been settled with the family yet?' Not that it would help them in their grief.

'Unfortunately not. Interior are still haggling. If they don't come to some agreement soon, it'll become critical and blow up in all our faces.'

I scribbled it down as the ninety-sixth thing on my 'to do' list, but moved it up to the top. In the uneasy atmosphere at the moment, we needed to remove any potential flashpoints.

'But it wasn't all police brutality. If anything, the *vigiles* were being extra careful as it was that nationalist lot – the toga toughs. A lot of ordinary people are impressed by their marching and how purposeful and disciplined they seem.'

I groaned. We all wore traditional dress, especially at home; a light tunic in the summer was far more comfortable than tight Western clothes. But these toga toughs, calling themselves the Roman National Movement, were a strange development. They paraded, metres of heavy cloth draped around their bodies as if they were in an old imperial triumph. Plico's people had reported how some bystanders actually clapped and cheered, even joining in their old marching songs. The *vigiles* seemed unable to contain them. Troops had been called out on one occasion but the toga boys had melted away. As well as their antics in the city and the bigger centres like Aquae Caesaris and Brancadorum, they'd had the nerve to march along my estate boundary at Castra Lucilla. I'd suggested to Severina that we ban them as they were becoming a civil order threat given the frequency and the widespread reach of their organisation. She looked at me vaguely and said she'd have it put in Any Other Business at the next imperial council meeting.

And that was tomorrow.

• • •

Marina eventually came out of her room. She sat at the table with me that evening, but she said nothing beyond a formal greeting and 'yes' and 'no'. She had really taken her separation from William Brown to heart. Silvia had invited her to the palace the next day and although she'd go in the car, I mentioned the toga toughs were out and about, so to be vigilant. She'd have Cassia, the under-steward's daughter, with her this time and their driver was a hostage-trained member of our security team, but Marina wasn't beyond doing something impulsive like ordering the car to stop in a dubious area and diving into a little shop because it displayed stands of colourful scarves.

'You do not need to be concerned, Mother. I know.'

I was more stung by her formal address than by her cold tone.

'Marina, I—'

'I will return at the correct time, Mother. Goodbye.'

I watched as she stalked out of the dining room, straight back radiating hostility, her earrings reflecting the morning light from the bull's-eye roof window and the copper shining in the soft brown of her hair.

Additional guards were on duty in the palace annex where Severina held council meetings. I rubbed my forehead to ease the stinging headache that had been with me since I woke up. Claudia offered me analgesic again, but I didn't want even the slightest part of my brain dulled today. I nodded as the Praetorian *optio* saluted me and we passed through the electronic scanner gate.

In the council room, sun streamed in through the floor-to-ceiling windows, casting diamonds of light in different shades through the sixteenth-century glass onto the dressed stone of the wall opposite. The air conditioning was humming, trying to combat the already hot day. Twenty-eight pads of paper and pens were set out along the table, a purple velvet padded chair drawn up precisely at each place. Familiar, but I sensed something wasn't right. I greeted the half dozen colleagues loitering around the refreshments table and we exchanged polite niceties as more joined us. Claudia Cornelia went to sit at the side with Tertullius Plico, her notepad and pencil ready.

The imperatrix's entrance was the signal for us to sit and as I took my place at her right hand, she beamed at me. I smiled back, on reflex, startled, but pleasantly surprised, and the hammer in my head struck a little less powerfully. A worm of doubt wriggled in my head wondering what she was up to, but I squashed it as ungenerous. She greeted us with the usual words, rather absent-mindedly, then pulled herself up straight as if preparing to say or do something contentious.

'Although we have good representation from the Twelve Families, several of you are also permanent members of the government.'

I quickly counted five heads or junior heads of families at the table including me. What on earth was she coming up with now?

'I feel those concerned must be burdened by the conflict of representing two constituencies – your functional duties as ministers and your Families representation.' She looked down at her notes. 'So in order to introduce an independent Families representative, I have invited the acting head of the second most important one to join us.' She raised her hand and a servant opened the door to admit Caius Tellus.

I nearly forgot to breathe. With all the other members of the council, I stared at Caius as he walked slowly to a space at the table. He rested his hands on the back of the chair, gave a full smile to the other council members, bowed to the imperatrix. He stopped opposite me. The smile died in his eyes. They became hard like green agate. We stared each other out for a full minute.

I hadn't seen him since the Families Council meeting when he stormed out. Now he was a member of the ruling imperial council. I shivered. Not because of the air conditioning. Only the interior minister's hacking cough broke the tension. Caius pulled the chair back and sat down. We progressed through the agenda, mostly without incident. But I couldn't stop glancing over at him, watching as he nodded at people's comments, and agreed with them; affability itself. Twice he caught me looking and gave me a knowing half-smile back. What in Hades was that about? As my headache grew worse during those interminable hours, I struggled not to feel sick.

Severina couldn't decide on the finance reform bill and called for further explanations. I thought the finance minister was going to fall on her pen as she explained each point again in careful detail, but Severina wanted more and it was postponed. But we didn't get the toga toughs banned. It came down to one vote and Caius voted against.

Fortified by a double dose of analgesic for my head and tea for my nerves, I tried to recover as my new driver battled his way through the rush hour. Apart from the thick heat of the day intensifying the dust and noise, there seemed to be a lot of police on the streets – *vigiles* cars were everywhere. As we reached the forum, we found it barriered off and took a diversion. When we finally reached Domus Mitelarum, I called Plico's office and asked one of his staffers to look on their system to see if there was a reason for additional vigiles presence. A march and rally of the Roman National Movement was taking place that evening, she said.

I dithered about, rang the palace comptroller who confirmed Marina was already on her way back. I glanced at my watch – it was only fifteen minutes in the worst traffic; she would be clear by at least an hour before the toga toughs set out. When she hadn't arrived forty minutes later, I checked again with the palace, then called the *vigiles*.

'I'm sorry, Countess, we've got more on tonight than a lost young woman to look for. I'll put the details on our system when I've got a minute.'

'When you've got a minute? What kind of answer is that?' Then I heard the noise in the background. Shooting. The phone went dead.

I snapped on the television news channel. It was a pitched battle around the forum. Rioters were setting fire to cars, shops, kiosks, anything. International shops' windows were smashed in and their goods spray painted. People were lugging things out of other shops. Alarms screamed, people chanted and shouted, placards jabbed rhythmically into the air. Against the flames, dark figures, their lower faces covered in scarves, and armed with sticks and metal piping, pushed and shoved amongst the demonstrators. The *vigiles* in riot gear were in retreat, their line broken.

And Marina was out in this.

8

———————

Upstairs, I tore off my day clothes, pulled on my old khaki combat trousers and para boots. My fingers trembled as I buttoned up an old shirt and buckled on my ballistic vest that I'd grabbed from the back of the cupboard. I was sweating already. Reaching up onto the shelf amongst gloves and hats, I stretched my fingers out for my service pistol. It was loaded, ready. I grabbed extra rounds and stuffed them in my pockets. My heart was hammering. Heaving open the top drawer of my cabinet, I snatched the PGSF gold eagle badge and stuffed it in the top pocket of my shirt.

I clattered down the stairs and belted out to the courtyard. Callixtus, the head of our domestic security, was briefing the night team.

'4 x 4. Two troops, armed. Now,' I shouted.

He frowned and opened his mouth to say something, but must have seen my look. I took some deep breaths while he waved a woman forward. 'Rufia, get the short wheelbase out, stat.' The woman ran to the garage, then he turned back to me. 'What's happening, *domina*?'

'Countess Marina, she's out in this.'

'What!'

'She left the palace nearly an hour ago.'

'Jupiter's balls.'

He pointed to two of his team and flicked his fingers at the porter's

62

lodge. They ran in, emerged with weapons and clambered into the now ready vehicle. Callixtus reached into his pocket. 'Here, *domina*, take this.' He thrust his reinforced black field cap at me. Barely minutes later, we were driving up the Dec Max towards the noise and flames.

Spotting a police barrier, we veered right into a side street. Snaking through the backstreets we only once came across rioters. Callixtus brought his rifle up and fired one round over their heads. They ran like rabbits, dropping everything. The noise faded as we neared the palace. Rufia turned the vehicle back onto the main approach road. No rioters or *vigiles*. No rubbish or burning wrecks.

'Okay, we trace the normal route the chauffeur would take to Domus Mitelarum.'

Rufia and Callixtus exchanged glances.

'Wherever it takes us,' I added.

It was always the noise: the screams of excitement, of triumph, cries of pain, the crash of plate-glass windows falling to the ground, the roar of flames consuming cars and the *whoomp* of fuel tanks exploding.

Rufia slowed down as we approached the centre. Wild faces with blood and smuts peered in the vehicle windows, but she got us through. I stared around as we reached the forum. The barriers were destroyed and the rioters swarmed everywhere, taunting the *vigiles* who tried to contain them. How could we find one slight girl in this hell?

Callixtus touched me on the shoulder and pointed to a blackened Mercedes, warning lights flashing, rear door open. Too many milling figures in the way to see the number plate. No, please not, I swallowed hard, but I opened my door and slid out.

'Stay here, Rufia, but watch for my signal,' I said.

She nodded.

'Callixtus, with me.'

We advanced toward the Mercedes, weaving in between the shouting, wired rioters, crunching broken glass and rubbish under our boots. Some gave way, others looked at us with a moment's curiosity, tensed, but turned back to their friends as soon as we had passed. Maybe Callixtus's assault rifle, my pistol and our grim faces decided them to find easier prey.

The Mercedes' door drooped, the paintwork sported a large dent as if it had taken a direct side impact, but worst was inside. In her grey uniform, lying legs akimbo, one hand on the wheel, the other flopped down at her side, was my driver. Her face was white; the flames in the street cast sickly yellow light across it. Her eyes were open, gaze forward, below a perfect red hole in the middle of her forehead.

'Marksman. No GSR,' Callixtus said, his voice devoid of emotion. His face was tight; the anger in his eyes reflected the firelight around us.

I nodded. A sour taste rose up into my mouth, but I clamped it shut. On the back seat, I found a worse horror; Cassia, my assistant steward's daughter, her throat slit and a pool of blood coagulating on the leather seat. I spun round to the street, bent over and threw up.

We had no time to think. The boom of a massive explosion. Hot flying metal. We threw ourselves on the ground and scrabbled under the damaged car. I glanced over at the 4x4. Rufia was stretched out underneath. As soon as the debris stopped falling, Callixtus and I ran for our vehicle, Rufia scrambled up into the driving seat. The tyres screeched as she threw the car into an emergency turn and drove away like a Fury.

In the first calm street, we slowed.

'Stop here, Rufia. You two, wait here. I have to go back.'

'No, *domina*, you can't.'

'You forget yourself, Callixtus.' I gave him a hard stare.

'No, you do.' He gave Rufia a nod, but she was already on the radio to the house. 'You cannot go back into that by yourself. We wait for reinforcements.'

He was right, but this was my child. Her driver and companion had been murdered under cover of the riot. And there was no sign of her. I gripped the car door handle until my hand hurt.

The reinforcements were there in four and a half minutes. I shot out of the 4x4.

'Report,' I said tersely to the nearest newcomer.

'The house is locked down. I've brought the night team plus my sister who's ex-infantry.'

'Right.' I panned round all six faces. 'Countess Marina is out there somewhere. The driver and assistant steward's daughter are dead, murdered, so we assume this is at least a kidnapping.'

'But, *domina*, they'd know we wouldn't pay a ransom,' Callixtus said in a soft voice.

'Exactly, so I have to assume it's an attack on the Mitela family, or at least on me. And they've gone for the softest part.'

I had to hold it together. For my child's sake and for my people I was leading into danger. My old training kicked in and kept me focused. While the others guarded us, Rufia and I searched the Mercedes as thoroughly as we could by torchlight. Rufia took photos despite the poor light. When I jolted the steward's daughter by mistake, her head rolled over at such an acute angle I thought it would part from her body. I caught it and stared. I stifled a sob and shot a plea for help at Rufia. She looked as terrified, but helped me lay the body down along the back seat. This was no time for scene of crime niceties. The only thing I found was one of Marina's crystal earrings. I nearly crushed it as I gripped it.

We split into two parties, continuously in radio contact, and set out in a ninety-degree arc, travelling twenty metres. We regrouped at the car and did it three more times, covering the remaining quadrants.

'Okay, we go to forty metres, but exercise extreme caution,' I said. 'You will inevitably confront rioters at that range.'

Callixtus, the infantry sister and I took the direction of the forum. As we eased towards the flames and the noise, I couldn't help thinking we could be wasting our time. Marina might have been taken away, she could be imprisoned in a building or, the gods forbid, lying dead somewhere. I shut my eyes and took a deep breath to steady myself. And where in Hades were the *vigiles*? We hadn't seen one for over half an hour.

Then came the throb of heavy engines. Armoured vehicles. I snapped my head round in the direction of the noise. Troops were marching towards the open side of the forum. Praetorians. They wouldn't stop for anything. On a night like this, the 'shoot first' protocol would apply.

I signalled the other two back against the wall. We scurried into a shop porch and froze. We killed the radio – they would detect the signal. Hardly breathing, we waited for them to pass. I could hear Callixtus's heart thumping as my head was squashed up against his chest. The infantry sister's hair tickled the back of my neck and her breathing, although shallow, brushed my cheek.

We were a good twenty metres away. Perhaps we'd made it to our hiding place before they had seen us. Fifty per cent chance either way. The regular Praetorians were not as specialised as the PGSF, but their purposefulness was just as strong. Four armoured vehicles and at least eighty personnel were coming in our direction. We daren't continue searching until they had gone past.

At the edge of the forum, one vehicle and around twenty soldiers turned down our street. Five metres away. They paused, scanning for rioters. Several figures scurried past us, some with looted goods, some just running. A shot cracked out. One dropped. The others picked up speed, terror on their faces. I closed my eyes for a second. Juno, grant the Praetorians pass us by. We were on the street, in a riot and armed, so prime suspects.

In the next second, a slender figure, hair loose, torn tunic, stumbled across my line of sight right in front of the advancing line.

Marina.

Pluto in Tartarus.

I started forward, but an iron grip held me.

'No, they'll pick her up.'

'Let go of me. That's an order,' I hissed at Callixtus and pulled against him.

'No, *domina*, it's insane.'

I looked up – his face was implacable. Asking Mars to forgive me, I thrust my knee into Callixtus's groin, stamped on his foot and stepped out into the street.

Immediately, several weapons were trained on me. I crouched down and laid my pistol on the tarmac. And nudged it away with my foot. I held both hands up.

'Hold your fire – PGSF,' I shouted.

A ripple of relaxation, but the weapons stayed focused on me.

'I am here to find this civilian,' I said, pointing at Marina. Counting slowly to calm myself, praying they wouldn't shoot, I closed the few metres between us very slowly. I grabbed Marina and pulled her into my arms the same moment two soldiers seized me.

Somebody put a blanket around Marina as she sobbed hysterically. Callixtus, still half bent in agony, the infantry sister and I were thrust against the wall and searched by brisk, ungentle hands. The one searching me stripped my ballistic vest off and paused when she found my gold eagle badge. When I started to explain, another thrust a weapon at my head and told me to shut my mouth. Hands cuffed, the three of us were thrust into the back of a short wheelbase support vehicle. Our weapons had disappeared. Marina was treated more gently, but she huddled into her blanket and stared out like a frightened rabbit on the short journey.

In the barracks courtyard, we were made to jump out. A white-coated medic helped Marina out.

'Where are you taking her?' I struggled against the guard who had grabbed my arm.

'To the sick bay, if it's any of your business,' the medic answered.

'Yes, it is – she's my daughter. She was attacked and her escorts murdered.'

His hard gaze softened. 'You can visit her later, if you're free.'

I couldn't reply as we were dragged away. In the custody suite, I gave the grim-faced sergeant my name, status and confirmed the other two as members of my household. He stared at me, his fingers frozen in the air above his log pad. He looked like he'd touched a poisoned fish. He jerked his hand at one of the guards and they removed the handcuffs.

'*Consiliaria*, my apologies for the robust treatment. Difficult days.'

'I understand, no hard feelings,' I replied, 'but I presume we can go now.'

'Not quite yet, *consiliaria*,' a voice came from behind me. I whirled round.

Older, one or two kilos heavier, in combat suit, but minus webbing, and sporting a major's badge, was my comrade from the Berlin legation detail.

'Pluto's teeth! Fabia. How are you?'

'Very well, *consiliaria*, but I want to know why the foreign minister was out on the street during a riot, armed and leading some kind of mission.'

9

I glanced around at the faces full of curiosity. 'I'd rather continue this conversation in your office.'

I followed her up the stairs into the admin area. It was very like the old PGSF one I'd known, but a far newer building with clean, sterile lines. When I'd given Fabia the whole story, she picked up her phone and ordered the team in the area to guard the Mercedes and wait for a *vigiles* support team to recover the vehicle and the two corpses. She frowned as she listened to their reply.

'Bring it back here, then,' she said into the handset. 'You can't leave two people killed in suspicious circumstances out there until they find a convenient gap in their schedule.' She slammed the handset down. 'Bloody *vigiles*. Couldn't even put a fire out these days,' she said, derision coating her voice.

'Fabia, I want to see my daughter now.'

'Of course, but first of all, you'll need this back to get through security.'

She reached into her pocket and laid my badge on her desk. They'd taken it when they'd arrested us in the street. Now it glinted in the artificial light, the crowned eagle seemed fiercer than ever. I hesitated for a few seconds, then reached out and took it.

Fabia smiled to herself as she looked down, signed a document on her desk and threw it in her out tray. She stood up and led me upstairs to the sick bay. The duty medic checked our security and pointed us to the third room along the corridor. I opened the door gently, slipping in with Fabia behind me.

'Pretty girl,' she whispered.

I went over to the bed. Marina was asleep, thank the gods. I turned to Fabia. 'I'll stay here if you don't mind. Would you tell my people and give them transport back to Domus Mitelarum?'

'Very well, but I'll come back later.' She nodded and left.

I pulled a chair up to the bed and waited. Nothing moved in the room. The monitor panel lights glowed softly. Thick curtains kept the street lighting out. It was warm to the point of being soporific. We were in a safe cocoon. Marina's face reminded me of when she was a baby; plump, soft, relaxed. But the bruises and cut on her forehead were entirely an adult experience. The ovals of her eyelids were calm, showing no sign of any disturbance behind them. The drip line into the back of her far hand ensured that. I took her near hand and kissed it. Then I saw dark red weals forming a ring around her wrist. I looked at the other one. Identical. I shuddered. What horrors had happened to her only a few hours ago?

Screaming.

I jerked awake.

Marina, struggling up, her body rigid, eyes dilated and a soul-piercing howl tearing out of her mouth.

I seized her, enveloping her with my arms and body. She shook, collapsed into sobs with her cheek against my chest. I rocked her gently like the child she was. A medic pushed through the door, frowning.

I shook my head at him, but he hovered there, then went to check the monitor and drip.

Marina raised her face to me. I wiped the tears and snot away and smiled at her.

'You're safe. You don't have to worry any longer,' I said and pulled the blanket from the bed, draped it round her shoulders and hugged her. 'I'm here. You can rest now.' She blinked, gulped and gave me a little smile. She closed her eyes and relaxed into an instant sleep. I laid her gently back in the bed and drew the blanket up to cover her.

The medic beckoned me outside and we crept out. I pulled the door to, hardly letting the latch click as we slipped into the corridor.

'I was coming to find you, *consiliaria*, when your daughter woke up. The doctor would like to see you.' He looked away, then back at me. His gaze was not quite as steadily professional as it had been.

'What is it?'

'I think it's best that she speak to you.' A lump of cold settled in my stomach as he opened the doctor's door.

A figure in khaki combat trousers, boots and a white coat was sliding a folder into a tall filing cabinet. She pushed the drawer shut and turned. Her mouth was a straight line.

'*Consiliaria*. Please, sit.' She picked up a pen on her desk and rolled it between her fingers. 'We've made your daughter comfortable, but because of her injuries she should be carefully monitored by her own medical practitioner. I suggest in three days' time, then a week after that.'

She paused and looked down at her desk.

'Tell me,' I said.

'Very well. She has linear contusions around her wrists and ankles which suggest restraints. From the discoloration around them, she must have struggled. As you saw, she has cuts and more bruising to her face. These will all fade in time.'

'And?'

She looked straight at me.

'She has further contusions to her abdomen and thighs. Her genital area is swollen and bruised, but not torn. We found three different semen samples in her vagina.'

Marina woke three hours later.

'Mama?' Her face, lost in a sea of white bedding, turned towards me.

I jumped up off the chair where I had been nursing my fury and hurried over.

'I can smell coffee. You only drink it in the evening when you're worried.'

I stared at her. How could my damaged child think of such a thing now? I reached up to touch her forehead. She flinched.

'What happened, Marina? Can you tell me?'

She shook her head and looked away. Fresh tears leaked out of her eyes onto the pillows.

I folded her hand into mine to stop it trembling. 'That's okay, darling. Just rest.'

Outside Marina's room, I paced the corridor, not caring who or what was in my way. I crashed into an innocent instrument trolley and overturned it. Metal and plastic shards lay all over the floor. I cursed at an orderly trying to approach to clear it up. Numb inside, I was ready to tear those three bastards who'd violated my daughter apart. Slowly and bare-handed. Then Fabia found me.

'*Consiliaria*, you must stop.' She stood in front of me. I went to push her away, but she was too quick for me. She shot out a hand and grabbed my upper arm. The pain from her grip on my radial nerve shocked me out of my frenzied pacing. She hauled me into an empty room and pushed me down onto a chair. When I started rising to my feet, she extended her upright palm and a hard grey look at me.

'No,' she said flatly. 'You've lived the soft life for far too long. You wouldn't have a chance. I'd rather not knock you unconscious, but I will if you don't stop.'

We stared each other out. After a minute, I gave in. I slumped back on the chair and covered my eyes with my hands. I shuddered and broke into sobs.

Fabia gave me a paper cup of water from the machine and waited until I had finished.

'Thank you,' I said and swallowed hard. 'I apologise for my behaviour.'

'I haven't a clue how badly you're hurting,' she replied, 'but you're going to have to hold it in control. There's a war out there and we haven't any time for the personal.' She placed her hand on my shoulder for a few seconds. 'Sorry.'

'Well, *consiliaria*, I don't know what to say to you. I know your daughter's suffered a deep personal injury, but if you were still a serving major and under my command I'd have you broken to junior lieutenant for such an escapade. But I'll settle for expressing my deep concern that a senior minister saw fit to take things into her own hands and waste the time and resources of a law enforcement agency.'

Colonel Marcella Volusenia was small, fierce and craggy. Her face was all features, particularly her grey eyebrows and long nose. She reminded me of a cross vulture. I'd met her once before, thirteen years ago, and she'd been formidable then as a senior lieutenant.

'With respect, Colonel,' I said, 'you're not a law enforcement agency. That's the job of the *vigiles*. And they refused to help. I did what any other mother would do.'

'Hardly.'

'I wasn't going to sit at home waiting for them to bring my daughter's corpse back four days later. I will be questioning the interior minister closely about the behaviour of the *vigiles*. No citizen should be fobbed off like I was.'

'Stupid of them to piss off a senior minister like you. They're a complete waste of government budget.'

'There have been concerns expressed at the highest level about their competence and internal organisation,' I said.

'Ha! Don't give me weasel words.'

'I will report the deaths of my staff and the rape of my daughter to them, but no doubt they'll say it was collateral damage from the riots.'

'You don't think so?'

'A long-distance marksman shot that killed my driver instantly, a professional throat-cutting of a young harmless servant? Not the work of a casual rioter, I think.' I couldn't stay still. I stood up and starting circling her office. I stopped halfway round and looked back at her. 'This was a targeted attack on my family carried out by brutal cowards. I'm sure I've annoyed many people in my life, but I'm only aware of one person who hates me this much.'

I took a deep breath to steady the rage climbing up through me. Volusenia wouldn't tolerate hysterics. I had to hang on to balance if I was going to get anywhere.

'If you don't mind having the Mercedes in one of your garages for a few days,' I said, 'I'm calling in a private forensics team to examine it.' But I wasn't optimistic it would produce any evidence useful enough for a court; he'd have been too careful.

'Of course. Safer here, no sticky fingers to interfere.'

'You think that's a problem?'

'You're the minister, you tell me.' She looked at me, her eyes hard. 'You've seen it first-hand out there. Personally, I would guard my daughter well and bury my treasure.'

Marina woke in the early afternoon. She managed to eat a sandwich and fruit. The bruising on her face had started to fade to yellow, but she was still tense and nervous.

'Take me home, Mama,' she said in a tiny voice.

Callixtus collected us and a second car escorted us in the 4x4. I folded Marina in my arms as if I could physically shield her from the hurt in her mind and body. She shot glances out of the windows, her eyes darting everywhere as if watching for something or somebody. As the tall gates of Domus Mitelarum shut behind us, she shuddered.

'You won't let me be hurt again, will you, Mama?'

I didn't talk to her about that night until I had the forensics report in my hand three days later. She slept in my bed with me, but even the sedative medication couldn't stop her nightmares punctuating the night. She was my frail child again, nervous and frightened. The trauma therapist I hired hadn't been able to get her to open up – neither had I – but Marina seemed calmer in the following days. She watched films, laughing and crying exaggeratedly, but the therapist said that was perfectly normal – a kind of release. Marina even helped in the kitchen, which surprised me. She showed absolutely no desire to go out to see any of her friends or even to receive them at the house.

I wrote to Miklós. He hadn't just been my lover, my companion; he'd been my friend. Flowers arrived two days later. For Marina. She picked the note out of the bouquet and read it. I burned to know what was in it, but she said nothing and pocketed it. A formal letter arrived the day after for me. It wasn't unfriendly, and he expressed his sorrow for what had happened to Marina. His father had died that morning and he was staying for an undefined period in Hungary. I held the letter in my trembling fingers and bit my lips along with my regret.

Claudia Cornelia brought my most urgent work to me and told me in her calm and efficient way that she had deflected the rest *pro tem*.

The third day, when she mentioned the emergency imperial council meeting called for the following morning, she kept a serious gaze on my face. I knew I couldn't neglect my public duty any longer.

After a quiet lunch at home, I asked Marina to come and sit with me in the atrium. She glanced nervously at me and her hand started to shake. I took it in mine and smiled at her.

'Darling, we have to talk about it. Two of our people were killed and you were attacked. Take your time, but start. You'll feel better afterwards, cleaner, I think.'

She didn't say anything for a minute or two. She stared down at her hands, then took a deep breath. 'There was a big group of them, six or eight, those toga people. We were driving back, trying to keep to the back streets, but you know you have to cross the Cardo Max at some stage. There was some debris across the road and the driver got out to clear it. She was careful, she looked around, but there was nobody. Nobody, Mama.' Her voice went up several tones.

'It's all right, darling. You couldn't do anything. She was doing her job properly.'

'She got back into the car and was closing the door when we heard a shot and she fell back. Cassia and I couldn't believe it. We just sat there. Cassia scrabbled in her bag to find her radio transmitter. She told me you said she had to carry it. She shook her bag upside down. Everything fell on the floor and she knelt down but she couldn't find it. I'll never forget how scared she looked.'

Marina brought her hand up to cover her mouth. She shook her head. 'Then they appeared, a whole crowd of men. Two of them dragged me out of the car. One shone a torch in my face and said, "That's her." I couldn't see anything properly for a minute. They pushed me into another car. I heard Cassia scream, then nothing. They stopped at a block of flats. In the Via Nova, I think. Two of them grabbed my arms and marched me up to a door on the first floor. They pushed me in and shut the door.'

'What happened then?'

She shook her head and closed her eyes.

'Marina, tell me.'

She bowed her head and muttered, 'I can't.'

'Has somebody told you it was your and their little secret, that something bad would happen if you told?' I lifted her head and searched her face. 'Has somebody told you that you were dirty or you should be ashamed?'

She shook her head. I pulled her into a hug and she broke down into hysterical sobs.

10

———

I couldn't get any more out of Marina. The therapist couldn't get her to open up any further. He said she should be kept quiet, allowed to rest, do simple, practical things and never be allowed to feel threatened or in danger. He thought she would talk eventually, but it could be weeks, months or even years. Pressuring her would hinder the process.

As I walked down the house steps on Saturday morning to the car waiting in the courtyard to take me to the council meeting, I nodded to Callixtus. He glanced down at his watch and a second later the gates swung open in the tall archway. A military short wheelbase roared in and jerked to a stop. To my amazement, Fabia climbed out in full battledress. After she sent a death look at her driver, she pulled herself up and snapped a salute at me.

'*Consiliaria*, my apologies for not being here earlier.'

'I didn't know I was expecting you, Major.'

'The Colonel's ordered an escort for you on official duties. She considers an attack on the foreign minister to constitute a national security threat.' She half smiled and said in a lower voice, 'Besides, she's taken a shine to you.'

The duty Praetorians saluted Fabia as we made our way through to the meeting room. Clever of Volusenia to detail her to accompany me.

Praetorians were the only armed force allowed to enter the palace precinct and had the right to be admitted into any part of the palace for any reason.

The pre-meeting murmuring stopped as I walked in with her two paces behind me. My fellow councillors stared at her tall figure as we passed them. I stood at my place to the right of the imperatrix's chair and Fabia stationed herself behind me.

'Dear me, Aurelia has brought her own toy soldier.'

Only Caius could have made such an undermining remark. My pulse rocketed. I gripped the back of my chair. It took every ounce of my self-restraint to face him across the table. Even more so when he gave me a little smile. I had no doubt in my heart that he was responsible for Marina's rape and the murder of my people. I wanted to kill him for it. But I had no proof and without it, he would twist every word of my accusation round. I had never felt so powerless. My logical brain knew there was so much else to occupy our attention, so painful as it was I had to push it aside. But once this crisis was over, I would focus all my resources – emotional and financial – and call in every favour and make any alliance to prove it beyond doubt and see him brought to trial.

We stood like marble statues until the tension was broken by the door opening; Imperatrix Severina entered. She cast around and blinked when she saw Fabia standing behind me.

'What on earth is this, Aurelia? Are you starting a coup?' She tittered and her hand jerked nervously to sign us to sit at the table.

For the thousandth time, I asked myself how we had come to be led by such a ninny. A half-second later, I trod on that; warmth crept up my neck into my face at such a disloyal, not to mention discourteous, thought. She was my ruler and I owed her my best guidance. And my full support.

'No, of course not, *domina*. I'm too busy.' More nervous tittering, this time from two of the other councillors. 'I'm sorry if it disturbs you, but the Praetorians have assigned me a guard in light of the vicious attack on my household and the rape of my daughter.'

A stone cold silence fell. The interior minister brought his hands up to his head and slumped. Some councillors sat with fixed faces and part-open mouths. Two muttered oaths. All looked shocked apart from Caius. He sat relaxed and doodled on the pad in front of him.

'My dear cousin,' Severina said and touched my forearm with her fingers. Her eyes stared almost out of her head and shone with sympathy. 'Gods, Aurelia. I apologise for my stupid remark. How is Marina? What can we do for her?'

'She is being cared for, thank you, *domina*. I hope she will recover eventually.' I looked at the interior minister, still sheltering behind his hands. 'I have reported the whole incident to the *vigiles* prefect and he seemed almost interested. But on the night of the riot, I regret to say, he couldn't have cared less.'

'Such an insult to the heir of the senior of the Twelve Families cannot be tolerated,' Quirinia piped up.

'No young woman should be so insulted, whatever her status,' I replied coldly. 'The *vigiles* lost control of the riot. And I didn't see a sign of the Urban Cohorts where I was. Only the intervention of the Praetorians was effective. But the riot should not have been allowed to develop in the first place. Where the hell were the stewards supposed to be provided by the demonstration organisers? Where were the *vigiles* and UC patrols to police it?' I looked around the whole table. 'I have urged the reform of the police services many times in this room. Perhaps now some action might be taken.'

'Really, Aurelia,' Caius interrupted, 'there is no need to become hysterical.'

I think even he flinched at the violence of the look I shot at him. I half rose out of my seat, ready to confront him and hovered there, ready to spring.

'You know nothing, Caius,' I threw my words at him. 'Or perhaps you know everything.'

'I haven't the faintest idea what you are alluding to, my dear Aurelia.' He turned to Severina. 'Perhaps, Imperatrix, we can move to the calm of the agenda after this, er, diversion.'

Severina nodded like an automaton; the others fidgeted with their papers. I sat down, defeated again. If I said more, I *would* look hysterical.

I tried to relax on the way home; Marina did not need me tense and upset. As we approached the house, I noticed a line of barbed wire had been added along the top of the stone wall that ran along the street side of the house. At the archway, a new camera peered out at us. The driver used the standard remote control and as the gates swung open to admit the car and Fabia's short wheelbase behind us, an alarm screeched out. Two armed guards I had never seen before trained their weapons on us. Gods! Was this another attack? I swallowed hard. Marina. Was she safe? Had the household hidden her in the cellar room?

Fabia and her driver rolled out of their vehicle. He dropped to the ground in classic kneeling position, she tensed, ready, with her back against the vehicle, left foot forward, her weight balancing on both feet. I heard the safety click off on both combat rifles.

I was never more relieved when I saw Callixtus step forward. I opened the window.

'*Domina*. I hope we didn't startle you.'

'Startle me? I nearly had a cardiac arrest. What in Hades is going on? You've turned my house into a fort. And who in hell are these people?' I waved my hand at the two grim-faced guards as the gates shut behind us. Fabia's driver had got to his feet, but both kept their weapons trained on the newcomers.

'I've brought in additional security. Let me show you.' He opened the car door and ushered me towards the inner wall of the archway. 'This is one of the new bioscanners. If it doesn't recognise your eye, voice and palm imprint it will alarm. Let me enter your details.'

I stood impatiently while the machine scanned me. I recited one of my latest speeches into it plus a few standard greetings and eventually it flashed a green light. Although the new scanning panel was within the courtyard gates now, contractors were coming tomorrow to replace the hundred-year-old wooden ones with new metal security gates recessed back from the road. Any vehicle approaching would be forced to stop for scrutiny. I motioned Callixtus into his office on the far side of the courtyard.

'I'm pleased you've increased the level of security, Callixtus, but do we need such sophistication?'

'Yes, after the attack on Countess Marina and the instability out there.' He looked out through the lodge window onto the courtyard, tilting his chin towards the guards. 'My team are carefully selected. You know we investigate their backgrounds in minute detail and make them swear an oath to the Mitela family. But many of them come from, shall we say, tough backgrounds, sometimes criminal ones.'

I would have been naive to think otherwise, but I wondered where this was leading.

'They talk among themselves about their friends, cousins, about who's doing what, what's happening in their families and sometimes they report things to me and ask my advice.' He brought his gaze back to me. 'It's not formal intelligence, some of it may be exaggerated.'

'Yes?'

'The news from Aquae Caesaris, Brancadorum, even Castra Lucilla is the same. Strangers coming into the towns, delivering pamphlets, giving political speeches calling for jobs, stability and order, knocking on doors. These toga wearers seem to be parading as well. My brother-in-law's a *vigilis* in the countryside outside Aquae Caesaris.' He snorted. 'A real yokel. Normally you'd have to push his fat arse off his bicycle before he sees anything's wrong, but even he's noticed. And he seemed frightened by it all. Only him and another *vigilis* cover their beat at any one time.'

'Has he reported it?'

'His captain told him to get on with catching apple thieves and not to meddle in things he didn't understand.'

'Sounds as if the captain doesn't want to take any action, like that station *vigilis* on the night Marina was...' I couldn't say it.

Callixtus laid his hand on my shoulder for a brief moment. 'Personally,' he said, 'I think they're either stupid or as corrupt as all Tartarus.'

Silence hung between us. I heard the car being driven into the garages and the diesel engine of Fabia's vehicle throbbing in the courtyard, preparing to leave.

'Very well,' I said. 'Prepare a convoy to Castra Lucilla. Send the scout vehicles out tonight. Tomorrow we sharpen our spades.'

<h1 style="text-align:center">11</h1>

I called my business manager, our lawyer and the family recorder to the house ostensibly for dinner. We didn't stop working until two the next morning. We drove the secure telex lines to Zurich, London and New York to their capacity. Even though it was Saturday, our overseas correspondents received our instructions without protest. But then, we were moving millions.

I sent one last telex to the post office in Hungary nearest to Miklós's family home with a high priority marker to warn him not to come anywhere near Roma Nova, for his own safety. I suggested we could meet in Vienna once the situation in Roma Nova had stabilised. I only hoped we had something of our relationship to rescue.

Once that last telex tape had run through, the security team destroyed the terminals and burnt the coding units under Milo's supervision.

Five hours later in the blessedly fresh dawn, I looked back at his stern figure resembling the centurion he had always seemed; legs braced, arms crossed, standing in the gateway and flanked by two of the security detail remaining at the house. He would not only keep the household running and supervise the contractors in our absence, he would defend the house against all comers.

. . .

Our small convoy wound through city checkpoints, mercifully staffed by military rather than the damned *vigiles*, and made for our farm at Castra Lucilla. Our standard 4x4 was accompanied by an older, slower version that crawled along, mostly because it was lined with armour plating and glazed with bulletproof windows. Marina slept on the back seat. Despite the new security, I wasn't leaving her in the city.

The first scout car was parked under a tree in front of a *mansio*, a roadside plain hotel. No sign of the driver. Or his two escorts. Callixtus tensed, radioed to the other vehicle, then grabbed his rifle and slid out under protection of the door. I panned around with binoculars as the two men and one woman scurried forward from the other vehicle and spread out. I could see no movement through the *mansio* windows, nor any lights. Inside, they should have been clearing up after lunch.

I wanted to be out there, but I had to stay and protect Marina.

'Two dead,' Callixtus's voice hissed from the radio.

Hades.

A click. Safety off.

I turned slowly. At the far left, by the garden fence, half-hidden by a shrub, a man was holding a hunting rifle aimed at Callixtus's head. He was barely fifty metres away from his target – impossible to miss. I was twenty, less than half the distance. If I radioed Callixtus, the man would hear. His finger caressed the trigger. Praying Mercury wouldn't spoil my aim, I raised my pistol, aimed and squeezed.

As the man fell, his gun fired. A scream behind me. Marina. I stretched my arm back and squeezed her hand with mine. She gulped, but nodded. I counted to twenty. One of Callixtus's troops scurried back to my vehicle.

'*Domina*?' she said.

'All safe here. Report!'

'The owner's dead, but her husband's still breathing. We found the other staff locked in the cellar.'

'Very well. Tell them to call it in to the local *vigiles* if the line's not cut, then secure the building. Grab some food and water from the kitchen. We'll stay with the vehicles.' As she hurried off, I wondered how long we had before we were attacked directly.

Only clucking from hens and bleating from goats in the paddock behind the *mansio* interrupted the silence. We ate quickly, ignoring the rising heat from the afternoon sun. After I'd finished my bottle of water, I jumped down from my seat, turned and spread the map out on it. I glanced at the retreating backs of the two remaining members of Callixtus's detail as they made their way back to the *mansio* front door. I wanted to make completely sure they were out of earshot before I spoke to Marina and Callixtus.

He followed my look, raised an eyebrow, but shrugged when I said nothing.

'We have several options. We abort our mission and go back to the city or we carry on as planned. Both of these are inherently dangerous as I have no doubt the opposition will be waiting for us whichever we choose.' No change of expression on either face.

Marina tensed. She grabbed my arm. 'What do you mean, Mama?'

'Darling, somebody wants to stop us reaching Castra Lucilla. They killed our people to frighten us, to show how ruthless they are.'

'But nobody knows what we're doing,' she said.

'I had hoped not, but somehow they've found out or they've guessed. If it's who I think it is behind this, they have a lot of manpower at their disposal, certainly enough to overpower us.'

'Oh, gods.' She put her hand to her mouth.

'Or we go a different way. The problem is that the "different way" I'm considering is not the easy option, but we may all survive.'

Marina stumbled against me in the dark as we trudged along yet another gully. I checked my watch. Half past one. We'd been marching nearly three hours since the last stop. I clicked my fingers. Callixtus froze, then dropped into a crouch. I pulled Marina down. I panned round with the binoculars. No sound either. Thank Diana, the moon was a crescent.

'We'll rest here for thirty minutes,' I whispered. There was some shelter from the gully wall, but we huddled close. At least we were wearing boots and walking clothes, and had our parkas. We placed our backpacks in the middle, like a cluster of brown misshapes. Callixtus stretched out and closed his eyes. Marina let out a huge sigh. I handed her a bottle of water.

'Slowly,' I whispered. I wrapped her in a trekking blanket, tucking it between her body and the rocks. Leaning over, I put my mouth up to her ear and said, 'Shut your eyes and try to let your muscles go, as if merging into the rock.'

She stared at me for a few seconds, then lay back, gave a huge sigh and fell into sleep. She'd been medium fit before that dreadful night and I knew she'd used the gym and pool at the house since, but she wasn't used to a route march with a heavy backpack. And I'd given her the lightest one.

I leant back against the gully wall and drew my knees up under my own blanket. Time was against us. We'd left the vehicles with the two security guards by the *mansio*. At best, the opposition would think we'd decided to spend the night there, but when we didn't appear on the road in either direction by midday at the most, they'd start hunting us.

I really hoped they wouldn't think first about the mountains. Only a fool would come up here looking for refuge. Sheer edges, countless blind ends, lethal scree banks and rocks full of iron to confuse the best compass. And glacial. But I knew this; I'd trained up here for years. The problem was it was twenty years ago. I didn't tell Marina about the wolves, either.

It seemed like only five minutes had passed when my watch pulsed against my skin. I prised myself off the rock and stood. I bent and shook Marina's shoulder gently. 'Come on, we have to go.'

She blinked. She glanced around; Callixtus was on his feet and stretching, warming his muscles for the next stage. I held my hand out.

'How far now?' She looked exhausted already.

'We have to walk another three hours. The night is our friend. It's just gone two, so we can put another twelve kilometres behind us before the sun rises. Then we'll have to take more care.'

Marina nodded. She looked down at her bag, took a deep breath and reached for it, but before she could pick it up, Callixtus had it.

'I'll take it for a while,' he said and swung it up, threading his arms through the straps so it rested on his chest. I smiled my thanks at him; he'd already loaded the heaviest pack on his back.

The cold crept in at our necks, our wrists, our noses as we ascended. Heavy plumes of warm breath left us and cold air flew into our lungs. Next stop we had to eat, or our bodies would lose the battle against fatigue and chill. But now it was the task of one foot in front of the other, repeated thousands of times. Up, up, up. Nothing less than our ancestors in the legions had done, and we had more protective gear, but it didn't make it easier. We daren't break into any marching song to relieve the monotony; the echo would bounce around the whole range and pinpoint our location faster than any of the new spy satellites the British were using.

We stopped after another two hours. The pre-dawn wind skipped across the top of the range picking at us in small ice-carrying blasts. Sheltering in the lee of the summit, backs against the snow-covered granite and feet pressed on the ice and gravel, we chewed energy biscuits and drank water. Marina was almost too tired to eat, but she swallowed the last of the meat and fruit with the rest of us. She was the first to stand ready afterwards and reached out for her bag. She seemed to have dug out some deep strength.

'We have about five kilometres to go,' I said, 'and just over an hour before the sun gives enough light to spot us. It's downhill, so we'll get warmer, but we can't relax. We may have to fight once we're back in the plain.'

Two faces – lined, red-eyed and grim – stared back at me.

I tipped my head up. '*Eamus.*'

Within forty minutes, the navy blue sky with its slim crescent moon was broken at the horizon by a thin line of dawn. It was August and the full day would come very quickly, but we marched on. The gradient was dropping fast. The loose gravel turned and twisted under our boots. I worried that we were so tired, one of us might sprain, or worse break, an ankle. We slid into the shelter of the first trees before the full light could betray us. Marina dropped to the ground and closed her eyes. Her breath came in sobs. She tried to push the water bottle but I made her take a few sips, before she curled up and closed her eyes.

Callixtus and I crawled forward to the edge of the trees skirting the fields. It was hellishly hard dragging myself those few metres after such a night. I swallowed, struggling to get my breath back. If I stopped and laid my head on the ground even for a minute, I'd fall asleep.

I panned around with the binoculars. The Castra Lucilla estate complex covered a large area with the *pars domenica* – the main house – on the south side. The farm office and dormitories for the farmworkers occupied the next section and the *fructuaria* – the production area where they processed butter, cheese and yoghurt, and packed and bottled everything – lay beyond that. The vinery was at the far end. Barns, milking parlour and all the poultry runs stretched out on the other side. No sign of life from the house, but it was normally closed when none of us was there. Now, shutters hung open on the front.

'Anything?' Callixtus asked.

'Nothing. Not even a vehicle outside the farm office, no barn door open.' I glanced at my watch. 'It's half-seven. People should be swarming all over the place. The *fructuaria* should be open and running – it's market day tomorrow in Castra Lucilla and they need to pack all the produce today. We've still got wheat and spelt to cut. And then prep work for winter sowing.' I swung the binoculars round to the fields. 'And the cows should be in for milking.'

I looked towards the town of Castra Lucilla, but it was too far for me to see clearly.

'Either they're waiting for us, your people had a big party last night or they've all buggered off.'

'Thanks, Callixtus, that's really helpful.'

He grinned at me. I relaxed my shoulders and smiled back, but only for a second.

'I think I can discount the third one, the second one's possible, but if it's that, the farm manager's going to have an uncomfortable half-hour with me.' I took another look through the glasses. 'Unfortunately, given everything that's happened, it's likely it's the first.'

12

———

We crawled back to Marina. At least the physical effort absorbed some of my anger. Who were these bloody people who dared attack us, come onto my land and take my farm? The steward and her staff would try to keep the farmworkers calm, but they'd be terrified.

'Our main problem is that if we walk in from here, they'll see us coming,' I said.

The farmland was open but the estate complex was built on a slight rise. All very well in previous centuries as a defensive position, but now we'd be picked off by anybody with a sniper rifle before we'd gone ten metres.

'What can we do, Mama?'

'Oh, I have a little surprise they may not be expecting.'

Callixtus jerked his head up. His eyes narrowed. 'What kind of surprise, *domina*?' His voice carried a resentful tone. Odd.

'Come with me,' I said.

We trudged along the mountainside limit of the treeline about four hundred metres west of where we had dropped down from the mountains. I turned to face the mountains and squinted in the morning sun. In front of us grew dense scrub, dwarf birches and hawthorns sheltering between two hillocks.

'You see that little gully?' I said. 'Between those two rocks?'

'Yes, but it's a blank end.' Callixtus shrugged.

'Not quite,' I replied and headed straight for it. Peeling back the

87

thorns and fighting our way through the brambles, we reached the base of the back wall. I turned and took three paces forward, stopped and stamped hard. Nothing happened. I jumped on the spot several times. Callixtus frowned at me – he must have thought I'd gone mad. Marina looked desperate, no doubt hoping I hadn't. Several seconds passed. Then I felt it under my feet. I smiled at Marina to reassure her, then broke into a laugh. A straight black line approximately a metre wide appeared at the base of the rock. The rumbling grew and a grinding noise of a turning mechanism escaped from the gap now ten centimetres deep. Callixtus stepped back as the dark rectangle widened into a square.

'What's this?' He stared down into the darkness with a look of dread as if it were the pit of Tartarus.

'Our way in. Let's go.'

I fished the torch out of my backpack and started down the steps. Light footsteps behind me confirmed Marina was following. I squinted up into the morning light.

'Callixtus?' A pause. 'Problem? You're not claustrophobic, are you?'

'No, no, *domina*, just surprised.'

He followed us in slowly, almost reluctantly.

I found the winding handle and gave the torch to Marina.

'Shine the light on that pulley at the top and tell me when the weight is halfway down.' I braced my feet and seized the handle. The wrist-thick rope looped around a series of pulleys with a massive weight hanging from the other end. After the halfway point, all I had to do was control the descent. To my relief, Callixtus recovered his wits enough to help me finish it.

The trapdoor slid shut with a final thump. All I could hear was my own breathing, Marina's gasps and some foot shuffling.

'Marina, torch, please.'

'Sorry, sorry.'

The beam skittered over the rock surface as she passed it to me. I found a cable and traced it back to a wooden box on the wall. I opened it and threw the switch. Tiny glows like Saturnalia lights barely lit the underground chamber, but they showed us the passageway.

'Where in Hades are we?' said Callixtus.

'Back in history. How far do you think it is to the farmhouse? On the surface, I mean?'

'About a couple of kilometres.'

'Thirteen hundred and fifty *mille passum* in old Roman miles, to be exact. Can you imagine how long it took to hack and blast that out of this rock?'

'This goes all the way to the house?'

'Mitelus's great-granddaughter had the first one dug during the late fifth century as an escape tunnel,' I said. 'It was about half the length. But we hadn't pushed the cultivated land out so far then.'

He said nothing more until I stopped at the eight-hundred-*passum* wall mark. A few metres on, the tunnel widened out into a bulge where a wooden table and half a dozen folding chairs had been pushed against the wall. To their right stood two large cupboards and a wooden chest carved in crude country style. Everything was covered in dust.

'We'll stop here. We're safe now. Nobody can track us this far underground, and we must have some rest. Juno knows what we'll find at the other end.' I pointed to the left. 'You'll find a bunk in that side cave, Callixtus, behind the curtain. Help yourself to blankets from the chest. Marina and I will take the one on this side. Leave the backpacks here – I want to sort through them before I turn in.'

He nodded.

'Marina, give me a hand to lift these.'

She stared at me for a few moments, then bent down and heaved the first bag onto the table.

Six hours later, rested and fed on tinned fish and dry emergency rations, I felt boosted and ready to carry on. But as I held the emergency water bottle to my lips, my hand trembled. I changed hands. I couldn't let Marina see me unnerved. In the dim light, she looked paler than usual, which emphasised her red-rimmed red eyes and the brown shadows under them. Callixtus gave an air of being ready, but the expression on his face was more set than usual. He merely grunted in reply to my greeting. I searched his face. He lowered his eyes and mumbled an apology.

We walked along in silence, no spare energy for talking. Five hundred metres later, steps started rising.

'We have to creep up here like granary mice avoiding the watch cat,' I whispered. 'Leave our packs here. We'll come back for them later.' If we survived. I fished in my backpack and held a black plastic handle, about fifteen centimetres long, in Marina's direction. I pressed on the depression at one end and a steel blade sprang out.

She flinched.

'Here, take this.' I folded the blade back into its handle. 'I don't expect you to fight aggressively – leave that to Callixtus and me. But you have to be able to defend yourself.'

She nodded slowly, her eyes staring at the thing I'd laid in her hand.

'I know it's frightening, darling, but you have to make this one last effort. We might be a little busy once we get into the farm.'

I stared at the door at the top of the steps. On the other side, it came out by the side of a stone bench at the back of one of the old abandoned barns. It looked like any other neglected storage cupboard door – peeling paint, warped, a distorted latch. I had inspected it regularly to make sure it stayed that way. When she was newly appointed, the farm manager hadn't understood when I refused to let the old barn be pulled down and replaced by a modern watertight one. I'd explained it had been there for many hundred years and was historic. I'd seen doubt on her face and had hastily arranged for a national monuments surveyor to classify it as a protected building. A slightly bored professor came for a few hours, then left a bevy of students who dutifully photographed and documented every stone and beam. It was annoying, but after a week they went away and left the barn in peace. None of them had found the passage entrance beyond the false back.

I doused the lights at the top of the steps and felt for the first catch. Of course, it refused to budge. I slid the point of my knife along the gap below and above the catch. Grains of dirt fell out to the ground but there was no give and absolutely no movement. I cursed myself for not checking before that the bloody thing opened from the passage side.

The flash of light from the torch startled me.

'Turn that off,' I hissed.

'With the door that fast nobody will see it,' Callixtus whispered, irritatingly logical.

'True,' I had to concede. But now I could see the problem; the wood panel which formed the false back of the barn cupboard bulged towards us. The damp in the barn and the passageway had warped it enough to jam it. We daren't risk making the least noise; we had to assume there were hostiles on the other side.

'Okay, Callixtus, you and Marina press on the panel by the catch. Perhaps we can ease the pressure that way.'

When I thought my fingers were turning numb with the effort of applying so much pressure, the latch gave way. The door creaked and more dust blew out from the jamb. I nodded at Callixtus. He hefted his weapon ready and stood behind me, the barrel of his hunting rifle pointed forward over my shoulder. A faint outline round the barnside door showed there was still natural daylight. I just hoped nothing big like a storage bin was in front of the door to block our exit.

I took a deep breath and pushed the door open. Nothing. No machine noise, no voice, no footsteps even. I climbed through, Callixtus following with Marina. We waited for a few seconds. Out of the line of sight of the large barn door, we were still safe.

'Farm office first,' I said.

We crept forward to the barn door, slid it open a metre, watching all the time. Still nobody. I glanced at my watch. 18:56. Normally, the staff would be sitting down to their supper. But what was normal? The farm office was across the yard. I sent Callixtus forward. He reached the door and to our amazement, it was unlocked. We were in within the next few seconds, but it was empty of people.

'What in Hades is going on?' I whispered.

Callixtus shrugged, Marina said nothing. She looked as if she was about to burst into tears. I touched her forearm. 'Hold it together for a little while longer.'

She jerked her head in a tight nod, but I reckoned she was near collapse point.

'Right, let's see if there's anybody in the dormitories.'

We crept down the corridor and at the end turned right down the long corridor. Men on the left, women to the right. There were two doors to each dormitory, separated by a fire door.

I beckoned to Marina and whispered in her ear, 'I want you to stay here in the corridor, until I say to come in. Understand?'

She stared at me with huge eyes, licked her lips, then nodded once. I pressed her hand and gave her what I hoped was a reassuring smile.

I put my head against the first women's door and listened for a full minute while Callixtus guarded my back. Somebody was moving around in there. No, several somebodies. But no voices. I looked at Callixtus and tilted my chin in the direction of the door that led into the far end of the dormitory. He headed off there. I glanced down the corridor to him and signalled with three fingers. He nodded. On the count of three, I thrust open the door.

A man in hunting clothes, his rifle lying on the table in front of him, rose to his feet. I ran full pelt at him and punched hard down on the bridge of his nose, breaking it. As he went to cry out, I spun him round and chopped his neck with the edge of my right hand, just catching him as he fell. I let his unconscious body slide to the floor as quietly as possible. Another movement. To my left. I grabbed my pistol, swung my arm in his direction.

'Drop it. Now!'

After five full seconds, he complied.

I glanced around the room. Where in Hades was Callixtus?

'Kick it towards me,' I said. 'Down on the floor, hands out.' He shot me a sullen look, but slowly obeyed. I kept my weapon trained on him until Callixtus eventually entered through the far door. I frowned at him, but he just shrugged his shoulders.

Several people started to talk; gasps and crying in reaction to the violence.

'Quiet,' I hissed. 'Any noise will bring more guards.' They fell silent immediately. There were nearly twenty women in a room with twelve beds.

'Any ex-military here?' I asked in a voice barely above a whisper. Four stepped forward; one was easily over fifty, another was badly bruised and nearly stumbled, but two looked reasonably fit. I pointed to the two male guards on the floor. 'Secure these two and also gag the conscious one. Check their weapons and keep a lookout for any sign of trouble. If there's an auxiliary medic here, check the unconscious one's vitals, please. And keep the noise to zero.'

I eased the corridor door open a few centimetres and waved

Marina in. She went to speak, but I held my finger up to my lips. She blinked but said nothing. Inside, I eased her down to sit on one of the beds. She stared at me with huge eyes. I pressed her shoulder.

Next, I looked down the far end of the dormitory and beckoned Callixtus to join me. He marched down the centre aisle, making no effort to move quietly. I opened the outward opening door to the small laundry room at my end and ushered him in. He was so confident he left his rifle, barrel end up, against the dormitory wall and entered the small room first. His mistake.

'Sit down,' I said and closed the door. I remained standing. 'Would you care to explain a few things to me? Why you were so slow through that door, for instance? A simple infantry move – a first-week cadet could have done it.' I waited, but he said nothing. 'And why didn't you bother to move quietly through the dormitory just now when you know we're working covertly?'

He hunched over, his elbows on his knees, clasped his hands together. I almost couldn't bear to ask the question.

'So how long have you been working for the opposition?'

He said nothing.

I crossed my arms and leaned back against the washing machines. And waited.

'How did you know?' He spoke to the concrete floor.

'I found it very strange that they'd reached that *mansio* before us and set up the ambush until I thought it through and came to the only conclusion possible. I hoped I was wrong, but your face confirmed it when I opened the concealed passage.'

He shifted on the wooden bench. I flexed my feet to be ready to meet his attack.

'Mercury knows I tried to protect you,' he said, 'in the riot, coming here. Even the new security at the house.'

'Why?' I demanded. 'Did you still have a sense of obligation to your patron, of honour towards the Mitela family?'

'They wanted me to kill you, but I wouldn't. I made a bargain with them. I'd do what they wanted, but they had to promise not to kill you. Only proscribe and exile you.'

'Exile me?' The worst fate for any Roman; a living death abroad, cut off from every connection, family and friends and forbidden to communicate with or see them. Even Marina, my own daughter. And proscription; stripped of my citizenship, all protection under the law lost. Anybody informing on me could be paid a reward plus a portion of my assets; the state would take the rest. All the Mitelae would be blighted. I swallowed hard.

'Only the imperatrix can do that.'

'She wouldn't be the one to make the decision.'

'What in Hades is that supposed to mean? It's an imperial prerogative.' Then the meaning of his words hit me. 'What have you got mixed up in, Callixtus? Who are these people?'

'We want a better way, a return to proper manly Roman values. We've had enough of weak government—'

'Are you a member of the Roman National Movement?'

'Yes, and proud to serve it.'

'So your assignment was to infiltrate my household, and allow a vulnerable young girl to be brutalised during a dangerous riot, and my staff murdered?'

'No, of course not. I mean, about Marina. That was collateral damage. Although—'

'Collateral damage?' I hissed at him. I grabbed his hair, yanked his head up and struck him in the face. 'You coward. You want to be one of these nationalist bastards, but you're not even a true man. No honourable Roman would let a child be harmed, let alone collude in killing her servants. You're a waste of the ink on your birth record in the Censor's register.'

He glared up at me, hurt and fury shining out of his eyes. He tensed, ready to spring up.

'Try it,' I said, my pistol already in his face. His shoulders slumped and he bowed his head. A soft knock at the door broke my stasis, but I kept looking down at Callixtus's bowed head.

'Enter.'

One of the farmworkers, the older ex-soldier, now carrying the unconscious guard's rifle over her shoulder, came around the door.

'All secure, *domina*,' she murmured, then looked down at Callixtus's drooped figure.

'One more for you,' I replied.

• • •

I slipped back out to the dormitory, a lead weight in my stomach. Callixtus had been my staunch supporter, now even he had been subverted. I couldn't think about that now. Although we'd taken just over seven minutes, the longer we delayed, the bigger the likelihood of discovery.

'Manager?' I whispered as loudly as I could. I couldn't see her.

'Here, *domina*.' The manager's daughter, a young girl about fourteen or fifteen, standing at the end of a bed halfway down the big room, pointed down to a figure lying still on the mattress. I hurried to the side of the bed.

'Gods, Priscilla, what have they done to you?'

My brisk, efficient farm manager looked like a hunted animal at bay. Her head was bandaged, her face and neck bruised and red weals splitting the skin across her arm and shoulder. The other arm was fastened in a crude sling.

'They used a leather whip on her and on some of the men,' her daughter said, her tone flat and eyes staring ahead. 'Then they raped her and made us all watch.'

Marina moved over to the girl and took her in her arms, but the child remained stiff. Nobody said a word. My hands hurt, I realised I had balled them so tight, my nails had almost punctured the skin in my palms. I stretched my fingers, took hold of Priscilla's uninjured hand and pressed it.

'I will find them and bring them to trial. They will be severely punished. You'll have the best care possible, Priscilla, but first we need to take the farm back.'

She closed her eyes, then opened them again. 'Thank you,' she whispered and closed her eyes once more.

I beckoned the two younger ex-military to join me by the dormitory door.

'We have to take the men's dormitory,' I said under my breath. 'Are you fit enough?'

'Albina, ex-II Apulia, same as Sentia here. We're fit.'

I nodded. At least I had two from a good infantry unit with me.

'You two in the far door. Neutralise the guard and secure his weapon.'

As we crouched in the corridor, Sentia and Albina each side of the far door, I listened. Nothing. Either they were completely unaware of our presence or they were waiting for us.

We burst in. Complete surprise, thank the gods, but my opponent didn't go down easily. Tall, solid and grinning as if he relished the fight as I attacked him, he grabbed both my upper arms and squeezed, right on the radial nerves. The pain shot up into my shoulders but I managed to swing my leg and kick him in the groin. As he fell back, I searched for anything to use as a weapon against him. Nothing.

I readied myself for a disabling chop to his neck. Then I heard a cracking sound splitting the air and felt the whoosh of leather flying past my cheek. Half a second later, the big man's face was sliced open, red flesh gaping each side of the long cut. The tail of the whip, dropped after the cut, glanced off me. I jumped back and whirled round.

'That, you bastard, is for Priscilla.' Gavinus, the farm technician, was grasping a bullwhip with his bony fingers. His breath heaving, the whole of his slight frame trembled. He raised the whip again, his eyes fixed on the man on the floor.

I put my hand up in front of him, palm outward. 'No.'

Gavinus, fired up with adrenalin and hate, pulled his arm back, ready to strike again. I lunged forward, grabbed his wrist and yanked it down. 'No, Gavinus. Leave it.'

He stared at me, as if he didn't recognise me. His eyes bulged, his face set in a snarl. Then the fire subsided and his face relaxed.

'*Domina*, I—'

'I know.'

Sentia and Albina had secured two other guards and locked them in the men's laundry room. They tied the big man up and bandaged his face. I reckoned he'd lose an eye, but didn't really care at this moment. I cared even less when I found many of my men had been beaten. Two were dead.

Gavinus was one of the few uninjured apart from a few bruises. He trembled now in post-action fatigue and I told him to sit down. He was no warrior. His slender fingers were trained to delicate tools, engines and electronics, not weapons.

'Are there any other of these scum around?' I asked him.

'Not now. About twenty of them arrived yesterday morning in two lorries.' His shoulders drooped. 'Mercury, we were pathetic. They had us herded like stock within twenty minutes. Then they started hitting us, calling us—' He looked up at me.

'I get it, Gavinus. Don't upset yourself. I know it's not true.'

But I let him talk it out. The opposition had driven up to the farm manager's office, walked into her office, told her at gunpoint to summon all the personnel. While most were coming in from the fields, they rounded up all the home staff, herded them into the courtyard, picked out one of the younger men and shot him point blank 'as an example', they said. When the doctor tried to rally them, they shot him next. After that the rest of the staff were cowed and the intruders started beating the men, calling them pussy-whipped. Priscilla was their next victim.

'They were so cold and mechanical, *domina*,' Albina said. 'More would have suffered if we'd reacted.' She looked down at the ground. 'There just weren't enough of us.'

'I understand, Albina. Truly.' I put my hand on her shoulder and gave her a little shake. She looked up and searched my face. 'Believe me,' I said. 'I'm going to make damned sure nothing like this ever happens again. Whatever it takes.'

13

———

All the telephone cabling had been cut, and the radio smashed, so first thing next morning I dispatched a party of six, two armed with the intruders' weapons, to the *vigiles* station at Castra Lucilla. Their captain looked shocked as I walked him through the scene an hour later. In a peaceful country district most of the dead were rabbits or the odd stranded bovine.

'I've tried to question these men, but not a word. You will obviously submit them to more formal interrogation. I will sign the accusations this afternoon if you will prepare charges for murder, attempted murder, rape, aggravated trespass.'

'I don't know if I have the staff for all this paperwork, Countess,' he protested.

'Then call in your auxiliaries,' I said, trying not to let my impatience leak into my voice. I'd been up most of the night patrolling with Sentia and some of the men. 'This is a severe incident.'

When he seemed frozen by indecision, I played the weasel card. 'Obviously, it goes a lot farther than a brutal attack on a rural community. As foreign minister, I shall be reporting it direct to the imperatrix, who will naturally want to know that her cousin had every assistance from the police authorities.'

He gabbled into his radio. I turned with relief to Gavinus, who had started organising clean-up parties. I told him to leave the main house until the working parts of the farm and the dormitories had been cleared. He was astute to have asked Marina to look after Priscilla. I took him into the farm office later that afternoon and shut the door. After he gave me his report in detached tones, he looked up, questions and hurt in his eyes.

'Very satisfactory progress, Gavinus. I'm appointing you farm manager until Priscilla recovers. If she wishes to resign, then you'll take over, but I think it would be wise for the two of you to work in tandem if she wants to continue.'

He nodded.

'Next, security. Obviously, you need more armed guards. Albina seems a likely candidate for detail head – she has experience. Sentia can be her deputy. Check if any of the other personnel has experience and is fit enough. Two of the men on last night's patrol had reservist experience. If you decide to take on anybody locally, double-, quadruple-check their background. They must be prepared to work on the farm as well. I won't have an idle armed force eating their heads off and making the farm hands' lives a misery.' I paused. 'I would have asked Callixtus to help with selection and training, but—' His betrayal made my saliva sour in my mouth.

'I understand, *domina*,' he said and gave me a tight smile. 'I think we'll train everybody, though, as a precaution.'

'Very well. I don't like militarising the farm, but people must feel protected. We can introduce regular contact and security protocols, but obviously we'll have to find alternative transport and communications. See if you can procure some heavy-duty vehicles. Enough to evacuate everybody. Keep them in full readiness at all times with food and water supplies. And run some drills. It's a pain, I know, but you must have an escape route prepared. There's an alternative for absolute emergency, but I'll explain that later.' Somehow, I didn't want to talk about the tunnel yet. 'Leave the communications to me,' I continued. 'The expert I have in mind will solve our problems.'

I used the *vigiles* radio to call Fabia in. All I had to do was speak one of the old PGSF codewords and "CL" and she was there within two hours with two helicopters and twenty troops. Unfortunately, she brought Tertullius Plico with her.

'He insisted,' she said, and made a face as she ran out under the dying swish of the blades.

I made a sympathetic face back, but returned my features to neutral as the short figure trudging along beside his young military escort stopped in front of me.

'I'm working my last three months, looking forward to a quiet retirement and a bit of fishing, then I hear you need rescuing again.' He spat on the ground. It was dusty. 'Women!'

I sent him a sharp look. No, not Plico, surely?

He grinned. 'Joke. Got you, though.'

'Don't be a pig's arse, Plico. Come inside and leave those filthy cigarettes in your pocket.'

'Spoilsport.'

He was shocked when he saw the inside of the villa itself. Almost all the furniture was damaged, including the doors wrenched off the eighteenth-century solid mahogany dresser my mother had loved. Slashes across paintings and hangings on the stone walls ripped, porcelain shards scattered at the foot of stands. Bullets had nearly destroyed what had been a poker-faced portrait of the dead Imperatrix Justina. No great loss; my mother had thought her friend looked lifeless in it. And from the smell, the invaders had left the usual vandals' signature behind them.

I dismissed it. 'It's only furniture, and it's mostly old stuff from the city house. Come into the kitchens.' I preceded him along the corridor and down the steps into the older part at the back of the house. Even when they rebuilt this house in the 1100s they'd followed the traditional *villa rustica* pattern. The old stone range was built into the wall. Only Tartarus falling would have dislodged it. I picked up pans and cutlery from the floor, grabbed a brush and swept glass into a corner of the tiled floor.

'Bit old-fashioned, isn't it?' Plico said.

'It's called traditional.'

'From which century?'

I turned the regulator on the gas bottle and boiled a kettle of water. As I set the mugs of black tea down on the long kitchen table, I looked him direct in the eye.

'Now, Plico, suppose you tell me what in Hades is going on?'

Terrifying as the attack on our farm had been, it was minor compared with the trouble in the city. By the time he'd flown out to see me, Plico had compiled the full picture. A parade of thousands of men from the Roman National Movement marching in full toga order from the forum had ended as a rally in front of the amphitheatre with twice the number they'd started with. There'd been declamatory speeches which some of Plico's operatives had listened to while mingling with the toga toughs.

'The speakers called themselves Gracchus, Sulla, Clodius and so on.' He snorted. 'Pseudonyms, obviously, but they got the crowd fired up. My people said they pushed emotional words at the crowd, repeating over and over again stuff about land, virtue, tradition, strength, order, manliness, grabbing every popular reference they could from history. They called for stability, jobs, respect – all the usual stuff – without any explanation about how they were going to deliver them, of course. The cheers and shouts back from the crowd became louder and louder and rippled through the crowd. And when drumming started at the back, the crowd started chanting and stamping on the ground. After a good twenty minutes of this, there were thousands of them all lathered up.' He shrugged. 'Clever, very clever. There's some smart bastard behind this. I don't know whether I want to wrap my hands around his throat or clasp forearms in admiration.' He must have seen my face. 'No, I do know really.'

'And then the rioting started in earnest,' he continued. 'Oh, not anybody in Roman Nationalist get-up, just ordinary clothes. They're too bloody clever for that. They ran back through the city, tearing everything down in front of them. The nationalists just stood to the side, not even attempting to stop any of it. Thank the gods, the troops had been stood to and slowed them down. The Praetorians under Volusenia were waiting for them in the forum. Jupiter, she's a bloody terrifying woman, but she stopped them.'

He scratched his head.

'The Praetorians can't keep turning out like this. Their prime duty is to protect the imperatrix. I just hope it's a summer flare-up and it'll calm down in a few days. The regular forces are controlling transport movements and the public radio and television are broadcasting "keep calm" messages. Can't do anything about the commercial media, more's the pity, but we've asked them to cooperate.' He curled and stretched a piece of string between his fingers. 'But after an inquiry, we're going to have to crack down on these thugs. And the imperatrix will have to sign a controlling order, *volens nolens*.' He glanced over at me. 'Your bruised face at the council might help.'

'I doubt it. Nothing happened when Marina was attacked.'

'She's had a crap time.'

'Yes. I'm going to do my damnedest to make sure it doesn't become any worse.'

Fabia was called back with Plico the next day, but gave us another day's grace, leaving the second helicopter and half the troops. At least the journey by air would be faster as well as safer. She also assigned four Praetorians to stay for a week to assist Gavinus in training the farm staff. The hands looked terrified of the confident, self-contained troops but they'd settled down by the next evening when we left.

The rhythmic thud of the helicopter engine drowned out any possibility of talking normally, but I had plenty to think about as we rode back.

There was no charge I could bring against Callixtus; dereliction of duty and negligence were civil torts, private matters. He'd been hired to protect a family and home, not an official person. I brought him back to Domus Mitelarum under guard to dismiss him formally. I was repelled at sharing transport with him, but I refused to let him see my bitterness at his betrayal.

'I'm not going to waste my time and effort chasing you through the civil courts – there are more important things for me to do at the moment. You broke my trust. That's worse than anything.'

He had the grace to look away.

'You'll be escorted to your quarters to collect your personal effects. You have an hour. You will not speak to anybody else. After you exit through the house gate, if I ever hear of you anywhere near me, any member of my family and household, any of my friends, colleagues or businesses, I will take permanent measures. Do you understand?'

He nodded.

After I'd turned him out of the door and cancelled all his access codes, I told Plico to have Callixtus's weapons licences, both personal and professional, revoked with immediate effect and to put him on the watch list as a member of the Roman National Movement. I made an international call during that night. Eighteen hours later William Brown arrived in Roma Nova.

103

14

I hadn't told Marina. We were sitting in the atrium drinking our coffee after dinner when he was announced. She jumped up, then stood bolt still watching him approach. He smiled. She smiled back, then walked up to him and put her hand in his outstretched one. They said nothing. After some seconds, he broke his gaze and looked at me.

'Countess Mitela.' He nodded, but didn't smile. 'You said you needed me. How can I help?'

He stayed for six days, upgrading and reinforcing every aspect of our electronic defences and communications. On the third day, two nondescript men speaking EUS English and carrying black leather messenger bags arrived with a small crate. The three men worked silently most of the time, wrapped in their own bubble of technology. I commissioned a helicopter to take them out to Castra Lucilla for a day. In the evenings, William Brown sat quietly, his face tight with the fatigue of working fourteen-hour days, but he seemed content just to be near Marina.

Driving to the Monday morning imperial council, we had to go through several new checkpoints, staffed by mixed *vigiles* and troops, and negotiate builders, glaziers and street cleaning vans. Rubbish, burnt vehicles and abandoned loot from shops scattered over the roads and pavements gave the city a sombre look, almost like a war zone. Nobody said a word when Fabia trooped in behind me. I noticed Interior had a *vigiles* officer shadowing him, and the *magister miletum* was accompanied by a senior infantry tribune trying to look nonchalant. Unlike Fabia, though, none of them was allowed to be armed inside the palace precincts.

Instead of milling and gossiping as usual, some of the councillors stood in a glum patch, faces dejected, glancing across the room at others who had already taken their places behind their chairs. Not a sign of the usual banter. Some fidgeted with their folders or papers, others changed their weight from foot to foot. No sign of Caius Tellus. That was odd, very odd. I looked at Fabia and we shifted into an alcove out of general earshot.

'Find out where Caius Tellus is. I want him tracked. I wouldn't put it past him to burst in here with a crowd of toga toughs and take over.'

'Isn't that a little extreme?' She hadn't used the word paranoid, but I was certain she was thinking it.

'No. Let's be sure. Do it.'

We'd been waiting fifteen minutes when Severina entered the council room with Plico and the *praetor urbanus* in tow. What was Roma Nova's most senior magistrate doing here?

'Please, sit,' Severina said with no trace of her usual vapidity. Her mouth was tight as if she had been eating lemons. As we scuttled into our chairs, the *praetor* took his place to one side and behind the imperatrix. Without looking back he held up his hand and flicked his fingers. A staffer handed him a purple leather folder. To my surprise I saw it was Quintus Tellus. Of course, he'd scraped in as a deputy *praetor* at the last judicial elections, despite his convict brother.

'You can hardly be unaware of recent disturbances, the parades, riots and that rally by the amphitheatre,' Severina began. 'The attack on Aurelia Mitela's farm is not the only one.' She waved her hand in my direction in a half-hearted way. 'No others have reported deaths, though, according to the *vigiles*.' She stopped and half emptied her glass of water. 'I don't understand what's happening,' she continued. 'Why are these men so discontented?' She looked around the room for a few seconds. Nobody answered.

'I have been persuaded—' she glanced up at Plico and the *praetor* '—to introduce a temporary control order with curfew.' She pulled her shoulders back. 'I am very unhappy at doing this. It seems brutal to impose such constraints on normal law-abiding people. If you as my council are equally unhappy, then I will not sign it.' She looked at us one by one, almost pleading. Some looked away, but most returned her look with grim expressions, only one or two councillors nodding in agreement with her.

We dropped our pebble ballots into the marble jar as it passed around the table; silver for consent, obsidian for dissent. At the end, Quintus came forward to count them. He picked up the voting urn as if it was a cauldron of hot writhing snakes. As he stood by the table at Severina's left, all our stares focused on the pile of ballots. Only three obsidian. I let out a sigh of relief, careful for it not to sound too loud.

Severina's face looked like thunder. 'Very well.' She flicked her hand as if batting a wasp away. But the *praetor* dodged her fingers and dutifully slipped the control order on to the table. She scribbled her signature in half a second and threw the pen down like a child in a tantrum. 'I hope it works as you want it to.'

'Whatever the reason behind this unrest, it must be stopped,' ventured the *magister miletum*. 'I have neither resources nor manpower to field enough military to do the *vigiles'* job in keeping order.' The interior minister started to rise to his feet at that, but Severina waved him back. The *magister* continued, 'Despite standing orders, Colonel Volusenia took the initiative. She performed magnificently. I'm proud to have troops like her at my disposal.' He sent a belligerent look at the interior minister, then leaned back and crossed his arms with apparently no more to say.

'Imperatrix, I must contest the *magister*'s remarks.' The interior minister flapped two sheets of paper he was holding. 'The *vigiles* are understaffed in most areas and have suffered a high level of sickness and injury in the past twelve months.'

'Then why didn't you ask for extra budget and recruit more as soon as you had three months' trends?' Quirinia shot at him. As deputy *quaestor* she knew the government budget inside out. 'You know we have a reserve allocation for law and order.'

'My people thought it was a temporary blip.' He glanced at her. 'We've tried to contain it, but we don't seem to be getting anywhere.'

This was insane. *Vigiles* enjoyed many privileges apart from good pay and a government pension – they were housed free, paid nothing for transport and enjoyed free passes to all games. Recruiters were always turning people away.

'Show me the figures.' I stretched out my hand. I felt rather than saw Plico peer over my shoulder.

'Jupiter! What's this?' I said. The column for recruitment showed a twenty-nine per cent decline in the past six months. Sickness and injury had risen by seventeen per cent and the resignations rate for personal reasons was an astounding twenty-one per cent.

As I recited the figures, shocked faces stared back at me. Silence was their only reaction. The *praetor urbanus* beckoned Plico back to his side and whispered something to him. Plico stood up to his full height, bowed to the imperatrix, who nodded. He looked the interior minister straight in the face.

'Your police force is being eaten up from the inside, *consiliarius*. And it's been going on right under your nose. You either have totally incompetent direction or a significant proportion of the *vigiles* has been corrupted. The *praetor urbanus* has instructed me to carry out a full investigation. All proactive policing is suspended. Your role is containment and all *vigiles* will return to barrack quarters whether they live outside with their families or not.'

He looked at the head of the armed forces. 'I'm sorry, *Magister*, but your troops are going to have to be deployed in a central role while this investigation is carried out.'

Fabia was waiting for me outside.

'Nothing,' she said.

'What do you mean, "nothing"?'

'We can't find him. He's not at home, or the Tella office in the financial quarter. I'm sorry, *consiliaria*, I couldn't go further.'

Unreasonable of me to expect anything else. The Praetorians were military. They were forbidden to cross the line and deal with civilians. Even with their extended authority, the PGSF couldn't trespass on *vigiles* turf. Gods, it was so frustrating. We had work to do, and urgently. We had trained and competent people to do it. But everything was locked up in rigid, jealously guarded institutional territories.

I waited until Plico had finished talking to the *magister miletum*.

'Odd, that,' he commented on Caius Tellus's absence. 'I don't like it, but I haven't any spare capacity with all this unrest.'

'Can't you draft some others in? Use the PGSF?'

'Oh, that would go down well, wouldn't it?' He gave me a 'don't be an idiot' look. 'We're dealing with egos and bruised sensibilities and you're suggesting we use the do-or-die brigade to do intelligence work? Oh, spare me, do.'

'Come on, Plico, use the brain you've got underneath all that attitude. They're tough, persistent and motivated. And they're not stupid. You don't know how bloody hard it is to pass the entrance tests. You know I came from the PGSF.'

'Yes, and look at the trouble you've caused me,' he grumped.

'Oh, please! Look, I know you're in the arena with lions on every side, but think about it. If you hand-pick them, form them into a small self-contained squad and give them some intelligence basics, they'd be invaluable.'

He made a face, but said nothing. His gaze flickered around the anteroom. 'Okay, I'll get somebody onto Caius Tellus. It'd be stupid not to, but I haven't time for your other idea.'

I watched, frustrated, as Plico waddled down the corridor. I knew if I made it a formal ministerial request, he'd find some way to sideline it. I beckoned Fabia to me and asked her to fix me an appointment with Volusenia.

When William Brown announced the next evening he'd finished his work installing the new systems and was flying back to the EUS the following morning, Marina was standing next to him, a suitcase either side of her. My heart was sore. I knew what was coming.

'I'm going with William, Mama.' A bald statement. A fact. I was losing my child.

'Yes, I see you are. And I know he will be kind to you and protect you.'

'It's not that – we love each other,' she protested.

'I know, darling. Of course.'

I looked at him. He returned it as steadily. He understood exactly.

She had no idea of what she would be facing. She'd be protected physically and William Brown was comfortable financially. He didn't only have contracts with the Roma Novan government, but with the EUS, the United Kingdom and many other European states. And he'd divorced his first wife a few years ago with a generous settlement – an unfortunate alliance, according to Plico. The file had said honey trap; older woman, inexperienced young man. It was the regressive society he would be taking her into that worried me – the casual sexism, the pressure to conform and their brutal crime rate. She would be crushed by it.

When she'd gone to bed, he came back down and sat with me. I poured us both a large brandy.

'Mr Brown,' I began.

'William, please.'

'Very well. You know I'm grateful to you for responding so quickly, but I think it wasn't for me that you were here in less than twenty-four hours.'

He tilted his head and nodded.

'Despite the dreadful attack on her, Marina is an innocent, without any instinctive sense of self-preservation. She has a tender heart but often a child's viewpoint. I—'

'Please, Countess, don't disturb yourself. I know what she is and I love her even more for it.'

'Being frank, I worry what pressure your government may bring to bear on you and ultimately her. I know through my contacts in the EUS that the administration would like to control Brown Industries. If they try to get at you through her, she has no guile to—'

He laid his hand on mine. 'I will take every care of her and they won't touch her.' His face tightened and his hazel eyes became like twin agates. 'But if I ever track down who hurt her in the riots here, I'll kill him.'

'No, you won't.'

He flashed an angry look at me.

'I will have got there first.'

I embraced Marina so hard at the foot of the steps to the plane that she protested.

'It's all right, Mama, I'm not disappearing from the world. I'll fly back and see you soon. Or you can come and see William and me.' She gave me a little smile. 'Who knows? There may even be three of us.'

I stopped hearing the engine noise, feeling the wind flapping my hair on my face. I replayed her words. And I realised she was slipping from me, possibly taking my grandchild with her. Surely, it was too soon.

'Marina, are you sure?'

'That I want to go? Of course.'

Had she deliberately misunderstood my question?

She smiled up at William Brown who kissed the top of her head. He looked at his watch.

'We must leave now or the pilot will lose his window. Goodbye, Aurelia.' He shook my hand briefly, caught Marina's in his and guided her up the steps. Marina turned and gave me a last wave.

My throat sore, I could hardly swallow the hard lump in it. I lifted my hand to wave, but only managed a feeble gesture. I stayed on the tarmac, still as a column in the forum, until the plane vanished into the clouds.

PART III

ERUPTION

15

───────

I went straight to the Foreign Ministry where I would find so much work I'd hardly be able to breathe, let alone think. If I went home, I would see Marina everywhere.

Claudia Cornelia handed me a summary of events while I'd been absent and another sheet with the rest of the week's work schedule. It had been just over two weeks since Marina had been raped and eight days since the murderous attack on the farm. My daughter had been traumatised and my staff terrified and forced to live under armed guard. And now I was supposed to shuffle paper and run meetings.

'Enough!' I thumped the desk so hard everything jangled. Claudia flinched. I stood up, strode to the door and wrenched it open. The Praetorian outside stood to attention as I approached her. 'Get Major Fabia on the secure net, stat,' I snapped.

Back inside my office, I apologised to Claudia. 'I can't sit here and do nothing, Claudia. I know something fundamental is threatening us and we have to find out what.' I glanced at her. 'I may have to ask you to do things outside your normal duties, possibly risky, even dangerous. Your career could be seriously compromised. I completely understand if you decline, but I need to know now.'

Dull red patches and a tight mouth on her grave face – she looked angry. Her whole body stiffened. Damn. I'd insulted her by asking. She was a Cornelia, probably the proudest and most proper of the

Twelve Families. But when she spoke, her voice was as controlled and polite as usual.

'I am unhappy that you had to ask, Aurelia Mitela. I hope I have not given you any cause to doubt my service. If you are dissatisfied, then I will tender my resignation immediately.'

Gods. Proud was an inadequate description.

'Claudia,' I said gently. 'I didn't mean to insult you or your integrity, but while I might risk myself, my family and my name, I can't possibly expect you to do the same without offering you the choice. It wouldn't be honourable.'

She relaxed slightly and took a half-step towards me. 'I will serve you until I am no longer useful.' She looked away only when the knock on the door interrupted the silence. The guard came in and proffered me a crackling radio.

Volusenia hadn't softened a whit since I'd seen her the night of the riot.

'It's fortunate timing you asked me now, *consiliaria*,' she said. 'You may not have had time to read the circulars, but I've been asked to step into the PGSF branch as deputy legate. That idiot Opsius crashed his car and has landed himself with a plaster boot and his back in traction. I move office tomorrow.'

'Then you can authorise the formation of a small intelligence unit.'

'Under whose authority?' she barked at me.

'The imperial council has issued a ninety-day control order. The *praetor urbanus* has assumed emergency powers on the imperatrix's instructions.'

'He's sound enough but unimaginative.' She frowned. 'What's Tertullius Plico's role in this?'

'He's been appointed the *praetor*'s executive.' I wasn't going to give her details.

'Ha! His dog, you mean.' She glanced up at me. 'And you're pulling Plico's leash.'

I said nothing.

'Very well, I'll sort you out a few people. Fabia will head them up – you seem to have worked well with her in the past.'

'I suggest you make it a priority,' I replied.

Volusenia selected a first group of twenty ready for training within a day. I insisted on Plico seconding two good retired operatives, but he grumbled he could only spare one. He was too pushed to even do that.

'Look, it's an investment for you,' I said. 'Two instructors will get them through in half the time. In two weeks you'll have them ready to go out in the field. They're not exactly beginners. You pair each one with an experienced operative. They'll soon learn.'

'Are you trying to teach me my job?'

'Somebody has to shock some sense into you.'

'I don't think it'll make that much difference.'

'What do you mean?' I said.

He heaved himself to his feet, went off to his filing cabinet and took out a file.

'Read that,' he said quietly and sat down in his office chair.

The report was written in an emotionless style, but I was nearly sick when I put it back on the table.

'When did you find out?'

'This morning,' he replied. 'It took the local military camp a day to discover the bodies and another day to bring the news in here.' He slumped, elbows on desk, his hands pushing the hair back at his hairline. 'The border post hadn't reported in to the local camp on the regular evening radio check but they knew was a big party going on at the camp so it seems they didn't bother. When the camp had no answer from the border post the next morning and couldn't raise them on the phone either, the commander eventually sent a patrol out.' He snorted. 'A crowd of pissed-off troops with hangovers.' He glanced down at his notes 'He put an *optio*, a woman called Junia Sestina, in charge of that patrol. She'd got on their wick urging them to raise the alarm the evening before. Apparently, they thought it would teach her a lesson. Anyway, they found all twelve border guards stone dead. I'm flying up there in forty-five minutes with the *magister miletum's* investigator.'

'Cause of death?'

'Not formally recorded, but gunshot.'

'What's your feel – internal or external?'

'Too early, but given all the other crap that's been happening, I'd say internal.'

I walked over to his bookshelf, scanned the leather-backed collections, but didn't register their titles.

'Did you track Caius Tellus down after we talked at the council meeting?'

'Yes and no. I insisted on seeing old Countess Tella, but to be honest and no disrespect, she's gone a bit gaga. I think Constantia Tella's sudden death hit her very hard. I was getting nowhere. But I caught the under-steward after I'd asked to use the facilities. She was nervous, but indicated Caius had hopped it abroad. We think we've found the flight he went on. The video picture's fuzzy, but his walk gives him away.'

'And?'

'The flight arrived at IAD – Washington in the EUS.' He grunted. 'Pity they don't have cameras there.'

'You've asked the legation to help?'

'I told them to send a team of ferrets out to find him. They ID'd his hire car, then the apartment where he was staying and guess who owns it?'

'Plico...' I scowled at him.

'Sorry. Langley.'

'Hades.'

'Quite. I've put out a couple of feelers to find out what the hell the Yanks are doing talking to our chief headache, but I haven't heard back.'

'Talk to their head of station here – Farrow, isn't it?'

He nodded.

'They know how hard our attitude is towards foreign interference. Give him a gentle reminder, please.'

He tipped his head in acknowledgement, then glanced at his watch.

'Yes, you must go.' I looked at the floor for several long seconds. 'You know something, Plico? This level of surgical brutality is deliberate, planned. And I don't think it's unrelated to the recent riots or Caius cosying up to foreign intelligence organisations. I'm calling another Families Council – I feel in my gut we don't have mere actions by discontents but a threat to our very survival.'

Once again, the descendants of the founding families sat in the atrium at Domus Mitelarum facing another struggle to survive. The only one missing was Tella. I'd dispatched each summons by courier with two escorts. I was about to call order when there was a loud rap on the locked door. Quirinia opened it and Quintus Tellus appeared in the doorway.

'Quintus? Where's your great-aunt?'

He bowed to the group. 'I apologise, Aurelia, she's unwell.' He took a deep breath. 'She's dying.'

'Pluto!' muttered Quirinia at my left. I exchanged a glance with her. Ignoring the dead Constantia's child, Conradus, Caius would have a clear field to become the next Count Tellus.

'I'm sorry to hear that, Quintus. Please accept the Families Council sympathy. Are you staying to represent the Tellae?'

He hesitated. He must have felt pulled from all angles: his role as an elected public servant, being the brother of a convicted criminal, staying with his dying aunt and head of family and his right and duty to represent his house at the most ancient and powerful forum in Roma Nova.

'I think I must stay, but please understand if I'm paged and have to leave during the session.'

I waved him to the empty seat on my right.

As he settled in and the others were talking amongst themselves, I leaned over and whispered, 'What's happening to the child, Quintus?'

'I went round yesterday and saw Caius's steward. He's a lazy slob, but the cook's not too bad. She's looking after Conradus in a rough way – lets him sleep by the kitchen fire instead of that bloody dog kennel Caius put him in.'

'Gods, it's like something out of ancient times. Can't we do anything more?'

Quintus pressed my hand. 'No, it's that testament he made Constantia sign. I'm keeping my eye on him, Aurelia. Please don't worry – you have enough to do.'

I outlined the steps the imperial council had taken, shared the reports from ministries, and asked Quirinia and Quintus to share their knowledge. When I invited questions, nobody asked any. Their shocked faces said it all.

'My sister's been working like a contracted worker – all hours – especially now she's transferred to the PGSF,' Volusenia the Elder said. 'I thought I was going to be ordering her bier when she faced those rioters last week.' She had the same strong features as the colonel, but a fleshier face and a head of white hair instead of grey-brown. She was easily fifteen years older.

'Well, Severina's not up to providing leadership in this,' Livia said bluntly.

'I've never been that impressed by her,' Cornelia commented, 'but we owe her our duty to support her.' She fixed her stare on me, almost challenging.

Quintus fidgeted at my side.

'As I've outlined, the imperial council is attempting to steer a middle course, but I want to be able to give our help and influence to stabilise the situation.' I panned around the twelve faces. 'So what can you offer?'

'It looks as if we should check for any Roman National Movement people within our own households and spheres of influence, and try to dampen down this irrational rhetoric,' Cornelia added. She waved vaguely. 'I have to admit I hadn't taken too much notice of them before.'

'Oh, come on,' I replied, 'it's been all over the news.'

'I have better things to do than check what the rabble are up to.'

'You know something, Cornelia, that's exactly the attitude that's firing them up. And it's well beyond a few discontents.' I felt anger at her dismissive attitude. This kind of wilful blindness was so dangerous.

'When will you get Plico's report about the killings at the border post?' Calavia said.

'Within a day or so. Why?'

'My son and granddaughter are both serving officers. I'll ask them what the feeling is in their units.'

The others followed with offers to contribute information and we agreed to meet up in five days' time to coordinate our findings and produce a proposal to submit to the imperatrix.

'Two final things,' I said. 'First, you may think I'm being paranoid but as a precaution, I suggest you secure your family archives and treasure somewhere deep, and spread your investments. Obviously, as unobtrusively as possible or it may unnerve people.'

'Is it that bad?' Cornelia asked. She didn't quite scoff, but her look was full of doubt.

'If it isn't, then you can censure me formally. If it is, then you will have taken a wise step.'

'And the other?' asked Calavia. She may have been ninety, but with her eyes shining and her chin forward, she looked ready for anything.

I glanced at Quirinia, who nodded. I cleared my throat.

'Caius Tellus failed to appear at the imperial council meeting before last as well as the last one. My intelligence department reports he's in the EUS. Our local agents have tracked him down to a building owned by the CIA. He's been there for two weeks and has had several visitors identified as employees of the CIA. What this signifies, I don't know, but we're monitoring it closely.' I glanced around the table. 'Personally, so many alarm bells are going off in my head, I can't think. Caius's support of the Roman National Movement and his absence at a time when the Families should be rallying round in the crisis are bad indications. If he's conspiring with overseas intelligence agencies who are not particular friends of Roma Nova, then I think the danger is more than grave.'

16

———

'He's back.'

I didn't need Plico to elaborate who. 'When?'

'Flew in last night.'

'Follow every move. I want to know when he takes a breath.'

'I'll use some of your PGSF people. They're turning out to be quite good.'

'Careful, Plico, you said something nice.'

He snorted. I almost heard him grin. Which made a change. His investigation of the border troops massacre hadn't led anywhere. Forensics had shown that the weapons used and the rounds themselves were standard military issue which made the whole thing even more depressing.

But the demonstrations and parades had stopped, thank the gods, and the interior minister's new deputy had sent a full inspection team into the *vigiles* with a reform programme in their pockets. Apparently, the reaction had been sullen but they complied.

'By the way, did you have a word with the American head of station here about non-interference?'

'He just looked at me surprised and hurt, and denied any interference, so they're definitely involved.'

Merda. We'd refused to take part in the EUS superpower politics struggle with the eastern Reds. A policy of mostly non-alignment had saved us for the past fifteen hundred years and we would not compromise our neutrality. I wouldn't call in their ambassador yet, but I'd keep it in reserve.

'Well, check for an increase in their embassy staff or an unusual number of tourists.'

'Oh, I'd never have thought of doing that.' His voice was tight and sarcastic.

'Sorry, Plico, that was tactless. Just a bit tense here.'

'Stop trying to micro-manage everything and toddle off to your meeting.'

Bastard. But a tough and ultra-loyal one.

'Well, I do seem to have missed some excitement while I've been away.'

Caius sat opposite me at the imperial council table playing with his pen and doodling on his paper pad. Plico's report had shown that Caius went to see Severina the day after his return, and had taken her gifts. Apparently, he'd been all humility but coated his words with a patronising tone.

'How do you know that?' I'd asked Plico.

'Need to know,' he'd replied and tapped the side of his nose. So Plico was listening in to the imperatrix again. I pretended I hadn't made that connection. Whatever he'd said, Caius had cajoled or manipulated Severina into letting him keep his seat on the council.

'With the *vigiles* in disarray and the military incapable of even defending themselves,' Caius said, before Severina could start, 'I suggest, Imperatrix, that we call upon loyal and right-minded citizens to assist in the current crisis.'

'What are you proposing, Caius Tellus?' asked Quirinia. She looked as if she had a bad smell under her nose.

'It won't cost your precious budget a single *denarius*, my dear Quirinia. I know how anxious you become about tallying your figures.'

Dull red patches appeared on her cheeks. She tightened her lips for a moment before answering. 'A budget of over thirty billion *solidi* is hardly something you tally on an abacus.'

Caius just smiled at her as he would a recalcitrant child. 'Whatever you say, Quirinia.'

I thought she was going to explode. She looked caught between venting her anger and not wishing to lose her dignity.

'I think we should at least hear Caius Tellus's proposal,' piped up the junior commerce minister. He'd only been in post six months and was representing his minister today. 'No help should be refused in a crisis,' he added in a sententious tone, and turned his full attention to Caius.

'We're starting to come out of it, Felinus, if you read the report thoroughly,' I said. 'Which aspects in particular do you think need special help?' I smiled at him and waited.

'I... I would prefer to answer after Caius Tellus has outlined his proposal, Foreign Minister.'

'Really?'

'Come now, Aurelia,' Caius intervened. 'Don't tease the boy – he's trying to be positive.' He shot Felinus a ferocious look. His stooge flushed and looked down at the table and wriggled in his seat.

'But it's a fragile recovery,' Caius continued, leaning back in his seat, completely relaxed. 'I've been consulting with American economic and political experts in the last few weeks...'

Severina stared at him. Her mouth didn't quite drop open.

'... obviously in an informal and confidential way. They are willing to lend their help, but a condition is that order is restored.' He smiled at the stunned faces around the table. 'The Roman National Movement has disciplined organised cohorts. I have some open channels to them. I propose we ask their senior leadership in for talks to see what help they can offer.'

'Over my dead body!' I was on my feet hurling my voice across the table at Caius's unctuous face. Quirinia and Calavia shouted 'No' almost in unison. The room erupted. Caius shot me a look of pure malice and smiled. Through the shouting noise, I heard him say clearly, 'That could be easily arranged, Aurelia.'

Back in my Foreign Ministry office, I went straight to the tray and poured myself a stiff measure of French brandy. I should have known better than to rise to Caius's provocation. Of course, it would be stupid to dismiss his threat but I had my guard and despite being in my forties, I wasn't a complete pushover if attacked personally.

A buzzer on my desk interrupted my negative thoughts.

'The interior minister and *magister miletum* are here and ask if you have a few minutes.' Cornelia's voice sounded as assured as usual. How could she remain so cool?

'Of course. Show them in.'

I waved them both to easy chairs at the side and joined them. The interior minister coughed and attempted to recover his breath. He couldn't have been more than mid-sixties, but looked as if he'd spent the last ten years in the silver mines at Truscium. He'd lost weight over the past six months and I thought he wouldn't last much longer, but he refused to give his post up to his number two. Apart from formalities in council, we'd hardly spoken since Marina's attack. Although I knew in my bones it was Caius, I held this old fool partly to blame, and for the poor investigation. He avoided meeting my eye and gestured at the *magister* to speak.

'Foreign Minister, we find ourselves in a quandary.'

The *magister* was punctilious as always, but I was wary of the way he addressed me by my function rather than my *praenomen*, Aurelia. What the hell was coming next?

'I'll be blunt,' he continued. 'Caius Tellus. He's obviously looking for a power grab.'

Blunt indeed.

'He's obviously in cahoots with these nationalist people – any fool can see that. The imperial council is the only way to stop him within the law and it has to do it now.'

'I would remind you, *Magister*, the imperatrix is the legal ruler of Roma Nova, albeit with the consent of the council, Senate, and the people's tribunes.'

'All due respect, Aurelia, Severina Apulia couldn't open a jar of beans.'

'Careful, *Magister*,' I said.

'We're stable as long as she has strong advisors like you and Quirinia and is backed by fixers like Plico, but what would happen if you were all removed?'

'What are you saying?'

'After Caius's outrageous proposal,' the *magister* continued, 'Interior and I met and looked at the figures.'

'Mine aren't the only shocking ones, Aurelia,' the interior minister added and coughed violently. When he recovered, he shuffled some stapled sheets across the table. 'Look at the Curia stats for the local elections.'

I scanned the districts' returns. Nearly forty-six per cent had a Roman National Movement councillor and a dozen a deputy leader. No leaders, though. With all my personal and security problems, I hadn't noticed. What an idiot.

'Very well. Suggestions?' I looked from one to the other.

'If he succeeds, the military and *vigiles* will have no option but to obey him,' the *magister* said. 'That's the law. I'd resign, but that would allow him to appoint a stooge. The same for everybody. We're caught whatever we do.'

'You can always mutiny,' I half joked. This was too fantastical to take seriously.

'And have my troops decimated? I think not.'

'You're not serious?' I said. 'That's not still in the codex, is it?'

'Unfortunately, yes.'

'Mars' balls!' I closed my eyes for a few seconds and leant back in my chair. Picking out every tenth soldier and ordering her or his comrades to beat them to death on pain of suffering the same fate was a barbarity beyond imagining.

'The ancients only used it occasionally *in extremis*.' The *magister* shrugged. 'A pragmatic way to punish a large group of offenders.' He gave me the grimmest look I'd ever seen on his craggy face. 'Nobody's used it in Roma Nova for nearly a thousand years but it's never been rescinded. A bastard like Caius Tellus would know that, and use it.'

'You've looked into this in detail, haven't you?'

'I like to be ready.'

'So no commander, even at centurion or *optio* level, is going to risk it.' I was stating the obvious, but it was a perfect trap. 'Terror by numbers.'

'Exactly,' the *magister* replied.

'Rescinding that provision is the top of the next council meeting agenda.' I scribbled it on my notepad, underlining hard.

'You think that'll stop him?'

'For the gods' sake, why are you so sure it's going to happen?'

'I can add up.'

'Interior?' I said. 'Anything to add?'

He bowed his head and didn't speak for a few moments.

'I can't disagree with the *magister miletum*.'

'Very well,' I said. 'I admit, privately, I've had my fears, but I'm well aware I could be allowing my personal view to taint my judgement. Caius and I have hated one another since we were children. I was responsible for putting him away in a Prussian jail for twelve years. His criminal partner tried to kill me at the time and Caius threatened the same when he came out. I also think he was behind the attacks on my daughter and my farm. But I have no proof. Now my people live and work under armed guard and my daughter has fled to America.' I paused for breath. 'I've been too distracted, maybe with deliberate intent.'

Their faces said it all.

'I don't suppose you could suggest one of Plico's people, er, fix things?' the *magister* said, a hopeful note in his voice.

'Extra-judicial murder?' I frowned at him.

'I agree that in normal circumstances it would be deplorable,' he said, 'but it would be a quick solution.'

'I do understand your point, *Magister*,' I replied. 'Years ago when we were hunting Caius Tellus for murder, my senior centurion asked if he could shoot to kill if he had Caius in his sights. I was strongly tempted, believe me. Now I wonder if should have bent the rules for the sake of Roma Nova.' I let out a long breath. 'But that would have made us as bad as him.'

Two years ago, I'd turned down Miklós's offer for the same reason.

'Then what do you suggest, Aurelia?'

After they left I sent for Plico, but he was busy with the *praetor urbanus*. He'd drop by my office first thing tomorrow, his assistant assured me. I hesitated. I could insist, but one thing about Plico, he knew how to prioritise. If he thought whatever he was doing was more important than reporting to me, then it would be that important.

Claudia handed me a report off the wire. Now I knew where Plico was. A riot had broken out in the harbour area and a fierce fire was threatening to reduce the state food warehouses to ash. I could hear multiple sirens through the windows. What on earth was going on out there? I grabbed my telephone handset. It was jerked out of my hand.

My chair moved under me. No, the floor had moved. Claudia stumbled and grabbed onto the desk. The whole building was shaking. We staggered to the window. The boom of the explosion slammed down on us. Windows bulged inward, then crazed into glass webs. Claudia fell back on the carpet. I grabbed a chair and steadied myself. Only the windows being strengthened security glass saved us being ripped to shreds. Outside, flames raged high into the early evening sky. The roar thudded in our ears. It was the petroleum plant across the river. Black billowing clouds followed, then more fire vehicle sirens.

'Gods, oh gods,' Claudia shouted, her face streaked with tears. She sniffed, grabbed a tissue and started to wipe her face. Before she'd finished, a Praetorian burst in.

'Major Fabia has radioed you're to be escorted to the safe bunker, Minister.' He looked as grim as if he was in a war zone.

'Wait five,' I snapped back at him. 'Claudia, telex. Cipher blocks. Now!' I grabbed my blue minister's box, stashed the legations' lists and codes in it, the contents of my personal safe and my file on Caius Tellus. I flung my photo of Marina on top.

Claudia ran to my personal secure telex, flipped the control panel open and reached inside. She extracted two rectangles with twin circuit boards and cables, rows of multiple connector pins each long side, and handed them to me.

'It's like the Great Fire out there,' she whispered, looking through the crazed window.

Gods, I hoped not. Apart from the hundreds of lives lost, it had destroyed half of ancient Rome.

The guard's radio crackled and he thrust it at me.

'Mitela, Fabia. Relay from Volusenia – it's started. Out.'

17

From the bunker control room, we watched the public news reports and the CCTV, although it was blurred and full of static. I'd initiated our emergency plan and until the situation clarified we'd run the ministry from here. Claudia, now restored to her cool efficiency, supervised incoming information and liaised with the foreign delegations in the city as well as our legations abroad. Banks of desks were now occupied by my people, a little uncomfortable working in such close quarters, but quietly getting on despite the tension you could almost taste in the air.

I couldn't sit still. I walked up and down in front of the black and white screens, seeing twenty *vigiles* tenders spraying foam at the petroleum fire and tackling the warehouses. Others, plus some military, had barriered off the docks area. As we watched the images flicker from one part of the city to another, we saw more military patrolling in groups. People were panicking, running and screaming, trying to rescue things as fires sprang up in several districts.

'Where did those fires come from?' Fulvia, my diplomatic security chief, so suave and calm normally, jabbed her finger at different screens. 'What in Hades are the *vigiles* doing?' She was right – it was bizarre.

'Find me a city map,' I said.

She instructed one of her staffers to call out the locations and we plotted the fires. We got there at the same time.

'Some bastard's setting the fires,' she growled.

'Give me your radio,' I ordered the guard. 'Fabia? Mitela. Somebody's deliberately firing the districts. If the *vigiles* can't cope, tell the *magister* to get his engineers there with their auxiliary fire vehicles. Stat.'

Her answer made my blood run cold.

'What do you mean, they've been confined to barracks? Who the hell gave that instruction? It's an emergency. Tell him I'm ordering them to turn out.'

It was chaotic in the streets and the thick smoke was obscuring everything, including the CCTV. I had to hope the interior ministry had initiated their disaster plan, but I realised that was a false hope. Even from the blurred images, we watched helpless as looters moved in. And the *vigiles* seemed to have melted away.

We were interrupted by a telephone call from the palace, summoning the council to an immediate emergency session. The guard lifted his radio to call for secure transport.

'No, there's another way. Give me a minute.'

I beckoned Claudia and Fulvia over and tore off a length of paper from the nearest teleprinter. I wrote as I spoke. 'Listen. It's all going to Hades out there. I have to go to the palace now. If for any reason I'm not back within twelve hours, here's my temporary authority to keep the ministry going. Do what you have to do.'

'*Consiliaria*, I must come with you,' Claudia protested.

'No, I need you to stay with our people.'

Fulvia nodded and I went.

'What's your name, soldier?'

'Atrius, Second Cohort, *consiliaria*.' he replied from his considerable height.

'Very well, Atrius, you are to completely forget where we are going once we've got there.'

'Yes, ma'am.'

We hurried along a secondary corridor to the service area then down a flight of steps to the engineering plant room. I entered the combination into the keypad and pushed the door open. At the back, almost hidden by the main boiler was a plain door with a chemical hazard sign and another keypad lock. It opened to reveal racks of plastic bottles and a janitor's sink. Flicking the light on, I pushed the door shut behind us. I grabbed the fire extinguisher and swung it away from its wall bracket, revealing a small compartment in the base. Inside was a large, old-fashioned key.

I pressed a moulding on the bracket and the wall slid back to reveal a wooden door, plain but clearly old. Hefting the key, I unlocked it. A long tunnel stretched ahead of us.

'Switch the cupboard light off, Atrius.'

A grim-faced Fabia met us at the other end of the tunnel which came out in the old palace kitchens, now used as utility and storage areas. We walked in silence through the domestic hall, not looking at any of the staff casting curious looks at us. As we approached the anteroom I saw at least a dozen PGSF in the corridors and another two at the door.

'Eight councillors are here. We're expecting at least three more,' she said tersely and glanced at her watch.

'Wait a minute, Fabia, that would make only twelve out of twenty-eight. We wouldn't be quorate.'

'I'm expecting the colonel in the next half-hour. She's hoping to find another two, but to be honest, I think we're past that.'

'What do you mean?'

She looked uncharacteristically nervous. 'I'd prefer to let the colonel explain.'

'Now wait a minute, nobody can suspend the legal decision-making process arbitrarily.'

'It seems that somebody can.'

We hurried through to the council room. Even here at the back of the palace, the glow from the fires raging down in the city shone through the tall diamond-paned windows.

Severina looked haggard. Her hair was messy, her dress wrinkled as if she'd been lying down in it. I bowed, but she waved her hand as if dismissing such niceties.

'Thank Juno! Aurelia. You're my cousin. You won't let me down, will you?'

'Of course not, Severina. What's the matter?'

'I've done something stupid.'

'What?'

'Caius.'

'What have you done?

She shook her head.

I seized her hands and shook them. 'Tell me, Severina. Now!'

'It's all falling apart. People are rioting. It's like Hades. I didn't know what to do.' She looked up. 'Julian was shouting at me, Silvia begging me not to give in to Caius. It seemed the only way. He's strong, he knows what to do.'

I looked at Fabia. She nodded.

'Severina, I want you to stay here with Major Fabia. I'll be back shortly.'

I ran like the Furies were after me into the family quarters. I burst into the living room, only to find the barrel of a hunting rifle in my face. I froze, then relaxed when I saw who it was.

'Julian! Where's your sister?'

'I'm here, Aunt Aurelia.' Silvia emerged from behind her mother's china cabinet.

'Thank the gods!'

'Sorry about the gun, Aunt Aurelia, but I thought it was that bastard Caius Tellus.'

'Look, I know it's rough at the moment, but tell me as quickly as you can what in Hades your mother has done?'

They exchanged terrified glances. Then Silvia drew herself up.

'She's given him plenipotentiary powers.'

Pluto in Tartarus.

'Why in Hades didn't she give either or both of you that? You're both emancipated!'

Young as they were, they had more strength of character than Severina would ever have. The imperial council would have supported and advised them. And Silvia was her mother's natural heir, not bloody Caius.

'He's played on her like a fool, before and after he went to the EUS. She wouldn't take any notice, saying we didn't understand. She wouldn't listen to Dad either.'

'Where is Fabianus?'

'He went to see Caius to try and reason with him,' Julian said. 'I told him it was a waste of time as well as dangerous, but he went.' He looked over at the far wall at a portrait of his father and said nothing more. Fabianus always believed reason would solve everything. Too much of an optimist for these times.

Silvia's face was white. Then I noticed she had a knife in her hand, like a *pugio* dagger carried by ceremonial guards. She saw my gaze.

'It's Julian's.' She glanced at her brother. 'I have to feel I can do something when that man comes after me.'

'What do you mean?'

'The night before last, he was here with some of his weird friends. For drinks and dinner. Others were there, normal people, but he was dominating the whole thing. Mama seemed cowed by him – she was tongue-tied in talking to him.' She shivered. 'He was overpowering in an uncomfortable way. He stroked my arm. I couldn't bear it and pulled away. He smiled at me. He knew exactly how revolted I was. He whispered to me, "Soon". Then Mama took me aside and told me he was proposing an alliance between our families. I had to sit opposite him through the whole horrible dinner.' She looked away.

'She can't make you do that, Silvia. Didn't your father say anything?'

'Of course, but she wouldn't listen. She said I was being selfish by refusing. That's why Dad has gone to see Caius – to tell him to keep away from us.'

'I'll shoot the bastard if he comes near her again,' Julian added.

'Right, come with me. Both of you.'

They exchanged glances, Julian nodded and both grabbed small backpacks.

'What are those?' I said.

'Things have been so unsettled the past couple of days I told Silvia to put a few essentials together. Just in case.' His brown eyes looked steadily into mine.

I nodded in answer.

Back in the council room, Fabia raised an eyebrow at the sight of Julian toting the rifle but said nothing. Silvia slid her knife into her backpack and dropped her bag as she put her arms round her mother. She must have loved Severina very much to do that after everything I'd just heard.

Fabia drew me aside. Without saying a word she handed me a

semi-automatic, military issue, which I thrust in my loden coat pocket. The weight of it distorted the fall of the coat. I felt awkward in my office suit and shoes.

'The colonel's on her way here. None of the three councillors would come with her.'

'Juno, they must be shit-scared to refuse Volusenia.'

'She said two were packing and preparing to go to the airport.'

'What! What in Hades is the matter with these people? Their place is here.'

'Apparently not,' Fabia replied.

'Jupiter give me strength.'

Almost as an answer, Volusenia marched in with half a dozen people in civvies. But their sharp eyes, stance and the strength radiating from them gave them away – PGSF. She nodded at me, saluted Severina and waited.

Severina glanced round the room, her eyes darting from once face to another. I didn't know what she was looking for, but eventually her butterfly gaze came to rest on me. She seemed to want to say something and her mouth moved, but no sound came out.

Volusenia took a step towards Severina, but the imperatrix still said nothing; she slumped in her chair and looked down. Volusenia's face tightened – the tiniest flicker of anger. The next second it was extinguished.

'Mama?' Silvia knelt down by her mother's chair. 'What is it?'

Severina looked at her daughter as if she was a stranger. Her throat constricted as she swallowed hard. She reached out and touched her daughter's hair.

'Silvia, you must go. Now. You must escape. Go.'

Severina stood up, hugged Silvia, then kissed the top of her head. She pushed her daughter towards me. 'Help her, Aurelia.'

Silvia looked at her mother, appalled at being pushed away. But Severina had covered her face with her hands as if hiding herself from the world.

We all stood frozen by the collapse of power and order. It was only broken by a crackle from a radio. One of Volusenia's troops lifted his set to his ear and listened intently. Then he bent and whispered in Volusenia's ear. She nodded and took the radio. She paused long enough to say, 'Caius Tellus is on his way. With a mob.'

The few councillors who had struggled through the fire and panic to get here gasped; Quirinia dropped onto a chair.

'How long have we got?' I asked.

'About ten minutes.' She looked at me steadily. 'We can extend that to twenty, perhaps twenty-five.' I knew what she was asking. I took a deep breath and let it out, releasing deep regret with it.

'You are authorised,' I said in the most neutral tone I could muster.

'Volusenia,' she spoke into the radio, her eyes on me. 'Code word Horatius. Execute.'

I closed my own. I might have just condemned twenty elite soldiers to their deaths. Like the ancient Horatius, these Romans 'on the bridge' would die before allowing Caius to succeed. I heard a step behind me. Julian had come to attention and saluted Volusenia.

'My station, Colonel?'

'You are excused, Julianus Apulius. You must guard your sister.'

'With respect, ma'am, we have discussed this. My duty is here with my mother. I shall stay.'

She tried to stare him down, but he refused to break.

'Very well. You guard the door to the anteroom and let no man or woman pass.'

'Understood.' He bent down, kissed his sister on her forehead, his mother on her cheek, bowed to her, then set off for the door.

I sat at the table and wrote fast and furiously. I waited until Volusenia had given her orders to Fabia, then gestured her over to where Silvia and I were standing.

'Volusenia Minor,' I said in a low voice, 'as the head of the senior family, I require you to escort Silvia Apulia away from here and take her abroad to Vienna. You must leave now.' I handed her the written order and a small pouch. 'Memorise this address.' I handed her a slip of paper. 'Wait for me there. Do not approach the Vienna legation at present.'

'Are you joking, *consiliaria*? My post is here. Now, if you'll excuse me…'

'No, I will not. I am giving you an instruction as the imperatrix's senior minister and you will comply.'

She looked as if she wanted to tear me into scraps and feed me to the animals in the arena.

'Colonel, I need somebody tough and determined enough to get

Silvia Apulia away. I know I can trust you to do this.' I lowered my voice almost to a whisper. 'It's only a matter of time before Caius Tellus comes through that door and you're wasting it. Fabia is perfectly capable of commanding the troops here. Silvia will need your skills and resolve to get her through this. Come with me.'

She hesitated.

'Now.'

She grumbled all the way down to the old kitchens, but followed. I held Silvia around the waist to steady her; she traipsed alongside me like an automaton. As I opened the tunnel door, she stopped and pulled away from me. 'I can't. I can't leave her.'

I grabbed her by the arm. I was going to hate myself for my next words.

'Silvia, you have to accept your mother's cause is lost. We cannot allow Caius to get hold of you. I understand your instincts are to stay with her. But Severina herself told you to go and me to help you. If you hesitate now, those left behind fighting to delay Caius will have wasted their lives in vain. And you don't want to live with that on your conscience.'

She threw me a look of pure anguish, but said nothing. I pulled her into the tunnel. As we hurried along in the semi-dark, I heard sobbing and when I turned to glance at her, saw tears running down her face. After a kilometre, we turned into a side tunnel and stopped in a recess with a small table, two chairs and a large cupboard.

'There are rations, water, torches, batteries, field clothes and supplies. Take everything. You'll need it.'

I thrust a combat jacket, scarf, gloves and wool hat at Silvia. She had trousers and strong shoes on at least.

'You have funds – there's enough in gold in that pouch, Colonel, to bribe or buy your way through. If not, you'll have to use your initiative. Nothing, or nobody, must stop you. Assume you are now in enemy territory.'

Volusenia said nothing, merely set about packing the supplies. Silvia looked completely bewildered.

'Aunt Aurelia, why are we running away? Surely nobody will support Caius Tellus? He wouldn't dare hurt my mother.'

I glanced at Volusenia who shook her head.

'Silvia, we don't know what's going to happen. Our duty is to protect and keep you safe at all costs. Your duty is to stay alive. You are your mother's heir as well as her beloved daughter.'

'Gods, no. You don't mean—' She covered her mouth with her hand.

I pulled her to me and hugged her. After a few seconds, I held her away and looked into her eyes, her mother's soft brown eyes, now full of anxiety.

'I don't know. As soon as I do, I will let you know.'

'What do you mean? You're coming with us.'

'No, I have to go back and try to stop Caius.'

Volusenia stepped forward, her face projecting an angry vulture look. '*Consiliaria*, you can't go back. He'll kill you.'

'Maybe, but I'm not the easiest target. And my heir, my darling Marina, is safe in the EUS.' I glanced at my watch. 'You have about another five minutes' bought time. I don't know if Caius knows the tunnels, but let's assume he does. Carry on for another five hundred metres and you'll come to a half-height door. It's awkward but it comes out in a house in the Vicus Fabricensium outside the old city wall. It belongs to one of the former imperial armourers, but she keeps it available for, er, operations.'

Volusenia snorted at that. It was one of Plico's safe houses.

'She should hand over supplies and keys for the van in the adjoining garage. Use it as far as you can, then dump it. You'll probably have to walk the mountain route into New Austria – he'll close the road and railway crossings. You won't be the only refugees.'

I kissed Silvia's cheek, clasped forearms with Volusenia and headed back into the chaos.

18

___

Back at the palace end of the tunnel, I opened the door a couple of centimetres. I waited, Fabia's semi-automatic in my hand. A tap running, people moving, but quietly. I caught a gasp, sobbing, cursing. Then the smell of blood hit me. I opened the door only wide enough to slip out, but casting round all the time. Nobody was in this storeroom. I locked the tunnel door, drew the wood panel back across to hide it. Thank the gods, the only noise was made by the panel catches as they clicked into place.

I crept to the outer door and slid into the old kitchen. A servant was tipping the contents of a yellow plastic bucket into the back drain. Another bucket stood on the floor by him. It was the colour of diluted blood.

As I walked along the stone passageways of the older palace into the newer seventeenth-century ones, the smell grew along with the noise of people moving: footsteps on the marble floors, clothes rustling, things being picked up and put down. But worst of all, groaning and the odd shriek. As I approached the council anteroom, I heard arguing and shouting, and a woman sobbing. Severina.

I flattened myself against the wall and crept towards the door frame. The door was ajar and I peeped through the gap between door and jamb. Severina, still on her chair, streaked face. Fabia, bandaged sleeve, hair escaping from her severe bun, blood caking on her forehead, rifle slung across her shoulder, shaking her head, and two other Praetorians. Quirinia and two other councillors on their knees by bodies on the floor. And Plico, talking sternly to Severina. His face consisted of bruising with two eyes staring out.

I edged around the door. Two rifles were pointed at my chest and safety clicked off before I'd taken the next step.

'Stand down,' I ordered. They lowered their weapons a few centimetres.

Plico swung round, then all eyes were on me. But for only a second.

Gunshots rang out. A volley of return fire. Fabia signalled three guards to follow her and disappeared towards the fire. I never saw her again. The two remaining guards stood by Severina.

'Plico,' I hissed at him and beckoned him over to me.

'Did you get her away?' he whispered back. He was searching my face, a mix of doubt and worry on his own.

I frowned at him. 'Of course. I said I would.'

The sound of marching feet and doors banging.

'Here they come,' he said grimly. 'Run. I'll cover you.'

'Only if you do,' I shot back.

I knew he wouldn't.

'If they take you, Plico, they'll bleed you of everything.'

He smiled.

Oh gods! He wasn't one of them after all, was he?

'You should watch your face, you know, *consiliaria*. I can read every thought you make.' Unbelievably, he smirked at me. 'No, my capsule is in my mouth already. I just want to watch that bastard's face when I die on him.'

'Plico—'

'I know what I'm doing.' He held his arm out and grasped mine in the Roman salute. 'An honour to have known and served with you, Aurelia Mitela. Now bugger off out of here as soon as you get the chance. Your duty is to go and look after Silvia Apulia who will soon be imperatrix.'

I swallowed hard and couldn't find a word to say. I shook my head.

He shrugged.

A few groans, whispered reassurances, cloths being squeezed free of water, were the only sounds as we waited in silence. Apart from

Severina, who still looked down, we faced the door – guards, councillors, Plico and I.

First through was a man in his forties, slim, dark, wielding an old-fashioned revolver, and flanked by six other men carrying machine guns. All seven wore hunting clothes with a blood red armband with a symbolic *fasces* and a mailed fist on their left upper arms.

The slim man looked first at the imperatrix, then scanned the room.

'I'm Phobius and I represent First Consul Caius Tellus. You're all detained under the emergency order. Any disobedience will be dealt with summarily.' He looked at each of us in turn. He sounded straight out of the Septarium, that perfectly named cross-river district where runnels of indeterminate humanity oozed furtively around, filling up the fissures between the shabby buildings.

Quirinia, kneeling on the floor by a shot guard, gulped. The other two councillors just stared.

Phobius snorted in their direction. 'The council is disbanded with immediate effect.' He jerked his head at the Praetorians. 'The military are ordered to return immediately to barracks, including you two.' They didn't move.

'Immediately, I said,' Phobius repeated.

'We do not leave the imperatrix,' the woman *optio* said.

'Well, darling, there isn't an imperatrix any longer, so move it.'

She blinked, but stood her ground.

'You was warned,' he said. He brought up his revolver and shot her in the head. Blood spurted over her face, she swayed, then dropped to the floor. The other Praetorian had his semi-automatic out, flung himself forward. Plico and I threw ourselves in front of Severina. I fell back onto her, knocking us both to the floor as the machine guns cut down the last Praetorian.

The rat-tat was deafening. Severina screamed and screamed. I brought my hands up to her shoulders to try to calm her, to get her to stop. She carried on shrieking. I slapped her face. She stopped immediately, her eyes rolled back and she fainted. As I knelt back up, I noticed my coat sleeve was scorched by a bullet trail and red liquid dribbled down onto my white shirt cuff. I stared at it unbelieving. Then my arm started throbbing. More, I saw Fabia's pistol had slid from my coat pocket when I'd fallen. But Phobius couldn't see it from where he was standing.

'Get away from her,' Phobius shouted. A gun barrel tapped against my head. I stood up slowly. I didn't have to pretend to be dizzy but I stumbled back as if it was worse than it was and nudged the gun under the armchair with my foot. I held my arm with my other hand.

'Let me at least put a cushion under her head.'

'No. Who are you anyway?'

He didn't have a clue I was the foreign minister. I decided to bluff it out. 'I'm her servant, sir, her secretary,' I said, which wasn't technically untrue. I waved at Quirinia with my uninjured arm. 'Her too.' Then I looked away, and caught the eye of the male councillors. One of them gave me the tiniest nod and stepped on the foot of his colleague. I blessed him for his presence of mind.

'What's your name, fatty?' Phobius pointed his revolver at Plico.

I wondered what persona Plico was going to assume. When he drew himself up, I knew with horror that he wasn't going to pretend. He was going into the arena.

'I am Tertullius Plico, the urban *praetor*'s executive officer.' He looked down his nose at Phobius, even though he was shorter.

'Well, well, the chief spy. Consul Tellus will be pleased.' And he struck Plico across the face with his revolver. I winced at the crack of bone breaking but Plico kept his balance. Phobius signalled to two of his heavies and they dragged Plico away.

'Take the men,' he ordered his guards. 'Leave these women here. The consul will be along soon to see her.' He pointed at Severina. 'She'll wake up quick enough then.'

Quirinia looked at me, but I shook my head. We would just be shot if we attempted anything. But she lifted a cushion from the imperatrix's chair, knelt down and placed it under Severina's head.

'Get up, you stupid cow,' Phobius snarled at Quirinia and grabbed her arm. 'Sit on the floor over there, hands in front of you, with the other typist.'

He turned abruptly, nodded at the guard left to watch us, and left.

We huddled next to the wounded staffer Quirinia had been tending. He was lying unconscious, mouth open, breathing noisily.

Quirinia shut her eyes and shook her head, opened them again and stared around. 'Gods, is this it, then?' she whispered.

'No talking,' the guard shouted at her, striding over to her and lifting his weapon ready to strike.

'Please, please don't hurt us,' I begged. I could hardly keep the fury out of my voice, but we had to defuse this man's anger.

'Well, shut your mouth.'

'Of course, sir.' I left it a moment or two. 'What's going to happen to us? We just work here. Our families will be worried.'

'The first consul will know. Him or Phobius'll tell you.'

Merda. The last person we needed to see was Caius.

The guard's radio crackled. He frowned as he listened. I looked over at the carpet under the armchair where I could see the metal of Fabia's semi-automatic. I could lunge at it, kill the guard, but what then? My arm was stinging like Hades. I wriggled my fingers and flexed my arm. Only a flesh wound, but it was still dribbling blood.

'Nobody said nothing about medics, but I s'pose it's okay,' he spoke into the radio and glanced at us. Intense crackling, then a terse voice from the radio. 'All right, all right, don't burst your tunic. Over and out.' He said the last three words in a very exaggerated manner, and looked at the radio as if it were rotting fish. 'Uptight arse-ache.'

A knock at the door. He strode over and opened it. Two women, one pushing an empty wheelchair, entered. The older one, her grey hair falling out of a bun, clips half out, was dressed in a faded tunic covered by an apron with bloodstains. She trudged in, head bowed, and carried a cloth bag in her hand and a satchel over her shoulder, both printed with a red twisted-snake staff of Asclepius.

No. This tired old woman couldn't possibly be the person I thought I'd recognised. My mind was playing tricks. Perhaps I'd lost more blood than I thought. The younger one, taller, in a crumpled nurse's tunic and trousers, seemed more confident.

'You've got some wounded?' The guard jerked his head towards us. She knelt down by the three dead Praetorians first, felt each neck for a pulse, then shook her head. She stepped over to the wounded staffer lying next to us, and with her back to the guard, looked straight at me. Her eyes widened as if she was trying to convey a message. She mouthed 'Diversion, now.'

Juno. She was military.

I groaned loudly, grasping my arm and started sobbing, rocking as if the pain was unbearable.

The younger woman turned around to the older and thrust her hand out. 'Marcella, pads, quick.'

The older one fumbled and muttered, 'I can't find them. Here, take the whole bag.' She pulled the satchel off her shoulder and thrust it at the younger woman. Within seconds, the younger one caught the satchel, opened it and pulled out a semi-automatic which she thrust in the astonished guard's face.

The older one brought a torch out of her cloth bag and hit the guard at the base of his skull. He fell where he stood, poleaxed.

'Up, we have only max ten minutes before the radio check, if they keep to their pattern,' said the younger woman. Quirinia and I struggled up to see the older woman now standing erect and smiling at us. I'd been right first time. It was Senator Calavia, my mother's friend.

'Calavia. What in Hades are you doing here?'

'Coming to get you out, my girl. Felicia would never have forgiven me. This is my granddaughter, Pia. She'll see you through.'

'I'm not leaving Severina to Caius.'

'I'm staying with her.'

'No, you can't. He'll—' He'd kill Calavia on the spot, ninety years old or not, if he thought she'd helped me escape.

'Now listen to me. I'm nearly ninety-one. I don't have much time to go. Let me use the rest of my life doing something good. You're not the only one who can make glorious gestures, Aurelia. My granddaughter has risked her life to get you two out. The least you can do is appreciate it. Now sit in that wheelchair and do as you're bid.'

Pia had eased my injured arm out of my coat sleeve, ripped my shirt and bandaged the forearm. It was only a flesh wound. I glared at Calavia, but she just made shooing gestures to the wheelchair, then turned to Quirinia and started bandaging her face and neck. She pulled her hair down to hide the rest of her face.

'We have to take Severina's staffer with us,' I said. 'He can't stay here.'

'No, it'll complicate things,' said Calavia. 'Look, Aurelia, it's a hard decision, but it's more important for Silvia and Roma Nova that you two don't fall into Caius's hands. Go!'

As I hesitated, Pia pushed me down into the wheelchair, flung a blanket round me and twisted a bandage around my head and eyes. I could just see out from the lower edge of the bandage. I flinched as she shoved a blood-soaked pad up in front of my left eye.

'Has to look genuine,' was all she said. I heard her say, 'Limp hard and grab the wheelchair handle as if for support.' That must have been for Quirinia.

'Wait,' I said. 'Under the armchair. The pistol Major Fabia gave me.'

Pia crouched down and retrieved the weapon, checked it and handed it to me. I stuffed it under the blanket. Calavia senior opened the door and we left. I squirmed round in the chair, lifted the edge of the bandage. The last sight I had of my mother's friend was her kneeling at Severina's side and holding the imperatrix's hand up to her chest.

The terrifying, blind passage from the council room full of death to the palace door seemed to take forever. Every time I heard marching feet or doors slamming, my heart thudded. I knew I was dead the moment I was discovered – there was no chance of reprieve. Quirinia also, but Pia Calavia was putting herself in the firing line for us.

A door creak, cool air. We were outside, thank the gods. I heard shouting, men, cars and trucks revving engines. I lurched forward as Pia bounced the wheelchair down an uneven slope. A few seconds later, up a steep ramp into the quiet. I was in a van. No, it had to be an ambulance. Two pairs of hands lifted me out of the wheelchair and somebody pinched my wounded arm, hard. By instinct, I cried out.

'Careful, she's probably got internal bleeding.'

Gods. I hoped not.

I didn't know if Quirinia was with me or not. I touched the bandage over my eyes with my good hand to lift it, but somebody pushed my hand away.

'Don't touch the wound. We'll soon be at the hospital.'

So we were still pretending. The vehicle started up and I could visualise crossing the rear courtyard to the gate that led to the road down to the city.

'Are you all right, Lucilla?' Quirinia's voice, but flatter. She'd used the name of my home farm. Clever. She was still alive. And we were escaping.

The ambulance stopped. Raised voices. Aggressive shouting, a rush of cold air. The doors crashed back on themselves. I flinched at the noise and cold. A hand took mine and I shivered as a damp antiseptic-smelling pad passed over my jaw and neck. I groaned.

'Papers,' demanded a flat voice with the town twang.

'Can't you see we have an emergency?' Pia said.

I groaned again and contributed a deep shudder, almost a spasm. The semi-automatic was under my blanket, but ready, in my hand.

'Still need papers. Now.'

'Here, here's my medical ID,' Pia said.

'Here's our palace passes,' said Quirinia.

Hades, what was she doing? They'd ID us within minutes and all this disguise and acting would be for nothing. I counted over a hundred and twenty before someone said 'Pass'. They slammed the ambulance door and we were on our way again. To my shame, I started trembling and gulped, perilously near a sob.

'It's okay, we'll soon be at our destination.' Pia squeezed my hand and leaned over and whispered, 'They were genuine passes. Yours have been left on the bodies of the real staffers who were killed. It won't delay them long, but it'll buy a little more time and we need every minute.'

'Where are we going?' I asked.

'To the Central Valetudinarium – this is an official ambulance. I can't say more.'

We rode along in silence for another ten minutes. My head was full of questions, but now was the time to do as we were told. Pia was running a desperate operation well. The ambulance slowed down, braked and turned abruptly to the right. It wound through the hospital grounds and eventually stopped.

'Next hurdle. Deep breath,' Pia warned us as she guided me back into the wheelchair.

I shivered as the cool air and the smell of vehicle exhaust flew in when the driver opened the ambulance doors. People shouting, doors slamming, groaning.

Pia pushed me up the ramp in the reception. Quirinia limping beside the wheelchair pulled on it. We were booked in under our false names and told to wait. It was chaos. Shouting, people screaming, crying, telephones ringing incessantly, trolley wheels squeaking and rattling. The stink of blood and antiseptic engulfed us.

'I'm going to be sick,' Quirinia said in a small voice.

'No,' I hissed at her. 'You can't. It'll draw attention to us. Take some deep breaths.'

'It's all right for you, you can't see the bodies lying all over the place.'

'Where's Pia?'

'I don't know, she's disappeared. Oh, Pluto!'

'What?'

'*Vigiles*, with one of those nationalists. By the entrance door. They're checking papers.' She grabbed my hand and started to sob.

'Right, you two.' Pia, with an officious voice. 'X-ray.' Next minute, we were hurrying along the corridor.

The wheelchair stopped abruptly.

'Hades, the bloody lift's not working. We'll have to risk the fire stairs.'

I jumped out of the wheelchair, stuffed the pistol in my pocket. Grabbing the blanket, I wrapped it round my shoulders, pulling a fold of it over my head. I ripped the eye bandage off along with the blood stained pad. It was a relief to be able to see again. Quirinia and I hurried down several flights of steps after Pia.

'The *vigiles* are only checking women,' Pia said. 'And one of them gave me a strange look as I took you off. We have to assume they're following.'

Dull cream walls gave way to concrete as we approached the services area. I couldn't hear any pursuit, but we couldn't bank on staying undetected. At the bottom, a reinforced wire-glass door blocked the way. It was alarmed. We couldn't get out. We were trapped in the stairwell.

'Don't look so worried, *consiliaria*, I have the code.'

She stabbed the buttons with her index finger and pushed the door open into the basement engineering room. A subterranean world of ducts, cabling and half-light opened up in front of us. Steam, the smell of oil and clanking noises were the only accompaniments as we hurried along. At the far end, we climbed up a ladder to an observation gallery and through a service door into a garage.

Pia led us to a black utility van and wrenched open the back door. Four shelves, the top two occupied by grey, heavy-duty rubber bags about two metres long with a central zip. Even in the dim light, I could see both carried the contents they were designed for. On the bottom shelves lay two flat empty bags.

'Get into the bottom two, please. Not exactly first-class travel, but we should get you out alive, unlike the poor sods above you.'

Quirinia stood completely still and stared at the plastic rectangle as if it were indeed her shroud. Then she looked at the corpse-filled body bags above her. She shook her head and looked at me beseechingly.

'I can't, Aurelia. You go on, I'll find another way.'

'Quirinia, if they find you, they'll beat it out of you, and Pia and her colleague driving the van will be dead meat. And so will I.' I leaned forward and unzipped it. 'Come on, feet in first.'

After a long second, she climbed into the bag, cast her eyes up at the top shelves again and shuddered, but complied. Her expression of dread was like a pig going to the butcher for Saturnalia.

I had no idea how long we spent zipped up in the body bags, strapped in and helpless. Despite the three tiny breather holes Pia had made, the musty rubber sheeting sticking to my skin and the pitch blackness made me feel I was enclosed in a tomb. Pia had given us a small flask of water each and me some analgesic for my throbbing arm. I heard Quirinia sobbing for a few minutes, then nothing. She must have passed out or fallen asleep.

I couldn't sleep. I'd left the imperatrix and saved my own skin. I should have been ready to die with her. What use was I if I couldn't protect her? Being right about Caius was no comfort, but I was shocked how easily he'd succeeded on the day. He'd done it in under twenty-four hours. Perhaps I should have authorised Plico to terminate Caius as the *magister miletum* had suggested. Or maybe have let Miklós do it months ago when Caius had been deported from Prussia. But it would still have been murder. Oh, gods, Miklós. Even if I got out of here, would I ever see him again? Or Marina? At least they were both safe abroad.

But I'd run away from my ministry, my household and my people at Castra Lucilla. I'd let them all down. I didn't deserve to lead the Mitelae.

What the hell use was it running away to New Austria anyway? I should have been out there, forming resistance networks, leading the movement to overthrow Caius. As soon as I was out of this rubber envelope, I'd tell Pia to drop me off before the border and I'd get to work.

Quirinia should go on – she'd only done the minimum two years' national service as a twenty-year-old. She'd probably forgotten more than she remembered. She'd been driving financial modelling and counting beans ever since. I doubted she'd survive the harshness before us.

It would be a hard slog, but the sooner the better. Who was loyal and who wasn't? I started planning. My mind filled with so many possibilities chasing each other around my head that I became dizzy. Juno, it was hot in this damned body bag; the sweat was running down my face and neck.

A strange sound came from nearby, soft at first, then louder and more intense. I shuddered. My whole body shook as I gulped and realised it came from me, sobbing my guts out for myself, my people and my country.

19

I jerked awake. The van had stopped, the engine cut and I heard a deep rumbling followed by a thud. The sound of the van door locking mechanism turning and the hinges creaking as the doors opened. The straps holding me fast were released and, Juno be praised, the bag zip was undone. I gasped and snatched air into my lungs. Sweet air, mountain air.

A groan opposite as Quirinia struggled out of her bag and fell onto the flatbed of the van. 'Never, never again,' she said, bringing her hand up to her throat. She leaned out of the back of the van and threw up. I knelt by her, holding her hair back from her face. In her black hair there were white streaks that hadn't been there twenty-four hours ago.

'Here, *domina*,' said Pia, and handed Quirinia a cloth for her face.

'Where are we?' I asked.

'In a barn, on a farm near the New Austrian border. We've been from one end of the country to another to take the two bodies above you back to their families for burning.'

'Why? I thought we were heading to Vienna.'

'Our cover's funeral transport. It's the only reason we've managed to get a travel permit. There's so much confusion, the nats aren't checking properly. They just scribble a note and sign it.' She pointed to the empty upper shelves. 'Both were Roman Nat bastards, but we had to do it. It makes me sick to listen to the crap they spout, but I feel so sorry for the parents. All they care is that their son is dead.'

Perhaps it was the poor evening light, but her skin looked grey.

'I didn't want to stop until we got here. If we'd been asked questions or spot-checked, we'd have been stuffed. It's too risky for us to be out in the day without any bodies in the back. Anyway, we're here now, but Atrius and I must have some rest.'

'Atrius?'

'Yes, why?'

'He was with me at the palace. How did he escape?'

'I'm part of the Aquila fallback reserve,' he answered as he appeared from the side of the van. His eyes were red-rimmed and heavy lines ran from the side of his nose to each side of his mouth. 'Lieutenant Calavia and I have been awake for thirty-six hours. Will you stand guard for us, Major?'

I stared at him. I hadn't been called that in nearly twenty years.

'Of course,' I stretched out my uninjured arm and he gave me his rifle. He and Calavia climbed into field sleeping bags on the barn floor and were asleep within minutes.

I opened the barn door a crack, wide enough to see the approach road winding up the hills. Sloping grassland spread out from the barn until it dropped abruptly down into the valley below. Apart from a group of conifers about fifteen metres away, only rock outcrops broke up the smooth green waves of pasture. Grey mountain peaks, capped with snow, surrounded us on three sides. A sharp morning breeze made me shiver. Nothing was moving out there, and the sun was just starting to break the horizon. I slung the rifle over my shoulder, grabbed my brown hospital blanket, the despised but waterproof body bag and a water flask, and slithered out of the gap. I made it to the trees in a few seconds, crouched down and scanned in each direction. A few birds were singing, but there was no other noise. I made a bivouac with the blanket and some fallen branches and sat on the body bag. It wasn't textbook perfect, but I could cover front and side approaches to the barn plus a little of the far side.

Strange, slipping back into an older self. My arm throbbed from the flesh wound, my city clothes were dirty and torn, and my stomach begged for food. Despite this, I was calm, had my duty to perform and for the first time in twenty-four hours I had time to think clearly.

As soon as Pia and Atrius were awake, I'd explain my plan and leave. But I was curious about one thing – what was the 'Aquila fallback reserve'? I'd never heard of it. It sounded like some contingency unit. Atrius was a Praetorian – he'd been on duty at the palace – so was it some kind of sub-unit? Fabia had never mentioned it. Gods! Fabia. Another one to add to the body count. I bent my head onto my knees for a few seconds.

Crack. Someone or something was in the copse. I stayed crouched as I was. Probably an animal, but if it was on two legs, best they think me unaware. I glanced left and right without moving my head. Nothing. I could hear heavy breathing. I brought my head up very slowly and looked into two enormous eyes. I only just stopped myself from bursting out laughing. I was in such a state I'd been rattled by a high alps cow.

'Shoo!' I hissed at it and flapped my hands. It replied by licking and then munching the green leaves on my bivouac. When it tasted blanket, it stopped, gave me a last look and wandered off.

I watched contentedly enough for an hour, busying my mind scanning each sector of the ground I could see from the trees. The next hour I spent crawling along the sides and back of the barn and watching from there. But there was no road or even a path to the back of us, only the grey wall of the mountain. As a safe stop it was well chosen, but I wondered who owned it or used it.

The sun was stronger now so I settled back in the trees, taking occasional sips from the water flask. Just after midday, the barn door opened a few centimetres to reveal Quirinia's anxious face. I waved with my fingers only, then signalled with my hand, horizontal and pushing down parallel to the ground. She nodded. She hadn't forgotten her basic military skills after all. She waited a few minutes, then crawled over to the trees.

'Are you all right out here, Aurelia?' she whispered.

'Yes, fine. All quiet.'

She smiled at me, then flicked her coat. 'We must look like a pair of idiots in our city clothes, toting a gun and crawling around in the trees like runaway kids.'

'Well, runaway is right.'

The laughter fell out of her eyes.

'I couldn't stop thinking about Severina last night,' she said. 'Did we do the right thing to run?' She looked down at her despised city shoes, now caked in mud and grass.

'You're asking the wrong person,' I replied. 'Whatever Calavia, and Plico before her, said and even Severina herself, I'll never know in my heart.'

She said nothing for a few minutes.

'You could do worse than remember the words you said to Silvia when she almost refused to go into the tunnel.'

'What do you mean? How did you know what I said? You weren't there.'

'We all heard it over the house intercom when you told Silvia to accept her mother's cause was lost.'

I opened my mouth to protest.

'And don't tell me that you delegated responsibility to Colonel Volusenia,' she continued. 'Severina ordered *you* to leave. She knew *you* would have enough grit and determination to make sure Silvia came back into her own. And think about this, Aurelia. As you yourself said, those left behind fighting to delay Caius will have wasted their lives in vain, including Tertullius Plico. And like Silvia, you don't want to live with that on your conscience.'

I rubbed my eye socket with the heel of my hand, drawing the palm, then fingers down over my face.

'Sometimes I don't know whether I love you or hate you, Quirinia,' I said and gave her a short laugh. I glanced at my watch. Half past four. It wouldn't start to go dark for several hours.

'I don't suppose there's anything to eat in that barn, is there?'

'I'll go and see,' Quirinia said.

I squeezed her hand; she smiled back and scurried back to the barn.

In the end it was Atrius who came out with two disposable mess tins of something brown, warm and mediocre looking. But to my empty stomach it was wonderful. He handed me a roll and a wrinkled apple.

'That's all the fruit the wayside shop had. The owner hasn't had her delivery for two days.'

'Have the others fed?'

'They're eating now. Lieutenant Calavia wants to talk to you once you've finished.'

We sat silently, looking out over the still landscape and finished our rations.

'I'm sorry, *consiliaria*, but I can't do as you ask.' Pia shrugged. We stood on the pressed earth floor, the last of the daylight seeping in between the slats of the barn walls. 'The colonel would have my hide. My orders are to bring you safe to Vienna. No discussion.'

'Very commendable, Lieutenant, but I'm not under her command and I'm going. I can't sit on my backside in Vienna when I could be putting my skills to use on the ground organising resistance.'

Pia smiled.

'What?'

'When we were allocated assignments in the Aquila fallback reserve several months ago, mine was to rescue and recover the head of the Twelve Families. As my grandmother is Countess Calavia, they thought I'd have good knowledge of Families procedures and personalities. When she briefed me, Colonel Volusenia gave me particular instructions about you.'

'Oh, really? Do tell me.'

'She said you might be reluctant to comply and that I should not hesitate to use whatever means necessary.'

'The Hades she did! Well, Tartarus take her and her instructions. You can try, Pia Calavia, but you won't be able to stop me. I'm not entirely past it.'

'That's what the colonel said you'd say. She also told me to ask you what your resources, networks, intelligence, analysis staff, weaponry, communications and strategy were.'

She crossed her arms and waited.

Damn the woman, she was right. I had nothing but my fury and my guilt. Nor could I access any resources until I reached Vienna. I didn't even know who had died at the palace, whether Severina was alive, who was loyal and who wasn't.

'Very well, I'll tap into this Aquila group,' I said.

'I can't comment on that, *consiliaria*. The colonel said she would explain everything once you'd arrived at the assembly point, i.e. Vienna.'

Clever bait, Volusenia, I thought.

'The priority is to get across the border and regroup,' Pia continued, 'and we should get ready. It'll be dark in an hour.' Before I could protest further, she walked to the back of the barn to an old storage cupboard. She heaved bags of animal feed out of the way to reveal three olive green equipment boxes.

'There's a selection of walking boots and warm clothing in these. You and *Consiliaria* Quirinia should change as quickly as you can. I'll prepare backpacks with some essentials.'

Thirty minutes later, we set off north in the direction of the mountains, walking poles in hands, loaded up for a survival exercise. But this was no exercise.

Scarcely a day after Caius had struck, we were hiking on a near moonless night into exile. If there was anything any Roman feared most it was being exiled, cut off from family, friends and community.

I marched behind Calavia, more comfortable now in countrywomen's clothing, but my heart was heavier than my backpack. Quirinia said nothing. All I heard from her was laboured breathing. I'd trained more to the west, nearer the Bavarian border and to the south, but I vaguely knew where we were. Calavia obviously knew the area well as she guided us along the narrow overgrown tracks, through dips and gullies without hesitation.

After an hour, just before a steep ascent, we stopped for a rest. I leaned back against the rock, my backpack a lumpy cushion, and took some deep breaths. Calavia had set a good pace. Quirinia looked exhausted. She hunched over and didn't move. She was, or had been, a government minister, not used to such physical demands. She probably hadn't been on such a strenuous hike since her national service. I reached over into the side pocket of her backpack and fished out her water flask. She grabbed it and I let her gulp the water down, but I took it back after a couple of seconds. Apart from her surprise, she looked cross.

'Slowly,' I whispered, 'or you'll get cramps or throw up.'

She took a deep breath, burped, looked embarrassed. She nodded, and I gave her the flask back. She drank more calmly.

Calavia hunkered down by us. 'We've come the short, direct way,' she whispered. 'We have to assume the main road will be barriered and they'll be patrolling the area.' She glanced at me. 'I don't know for sure but I reckon the guards will have been ordered to shoot on sight.'

'The border guards?' I was sceptical. 'They couldn't make an accurate shot at ten metres.'

'Ten metres would be enough to hit a leg and stop us.' She sounded impatient. 'Perhaps you've forgotten, *consiliaria*, what it's like to operate in hostile territory. We take no risks.'

I felt warmth rush up my neck into my face. I was furious and about to reprimand her for speaking to me like that. Then I realised she was right.

'I apologise, Pia Calavia. You are quite correct. It's been far too long. Please continue.'

'And I apologise for my abruptness. But you must realise the danger. If Caius Tellus is as well organised out here as he was in the city, you can be sure he will have sealed the borders and deployed reinforcements, possibly his own political troops.'

'But border guards are more used to stamping passports and confiscating coffee than actually shooting anybody.'

'Perhaps. But given the choice of shooting or being shot and possibly your whole family or work crew with you, or even both, what would you do?'

An hour later, it was sleeting in our faces. It was late summer in the plain – it had been a golden September – but here up on the mountain, it was a different world. The slice of the barely new moon on the snowfield gave us minimal light, eerie and neutral. The last time I'd been so high was when we had caught the Prussian smugglers, twenty-odd years ago. This time, instead of leaping around the arrêts and gullies, I was trudging behind Pia Calavia like a retired zombie. And the sleet had turned to snow.

After what seemed several hours, she stopped, leaned towards me and cupped her mouth with her hands near my ear. 'There's a hut up here,' she spoke against the wind. 'About a hundred metres on. I'm going to check it. Stay here until I get back.'

She took three steps and vanished into the blizzard.

Atrius, Quirinia and I huddled down in the shelter of a rock. He crouched in front of us, slipped on night vision goggles and watched the track, alternating between directions every few minutes. Barely visible between the wool hat underneath the hood of her jacket and the scarf covering her nose and mouth, Quirinia's eyes were dull. Tears had frozen on her face, on skin that looked grey. I pulled her to me and prayed that hut was unoccupied.

I wasn't quite dozing, just sitting in a neutral dream state, gently rocking Quirinia, wondering whether we were going to perish in this snowstorm. I nearly jumped out of my skin when Atrius tapped me on the shoulder. He pointed up the track. It was Calavia.

'Here.' I handed Quirinia a mug of the soup I'd made up from powdered rations on the tiny stove spotted with burnt-on food and rust. The chemical fuel blocks carried by most sport climbers and walkers as well as military made the hut smell like a petrol station, but they didn't produce any smoke. We helped ourselves to four of the emergency 'rat-packs'; Atrius stirred dried vegetables into tinned meat stew in an aluminium pan. Highly nutritious, but gastronomically dubious, it would refuel us before the most dangerous part of our journey.

I panned around the hut. Although rough wood on the outside, it was dry-lined and insulated. Six sleeping shelves along the walls took up most of the hut. We unclipped the folding table stacked flush to one wall and found unmatched base metal cutlery in the cupboard. I didn't count the chips on the enamelled tin plates and mugs; I was too hungry.

Calavia had pulled the blind down over the one window and fixed a blanket above it to cover the whole frame and glass.

'It's double-glazed, but that's not the problem. I don't want even the tiniest light leak.'

'I'll help you do the door.' I picked up the small hammer from the hut's toolkit and nailed the dark blanket along the top frame as she held it. 'If it continues snowing, all our footprints will disappear. Not that anybody with half a brain is going to come up here in this.'

'Still, I'll take the first watch,' she replied.

'Wake me in three hours. I'll do the next and Atrius can take over after that.'

She gave a little smile and settled back on the bench under the covered window, Atrius's rifle across her knees. We rolled out our sleeping bags on the other three benches, clambered into them and were soon asleep.

Someone was shaking me. I sat up, groggy, blinked to see Calavia looming over me. I started to drag myself out of the warm cocoon of my sleeping bag. She thrust a water flask at me.

'I left you another hour, it's just before eight,' she whispered. 'Nothing to report. Are you ready, *consiliaria*?'

My mouth tasted like glue, my teeth were furred, the flesh wound on my arm was itching like Tartarus under the bandage, my back ached and my legs were stiff, but I smiled at her.

'Yes, go and get your head down. I'm fine.'

Like almost all active soldiers she was asleep within minutes of zipping her sleeping bag up.

I spent the first half-hour taking the blanket down from the window and checking that nothing significant could be seen through the thin blind. Even the slightest movement could be detected from a distance. Leaving the blanket in place would have looked more suspicious, though. At the moment the others were sleeping. The danger would come when we were all up and moving about. I dragged my sleeping bag onto the floor and knelt and packed it up with the rest of my kit.

As I threw a couple of scoops of sawdust in the dry latrine behind the corner curtain and rinsed my hands under the trickle from the hand basin tap, I realised the weight of Calavia's words. We *were* operating in hostile territory, even though still in Roma Nova. The silence and the freezing cold merely reinforced my feeling of bitterness.

We'd been extremely lucky to use this shelter. Normally we would have replenished the water tank by filling the snow funnel, and reported and paid for ration packs used at the next village. That's what you did on the mountain – left a hut supplied for the next users. But it would have been like waving a location flag for any patrol to see. Another tiny but significant break in normality.

I wedged myself into the corner of the bench and wall, to the side of the window and out of sight. I'd forgotten how boring sentry duty was. Looking out from an oblique angle, all I could see was the snowfield, peaks, scree banks, all lit by a pale yellow sun in a cloudless rich blue sky. Pretty as a postcard.

An hour later it was snowing again.

20

'Pluto in Tartarus!' cried Atrius. 'On the floor. Now.'

Calavia threw herself down, grabbed Quirinia and pushed her under the lower sleeping shelf. I rolled off the opposite shelf where I'd been dozing after I'd woken Atrius, and scuttled underneath.

A buzz outside like an angry mechanical wasp. Then a faint thump-thump. Rotor blades.

'Faces to the wall. Don't move a millimetre,' Calavia ordered.

I breathed as lightly as possible, inhaling a mixed smell of wood, sweat and musty clothes. It had stopped snowing a good hour ago and it was two hours before the sun went down, so a perfect time window for a helicopter. Thank Juno, we hadn't cooked anything since last night. The heat sensor equipment on routine planes wasn't that sophisticated, but they may have had an upgrade for all I knew. I just hoped the snow on the roof would blanket us.

The whump-whump grew louder joined by the scream of the tail rotor. The hut shook as the helicopter hovered. Cutlery stacked on the table jumped. A fork fell onto the floor, tines down and narrowly missed Atrius's eye. He blinked, let out a breath, but said nothing. The thunderous rhythm of the blades beat against my eardrums, but I couldn't risk moving my hands up to cover them.

Suddenly, the noise dropped, then faded away rapidly. Within half a minute we could hear nothing but our own breathing.

'Oh, gods,' moaned Quirinia. 'Is it over?'

'Shh!' I hissed at her. 'We have to wait,' I whispered so quietly it was scarcely louder than a breath.

Pia Calavia signalled with her fingers that we would wait fifteen minutes, but ready our weapons. I slid my hand down to my jacket pocket and retrieved Fabia's pistol. If they'd landed troops, the classic tactic would be to wait five, then smash their way in. If they were being subtle it would be ten, so fifteen was a wise precaution.

Seventeen minutes later, Pia let out a sigh. 'I think we're clear,' she whispered, 'but let's just wait a few more.' She wriggled across the floor and touched Quirinia's shoulder. 'Are you all right, *consiliaria*?'

'Yes, yes,' Quirinia sniffed, rolling over to face us. 'Now I'm wondering what the next delightful thing will be.' Her voice was brittle, but I could see she was trying to keep herself calm. 'While we were waiting I was calculating the budget for sending that helicopter up here in manpower, fuel and opportunity cost. It must run into tens of thousands of *solidi*. And if I've got it right, today's the first of October, only eight weeks until close of expenditure period. Unless they've found a bottomless pit, they won't be back.'

The three of us stared at this accountant become budget minister as if she were an alien. She'd out-thought all of us.

We moved out just after the sun set. We'd had to dig a path out from the door through the snow and although we piled it back as best we could, until it snowed again we couldn't help leaving some evidence behind. But we were rested and in better spirits. Quirinia moved stiffly at first but seemed more alert and interested in the process, rather than being only a victim and refugee. After three hours, we descended through the treeline of conifers. We stopped at the lower edge for a few minutes' rest. Calavia handed me her field glasses.

'See those far lights? They're in New Austria. Now look right. That's our problem.'

The original border post on the *autovia* which ran from Roma Nova city to Vienna had been reinforced by a temporary camp. It wasn't just the ancients who could set up a camp in hours; it was a skill that had passed down over fifteen centuries. There were six eight-person canvas tents erected in a neat rectangle behind the post. Which meant there could be four separate four-person patrols out on a twenty-four-hour basis.

Hades.

'There's a track, of course,' Calavia said, 'a smugglers' route to the west, but the border force will know all about that. That's probably where they'll concentrate their patrols. So we'll go east.' She smiled brightly. Her confidence was almost too much.

We retreated back into the middle of the trees and struck east. It was silent around us. Calavia didn't have to warn us not to talk; the fear of being discovered so near to the frontier between death and life was too real.

As we neared the *autovia*, it was unnerving. The dual carriageways usually buzzed with freight lorries, cars and small vans weaving in and out. Now, I heard nothing. We crouched in the trees on top of the embankment looking down at four empty lanes, curving in a wide arc, the white road markings glimmering in the faint moonlight. Not a truck, nor tanker, nor private car. Zero.

Breaking the silence, the noise of an engine accelerating. It grew louder, deepening into the rhythmic thudding of a powerful diesel engine.

'Back!' Calavia hissed. But I was already lying flush to the ground and pulled Quirinia with me. An armoured personnel carrier, one of the new Agrippa wheeled models scarcely out of the factory, appeared, travelling at around 50 kph. Aside from the gunner, there was another figure, the commander, scanning both sides of the road with a pair of heavy night vision binoculars. She, or now more likely he, was looking purposefully. My stomach churned.

'Calavia,' I whispered as soon as it had disappeared into the distance. 'They know we're out here, but not where.'

'Agreed.'

'With their numbers it's only a matter of time before they find us. We have to move now and fast.'

She nodded.

'First thing is to get across this bloody road,' I said. 'I suggest Atrius goes first taking Quirinia, then me then you.' The theory was slowest first, fastest last.

'If they stick to standard patrolling they'll be back in twenty-five minutes.' She looked at her watch. 'Best cut that in half.'

We scrambled down the bank and crouched at the side of the road. Unluckily, we were inside the concave arc, so our field of vision was restricted at each end. Once Atrius was across, he could spot for us. He and Quirinia ran for the central reservation, waited for a few seconds and scuttled over to the far bank and started climbing it. Atrius heaved Quirinia over the ridge and they disappeared. I was on my toes to sprint across when I caught the buzz of vehicle engine. A scout car tore around the corner from the other direction and screeched to a halt. By then, Calavia and I were face down in the drainage ditch.

I turned my head very slowly and glanced sideways across the road. The figure beside the driver leapt out. On his left upper arm, I saw a pale armband with a darker indistinct design. I didn't have to see the symbolic *fasces* and mailed fist. He turned into the moonlight and I saw his face. Phobius. Caius's sidekick.

I started to sweat. Until now, despite the difficult journey, I hadn't believed we wouldn't make it. Now, doubt started to creep into my mind. Was it a coincidence Phobius was here, now? Was Caius hunting me personally? But I knew the answer. Phobius would have described us to Caius. Calavia's trail of deception had been temporary and fragile. Caius would have been furious at our escape and probably threatened to terminate Phobius if he didn't come back with us. Perhaps that was why Phobius had two heavies as armed escort. Or perhaps I had got it all wrong. Was I that important in reality? No, I was sure it wasn't my status. With Caius it was always personal.

Phobius brought a radio handset up to his face, spoke into it, gesturing with his hand while walking up and down the road in short, snatched lengths. He turned abruptly, jumped back into the vehicle and flicked his hand brusquely at the driver. They drove off as urgently as they had arrived.

'*Merda*, that was close.' Calavia rolled to my side. She extracted her field glasses from her jacket pocket and scanned the far ridge.

'Got him. Atrius signals all clear.' She stuffed the glasses back into her pocket. We crept out of the ditch and crouched by the hard shoulder. 'Care to make a bet who gets there first, Major?'

'Be a shame to take your money, Lieutenant,' and I launched myself across the road. It was a tie, but she beat me by two seconds to the top of the far embankment.

We marched on in silence but watchful for the least sound. Twice, Calavia raised her hand to stop us, and we'd hit the ground. Probably wildlife, foxes or the like. We shouldn't find wolves this close to the border.

A glimmer of light hesitated at the horizon. I checked my watch; just after four. Calavia directed us to the edge of the trees and scanned the fields with her glasses.

'Nothing moving out there.'

'How near are we?' I asked.

'Just under a kilometre. You see that farmhouse?' A traditional alpine building with shingle roof, windows shuttered. 'That's in New Austria.'

'Right, let's do it.'

Calavia nodded and beckoned Atrius and Quirinia forward.

'Atrius,' she said, 'take *Consiliaria* Quirinia along the hedge line west of that farmhouse. You have cover almost all the way. You'll have to belly-crawl the gaps, but there are only a few. RV at the taxi rank in Meintberg. Wait only two hours, then go on to the safe house in Vienna. The major and I will join you at one or the other.'

He handed Calavia his rifle and saluted.

Quirinia grabbed my wrist. 'Why aren't we going together, Aurelia?'

'We can't risk all of us being caught. Atrius is taking you by the safest route. Pia and I won't be far behind. We want to make sure you get to safety before we move. Now go. The sun will be up soon.'

We hugged and after a last, doubtful glance back, she turned and followed Atrius.

'She'll be all right, you know,' Calavia said. 'Atrius is very capable.'

I hadn't realised I was staring after them.

'Okay, Lieutenant, we'll wait until we see them reach the farmhouse. What about us?'

'We'll go a little further east. There's a direct pass through, but up a rather steep hill.'

Atrius and Quirinia made it to the farmhouse in twenty-five minutes. We watched the tiny figures walk along the verge of the road for another ten minutes almost out of our sight, then we continued east.

Calavia's idea of a steep hill was what I had expected – a nearly sheer climb. My legs trembled with the effort. I puffed up the steep slope almost on automatic, but was relieved to find myself not too far behind her. Or maybe she was being kind. But she was right. At the top, it came out just above Meintberg. A feeling of anticlimax and relief. We were already in New Austria, thank the gods.

Calavia and I reached the town ahead of Quirinia and Atrius. We sat in a bar, eating meat rolls, and savouring a beer. The early morning coffee drinkers gave us some strange looks but we ignored them. We'd earned it.

'We have to push on to Vienna as soon as the others arrive – we can't risk a snatch,' I said. 'Caius Tellus wouldn't let an international frontier interfere with his intentions.'

'Agreed. You and the *consiliaria* are far too tempting a target. In fact, you'll have to have a guard even in Vienna.'

'You're not serious?'

'I'm afraid I am. The colonel will bring you up to date when we get there.'

'You keep hinting at this mysterious bringing-up-to-date, Pia. What exactly do you mean?'

She looked away and was saved from answering by the appearance on the other side of the square by a forlorn, limping Quirinia leaning on Atrius's arm.

After the drama of our struggle to leave Roma Nova, the remainder of our journey was prosaic: taxi to the nearest mainline station, then high-speed train into the centre of Vienna. Our Roma Novan *solidi* notes were accepted by the ticket office clerk without blinking an eyelid. I still had some gold *solidi* as a backup in a money belt I'd grabbed from my personal drawer in the foreign ministry. I'd given Volusenia three quarters of it to get Silvia out. Pia Calavia and Atrius had their field reserve of two hundred each but Quirinia had only her purse contents.

'Did you export anything after the Families' meeting?' I asked her as we drove from the Vienna Hauptbahnhof to the safe house.

'I buried the insignia and histories in a steel box under the summer house,' she whispered. She glanced at the driver. She was right to be cautious; his sloppy appearance and casual driving style on the rain-washed roads didn't give us much confidence. 'When my mother told me years ago about the underground cellar there,' she continued in a low voice, 'I thought she was being dramatic. She told me not to be a fool, but to always be ready for the worst. How right she was.' She looked straight ahead for a few seconds. 'If you're asking if I have anything to live on, I have some foreign investments I can sell, plus twenty thousand I managed to transfer here. Who knows how long it'll have to last?'

PART IV

RESCUE

21

Vienna was much as I'd remembered from my last visit. Elegant, charming facades, but brittle inside. In the courtyards of many great houses, the stone would be flaking, windows dulled, paint curling from surfaces. I'd seen one where the inner windows had been modernised with white plastic-framed double-glazing; money-saving, possibly ecological, but much more jarring than the shabby originals would have been. The Ringstraße had been salvaged by generous private donations and Vienna's heritage status.

Pity the equally shabby taxi we drove in hadn't been renovated in the same way. It coughed and spluttered along the wide boulevards, its windscreen wipers smearing a mixture of rain and road grease across the glass. Quirinia and I exchanged looks when it shot through a red light. Atrius growled at the driver. We had no papers or passports. I shuddered at the thought of being picked up by the local police and deported back to Roma Nova.

Like ancient Rome, historic Austria had been golden, imperial and wealthy. Vienna had been the undoubted intellectual, cultural and social centre of Europe. Since the Great War of 1925-35, its consequent loss of empire and reduction to a rump state, Neuösterreich had to rely on its mountains, national costumes and undoubted genius for hospitality to survive. Apart from hosting countless international conferences, Vienna had the dubious honour of being the political dissident and exile centre of Europe. And we'd just joined it.

We stopped the taxi two streets away from the safe house and paid the driver off with no tip. We tramped through the rain, Atrius following the three of us at a thirty-metre gap as a backstop. As we turned into the street where the house lay, Calavia split away from Quirinia, now limping badly, and me to double-back and check nobody was tracking us.

At last, we stood in front of a two-storey, eighteenth-century Biedermeier town house, its arms at ninety degrees to each other and occupying the whole of a block in a quiet suburb. One of the arms housed a small bar and bijou restaurant on the ground floor. Opposite were a delicatessen, a coffee shop and patisserie. Very Viennese.

'Looks as if it needs some work on it,' Quirinia remarked, her accountant's eyes scanning the building, 'but the roof looks sound. How on earth did Colonel Volusenia get hold of it?'

'It was a surrendered asset from a reformed embezzler, *consiliaria*,' Pia answered. 'He gave it up as a condition of being granted leave to return to Roma Nova. He'd fiddled some defence procurement contracts, so the *magister miletum*'s department seized it and allocated it to the PGSF. The commander before Colonel Volusenia designated it as part of the Aquila fallback resources. The beauty is that we can get to the suburban station or onto the *autobahn* and out of the city within minutes.'

Calavia rang the bell at the side of the double doors. A couple of minutes went by without any response, so she thumped on the door, stepped back and stared up at the windows. On this dull, rainy October afternoon, a few lights were glowing at the upstairs windows. She raised her hand again, but before her knuckles touched the faded green paintwork, the door opened.

'About time, too,' she said and barged in. 'We're getting soaked out here.'

We shuffled past the young woman who had opened the door into a large hallway complete with split staircase and tall windows. A middle-aged man was leaning on a stick stood under a dull light. His face was bruised and his free hand bandaged, but I knew him straight away.

'Numerus! What are *you* doing here?'

'Major.' He gave me a semi-bow. 'I'm the logistics officer for this shambles of a fallback group.' He snorted and waved the end of his stick around a few centimetres off the floor.

'But you've been retired for years.'

'Somehow, nobody rescinded my orders.' He shrugged, but winced as his shoulders fell back. Numerus was as tough as Aquae Caesaris granite. I couldn't remember the last time he'd shown he was affected by pain.

'What in Hades happened to you?'

'Some of the local toughs decided kicking a retired PGSF guard around would be fun. I'm sure they were nats. Luckily, Maxima arrived and helped me see them off, but as soon as she'd bandaged her old dad up, we packed up and ran for it here. She's gone back to Roma Nova now, the silly tart. She's been troublesome since she was a kid, so I hope she gives them hell.'

I forgot about our wet clothes and studied my ex-comrade-in-arms. His face was grey and lined, and his eyes shone, not with pleasure, but with worry about his only daughter.

'I'm relieved they got you out,' he said after a few moments. 'That bastard Tellus never forgave you for banging him up in that Prussian prison.' He looked straight at me. 'You should have let me shoot him when we had him then.'

'Numerus, you know I couldn't have done that.'

'Yes.' He sighed. 'You always did have a too rigid sense of right and wrong.' He ran his eyes over us. 'Come on in, then, and we'll find you all beds. And there's somebody here who wants to talk to you urgently.'

'Volusenia, I presume?'

'No.' He frowned. 'Isn't she with you?'

My stomach fluttered. 'No, she came on ahead with Silvia Apulia.' I grabbed Numerus's wrist. 'Gods, don't tell me they haven't arrived!'

'Not yet, but somebody else turned up this afternoon looking for you.'

The figure was unmistakable; tall, tanned face, black curls. My heart thudded and I took a deep breath. My body knew him instantly even if my brain was half a second behind. No smile or word was necessary; he just reached forward and folded me gently into his arms, pressing me to him. I forgot everything except that I was safe again.

• • •

Numerus ushered us towards a door at the rear of the hall; the smell told me it was the kitchen before we walked into its warmth. Calavia drew me aside the minute we were through the door.

'Nothing personal, *consiliaria*,' she whispered, glancing over at Miklós. 'But he's a foreigner with a dubious background. He has no security clearance and no loyalty to Roma Nova. We should exclude him.'

'You forget yourself, Lieutenant. That isn't your decision.'

'With respect, you're allowing your personal feelings to rule your judgement,' she retorted.

'You have no idea what you're talking about, Calavia.'

'Ladies.' Numerus had come up behind us. 'Do we have a problem?'

'Him, the Hungarian.' Calavia jerked her head in Miklós's direction. 'I know he's the *consiliaria*'s friend, but in this situation, we can't take any chances with security. Suppose he goes running to Caius Tellus?'

As I opened my mouth to give her the full blast of what I thought of her accusation, Numerus touched my arm and gave me a warning glance.

'He won't,' he said to Calavia. 'I wouldn't want to breach security myself in giving you every detail, Lieutenant, but his role in the Berlin operation against Tellus was pivotal.' He looked her straight in the eyes. 'You'd have been packing your school bag and worrying about your first teenage crush at the time, so you wouldn't be expected to know.'

No obvious reaction showed in her stance, but her eyes had flickered as if flinching internally. She turned away without saying a word.

Quirinia, Atrius, Miklós and I clustered at one end of the large bench table in the kitchen with Numerus. Calavia joined us after a few minutes; she hunched over and frowned into her tea. A weak light from a conical shade gave little relief to the gloom. The smell of field stew and strong tea surrounded us. Over by the stove, people were stirring pans and cutting vegetables. The swish of stirring, the gentle roar of the gas flames and rhythmic chop-chop of vegetable knives were the only sounds.

Numerus leant back in his seat and crossed his arms. 'So what happened?'

'Silvia and Volusenia left two days ago, via a safe house,' I said. 'There was a van in the garage there, so they would have had a head start.' I looked down at the table. 'I should have stayed with them.'

Nobody answered for a second. Quirinia covered the back of my hand. 'You couldn't possibly have known what would happen, Aurelia.'

'We can't automatically assume Caius has got Silvia Apulia,' Numerus said. 'He'd have paraded her all over the television if he had.'

'Not until he'd terrified her enough to comply,' I replied. 'And she's a tough little thing.' I didn't add 'unlike her mother'. 'If he has her, he'll force her to marry him and his claim to power will be legitimised.' My imagination ran into a dark place where Silvia was in Caius's control. He'd make her life such a living hell she'd pray for death.

'I can't see Colonel Volusenia giving in easily,' Calavia added. 'She'd have died before she let anybody touch an Apulian.'

'Why do you all assume Tellus will find her?' Miklós's voice interrupted. It was the first time he'd spoken. We all turned and stared at him.

'You've seen how well this coup was executed, Miklós,' I said. 'Even Plico didn't see it coming.' I paused for a moment and closed my eyes. I would never see that grumpy, clever and honourable old tough again. I shook my head to dispel a grey lump of sorrow that threatened to settle in my head. He would have been the first to tell me to get a grip.

'The only way that Caius Tellus could have been so efficient is by building up a wide network of dedicated local groups, recruited one by one,' I continued. 'The individual group leader would report to a district leader, who'd be a member of a group in the next level up, and so on up the hierarchy. Classic revolution.' I panned around the faces. 'You can be sure he's faxed Silvia and Volusenia's descriptions to all of them. All it would take is for one member of one local group to spot the women and he'd have them. The chances against them staying undetected are minute.'

'If they're holed up somewhere in the countryside, they may find some sympathy, or possibly help,' Calavia said. 'The trouble is that if they're too well hidden, but can't move, we'll never find them.'

I looked round at the doleful, tense faces. 'But you know we have no choice but to go back and look for them. Or give up our own lives in the attempt.'

We ate a plain supper in silence, everybody absorbed with her or his own thoughts. Not quite twenty others sat in the kitchen at benches or picked chairs off a dusty stack in what had been a ballroom. With such small numbers, huddling in the kitchen was more comforting. Numerus had organised people into four groups and allocated tasks and shifts. Once a centurion, always a centurion.

'Gives them some kind of structure and purpose,' he murmured to me as we stacked our dishes in the sink. 'They've all done their national service, so they know how it works.'

'Thank you, Numerus.'

'Not a question of thanks, but of survival.' He searched my face. 'You know you can't go yourself, don't you? You'd be far too big a prize for Tellus.'

'Don't try and argue me out of it, old friend. It's my duty.'

'Sure it's not your ego?'

'How dare you!'

'Just a comment.'

'You can keep that sort to yourself, if you please.'

'I thought you might be motivated to stay here now.' He glanced over at Miklós talking to an uncomfortable looking Calavia.

'He's more likely to want to come with me.'

Numerus shrugged.

Miklós stood and left the kitchen, so I waved Calavia over to join us.

'So are there any rescue scenarios in the fallback plan?' I asked.

She exchanged glances with Numerus.

'Well?'

'There's one route in and another out from this side of the border, but we can't be sure they are still intact,' Calavia admitted. 'They were set up with the scenario of foreign invasion. Nobody expected internal rebellion. The people providing the support might now belong to the

Roman National Movement, so no longer sympathetic to us. We'll have to check each one as we go.'

Damn. People patriotic enough to be part of a national resistance movement against an invader could well be attracted by what looked like a movement that flourished on national pride, however spurious or illusory. This was becoming better and better. But there was no other option.

'Realistically, how many people can we muster to take part in this mission?' I asked her.

'Atrius and myself, and there are a couple here on the active reserve list that I recognise, but the rest, I haven't a clue.'

'Numerus?'

'Two of the women have just finished their twenty years and there's one young lad who's just started the Officers' Training School. He's worried stiff about his classmates, so I'm not sure about his nerves. The rest of them are full-time civilians.'

'Well, more than half a dozen of us would look suspicious.' I glanced at my watch. 'It's half-seven now. Get them all together for 20:00, in the ballroom, for a briefing, please, Numerus. We'll just have to work with what we've got.'

22

―――――――

'You're not going, are you?'

'I have to, Miklós. It's my duty.'

He sat cross-legged on his rolled out sleeping bag on the dirty floor of the room upstairs that Numerus had allocated us.

'Stop fiddling with that plastic bag and sit here with me.'

I thrust the towel, soap and toothbrush back into the bag so hard the thin plastic split and it all landed on the floor. Stuff it. I knelt down beside him.

'Going back is all very noble,' he said 'but your man, Numerus, is right. If Tellus has the girl, he might not be showing her because he knows you will try to rescue her. And we both know he wants his revenge on you. You'll be walking into a trap.' He stroked my hair, a straggly mess, and tucked a curl behind my ear. He pulled me to him and I nestled against his chest; I could feel his heart beating and his arms held me secure and safe.

'Don't go.' His warm breath on my face was so achingly familiar. I didn't want to go anywhere at this moment.

'Why have you come here, Miklós? I thought you'd left me for good.'

'When the messenger from the post office knocked on my father's farmhouse door with your telex, I could read the distress between the lines.' He pressed my hands and folded them in his. 'You're a strong, no, a tough woman, Aurelia, sometimes a little wild, but inside, there's a sensitive and vulnerable person hiding under that shell. I knew you would be hurting. You love Roma Nova more than anything.'

I went to turn and protest, but he held me tight.

He laughed and kissed my hair. 'Don't bullshit me, *drágám*. I know I come second.'

'You don't, Miklós, it's a different kind of love.'

'I don't understand it, but I know it's so important to you, you'd die for it. And you are so important to me, I'd kill for you. So I had to come.'

A knock on the door and a shout of 'five minutes' broke the moment. I sighed. He stood up and stretched a hand out to me. I took it, drawing on his strength. He pulled me to my feet, kissed the top of my head, then drew back and gave me the saddest look I'd ever seen.

'My name is Aurelia Mitela, serving until a few days ago as the imperial foreign minister to Imperatrix Severina. I was formerly a major in the Praetorian Guard Special Forces. With the help of Lieutenant Calavia and Guard Atrius, I intend to lead a rescue mission to find and recover Silvia Apulia. I have no right to ask you to go with me. You've struggled to get to safety and I'm asking you to go back into a lethal environment. It's no shame if you prefer not to.' I paused, waiting for any further reaction. I glanced over at Miklós sitting on a chair by the wall, arms crossed and a solemn expression on his face.

The two veterans didn't blink an eye, the reservists looked wary and the young cadet stared not quite open-mouthed. We sat in a circle on rickety chairs at one end of the ballroom. Dusty oblong rectangles stared down at us where once portraits had hung and the fashionable eau-de-nil had faded to a dirty greeny-white.

The lankier of the two veterans raised her hand. Her brown hair was bound up round her head and as she wriggled her shoulders, her body seemed to lengthen. 'I'll go. I'm thirty-eight and the legion is all I've known.' She glanced at her blond colleague who nodded. 'So you have two of us, ma'am.'

'Your names?'

'I'm Balia, she's Styrax, both served in the XX Victis.'

'Ha! Good legion.' I clasped her hand, then Styrax's. 'Welcome.'

'I'll come,' the boy chirped up. 'My name's Turturus.'

'How old are you, Turturus?' I said.

'I'll be eighteen next February, ma'am.'

Juno, he was far too young to take on this mission. He needed to finish his training, then be posted to a sound regiment to mature under the watchful eye of a centurion. His eager young face had hardly lost its soft adolescent bloom. I had to find a way to refuse that would salvage his dignity.

'What speciality have you chosen?'

'Infantry.'

Damn. Exactly what we needed. If only he'd been in a support arm, I could have refused him. But I wasn't taking children under any circumstances.

'Well, Turturus, I appreciate your enthusiasm, but I think Numerus will need you here to support him. He's still on the sick list and needs an energetic helper.'

'But—'

'Enough, young man.' Numerus flicked his hand and glared at him. 'Don't argue with the major.'

Turturus shot Numerus an angry look, then turned away. He hunched over and clasped his hands together. It was as if he'd been denied a place in the sports team. The woman reservist got to her feet. 'I'm a logistics specialist, Major. I don't think I'd be much help in this kind of operation – I'm not fit enough for a start.' Then she smiled. 'But I'll make sure you'll have the best equipment and papers that I can find you.'

In the end, we were six, comprising Balia, Styrax, the other reservist, whose name was Servlus, Pia Calavia, Atrius and myself. I gave us three days for planning and practice; every day the danger to Silvia and Volusenia would increase exponentially. By the end of day two, we had several scenarios, a handful of tactics and diminishing optimism.

On the third afternoon, Miklós and I lay together under blankets. I was awake, but he dozed in that almost half-unconscious way you did after good sex. We had the luxury of a mattress now, and two cardboard boxes for our clothes and meagre belongings. The sun was sinking, throwing light through the bloom on the old windows, giving an idea of warmth, but I shivered, even lying against his warm skin. His arm encircled my waist tightly.

'I'll come with you, of course,' he murmured, his eyes still closed.

'I can't drag you into this, Miklós.'

His eyes snapped open. 'I'm not going to risk losing you again,' he said.

'We have to settle this ourselves.'

'I'm a foreign national. I'll be able to move around more easily than you.'

'Caius knows exactly who you are. Do you think he'd respect your passport?'

He looked up at the ceiling for a long five minutes. 'I haven't been able to contact any of my people in Roma Nova. He must have cut the international lines. I'll give you the names and numbers of some people who might help if you get stuck. If they're still alive.'

I rolled over and propped myself up on my elbows. 'I don't want to endanger your contacts. This has to be a quick in and out. I'll be back in a week, ten days max.'

'You'd better be.' He stared at me, his dark eyes shining in the last of the day's light.

He pulled me on top of him and we made love urgently. I didn't know when, or even if, I'd see him again. Later, I ran my fingers down the side of his face and closed my eyes to commit the sensation of his skin to memory. When my index finger reached his mouth, I opened my eyes and found him staring at me. His brown eyes shone like liquid mahogany. He leaned in and kissed me with a soft touch, then more passionately until fire ran through me. I grasped his shoulders, hardly breathing as he entered me. Afterwards, I wept.

Dressed in hiking gear, backpacks ready, and a warm supper inside us, we were ready. My group waited in the hallway for Atrius, Balia and Styrax to go first; they would travel on the high-speed train bound for the free city of Trieste, but leave it well before and cross into Roma Nova from the west. Calavia, Servlus and I were to travel south on the train to Graz, then take the bus to the last town before the border. We'd go the hard way, back over mountains. It was a slight risk, taking the same route we'd used to escape, but at least we knew it. The logistics specialist had made us Helvetian Confederation ID; not perfect, she said, but it should pass muster in most circumstances and with Miklós's help she'd found us some personal transceivers.

If it all went well, we would meet up at the first safe house a kilometre west of Castra Lucilla. I had to hope that we could garner some support from my farm manager, Gavinus. If he was still alive.

I'd never forget the way Miklós held me in the grip of his arm as we waited thirty minutes after Atrius's team had left for the station. He knew it was useless trying to argue me out of going; he conceded, eventually, that I was better off with my own military team. He wasn't used to that disciplined mode and would jettison the mission the second he thought I was in any danger. I made him promise not to follow me into Roma Nova. For all his devious trading habits, I hoped he would be too honourable to renege on it.

Three days later on a moonless night at Castra Lucilla, I left Calavia to guard our backs near the crossroads before the farm entrance. Servlus and I crept along the farm boundary, avoiding the farmworker dormitories, and reached the manager's house. Thin lines of light ran along the top and bottom edges of the closed window shutters. I flattened myself against the wall by the opening edge of the door. Servlus waited opposite, clutching a thick oak staff disguised as a walking stick. Suppose Caius had already seized the farm out of spite and put an overseer and gang in? The memory of the brutal attack six weeks ago welled up. My people had been killed and beaten, and the farm manager raped, by a pack of unidentified thugs. I knew in my heart it had been Caius's thugs, but couldn't prove it. Please, Diana, I prayed, may you have protected my Castra Lucilla *familia*. I tapped on the wooden door and held my breath.

The door opened a few centimetres, revealing a dim light and an anxious face.

'*Domina!*' Gavinus's eyes nearly popped out. He yanked the door open. We slid in.

'Shut the door. Quickly,' I whispered.

I glanced round. At the end of the plain passage I could see a light coming from the living room and hear low voices talking.

'Company?'

'No, no, just the television. Some kind of public service broadcast.' He glanced at Servlus.

'He's with me, you can talk freely,' I said.

Gavinus led us into the living room. A half-glass of beer stood on a small occasional table by an armchair facing the set. A scene of toga toughs, fists clutched across their chests, marching across the forum towards a figure on a podium in front of the Senate steps. Caius. He was watching them with intense concentration. The commentator was describing the 'moving display of strength and patriotism'. We watched for a few seconds, mesmerised by the marching music and drums.

'Pluto in Tartarus.' Servlus swore. 'What a load of bollocks.'

I couldn't say a word. This was the worst of worst nightmares. I swallowed hard to try to relieve my parched throat.

'Sit, *domina*.' Gavinus pushed me gently into his armchair and gave me his glass of beer. I took a long swallow. The bitter taste brought me up sharp.

'Are you all safe, Gavinus? Has there been any trouble here?' I watched him jerk the remote control at the television and the image and sound evaporated.

'We haven't seen anybody these last few days, not even the postwoman. I contacted the local delivery office, but they told me they had nothing for the farm. That's odd in itself – there are always bills and catalogues.' He glanced at me. 'And the lorry I sent to the city yesterday with the weekly delivery to Domus Mitelarum hasn't returned. Sometimes the driver stays over with her sister, but she always lets me know. Then the telephone stopped working this morning. And nobody's answering the radio. I stayed up tonight hoping the driver would get back somehow. To be honest, I'm worried sick.' He handed me a printed notice without looking at me. 'One of the field workers found this pinned to the *mansio* door in the town today.'

By order of First Consul Caius Tellus

Due to the national crisis, the provisional government will apply the following emergency orders for the next 30 days.

1. All citizens must be indoors by 21.00 and will not leave their homes before 05.00.

2. We will respect citizens' rights but anyone instigating or committing a breach of these orders will be punished severely.

3. All orders given by the civil authorities or their authorised representatives are to be strictly obeyed.

4. Personal ownership of all rifles, guns, revolvers, daggers, sporting guns and all other weapons whatsoever including training blades of every kind together with any ammunition is now illegal. However, citizens have until 18.00 tomorrow, 7 October, to surrender any such items currently in their possession to the nearest vigiles barracks. Discovery of failure to do so will result in summary imprisonment even after the expiry of these emergency orders.

5. All service personnel on leave must report to the nearest military barracks by 18.00 tomorrow, 7 October.

6. No boat or vessel of any description, including any pilot, fishing or tugboat, shall leave the river harbours or any other place where same is moored without an order from the local Curia office.

7. All international flights and cross-border rail services are temporarily suspended and all road crossings are strictly controlled. Expect long delays for verification which will only be granted in exceptional cases.

8. Foreign citizens in Roma Nova will be respected, but should remain in their hotels or residences until they have either registered and obtained a permit to stay from the local Curia or applied for an exit visa. These will be issued via their national legations.

9. Emergency services including doctors, veterinary and social personnel will be granted fuel and supplies subject to registration. Agricultural units and food suppliers will be granted movement orders and fuel subject to registration.

10. For the time being, there will be no fuel allocation for private use.

11. Food shops will remain open as before; increasing prices is forbidden.

12. All television and radio organisations apart from the National Roma Nova Broadcasting Company have been switched off. Their male personnel will be integrated into the new national company and the female staff dismissed.

Signed this day 6 October

'What in Hades is going on, *domina*?'

I couldn't sit still, so I walked back and forth as I gave Gavinus a short version of what had happened in the past six days. He flopped down, hunched over and didn't say a word. I didn't know what to say to him. The horror of that notice hadn't sunk in. Our knives and my service revolver would condemn us out of hand if we were discovered. I couldn't imagine how miserable and oppressive life would become for all normal Roma Novans under these strictures. But the most ominous of Caius's orders was the last one – the wholesale dismissal of female workers. Surely he wasn't going to try to reverse over fifteen hundred years of history?

Gods.

'Gavinus,' I said, 'you must prepare for the very worst. I've always thought it was Caius Tellus behind the raid six weeks ago, but I can't prove it. They'll remember how we disarmed them and took the farm back. For your own safety, you should hand over to one of your deputies, somebody who didn't actively resist the raiders, if any will accept it, and disappear. Evacuate anybody who resisted, and take Priscilla and her daughter with you.' I scribbled down the Vienna address on a piece of paper I tore off his farm magazine and handed it to him.

'I'm not deserting Castra Lucilla,' he said. 'I can't leave everybody here in the lurch.' He looked at me steadily. Warmth flowed up my neck and I felt a wave of guilt all over again.

'Believe me, Gavinus, I've been through this myself. To be brutal, we don't have a hope in Hades of resisting effectively at the moment against such an organised coup. I'm surprised they haven't been here already. This isn't just a power grab, it's a sustained and wholesale attack on our values, and way of life. And knowing Caius Tellus, he'll pursue it through any means and not care how violent he is or the misery he causes. I want you to get out as soon as possible, tomorrow morning, and take our most vulnerable people with you.'

'Are you giving me an order?' His voice was as cold as the snows on the high peaks.

'If necessary. I want you to survive this.' I took his hand. 'We will take it back, but throwing your life away now would be futile. Please do as I say.'

'You are forcing me to make a bitter choice, *domina*.'

'Bitter indeed, but better than being dead, or worse. On second thoughts, we should evacuate everybody. I can't face the idea of *any* of our people being here when they come. They'll be left with little choice but to knuckle down to Caius's people – they'll have no way of escaping.'

I suddenly realised what I was doing. Hundreds of years of careful husbandry of the land, the exclusive breeding stock, the unique cattle herds, the world famous vineyards – all this would be ruined. And my people whose families had survived since the earliest times, even during the great migrations and the European religious and civil wars, would be wrenched from their homes, their inherited ties to their land, their very souls would be ripped and shredded. The alternative was brutality, servitude or death. The gods curse Caius into the black depth of Tartarus. My hand trembled as I touched Gavinus's forearm.

'Get everybody up before first light and explain the situation. If they can go to any relatives or friends and stay with them, then so much the better. If anybody wants to stay, then explain exactly what could happen to them. I don't want any false optimism. It will be vile. If everybody goes, you'll have to turn all the livestock out. Leave the troughs full.' Poor beasts, but they might survive in the wild. Perhaps the toughest would. I rubbed my forehead and tried to blank out the time as a child I'd helped to drive the cows to the milking shed and walked in the fields, patting the lambs, the time I'd popped a sun-filled wine grape into my mouth only to screw my face up at the tartness.

'Allocate anybody who wants to go a place in the trucks. You'll have to abandon the trucks and walk over the frontier. The western route past Aquae Caesaris using the old mountain routes is your best bet. You should have enough money to bribe your way through.' I shot a look at him. 'You've been doing the emergency drills?'

'Yes, and we have survival packs ready for everybody, but I never thought it would come to this.'

'Well, Tartarus has opened up and is trying to suck us all in.'

• • •

By the early hours, we'd packed and loaded the farm records and reserves plus money, food and filled water tanks. Gavinus would bury the steel boxes containing the records and reserves in the far sheepfold where there was an emergency shelter. Servlus went to the barns and sheds and filled the troughs by torchlight, and left piles of feed for the poultry, Ceres bless him. The foxes would get most of them, though, once the gates were open. As the electric clock beeped five, the three of us stared at each other, eyes wide with exhaustion. I ached for my bed, any bed. The two men didn't speak; they looked utterly spent.

I opened the front door of Gavinus's house a couple of centimetres. Nothing stirred that I could see. I heard the low moan of a cow in the distance. A cold breeze touched my face from the dark morning. The sun wouldn't rise for another hour. I turned to Gavinus.

'You'll have to start getting people up soon. I'm sorry I can't speak to them, but they mustn't know I've been here. They can't reveal what they don't know. This is a bad time when we're forced to behave against our instincts, but now our duty is to survive and endure.' I held my hand out. 'Goodbye, Gavinus. Look after our people, and *bona fortuna*. And I'll see you in Vienna.'

23

———

Servlus and I kept close to the hedge as we crept down the tree-lined driveway of the farm. I couldn't have spoken a word if I'd wanted. All I could do was swallow the sour taste that kept filling my mouth. I shrugged my rucksack, now heavy with supplies from the farm store, further up my back. Five metres before the gate, I flicked my hand downwards and we dropped to the ground. The pre-dawn gloom contrasted with the whiteness of the stars, but it was enough to see we were not alone.

'Estate guard,' I whispered into Servlus's ear and pointed towards the figure by the stone pillar supporting the right gate. She was turning her head, panning in a circle as if looking for something. Had she heard us? We had to either neutralise her or admit our presence. Hades, this was ridiculous. Couldn't I trust anybody? No, the less they knew, the safer they were. I reached into the inside pocket of my hunting jacket for my transceiver.

'Calavia, Mitela,' I whispered, my lips touching the mouthpiece. 'All clear?'

'Calavia. Affirmative.'

'Small problem here. Guard on the front gate, but I do not, repeat, do not wish to harm her nor acknowledge our presence.'

Calavia's laugh came back with some crackle. 'I should hope not – it's me.'

. . .

'You might have let me know,' I grumbled at Calavia once we had entered the woods a couple of hundred metres behind the farm. 'What did you do with the real guard?'

'She's probably back on the gate now. I persuaded her to take my place.'

'Persuaded?'

'Turns out she's a cousin of one of the *optios* in my troop. Well, one of the *optios* of my ex-troop. Gods, I hope he's safe along with the others.' She looked ahead and didn't say anything for a few moments as we marched on. 'Anyway,' she continued, 'I said I was on a mission and needed her to guard the crossroads for an hour.' The dawn light was enough to show her quick grin.

'Was her name Sentia, or possibly Albina?'

'Sentia. How did you guess?'

'She's one of the ex-regulars who helped me take the farm back six weeks ago.'

'She said to pass on her respects when I saw you next…'

Juno!

'… and that she and Albina would do whatever was necessary to save your people.'

On a slight rise just outside the town of Castra Lucilla sat an abandoned stone house, now encroached by the woods we were walking through. According to estate records, it had once belonged to the Mitelae, but was gifted away in perpetuity in the eighteenth century. I knew that earlier Mitela stewards, and later business managers, had tried to trace the owners to buy it back, but without success. I'd only ever run by on the outside, too spooked by my cousins' tales of the ghost who was supposed to wander there. In the early morning light, the peeling shutters and rampant ivy crawling up the wall and crumbling chimney stack reinforced its general air of dilapidation. This was our first safe house.

We pushed open the iron gate separating the woods from what would once have been a pretty garden. Skeletons of fruit trees interspersed with wild looking survivors. A slab path ran from the gate through the orchard and former vegetable beds, up three steps and through what looked like an open prairie with knee-length grass.

Tramping through it would easily show up on an aerial photo, so we kept in a straight single file in the hope it would look like a continuation of the path. At the house, we sidled along the house walls until we reached the back kitchen door and at my nod, Servlus pushed it open.

A shower of dust fell on us as we entered. Something scampered away, raising more dust. Calavia switched on her low-light torch and a time warp scene appeared in the glow. A dresser with china on the top three rows and a full set of Samian bowls below was flanked by wooden cupboards and a long table with benches stood immediately opposite. The floor was covered in plain slabs. Servlus and Calavia dived straight for the door in the far corner. I heard heavy bootsteps as Servlus ascended the stairs. Calavia pushed doors open along the corridor as I charged through to the next room. A dark wood sideboard, upholstered sofa, two winged armchairs and an elegant bureau and chairs greeted me. Three glass and gilt shades shaped like overripe plums and coated with a dull bloom of dirt hung in a group from the decorated ceiling. What on earth was such elegance doing in what was essentially a large country cottage?

'Clear upstairs,' Servlus shouted down.

'And downstairs,' Calavia agreed. 'But this is a strange house. Apart from being something out of a history book, both rooms on the west side of the house look as if they were abandoned in a hell of a hurry. There are plates and cutlery on the table with dried traces of food in the first. And a lot of vermin droppings.'

'Well, fascinating as it is,' I said, 'we don't have time to think about it. Let's grab some rest and wait for Atrius and the others.' Servlus took first watch. I unrolled my sleeping bag on the sofa and within minutes of climbing into it, I was out. What seemed like five minutes later, I felt a hand shaking my shoulder. Atrius. They'd made it. He thrust a hot drink at me. I blinked, shook my head, then took a sip of the delicious warmth. Balia and Styrax were talking in earnest whispers to Calavia.

'Any problems?' I asked Atrius.

'Not really. Some officious little nobodies with nationalist armbands stopped us at the frontier demanding ID but our Helvetian papers were accepted. However, we learned something interesting –

most of the domestic telephones are still working as normal, so I phoned my sister in the city.'

'You did what?' How could Atrius break security like that?

'Don't worry, ma'am, we have a secret code we've used since childhood – it's something twins do.'

'This isn't a childhood game, Atrius.'

'I know. That's why we have to pull in every favour. My sister runs a small dry cleaning and dyeing business inside the city. She's offered to put us up in the storeroom.' He glanced away. 'Unfortunately, Caius Tellus's thugs are patrolling with the *vigiles* and the new rules are being applied ruthlessly. Three traders in her street have been hauled off for questioning. None has returned.'

Everyone stopped speaking and stared at him. We'd heard of such things in the Russian lands in the east, but for it to be happening in Roma Nova…

'Six of us will be far too conspicuous,' I said and struggled out of my sleeping bag. 'Servlus, Balia and Styrax will stay here and set up exit routes. We could be eight altogether. Do not under any circumstances endanger yourself or compromise this building. But be ready to move at any time and expect us to be under hot pursuit.'

'What happens if the nationalists come to Castra Lucilla and take over your estate?' Styrax asked.

I swallowed hard.

'Plan a fallback position in the woods.' I almost mentioned the tunnel, then remembered Callixtus's treachery. 'There was an alternative, but it's blown. One of the nationalists knows about it.'

'How will we know you've been successful in the rescue?'

'Lieutenant Calavia will give you a radio check schedule. If we miss two, then assume we're down. Every day makes our mission harder. Whatever happens, if Calavia, Atrius and I are not back within four days, you must bail out.'

Keeping to the fields until we encountered the first houses at the edge of the city seven and a half hours later, we were able to make good progress. Calavia was kind enough to make a couple of stops so I could catch my breath. Everything appeared calm and normal; we could have been three walkers out on a pleasant evening country stroll. The soft autumn breeze, slightly humid, but warm and smelling of grass, earth and a hint of pine lulled and comforted us. Clusters of grapes reserved for late picking still hung from vines, maize leaves were just starting to wilt so the cobs were in perfect state for harvesting, possibly a week overdue. But nobody was working in the fields. We hadn't seen a soul in the past fifteen kilometres.

'Can you push on into the city, ma'am?' Calavia asked.

The sun was about to disappear and all I wanted to do was fall into the earth after it. I glanced at my watch. Seven thirty.

'Can we make it to your sister's tonight, Atrius?'

'Normally, it's about thirty minutes from here – she's in the Via Nova – but we're going to have to go through the backstreets and alleys. It'll be tight, especially if we run into any checkpoints.'

'Well,' I replied, 'we'd better get going.'

It was ridiculously easy, which was fortunate as we were bone tired. Systematic as Caius's organisation was, he hadn't achieved the critical mass yet needed to watch every street, house or *insula* block in the city. But if he managed to convince or terrorise his fellow Roma Novans, it would only be a question of time. My head was reeling with tiredness, but I was still so angry.

Calavia took photos of any changes with a miniature camera wherever she could. If we got back to Vienna, it would be valuable intelligence. Atrius and I waited, flattened against the wall of a building near the forum, while she took a series of shots. Suddenly, she jerked back.

'*Merda!*' She gave a violent jerk of her hand. We shifted immediately and ran, twisting around different buildings until we were three blocks back.

'What happened?' I asked. My heart hammered as I tried to catch my breath. Even Atrius was breathing heavily.

'I may have been spotted,' she gasped.

'Pluto! Let's get out of here and bunk down at Atrius's sister's without any more detours.'

We wound round the streets in a disparate pattern, avoiding the CCTV where possible. Luckily for us the new public feed plan hadn't been implemented, so it was still only installed in the main shopping streets and the Macellum market area. After winding through backstreets, eyes watching everything, we dived into a poorly lit alley. Atrius pressed on a bell push by an unmarked service door. A siren from a *vigilis* car pierced the silence. We jumped like cats behind bins.

Gods.

The door opened a few centimetres.

'Paula!' Atrius hissed. 'Open the bloody door.'

'Junius, thank Hygeia. Get in, quickly.'

We tumbled in and Atrius's sister slammed and locked the door behind us. Brother and sister hugged briefly. She was nearly as tall as him. He released her and nodded. 'Paula, this is—'

'Don't tell me any names, Junius. I can't tell what I don't know.' She stared at me, blue eyes blazing. 'But I know who she is.' Her face twisted in anger. 'How in Hades did you lot let this happen? What sort of government were you? Do you know what sort of shit you've left us in?'

'Enough, Paula,' her brother said. 'Nobody doubts the gravity of the situation.'

'Grave? Is that how you see it, Junius Atrius? It's damned disastrous! You haven't heard the latest, have you?'

'No, we've been trying to stay alive, if that's not seen as a frivolous occupation.'

'Ha! My twelve years of slaving away to build up this business is going down the well. Women have been ordered to sign their assets over to their nearest male relative and retire from commercial and public life. We have thirty days to comply or everything will be confiscated.' She slumped down on a stool and burst into tears.

24

———

Despite her harsh words, Paula Atria gave us food and shelter, but she wouldn't talk directly to me. She threw blankets and pillows down on the floor, turned her shoulder and left the storeroom. Twenty minutes later, she returned with a tray of soup and meat-filled rolls which she thumped down on the top of an old laundry machine. Atrius shrugged and gave me an apologetic look. We bunked down on the vinyl floor between tubs of chemicals and open boxes of plastic clothes covers.

The following morning, I intended to go to the ex-armourer's safe house in the Vicus Fabricensium at the end of the palace tunnel that Silvia and Volusenia had escaped down. The road to the armourer's house outside the city wall narrowed under an archway – a perfect bottleneck for the nationalists to check both pedestrian and vehicle traffic. Of course, there were other, less formal ways through the wall, but as the phones were working, it would be safer to make the first contact from within the shelter of Paula Atria's laundry.

'Yes?' A gruff female voice answered after ten rings.

'Marcia? That you?' I whined.

'No Marcia here. You've got the wrong number.'

'Sorry, love.'

• • •

'Plico's armourer is still there. Or somebody who sounds just like she should sound.'

'We don't know that, Major,' Calavia chimed in.

'No, but it's highly likely. So now we have to go and see what she has to say for herself.'

'It could be a trap, of course.'

'Perhaps, but I would think Caius has enough to do at the moment without drilling down to the level of retired supply soldiers.'

'To be sure, Atrius or I will go and check,' Calavia said.

'I haven't quite lost the ability to act covertly, Lieutenant.' I frowned at her.

'No, I don't doubt your skills and abilities, ma'am, but you are far too big a prize to be picked up on such a simple errand.'

'I'll go,' Atrius said. 'I'm probably less conspicuous.'

Calavia and I stared at the nearly two-metre tall, sturdily built man with black hair and blazing blue eyes. Hardly my idea of inconspicuous.

'If what Paula says is true,' he said, 'Tellus has already started implementing his old Roman policy. In that case, as a man, I'll probably pass through more easily.' His logic was impeccable, but uncomfortable; I hated splitting our tiny group.

As the back door closed behind Atrius, Calavia and I started gathering our things together. Fiddling with bags and blankets when I should be out there trying to find Silvia was frustrating. Calavia fidgeted around aimlessly. Waiting was always the worst part. I couldn't get rid of a nagging feeling that something was very wrong. Had Caius got Silvia or not?

The door opened to reveal Paula Atria. She kept her grasp on the door handle, but jerked her head at us. 'There's something on the news you should see.'

We followed her up a flight of open metal steps, inhaling by default the sharp chemical smell from the thrumming machines below. The rows of plastic-covered clothes on racks filled the front half of the premises which led directly to the shop. I caught a brief glimpse of the street beyond.

'Quickly,' came Paula's voice. 'I don't want any of the shop staff to see you.'

She fished out a key on a chain round her neck and unlocked a door marked 'Private'. Inside were a desk, chairs, filing cabinets and a sofa in front of a small television set from which came a commentator's voice.

'… and we are waiting with tremendous excitement for Caius Tellus whose chief of staff has hinted the first consul will be making a special announcement.'

I crossed my arms and looked down at the sculptured face of the reporter with his hairspray-fixed hair. Just fourteen days ago, he'd been grilling me about our relations with the European Economic Area; now he was smarming all over Caius. The press room in the Golden Palace looked exactly the same, but the whole press corps was male. Gone were the bright, shoulder-padded jackets and the big hair of the senior women correspondents. Instead, a tight-suited heavy with a nationalists' armband and a big name tag with 'press officer' printed on it hovered at the front and watched the reporters. I felt as if I'd stepped into an alternative reality.

Caius strutted onto the podium and, at a signal from the 'press officer', all the reporters stood up like children in school. No press pack had done that since the beginning of the 1960s.

'Please sit,' he said and gave them one of his saccharine smiles. 'Thank you for coming along today, gentlemen. I wish to make a brief statement about the Apulians, the former ruling family. With the demise of Severina Apulia, their rule has ended and their assets have returned to the state treasury. Unfortunately, the son was caught in the crossfire. We shall honour his funeral later this week. We have some news of the daughter and will update you as the situation becomes clearer.' He looked directly into the camera. 'Naturally, we wish to protect such a young and vulnerable female child from terrorists in exile who wish to stir up rebellion and threaten our hard-won stability and from misguided citizens who may have been persuaded to hide her out of a false sense of duty. I call upon all patriotic citizens to help us find her. Please advise your local National Movement coordinator or the *vigiles* in your area if you see her. All reports will be treated seriously and a significant reward offered. Thank you.' He smiled, nodded, then strode off the podium and out of the room.

Thank the gods. He didn't have Silvia, but as her photo filled the screen, I realised with horror he'd just recruited the national media and the whole population to search for her.

. . .

Atrius wasn't back by lunchtime; the armourer's house was twenty minutes away at the maximum. Of course, he'd have to be careful, but it was now nearly three hours. Calavia and I had absolutely nothing to do; we dozed in turn, but I jumped every time I heard a noise. It was probably just the laundry machinery clanking and thumping.

'I think we ought to move tonight,' I said.

Calavia glanced at the door. 'Why do you think that?' she whispered.

'I don't know, but we can't endanger Atrius's sister any longer. She's too tense. If one of these thugs presses her, she'll squeak.' It wouldn't be any fault of hers. She was a normal person under abnormal pressure.

'I'll get some bin bags to put our stuff out in the alley, ready,' said Calavia. 'I just hope it's not rubbish collection tonight.'

By two o'clock, I was really worried. Calavia radioed our situation back to Styrax and advised her we would move now. I was washing my hands in the back basin, when I caught sight through the tiny window of a group of figures in black clothing creeping up the alley.

Merda.

I burst into the storeroom.

'Enemy. In the alley. Up on the roof. Now.'

Calavia shot up and we ran for the service stairs to the attic. The door was locked.

'Fuck. Stand back,' she hissed. She raised her leg, bent at the knee and arched her back. She slammed her foot against the middle edge of the door. It shivered, but didn't give way.

Shouts and the sound of running feet came from below.

'One, two, three!' We hurled ourselves at the door, shoulders first and it buckled, making an almighty crack as it gave way. We scrambled up the metal ladder and onto the roof. I searched round desperately, spotted a splintering duckboard and jammed it against the roof door under the handle. It might buy us a minute or two.

Paula's shop was one of a terrace. We sprinted along to the end where it dropped onto a curved tile roof. We leapt, knees bent. I slipped and landed face down, spreadeagled on the tile roof ridge. Calavia grabbed my arm and pulled me up.

'No time to lie down, Major.'

We hurled ourselves along the interconnected roofs of the old quarter. I kept my eyes on every single step I took. Gods, nearly tripped on a cracked one. Feet slipping on lichen or dirt. One mistake and we'd be stuffed. Then we came to a dead end. A fretwork parapet, then empty space. And voices behind us.

Merda.

Calavia glanced over at the building opposite.

'We can make that. A run of two strides, third one on the edge of this parapet and throw ourselves over the gap. Fourth stride the far side parapet.'

'Juno, you're so bloody confident, Calavia.'

'Nope, just a question of maths.' She grinned. 'I'll go first.' She ran back, took a deep breath, two long running strides and launched herself, landing on the opposite parapet, then running another stride for balance. She whirled round and beckoned. I hesitated, then heard thumping at the roof access door. I had no choice. I ran at it, aimed at the other side and threw myself into the air. The parapet hurtled towards me and I landed in Calavia's arms.

'Well done, Major. Now let's get out of here.' We were in the Macellum, the market square, on the roof of a department store. We hurried down through the access door, thankfully only on a loose hasp, and slipped into the women's powder room.

'Stay here,' Calavia said. 'I'll go and forage some clothes. What size are you?'

I locked myself in a cubicle and took some deep breaths and the opportunity to relieve myself. Had we lost Atrius? Maybe I'd underestimated Caius's people. No, there weren't the numbers on the street and we were off the CCTV coverage. The raid was specific. The only people who knew we were there were the three of us and Paula Atria. Had she waited until her brother was clear, then called the nationalists in? A wave of cold dread washed through me.

Ten minutes later, I heard the outer door open, then a soft noise of carrier bags falling to the floor. Water from taps, then a roller towel machine yanked. Was it Calavia? I stayed quiet for a full minute then heard a few bars of a soft version of one of our marching songs.

'Alone?' I whispered.

'Completely,' came Calavia's voice. I unlocked the door.

She thrust a bag at me and a cardboard shoebox. We changed quickly and became two women on a shopping expedition. 'The clothes are a bit conservative, but I thought we'd blend in better. I got you a brown wig and headscarf.'

I shrugged on the shapeless dark green dress and grey anorak and transferred the things left in my jacket pocket to my new clothes. Thank the gods we had our money and fake ID on us. Sensible lace-ups and thick tights completed my outfit.

'Gods, Calavia, I look like my mother on a bad day!'

She grinned back, looking like a young country bumpkin, complete with below the knee skirt, knee socks and brogues. 'You can be mine,' she said and ducked as I flicked my fingers in her direction.

'Very funny. Tell me, why isn't the security detail in here, pursuing you for shoplifting?'

'I, er, liberated some loud-mouthed woman's purse. Her male companion had one of those vile nationalist armbands, so I reckoned she was fair game. And he seemed to be doing the buying.'

'Many people about?'

'Not so many as should be.'

'Okay, we'll take it slowly as we make our way out.'

'Where are we going?'

'Only one place, the armourer's house.'

Clutching shopping bags which now contained our walking clothes and boots, we dawdled through the ground floor, passing through the haberdashery and fabric department with their neat rolls of cloth, the wood and glass counter full of ribbons, and customer chairs in front. But nobody was buying. The solemn-faced doorman held the door open and nodded. Out in the street, the first thing we saw was a *vigiles* patrol car. Calavia's grip on my arm tightened, but we carried on as if absorbed in our chatter.

'We'll have to walk. If we get on a bus and they do an ID check, we're stuffed,' Calavia whispered.

'Our Helvetian papers should get us through a casual check, but yes, we're too poor and countrified to be genuine.'

We kept to the side streets and minimised our shoe noise on the pavement slabs, but it started to rain which accentuated the sound of our steps. After fifteen minutes, we reached the city wall at one of the former pedestrian gates. Locked, of course, but not guarded. I fished in my anorak pocket and produced a small black tool wallet.

'When I was working for Plico I always carried these in my pocket just in case I was ever separated from my field bag. Plico always said they'd be as much use as the treasure of Cathay if you didn't have it within finger reach.' Gods, I missed him.

Calavia watched the street, while I tackled the lock. The gate itself was recessed between two stone houses built after the need for defensive walls, so we weren't in full view. Nevertheless…

The lock was old fashioned, heavy and simple. The bottom edge of the door scraped on the cobbles as we tugged it open. We stopped and listened. Nothing but the sound of the rain in the grey and gloom of the late afternoon. We eased the gate open enough to pass through and heaved it shut behind us.

The Vicus Fabricensium was one block away from the wall, a series of old stone cottages, some still with sheds and workshops at the side. At the end, a rock outcrop sheltered the last three of these artisans' houses. The armourer's was the end one in the row, larger and with the back built into the rock. We dawdled along on the opposite side, but couldn't see any sign of *vigiles* or nationalists. Nobody was in the street; all the house shutters were closed. A few cars nested in drives here and there; one was already up on wooden blocks due to the petrol ban.

'Right,' I said, 'let's go and knock on the door, or we'll never get out of this blasted rain.'

Calavia stood to my right side and kept a discreet watch over my shoulder. The dull sound as I knocked echoed up the street. It probably didn't travel that far, but it disrupted the silence. Then I spotted a doorbell. Damn. Of course, an armourer would probably have a metal reinforced door. I jabbed the bell push.

The door opened, but was tethered by a chain.

'What?' A round face, veined, with dark eyes and topped with a grey bun stared out ferociously.

'Friends of Atrius,' Calavia said.

'Nope, never heard of him.' The door started to close, but Calavia had her foot in quicker.

'Plico sends his regards,' I added.

'Ha! From Tartarus, then. He's dead,' the woman said.

'And just how do you know that?'

'Who are you to ask?'

I pulled my headscarf back and turned my face into the light cast by the street light. 'Look at me. Do you recognise me?'

'Nah, never seen—' Her eyes narrowed, then widened. 'Oh, gods, you're—. You can't be.'

'Yes, I am and I'm wet and freezing out here.'

The door slammed, a chain rattled and she flung the door open. 'Come in *domina*, quickly, and your companion.' She ushered us into the vestibule and went back to secure the door. 'Please, this way.'

We followed her across the tiled floor into a side room. She bustled off with our outer garments. A fire crackled in the small grate and thick curtains made it cosy, almost airless. As she came back with warm honey drinks, she bowed. 'I apologise for my rudeness, *domina*. Times are difficult, as you must have seen.'

'I understand. The last thing I want to do is draw attention to you, so we'll go as soon as we've finished.'

'You're welcome to stay as long as you wish; I have two guest rooms, small but adequate. I'm not just being polite.'

'Thank you.' I studied her face for a few moments. 'Tell me, did a young man around thirty, tall, dark hair, blue eyes, call here this morning?'

She frowned. 'No, nobody's been here today.'

I exchanged a look with Calavia, who pulled the front window curtains back together after looking through the gap in the shutters.

'Not at all?'

'No, did he have a message for me?'

'He came to ask a few questions about events a week ago.'

'Oh, that.' She looked away.

'What do you mean "Oh, that"?' I frowned at her and crossed my arms. 'Sit down, Armourer, and tell me exactly what happened.'

'It was the evening of the fires. I heard the sirens, then saw the local *vigiles* fire section engines rush through towards the city gates. I can't remember last when they went out on a call – it's quiet around here. Anyway, I was a bit deafened by the noise – my hearing's not very good after all those years in the factories – and I didn't hear the calling coming up from the cellar.' She gave me an embarrassed look. 'I keep the cellar door locked. Nobody's used the tunnel in months. I went to the kitchen to bank the range and I heard banging on the cellar door and a child sobbing. I fetched my revolver, tweaked the key and stood back.'

'What happened then?'

'A woman burst out half carrying a girl. The woman swore and shouted at me like I've never heard before, and believe me, in the armoury, I've heard some.'

Volusenia, of course, and Silvia.

'I didn't know her from Juno. She wasn't one of Plico's people. She told me you'd sent her, she demanded this, that and everything, but she didn't have any password or token, so I sent them on their way.'

'You old fool,' Calavia shouted. She grabbed the woman's arm and shook her hard. 'You idiot, that child was Silvia Apulia, Imperatrix Severina's daughter, with Colonel Volusenia of the PGSF. They were running for their lives. Why in Hades did you think they were using the tunnel?'

'Don't shout at me! I was told to offer additional help only if they had the right password or token. Everything else was off limits. I've had some strange people through here over the years. Mostly, they just go without a word. Not even a thanks.' She sniffed. 'The woman wouldn't give me her name. Just insisted they had to have help. How was I to know?' She wrenched her arm away from Calavia's grip.

'Didn't you recognise the girl?' I said, keeping my temper caged.

'One girl's like any other.' She looked away.

I moved over to her chair and stood centimetres away from her so she had to crane her neck up.

'So you sent them out into a night of riot without resupply of food and water or transport, or equipment.' My voice was as icy as the wind off the northern mountains.

'I—'

'Yes?'

'I realised who it was after they'd gone and I rushed out to find them.' She bowed her head. 'But they'd disappeared.' She looked up. 'What's happened to them?'

The flickering firelight reflected the anxiety in her eyes.

'I wish I knew,' I replied.

25

───────

We raided the armourer's supplies and clothes stores, including a field survival kit and handheld radio; I was surprised the batteries were fully charged, but took a couple of spare sets and charger. We had to stay in contact with the others at Castra Lucilla. The armourer flitted around making us supper and drinks. I asked her to retire to her bedroom and close her door. Calavia looked as grim as I felt. We bent over the table to work out what to do next.

'On the good side, we're resupplied,' I said, 'but on the bad side, we have no idea what's happened to Silvia, Volusenia or Atrius. Not an even balance, I think.'

'How the hell did the nats know we were at Atrius's sister's?'

'Either she contacted them after he'd left this morning or we have a leak somewhere else. On balance, I don't think it was Paula Atria – she had too much to lose. They would have pulled her in as a matter of course and closed or confiscated her business. They may have done it anyway.' Juno, another casualty. 'Also, angry as she was at me, I don't think she would betray her brother's colleagues.'

'I'm not so sure. Too much of a coincidence.'

'If the nationalists have Atrius, we must consider the whole operation compromised. I can't imagine Caius's people would interrogate in line with standard operating procedure.'

Calavia drew her hand over her eyes. 'Poor sod.'

I poured her a glass of water and pushed it across the table at her. Her hand trembled as she lifted the glass to her lips.

'We can't go looking for him, Pia. We have to prioritise finding Silvia Apulia. That's our main mission.' I looked at her steadily. 'And if either of us is taken, the other one must push on with the mission.'

'Of course, ma'am,' she said in a dead voice.

'Now you know Colonel Volusenia. What do you think she would do in these circumstances?'

'She wouldn't let anything interfere with her mission… I think she'd go for safety, let Silvia Apulia rest, so as not to compromise security.'

'Are there any other safe houses? For this Aquila fallback plan, I mean.'

'Not that I know of.'

'Very well. She's not going to do anything obvious like going to her sister's house – that would be dangerous in the extreme. The next logical thing would be an old friend. She's aiming for the route over the mountains into New Austria, so she'd probably pick somebody on that road.' I looked at Calavia. 'Any thoughts?'

'She sometimes goes horse-trekking with a friend who has a stud farm about twenty kilometres from here, but it's north-west.'

'But safe. And they'll have been able to take horses from there.'

Calavia nodded.

'Right, we'll grab a few hours' sleep, then we set off for that farm. Check in with Styrax before we turn in.'

I asked the armourer for the van keys; it was kept for Plico's operations, so I reckoned I could take it.

'I can't, *domina*.'

'I beg your pardon,' I said, looking down my nose at her.

'No, I didn't mean you couldn't have it, of course not,' she stammered. 'But it's disappeared.'

'When?'

'The night of the fires when the woman and girl were here.'

'Show me the garage.'

She led us through the kitchen and outside down a narrow passageway to a low stone building. How on earth could a vehicle exit from here? The armourer flicked the light on to reveal a workshop, shelves to the side above a workbench onto which were bolted two vices. Tools were neatly stacked, boxed or hung on the wall with hooks. In the corner was a welding set with gas bottles and metal mask hanging above. More importantly, two large doors opposite us. But no vehicle, just a small circular oil stain on the slab floor. I crouched down. Nothing special. I glanced up at Calavia who shook her head. Just as I rose, I spotted the paper fixed with a piece of duct tape to the underside of the bench.

The vulture has flown with the eagle.

I smiled at Volusenia's use of the nickname her troops gave her. So she'd come back and taken the vehicle. Probably hot-wired it. But where were they now?

———

We slid into the night through the side garden of the armourer's house. The rain had turned to drizzle, but unlike our department store disguises our walking clothes kept the damp off. We crossed the scrub beside the houses, then past a small cluster of cottages, and finally on to open ground. Keeping to the field hedges, we made for a copse two hundred metres from the last house.

While Calavia checked the compass bearings, I looked back at the city, now under control of Caius's thugs. Somewhere in there, our comrade-in-arms was facing pain and humiliation and hundreds of thousands were anxious about their present and terrified of their future. We *must* take it back, throw Caius out and relieve the terror.

'Ready,' Calavia whispered. Tiny pale green dots glowed through the glass cover of the field compass she held – our only guide on our lonely mission.

An hour later, a helicopter passed over us and we flung ourselves into the lee of a hedge and waited a good fifteen minutes after it had gone. We traipsed on in silence. After about ten kilometres, my legs were losing strength; the short sleep hadn't been enough.

'Sorry, Calavia, I'm going to have to rest for a few minutes.'

We positioned ourselves at ninety degrees to each other to keep an eye out in both directions on the road in the valley below us. Calavia picked a grass stem and started chewing it. I took a long drink from my water bottle and studied her. Despite her competence, she was only a young girl, not much older than Marina, if that. I could have been her mother. My daughter was safe in the EUS, but this one was in as dangerous a place as she could be.

'Of course, I forget,' she said, taking the stem from her mouth.

'Forget what?'

'That you're more used to managing a desk.' She turned her head in my direction. Her eyes shone in the moonlight and I saw a smile. 'Although you're not bad for your age.'

'Cheeky bitch!' I elbowed her hard.

'I know.' She chuckled. 'My grandmother said I was bound to be thrown out for insubordination one day.' Then she went quiet and her mouth drooped. 'I miss her. She was so good to me all my life. I loved her so much.' She dropped her head onto her bent knees.

I stretched out my hand and grasped hers. I couldn't say anything to comfort her. It was very unlikely Senator Calavia was still alive.

Her granddaughter got to her feet and stretched out her hand.

'She would have been the first to tell me to pull myself together and attend to my duty, so we'd better march on.'

Thirty minutes later, we threw ourselves to the ground again behind a stone wall.

'Juno, that's the second helo flying low tonight,' Calavia hissed.

'They're looking for something specific. Silvia and Volusenia.'

'*Merda*, that will make our job harder.'

'Yes, but it means they don't have her.'

As we were about to stand, I heard, no felt, a soft rumble in the ground. A steady hum, then a growl and finally the clatter of diesel engines. We crawled forward using elbows to pull ourselves along until we found a gap in the wall. Strong headlight beams swung round in the road below us, piercing the darkness. Two troop transports and a *vigiles* long wheelbase tore round the corner and screeched to a stop.

Pluto in Tartarus. What was going on here? Two dozen troops formed a line each side of the road, back to back. At a signal from a short figure standing by the *vigiles* vehicle, they fanned out, weapons ready, and walked slowly away from the road up each side of the valley. A cold invisible hand clutched my heart. No, they weren't after Silvia and Volusenia; they were looking for *us*.

I flicked my fingers at Calavia and pointed to the course of the wall which rose until it skirted the crest of the valley. It was our best chance. My heart thumped and I gasped in breaths as we scuttled along as quietly as possible. They were getting nearer; I could hear shouts between them. The moon was obscured behind clouds, so barring our doing something stupid, they couldn't see us unless they fell on us. Calavia was increasing her lead, but she should be able to see our way out down the next valley. As I puffed my way up towards the crest, Calavia disappeared. I heard a thump, and a muffled cry. Had she fallen? I scrambled over the rock edge into the lee. Thank the gods, we'd made it. At least we could run upright now. And we'd need to run. As if the Furies were after us.

I looked around in the gloom for Calavia. She was stretched out on the ground, face down, her hands on the back of her head. Two troopers in full battledress pressed their gun barrels in her neck. Before I could open my mouth, or take a step, cold steel jabbed at my head. Fear rolled through me down into my gut.

'Hands on your head. No funny moves. On the ground. Now!'

26

———

I shifted my weight onto the balls of my feet. If I was fast enough, I could disable the trooper and run. The diversion would give Calavia a chance. As I tensed, ready, eight more of them, all men, advanced rapidly. Several cocked their weapons.

Merda.

'What is your authority?' I asked the one wearing centurion rank tabs. He didn't reply. 'You can't detain us – we're free citizens. I'm a Praetorian officer. I order you to stand aside.' One lowered his rifle. Two of them shifted from one foot to the other and glanced at the centurion. He hesitated for a second, then jerked his head at two of his troops. They pushed me to the ground and handcuffed me. As I ate dirt, I cursed them in every way I could, furious we'd been taken like this.

They pulled Calavia and me up and marched us back down the hill. As we trudged down, I caught her look. Anger and humiliation. She looked away. Our boots clattered on the tarmacked road at the bottom of the slope as the troops pushed us along to the waiting *vigiles*. And Phobius.

Caius's henchman took one stride towards me, reached up and struck me full in the face. The *vigiles* stood there expressionless.

'Not so hoity-toity now, are you?' Phobius squeaked.

'Are you speaking to me?' Although my face was stinging and the blood dribbling down my chin, I drew myself up as tall as I could and looked down my nose. Of course, he hit me again.

'You'd do well to remember you're a criminal, a terrorist, and that's just for starters. Once the first consul has finished with you, you'll be in for a lesson you'll never forget, you stuck-up bitch.'

'Aren't you the brave little man?' I said. Calavia closed her eyes and gave a tiny shake of her head. Phobius raised his hand again and I braced.

'One moment, Representative Phobius,' the senior *vigilis* said, 'First Consul Tellus specifically said no injuries with this one.'

Phobius lowered his hand slowly. His eyes narrowed and he turned to Calavia, then back to me. 'All right, then. Any more trouble from you, she'll get the beating.'

What a turd.

He took a step closer. The top of his head only came to my chin. I could smell the sweat and cheap hair oil he used. I couldn't help wrinkling my nose. Then I remembered Calavia and calmed myself.

'You nearly cost me my position last week when the first consul found out you'd slipped away on my watch. It's not going to happen again. Clear?'

'I hear the words you are speaking,' I replied. He tried to stare me down with his bitter, angry eyes, but I wasn't going to break. The *vigilis* behind him coughed and signalled to his junior to put us in the back of the lorry. Two military troopers were in there already and shifted to let us sit down, then looked anywhere but at us.

Bumping along in the back of the transport with a sore face and a split lip, I looked at the grim faces of the two male *vigiles* opposite. In the dim glow of the interior light, their faces could have been carved out of Aquae Caesaris granite.

Calavia closed her eyes, to shut out the horror of our situation, I imagined. Or perhaps from sheer tiredness. She slumped back against the ribbed frame and her body rocked with the motion of the vehicle. I was tempted to do the same, but wasn't prepared to let them see me cowed in any way. I stared at them all in turn, trying to read the *vigiles*' neutral faces and the troopers' confused ones. Their world had been turned upside down in seven days. One of the younger soldiers snatched a glance at me, but when he caught my gaze, looked down at his boots as if caught in a misdemeanour. Poor kid.

As we bumped along the road, I had no doubt we were in for a rough time at Caius's hands. Calavia's grandmother had blocked him and she'd helped rescue Quirinia and me from the palace on the night of the fires. He never forgave grudges. Me, he'd kill, I was sure. I just hoped it was quick. I would never see my darling Marina again, but she was safe in the EUS with William Brown, thank the gods. And my heart's love, Miklós, would mourn me. I blinked back prickly hot tears. My deep regret and anxiety was that I had not found Silvia and protected her against this evil.

After a stop, and what sounded like an ID check, the vehicle carried straight on. The canvas back flap of the lorry was tied down and it must have been between three and four in the morning so I wouldn't have been able to see anything anyway. But this was my city – we were driving along the Dec Max into its heart. A little further on, I swayed as we went round a large roundabout and fell against one of the troopers who put his hand out to steady me. Not easy to keep your balance with your wrists manacled. Two turns later, we slowed down and I heard large metal doors scrape open then clang shut behind the vehicle which stopped a few metres further on. Calavia jerked awake, her eyes searching instantly. I mumbled 'V*igiles.*'

'Silence. Out of the vehicle. Move!'

We shuffled to the edge and jumped down onto a rough concrete surface. We were in the back service yard of Vigiles XI station. It was the one nearest the palace. We were pushed through a barred gate, then a metal door. The duty senior *vigilis* took one look at us, grunted and scribbled two lines on his record sheet. So their sloppy procedure hadn't changed a scrap with the change in regime.

Phobius demanded they fetch their captain, who arrived five minutes later, tucking his shirt in the back of his trousers. He smelt of smoke and sweat. Phobius jerked his head at Calavia and me.

'These two women are to be searched and held in separate cells and maximum secure conditions. Two troopers and two of my men will stay here as extra guards. They'll need food.'

'What about these women?'

'Don't waste any rations on them.'

• • •

The station processing team, now only men, were more embarrassed searching us than we were being searched. They took away our warm clothes and boots in transparent plastic bags and left us in the standard yellow prison tunics, bare legs and plastic sandals. By the time we had been pushed into cells, I was shivering and my feet were numb.

About fifteen minutes later, my cell door opened. A young *vigilis* stood in the door frame. Behind and slightly to his side, an older one aimed his service revolver at me. What now?

'Stand back in the corner.' The younger man's eyes glanced at the corner where the slops bucket stood. Careful with my footing, I retreated there and watched as he tossed two coarse weave blankets and a brown paper bag onto the wooden bench masquerading as a bed. He kept his eyes on me as he bent and set a tin mug of water on the floor. He backed out and the door clanged shut followed by a locking and bolting sound.

I wrapped one of the blankets round me, sat on the hard bench, pulled my legs up and rubbed my frozen toes. The meat-filled roll from the paper bag tasted wonderful. Who knew when we'd get our next food? Anxious as they'd seemed, these station *vigiles* hadn't completely lost their humanity.

But how in Hades had Phobius and his thugs known where we were? That we'd been at Atrius's sister's? Or the armourer's? Calavia and I had only decided yesterday evening to take this route. Either somebody had developed telepathy or we had a leak. Or maybe unbearable pressure was being exerted on Paula or the armourer. Or maybe they'd broken Atrius. I shuddered at the thought of what they must have done to him. We hadn't used the radios yet, so they hadn't tracked us via signals. The only other possibility was that somebody had attached a tracker to our bags or clothes but we'd checked both before leaving the armourer's.

I couldn't stop the anger and frustration chasing round in my mind. Had we made a stupid mistake somewhere? I couldn't see one. And that made me angrier. My head was thumping with it all. Eventually, I gave up, exhausted by the sheer tragedy of the day and fell asleep.

. . .

Noise, a piercing whistle, banging on the door. I jerked up, half awake, and shook my head. Ouch, the hard wooden bench. The door was flung open. I jumped as it crashed into the wall.

'Out. Now!'

In the corridor, Calavia stumbled along, bleary eyed. Two *vigiles* took us back to the processing room where our clothes were piled in a heap on the bench, and instructed us to dress.

Calavia glanced over at the armed vigiles watching us.

'What's happening now?' she whispered into her boots as she tied them.

'Not a clue,' I muttered and shrugged on my sweater. 'But not good,' I added as that bastard Phobius strutted in.

'Sleep well? No? Good.' He smirked. 'Get a move on.'

'Why?' I said. 'What's happening?'

'Not for you to ask questions. I'll let it be a nice surprise.'

Calavia and I exchanged glances.

'I want a legal representative,' I said, forcing my voice to be steadier than my nerves. 'Now.'

He laughed in my face.

'That's all been suspended. We know who's guilty and if you're guilty, you don't need no brief.'

Handcuffed again, this time in front. Two *vigiles* pushed us into the back of a long wheelbase where two more chained us to separate corners of the vehicle frame. Were they being paranoid or did they think we were so dangerous? Apart from that gesture of the food and blankets last night, it was frightening to see just how compliant the *vigiles* were to Phobius, as if they'd slipped into being his personal police force.

The vehicle soft-top was rolled down completely, including the rear flap, so we could see nothing, or be seen. I concluded we were being taken somewhere for more permanent imprisonment, or possibly to be put up against a wall and shot. I didn't want to die. But at least if I was dead, Caius wouldn't be able to use me to further his power hunger. Many of my ancestors had died in battle, some as victims of political intrigues, but always well. Please Juno, I would remember them when my time came and draw courage from theirs.

Abruptly, the engine noise changed as the vehicle started pulling

uphill. We were going to the Golden Palace. This meant only one thing
– Caius.

PART V

CAIUS

27

———

Phobius led the unhappy procession through the vestibule. Two *vigiles*, their maroon uniforms and boots dusty, shuffled behind him and four of the troopers, porting weapons, followed us as escorts. I glanced around. Everything looked exactly as it had been eight days ago. Even the Apulian ancestors' busts and statues – the *imagines* – had been left here. Phobius nodded to an armed black-suited man with a nationalist armband, who leapt to open the double doors into the colonnaded atrium. Now we were here, fear flickered through me and I felt my courage seeping away. I exchanged a glance with Calavia. Her face was pale and her features pinched. But she pulled her shoulders back and looked forwards. Would I be as resolute as I thought I would be? The image of the previous imperatrix Justina flitted in front of me. Gods, how she would have given me a steely look and told me to pull myself together.

He stood at the far side of the atrium, arms crossed, legs braced, and gazing out of the tall windows to the side garden. His figure looked totally relaxed, but the early morning sunlight highlighted his features in harsh brightness and shadows, turning his profile into a fascinating, almost alien thing. I shivered, this time not from cold.

Phobius stopped about five metres from the oak desk at the centre back of the atrium. After about twenty seconds he coughed, but Caius waited another full minute until he turned to look at us. His gaze skimmed over the group, stopped briefly at Calavia, then rested on me. The hazel agate eyes were like stone. He frowned, and without looking away, said, 'Phobius, why is she damaged?'

'Sir, there was a struggle.'

I snorted.

'You have something to add, Aurelia?'

'Your subordinate is lying to you. He decided to vent his insecurity on my face *after* the military captured me. I do not *struggle* with five hundred millimetres of hard steel barrel from a service rifle in my neck.'

'How very sensible of you.' He flicked his fingers at Phobius. 'You will wait outside. First, dismiss your men. Oh, and put the Calavia woman in a holding cell in the Praetorian barracks. I will decide her fate when I have time.'

Calavia took half a step towards me, but I gave her a tiny shake of my head. They pulled her away and marched off. I was completely alone. With my nemesis. He went back to staring through the window.

'I can't decide what to do with you,' he said. 'You will undoubtedly try everything to oppose me under some delusion of duty, so it would be prudent to remove you permanently. And you caused me to rot in a Prussian jail for twelve years. I shall never forgive you for that.'

'You murdered a Prussian citizen and permanently disabled another. You ran a silver smuggling organisation that threatened Roma Nova's security. You got off lightly.'

He shrugged.

'And let's not forget your two attempts to kill me.'

'You were being irritating, Aurelia, and I dislike that.'

'Irritating!' I raised my hands to vent my frustration but the steel grip of the handcuffs constrained them. 'I was a Praetorian officer tasked to hunt you down. I'd hardly class that as irritating.'

'"Was". That's the correct word.' He turned and looked straight at me. 'You're finished. I've cancelled your commission along with that of every other female officer. You're no longer a minister, nor a senator, nor head of your family. You have become an irrelevance in the new Roma Nova.'

I stared at him. Irrelevant? He couldn't take away my identity like that.

'Don't be ridiculous. You can't destroy the structure of such an old country just like that.'

He strode over to me. I took a step back, but he was too fast. He grabbed me by the throat, pressed his thumb and fingers hard, and squeezed. I could hardly breathe. He pressed harder. My head swam and my vision blurred.

'Don't tell me what I can and can't do.' Then he dropped his hand and released me. I bent over coughing. Gods, his grip had been strong. I thought I was going to choke to death.

'You have two options – adapt or go under. There is no release for you, Aurelia. You will be guarded and tracked, and if you attempt escape, I'll execute one of your friends like Calavia. Maybe I'll do that anyway, if only to motivate you.'

'Only cowards let their friends take the punishment for them. Just call in the swordsman and I'll kneel in the sand.'

'Certainly not. You're far too valuable a political asset. And you do have a certain amusement value.' He smirked at me. 'Perhaps I'll keep you as jester, my own tame doomsayer. You'd look quite fetching in scarlet.'

I couldn't speak. The humiliation of what he suggested – how dare he?

He laughed. 'You should see your face, Aurelia. You always were quick to rise.' Then his mouth straightened into a crisp line. 'This is not a game. The old ways are finished, as is everybody associated with them. There is no more deplorable female rule. We need several clear months to recover the correct balance in this country and to turn it into a proper Roman one. After that, our neighbours had better pay attention.'

Gods, was he about to start a local war?

'The last thing I need is a dangerous maverick, who might have some residual influence, plotting behind my back.'

'Then terminate me.'

'Determined as you are to seek death, it will be far better for Roma Nova if you don't. I want a strong Roma Nova and you tell me you love our country. You might be just a woman, but you could help. Think about working together.'

'I'd rather end my days in Truscium than lift one of my little fingers to help you.'

'Always so dramatic. Phobius would throw you in there without hesitating after he'd had you and given his men a turn. Would you prefer that?'

Just for a second, something in his eyes united us as patricians, revolted at the thought of Phobius touching either of us.

'Quite,' he said.

'What will happen to my people?'

'I might, of course, have them all thrown into prison or deported. Perhaps I'll send all your first and second cousins to one of my new work camps. At least they'd be making a contribution. Their future depends on their behaviour. But most of all on yours, Aurelia.'

What the hell did that mean?

'For the moment, an acting head of the Mitel*us* family will be appointed in the next week,' he continued. 'The family recorders of all Twelve Families have been requested to submit the name of the senior male member. They'll run the Families organisation as a charitable and social body only.' He sighed. 'I really don't know why I'm telling you all this. You have no further role in the public life of this country.'

'And my comrades-in-arms?'

'Calavia will be tried for treason and sentenced accordingly. Your trooper we, er, interrogated, likewise. When he recovers, that is. The penalty for treason is execution.'

'No, please. They only followed orders. My orders.'

'Are you begging for their lives, Aurelia?' His eyes glinted. 'If you're trying to bargain with me, then I require something in return.'

I swallowed hard. Soreness and pain from my bruised throat almost made me choke again. I was dead meat but if I could bargain for Calavia and Atrius's lives, they could come back and carry on the search for Silvia. That was the prime objective of the mission. I would have to take my chances. But every cell in my mind and body revolted at the thought of even pretending to work with him.

'Let them go, put them over the New Austrian border, and I'll think about what you're proposing.'

'Do you take me for a simpleton?' He laughed. I flinched at the hard tone. 'You'll have to do better than that. If that's a demonstration of your negotiating skills, no wonder the last government crumbled.'

I hesitated.

'If you want your family to survive, and your friends, I need your total compliance. Now.'

In my head, I cursed him, I cursed myself and I cursed Severina and the Fates. I buried my dignity and went down on my knees.

'If you guarantee the Mitelae safety, and release Calavia and Atrius across the border, free to go—' I said, the taste of ash in my mouth and lead in my heart, '—then I will do what you ask.'

28

———

He pressed a buzzer on his desk and spoke into it. I bowed my head, not to him; after an exhausting day yesterday and three hours' sleep, I was so tired I could have collapsed in a heap. My mission had ended in failure with two comrades under death sentence. Now I had made my first act of collaboration. I did it knowingly and only to ensure the other two were released, but I felt unclean. No, I was disgusted with myself. All I wanted to do now was to hide in a corner under a blanket and close my eyes.

'Get up, woman,' Caius said. 'You look ridiculous.'

I struggled to my feet. I didn't care what I looked like, but it was pointless antagonising him. Had my surrender been worth it? Would Caius keep his word and leave my family and household alone as well as releasing Calavia and Atrius?

The door opened and a boy, no, a young man, hesitated just in the shadow by the doorway.

'You may be wondering how we knew you were here and what you were playing at.' He beckoned the young man forward. 'I'm sure you remember Turturus whom you met in Vienna.'

Juno, the cadet who sulked because I wouldn't take him with us on the rescue mission. This was getting worse and worse. The surge of anger running through me pulled me out of my stasis.

'Turturus was fed up with being told what to do by a woman, by having his masculinity stamped on, so he came here seeking a better way. He's been on active duty and done well on this first counter-surveillance operation.'

'He was a child. I wouldn't bring him on this mission because of that. I see now he's a treacherous little bastard.' I directed every volt of all my pent-up anger and frustration at Turturus. 'How could you do this? You're directly responsible for a loyal guard who befriended you being subjected to hours of pain and humiliation. And you put another one under sentence of death. *Macte!*'

The boy flinched.

'Be silent, Aurelia,' Caius said.

'No, I won't.'

'Remember what you promised two minutes ago and the consequences of disobeying me.'

I sucked in my lips and looked at Turturus, willing him into a heap of ash. But I had to be patient. Calavia and Atrius must be safe before I did anything.

Caius flicked his fingers in dismissal at the boy, who almost ran out of the atrium. After a moment's pause, Caius turned to me.

'Now, you will be housed here in the palace. You will be fitted with a steel wristband to show your reduced status. You will also wear an electronic tag which will track you and alarm if you leave the palace building. If it beeps and flashes orange, it means I require your immediate presence. I stress the word "immediate". Only by concentrating will you prevent your friends' execution. It will also teach you some humility.'

Gods, I didn't think I could hate him any more, but at that moment a shaft of pure red light invaded my mind that I wanted to aim at his face and destroy him.

He turned away, pressed a button on his desktop set again and two troopers entered. Regulars, not palace Praetorians. Where were the Praetorians?

'Take this woman to the guardroom, tag her, level 1 security, plus a steel wristband, then instruct the housekeeper to allocate her a room in the domestic quarters. Oh, and find her some decent women's clothing and burn those trousers.'

. . .

The leading trooper hesitated by the service stairs and looked at his companion, who shrugged. They didn't know the layout. It was tempting to mislead them, but I thought of Calavia and Atrius.

'If you're looking for the guardroom, it's down the first flight, turn left and second right,' I said in a deadpan voice. 'At least it was when I last commanded the palace guard.'

'Quiet. Nobody asked you.'

He grabbed my upper arm and pushed me towards the stairs.

In a small act of defiance, I pulled away, scampered down the stairs and sprinted along the corridors, arriving at the guardroom door several seconds before my escort. As they came running after me, I stared at them as I would at incompetent recruits. The first one's face clouded and his mouth tightened.

'Leave it, she's just winding you up,' the second one said and pushed me through the door. Three temporary workbenches with tools had been set up in the open area. Shouts, crying, people and the clatter of metal filled the space. A burly man, with a bushy moustache and mean eyes was sitting behind the nearest table with a clerk writing notes beside him and a younger man fiddling with what looked like metal loops. Several other women and two teenage boys stood to one side. One of the women was comforting the younger boy, who was shivering and weeping. The man consulted a clipboard with a list.

'Next!'

The woman and boy went forward.

'One at a time. Back in line, woman.'

She retreated, casting the terrified boy an anxious look.

My first escort stepped forward. 'Priority, direct from the first consul.' He pushed me forward. The man looked up, waved the boy back. I was conscious of people looking in my direction. One nudged her neighbour. Perhaps it was my dirty clothes, the handcuffs, my swollen face.

'Name?'

'Aurelia Mitela,' I said in my clearest voice.

Faces jerked round, work stopped and the room fell silent. Even the moustachioed man gaped at me. I looked round the room slowly. One or two bobbed or half bowed and I heard the word '*Domina*' whispered. My two military escorts stepped back. One looked shocked. He hadn't realised exactly who I'd been. No, who I still *was*, I told myself.

'Let's get on, then,' the first escort said, breaking the tension.

'Are you sure?' the burly man said.

'Are you questioning the first consul's orders?'

'No, no, of course not.' He jerked his head at the clerk to write my name down. The clerk was still staring at me. The burly man nudged the clerk who scribbled wildly. The younger technician stood and brought a chair round and gestured me to sit. My second escort leaned over me and unlocked the handcuffs. I rubbed my wrists and flexed my shoulders.

'If you would give me your right wrist, *dom*— I mean—'

'Please, don't worry. Do what you need to,' and I stretched my right arm out. The metal mesh band with the tracker tag pinched as the technician locked it on my wrist, mostly because his fingers were trembling. He glanced up, blushed then looked down. Then the burly man selected an open steel bracelet around two centimetres wide from a plastic tray. What was that for? Was it some kind of category? I drew my arm back; I wasn't going to be slotted into Caius's system. The burly man looked horrified, glanced at the watching guards with such fear, then at me. His eyes pleaded. Slowly, I lay my forearm back on the table. He fitted the steel ring round my wrist, not looking at me. He slid a cloth pad underneath, pinched the two ends together and sealed it with a high impulse electronic tool. The heat was intense but didn't burn me. The join left a ripple on the shiny surface of the bracelet and a red mark on my wrist.

'Forgive,' the burly man whispered, glancing to see if my guards had heard.

I nodded. Of course I did. None of this was these people's fault. It was Caius's brutal orders that forced them to do this work. I stood and raised my wrist so everybody could see.

I looked round the room and smiled at these anxious people.

'Very pretty,' I said wriggling my wrist, 'and I haven't even had to pay for it.'

A few smiles, one or two chuckles, then a few shouts of *Ave Mitela* and *Macte!* I bowed to them, turned and left, my two guards trudging in my wake. I might have been forced to wear this band, but at least I had shared a few moments of solidarity with people in the same plight.

I recognised the housekeeper, Drusilla, of course. Under the guards' scrutiny, she allocated me a room in the domestic hall, but they didn't know it was the under-housekeeper's, so a lot more spacious than a standard room and with that blessing, a small bathroom, attached. I wouldn't need to go to the communal palace bathhouse. Their duty done, the two men left and we watched them disappear up the stairs. I stretched my hand out and staggered against the wall.

'*Domina*, when did you last eat? Or even drink?'

Drusilla brought me milk and a bread roll plastered with butter and honey and a bowl of fruit, nuts and olives. She eased me down onto the bed and took off my boots and socks while I devoured everything. I stretched out, closed my eyes and sank into the void.

I woke to a loud buzzing. As I half opened my eyes, a flashing orange light violated them. Gods! Bloody Caius. Stuff him. No, for my comrades and family's sakes, I had to comply. I swallowed the bitter taste in my mouth. I dragged myself up and found myself without a stitch on. At the side of the bed were my underclothes and two tunics – one light green and long sleeved, the other dark red and shorter. I scrambled into them, grabbed the belt and slid my feet into the sandals by the bed. Although I often wore traditional dress in the country, this was comic opera style in the city. I pulled my hair back and tied it with one of the ribbons on the dressing table. I wiped my face with a corner of the towel; the blood from my split lip had dried, but half my face was purple from Phobius's beating.

My watch had gone. I had no idea what time it was, except that it was light, probably mid afternoon from the sunlight shining through the half-basement window.

I trudged up the service stairs to the atrium. My legs seemed full of sawdust instead of muscle and a soft pulsing in my head threatened to become a full-blown headache. At the atrium entrance, I ignored the nationalist guard and grasped the handle of one of the double doors. I took a deep breath and counted to five. Please Diana, let me keep my temper.

Caius was studying his watch. He raised an eyebrow theatrically.

'Ten minutes. Not immediately, as required.'

Should I reply? No, it would only provoke him. I looked steadily at him, trying to convey how much I despised him. After a few seconds, he looked up.

'Very well, I will overlook it this one time. I am holding a small reception tomorrow evening for leading men to inform them how things will be in the future and invite them to participate. You will assist in serving drinks.'

He watched me, a smile hovering on his lips. He was daring me to react. I wasn't in the mood to play his game, so I stood there unmoving and silent.

'Do you understand?'

I nodded.

'You will address me as First Consul at all times.'

I'd see him in Tartarus first.

'Report to the senior steward at six tomorrow evening. And have a bath and wash your hair. I dislike servants who smell as if they've been traipsing around fields full of shit.'

As I stumbled back downstairs, I wiped tears away. He was determined to humiliate me on every level. I'd had no time to bathe and he knew it. I went to the kitchen to make a drink. Honey and lemon were always soothing.

'What do *you* want?'

A brown-haired man in chef's whites blocked my way to the sink. The other kitchen staff looked round.

'A drink. I'll make it and get out of your way in a couple of minutes.'

'We're busy preparing dinner. Clear off.'

Somebody gasped.

'Just a glass of water, then?'

'Out.' He pushed me away then looked at the other kitchen staff. 'And what are you lot looking at? Get back to your work.'

In the bath, comforted by the warm water, I worked through scenes in my mind where I had Caius at my mercy, begging and grovelling. I relived that terrifying day thirteen years ago when he'd held Marina as hostage in my own house. I'd fought and defeated him then. Any residual guilt about kicking him when he was injured and defenceless vanished down the plughole with the waste water as I clambered out of the bath. I had to let my anger cool – he fed on my reactions – and work out a way of surviving and then claw my way back.

Caius and I had so much negative history. Not the small things like spitting on my favourite cake when I was a small child or holding my head down the kitchen sewer when I was eight or even when he attempted to rape me at sixteen. He'd disgusted me when he'd thrown up noisily at my emancipation ceremony, an important moment in any young Roma Novan's life. The trouble was he had charm and laughed off all these things as horseplay or jokes. But his eyes had betrayed the calculation behind each act. I couldn't deny the pleasure that went along with duty when we caught him and had him sent to the Prussians to be locked up for murder.

It wasn't mere hate; he wanted to dominate, to crush me. Somehow I represented something he resented deeply, perhaps something he secretly longed for. For now, he had his way, and I would comply to save my people's lives, but as I fell into my bed, I vowed it would end the instant they were safe.

29

———

I swallowed a yawn. I'd been up since five that morning, first fetching Caius coffee and rolls, then he sent me to empty his bin, take drafts to the typists on the floor below. More coffee. In between, he ordered me to stand by the wall while he worked in silence for hours. A messenger came through the double doors on the hour to deliver and take work, but Caius worked at files or read in solitary state in the three-storey high atrium. Once he answered the telephone call with one word. 'Yes'. It was so boring I almost dozed off. He knew I would hate it; I'd been active and busy every day of my life.

Two armed guards in mismatched dark clothes and red Roman National Movement armbands stood by the doors as if they were Praetorians, but fidgeting now and again, something that Severina's guards would never have done. One of them raised his hand to his mouth to cover a yawn. Caius's head snapped up. He stared at the young man for a few seconds. The guard flushed, then looked straight ahead like an automaton. Caius wrote a note, placed it to one side and handed it to the next messenger. Within five minutes, Phobius appeared, struck the young guard in the face and dragged him away. Another automaton took his place and the only thing that he moved were his eyes. Caius went on working as if oblivious to the whole episode.

By one o'clock my stomach was rumbling and I was dying of thirst; my legs and knees had almost locked up. When he went out for a meeting, for an hour, he said, I fled downstairs where Drusilla gave me some soup. The damned buzzer went as I was gulping down the last of it. Just as I reached the atrium door, I found my way barred by Phobius.

'In a hurry, darlin'?' He reached out for my breast, but I smacked his hand away. He pushed me against the wall, his arm across my throat, and fumbled for the hem of my tunic. I brought my leg up and kneed him hard in the groin. 'You cow,' he croaked. He bent over, panting hard. He clicked his fingers at the two nats guards. 'Take her to the punishment cell and chain her up. I'll flog her myself.'

I opened my mouth, but words wouldn't form. I couldn't believe what I'd just heard. Flog? The nearest guard went to grab my arm, but out of sheer instinct, I feinted and brought my arm up and chopped the edge of my hand right across the jugular in his neck. He staggered back, right against my outstretched leg that I bent up at the knee just as he went over. He fell like a dead weight into an unconscious heap. The second one ran for me, but I spun round and dodged at the last minute. He hit the double doors. When he came back, I chopped the bridge of his nose, hard. As he crouched over, my elbow hit the soft spot in front of his ear and he collapsed screaming in pain. Phobius had recovered enough to snarl at me.

'You cow, I'll tear your limbs off one by one.'

I flexed my legs, shifting my weight on the balls of my feet, ready to lunge at him. I beckoned him with my four fingers in parallel.

'Come on, then. You wanted to touch me. Here's your invitation.'

He hesitated.

'No? Not so brave now, little man, are you?'

'Don't call me little. You'll find that out when I fuck you.'

I burst out laughing. 'Wrong, Phobius. You haven't got a tenth of the strength to satisfy a real woman.'

He went red, the vein on his forehead throbbed and a feral look shone from his eyes. He charged me, but I sidestepped and punched him in the ear. Grabbing his wrist, I yanked it hard, causing him to shriek and collapse onto his knees.

'My reply is no,' I said.

The door opened. Caius.

Merda.

I swallowed hard. The elation of winning fled and I shivered. I had just condemned Calavia, Atrius and my whole family.

'This is the second time you have been late when I summoned you,' he said, looking at me.

I stared at him. What world was he living in? He looked briefly at the three figures struggling to their feet, then back to my face. 'Inside,' he commanded. He shut the door behind me. I crossed to the drinks side table and grabbed a glass of water. In between gulps, I caught my breath. My right hand was starting to throb so I plunged it into the ice bucket.

After five minutes, Caius came back into the atrium. He stood by the doors, hands behind him and studied the floor.

'Having been on the receiving end of your, er, talents several years ago, I have a great deal of sympathy for Phobius and his men at this moment.'

'He threatened to flog me for defending myself!'

He looked up.

'Harsh, of course, but one of Phobius's responsibilities is maintaining discipline.'

He walked over to me. I went to speak, but he held his hand up.

'I will let this pass this time. You will not attack any more of my staff or colleagues for any reason. If you do, regrettably, I will hand you over to him.'

'But—'

He slapped my face, not hard, but stinging.

'Do not interrupt me, Aurelia, I dislike it intensely.' His agate eyes burned. 'But you can be reassured that Phobius will not touch you in the future.'

I stood by the service table that evening and occupied myself with pouring drinks for two other women to take round on trays. My hand was bandaged so nobody could see the bruising from earlier. Neither woman had said a word to me. Had I offended them somehow? Or were they just as nervous as I was? If Phobius was prowling round terrorising the staff, no wonder they kept their eyes down and said nothing. And it was only women who carried out domestic tasks now. The only men were clerks, two grumpy maintenance men, the boorish cook, nationalists everywhere, and armed male military. It was so unnatural.

When my former ministerial colleagues – the male ones – filed in with representatives of the Twelve Families, the Senate and local businesses, I kept my back turned. I was reluctant to show myself. Pride? Possibly. Embarrassment, certainly.

Ten minutes after the appointed hour, when the men were busy greeting each other and chatting, Caius made his entrance. His tall, impeccably suited figure had presence, I had to admit. He walked slowly, nodding to this one, saying a few words to that one, smiling to all. One of the serving women approached him and handed him a drink. He took a sip, then scanned the room and found me. He raised his finger and beckoned. I couldn't pretend I hadn't seen. I walked over slowly. One or two half turned in the way people do when they become aware of another's presence. One by one the others stopped talking and stared. Then they all broke in at once.

'Aurelia—'

'*Consiliaria*, what—'

'My dear Countess, are you—'

'Senator Mitela, where—'

Caius placed his hand on my shoulder; his fingers gripped into the soft flesh by my collar bone. 'Aurelia no longer holds any of those positions. She now serves in my household.' He released me and tipped his chin at me. 'Go about your duties. Replenish these gentlemen's drinks.'

They watched us, as if mesmerised. Wide eyes, shocked expressions, some frowning, some opened their mouths, but none said anything. Warmth crept up my neck into my face which made the bruising hurt like Hades. Then one by one, they turned their eyes away and started talking to each other again.

I walked back to the side table, pressing my lips together and blinking back my public humiliation. One of the other women glanced at me, this time not unkindly. She handed me a jug of wine and picked up another for herself. She cupped her hand round my elbow as a friend would and together we walked back to the group. Furtive smiles and nods from my ex-colleagues greeted me as I circulated. One or two muttered 'so sorry'. But nobody spoke up for me. They were like sheep, all too frightened of Caius and his bullies.

He called for their attention and they stopped talking almost as one.

'Gentlemen, thank you for coming here this evening. This is an informal evening, so I won't hold you up too long from your networking.' He gave them a full teeth smile and some gave a chuckle in return. 'I wanted to clarify the situation now and outline the future. Public notices were posted an hour ago and details will be flowing out from my office over the next few weeks, but here are the basics. The female Apulian dynasty is finished. The eldest son is, regrettably, dead and there is no trace of the daughter.'

So Caius still hadn't found Silvia. I was so pleased I nearly smiled, but remembered just in time where I was.

'The female heads of the Twelve Families have been dismissed as have the female senators, lecturers, judges and civil servants. All commissions previously held by women in the military, *vigiles* and other forces have been cancelled and women personnel of all ranks dismissed. My colleagues from the Roman National Movement auxiliaries will step into the breach in the meantime.'

'Mars help us,' the *magister miletum* muttered.

Caius frowned, but continued.

'Women who own businesses or significant shareholdings have been sent notices to sign them over to a male relative within thirty days. Inevitably, there will be some readjustments needed, but at the end of six months, I expect to have the transition fully in place. New laws are being introduced to assist this process and they will be strictly enforced. Married women and mothers will take up their traditional roles and nurture the next generation. Single women will be permitted to work in subsidiary roles, but resign on marriage.

'We have restored order, structure and stability to our country. These are essential to true Roman values. They powered the ancients for over a thousand years. We will restore the natural balance and make a stronger Roma Nova both at home and in the world.'

He raised his glass. '*Vivat Roma Nova.*'

Like me, they were trapped, so they duly raised their glasses and returned the toast.

We three women watched from the side as the men mixed and mingled, talking about Caius's announcement, a few laughing here and there. For most of them it was business as usual. I despaired. Had the former ways been so difficult and oppressive? Wouldn't they at least make an effort to counter this coup?

Despite the noise that inevitably increased with alcohol, I heard something else. It was coming from outside. I looked through the window that overlooked the front courtyard of the palace. Shouting and chanting, banners strung across groups and placards jiggled up and down. A crowd of women and men had gathered in front of the closed palace gates and more were joining from the sides. Mixed military and nationalists porting weapons faced them from the inside. They were pointing barrels directly into the crowd. Gods, somebody had better diffuse it soon or there'd be a full-scale riot with the inevitable casualties.

I searched for Caius. He was nodding his head as if taking in what the new head of the chamber of commerce was saying. He must have felt my gaze on him as he turned and raised an eyebrow at me. I flicked my eyes towards the window, casting him an urgent look. He creased his eyes and turned away, but I saw the cruel hard line of his mouth, then a little smile.

Oh, gods, he knew. He knew and wasn't going to do anything to stop it. The noise grew louder and a few on the edge of the group of drinkers looked over. The *magister miletum* came over to the window. He studied the crowds below, then grabbed the radio from his belt and barked orders into it. Only static answered him.

'What the hell's wrong with this thing?' He shook the handset.

'No signal. The transmitter isn't working,' I said as quietly as I could.

'Why not? The relay is here at the palace. It's normally signal strength five.'

'Precisely.'

'What do you mean, Aurelia?'

'Obviously, it's been turned off.'

'The bastard.' Others had clustered by the other windows and were gaping down.

'I'm so sorry about your situation,' the *magister* whispered. 'I'll try and buy your contract from Tellus, but I doubt he'll sell.'

'What do you mean, contract? I'm a detainee, a terrorist according to his sidekick.'

'You don't know what that steel bracelet means?'

'It's part of Caius's tagging system. Look, I've agreed to do what he says if he spares the two Praetorians who came with me,' I whispered. 'Once they're safely across the border, I'll be out of here.'

'No, you won't, my dear. That steel bracelet marks you as Caius's property. Technically stands for "state contracted worker", but slavery by any other name.'

Before I had time to digest what he'd said, shots rang out from the courtyard below. The rest of them rushed to the windows and I was jostled out of place. I looked over at Caius, but his face was almost serene. He walked towards the windows in a measured pace, grasped my arm and pushed me forward to the glass.

'That, my dear Aurelia, is what happens to opponents and rebels.'

I looked down in horror at the twitching and then immobile bodies on the ground, at the shattered flesh, hopes and lives.

30

When the last of Caius's guests had gone, he strode over to the window and looked down to where the ambulances and funeral service vans were clearing up. He fished in his inside jacket pocket and drew out a silver case, took out a cigarette, tapped it and lit it. He took a deep draw then released it in a long, slow stream of smoke.

My companions and I finished tidying up and loaded the dumb waiter. I wanted to leave and find a window that let in fresh air, not because of the smoke; I needed to get out of the atrium away from this monstrous man.

'Aurelia. Stay where you are. You other women, out.'

He finished his cigarette and stubbed it out in one of Severina's crystal trinket trays. 'You played your part well this evening.'

I said nothing.

'Wolf bitten your tongue out, or are you just sulking?'

'Just leave me alone, Caius.'

'Dear me, and after the effort I made to make you part of the evening.'

'You shamed me in front of my peers and colleagues.'

'Your "peers and colleagues" now are the women in the domestic hall.'

'Not in my head and my heart. I know who I am and you'll never change that, whatever steel rings you put on me.'

'Yes, the *magister* was rather busy explaining that this evening, wasn't he? I really must think about replacing him. But he's a good soldier and the troops are very loyal to him.'

'Was that what was happening in the guardroom? No wonder they were terrified and crying. How can you enslave free citizens? It's never been permitted in Roma Nova. Apulius specifically excluded it from the Twelve Tables.'

'Times change and we need the labour of all these unemployed people.'

'Then pay them.'

'What a quaint idea.'

'And slaughtering innocent demonstrators? What would you call that?'

'That was a demonstration for my guests and for the general population. My rule will be strong, but fair.'

'Fair?'

He held his hand up. 'Enough. You are becoming irritating.' His eyes gleamed, the strange green-amber colour darkened. 'And I was thinking about releasing your two friends tomorrow. Perhaps I won't now.'

I took a deep breath. 'I apologise for my harsh words and will retire with your permission.'

'Much better.' He clapped his hands slowly. 'But don't bottle it up to the point of imploding, Aurelia. I need you alive for a while longer.'

I struggled to get to sleep that night. The bed was plain but comfortable, the window brought in crisp, refreshing air and I was exhausted with the mental strain of my existence. Eventually, I suppressed the horrendous images of last night's slaughter enough to doze off.

I woke at first light, feeling like a sack of lumpy, uncoordinated flesh. Just as I finished my quick bath, the damned bracelet buzzed and flashed. I'd tried keeping it under the water in the bath yesterday so the water would leak in and stop it working, but the bloody thing was obviously well waterproofed. I pulled on my clothes and sandals and hurried up to the atrium. I knocked and entered. A slight figure in outdoor clothing stood this side of Caius's desk. Sitting on a chair and holding a walking stick was a tall man. My heart pounded with delight – Calavia and Atrius, dressed for travelling. He really was releasing them. The mission would be reactivated, thank the gods.

'Ah, Aurelia, my dear, do come in.'

Caius's tone was warm and inviting and he smiled at me as if we were lifelong buddies. Of course, he was doing it to pollute their memories of me. Bastard. Two of his nationalists, fully armed, stood at the wall behind him.

'You summoned me, First Consul?' I kept my voice as neutral as possible.

'You're very formal this morning.' He smiled again. I wanted to smack it from his face. I ignored him and put my hands out to Calavia. She looked at my clothes, searched my face and looked at my hands, hesitating before accepting them. I pressed hers hard and willed her to believe in me. I held my hand out to Atrius. His face was pale, bruised, one eye half-closed; he looked thirty years older than he should. What in Hades had they done to him? Eventually, he took my hand, but released it as soon as he could. What had Caius been saying to them?

'Your friends are leaving for exile,' Caius said. 'I thought you would like to bid them farewell.'

'Would you give us a few moments alone, First Consul?'

'I'm afraid that won't be possible. Make your farewells; they have a train to catch.'

I swallowed, trying to think of some way to convey a message. 'Travel safely, my friends, and may Mercury speed you on your way. Give my regards to Numerus and his daughter. Tell him I'll drink a toast to Maxima.'

Calavia shot me a strange look but Atrius said nothing.

Caius flicked his fingers and the two nationalists stepped forward. Caius stood up, came to my side and to my horror slid his arm round my waist. I tried to pull away, but his grip was more than firm. Warmth crept up my neck into my face.

Atrius cast me a look of disgust and Calavia looked away. They turned and walked to the door, Atrius leaning heavily on his stick. I wanted to run after them, to explain, but Caius held on to me like Pluto himself.

'Steady, Aurelia, don't spoil it now,' he murmured. 'They're not over the border yet.'

As I watched them disappear through the doorway, I felt his warm breath on the skin of my neck and shivered. I made myself look into his eyes, trying to see any honesty in them. I saw nothing but an intense stare back.

'How do I know you'll do as you say?' I said. 'You could just drive them up to Truscium, dump them there and I wouldn't know.'

He released me and gave a theatrical sigh. 'I will ask my men to take a photograph at the border. But I don't think your ex-comrades will be sending you a postcard when they reach Vienna.'

No, they'd think I really was a collaborator, especially after Caius's performance just now. I'd fought so hard to ensure Calavia and Atrius would be released and they'd literally turned their backs on me.

Down in the domestic hall, Drusilla made me drink a cup of coffee – I couldn't face breakfast. Caius had told me to get out of his sight. Somehow I'd 'irritated' him again. I didn't care now.

'How are things here, Drusilla? You must be struggling with your deputy missing and so few others to help.'

'My deputy has been removed – they said he shouldn't be doing women's work. They've given him an accounts job in the comptroller's office. Poor Marcus, he hates it. Half the domestic staff were dismissed the day after the first consul moved in. The senior steward lost her job and her deputy who's taken over keeps grumbling about managing the whole palace with only three of them. The imperatrix's private secretary was kept on for two days and ordered to hand over all her files to the nats. They dismissed *her* two secretaries, then gave her the option of staying on as a typist. She told them to stuff it.' She glanced around and bent her head towards me. 'People are so frightened. The new chef is a hard, cruel man. He's one of these Roman nationalists. He beat two of the younger girls yesterday just for spilling flour when they were making bread.'

'Don't worry, Drusilla, I have a worse one to deal with upstairs.'

She gave me a strange look.

'But everybody knows you're under the first consul's protection.'

'What do you mean, "protection"?'

'All the security staff, and the heads of services have been forbidden to stop you going anywhere within the palace and none of them are allowed to touch you. I heard yesterday that that nasty piece of work Phobius wanted to flog you for cheeking him but the first consul said that if Phobius laid another finger on you, he, the first consul, would personally cut Phobius's hand off. *I* know you sleep down here, but others draw different conclusions.'

Pluto in Tartarus. Not only did my comrades-in-arms think I was a collaborator but apart from Drusilla, nobody here, where I thought I could find some help, would come near me now because they thought I was Caius's tart.

I took myself off around the palace to see if what Drusilla said was true. Whether from the remaining staff, military or the nats, resentful looks followed me. I escaped into the room where we'd held the imperial council meetings and where so many had died on the night of the fires. Autumn sun streamed in through the floor-to-ceiling windows, casting diamonds of light through the glass onto the stone wall opposite. The purple velvet padded chairs were still strewn all over the room. Dark stains on the purple carpet could only be blood. Severina, Fabia, Tertullius Plico, Julian, Calavia senior, the brave Praetorians – all gone. Tears rolled down my face. I dropped into a chair and waited until I became calmer. I couldn't allow myself to look weak in front of these brutal people who had usurped all we cared about. I closed the door softly as I left this sad and abandoned place an hour later.

In the side corridor, I looked to see if I could reach the tunnel entrance I'd pushed Silvia and Volusenia down on the night of the fires, but there were two guards at the corridor entrance. It didn't mean Caius knew about the tunnels, but it was safer to assume he did.

Back in the vestibule, I was about to return downstairs to the domestic hall when I saw an elegant figure handing his coat to a steward.

'Quintus. Oh, gods, I'm so pleased to see you.'

'Aurelia. Are you well?'

He spoke in a measured, cool tone and looked over my shoulder as if he couldn't bear to look at me.

'Well? A prisoner, no, a virtual slave in this hell-hole, at your bastard brother's beck and call?' I shook my arm, letting the tunic sleeve fall back to reveal the tag and slave ring. 'And considered a collaborator or a tart? Yes, I'm wonderful.'

He frowned, took my arm and led me back down the corridor to a small office strewn with abandoned files. In the corner, he opened a flush door ostensibly to a cupboard, but which led to another, smaller room for confidential work. He looked around, then lifted the desk lamp and examined the telephone. I shook my head.

'There hasn't been time to seed bugs everywhere,' I said. 'Not down to this level. You and I know this place inside out. Caius's people won't get to this small office for weeks.'

He perched on the edge of the desk and crossed his arms.

'Kindly explain exactly what you meant.'

I plumped myself down in the chair behind the desk and told him the whole story.

'I see,' Quintus said. 'I apologise for my frosty greeting. Caius told me you had returned voluntarily and had reconciled with him. Apparently, you, too, had despised Severina and were ready to go along with his plans for the sake of Roma Nova.'

I leapt up. 'Is that what people are saying? Dear gods, your brother knows how to twist everything, doesn't he?' I seized Quintus's hand. 'You must believe me. I only complied to save my comrades so they can come back to look for Silvia. Although Atrius looked in bad shape…' I glanced at him. 'You haven't heard anything about Silvia, have you?'

'Nothing. I *had* hoped she'd got away with you.' He tapped his fingers on the peeling leather top of the desk. 'I'm sure Caius hasn't got her. He'd never be able to keep it to himself.'

'Agreed. So the search must go on.'

'What about you, Aurelia?'

'Once I know they are safe, Caius can whistle.'

'Be very careful, he doesn't let anything go. He's not stupid. Look how he's outmanoeuvred you.'

'But he doesn't know *why* I'm doing it. He thinks I've given in.' All the same, Quintus wasn't entirely wrong. Everything I said, every public gesture I made was carefully choreographed by Caius. Through his threats, he'd pushed me into apparent dependence on him.

'Why are you here, Quintus? I thought you hated him as much as I do.'

'I'm going to try and get Conradus away from him.' He sighed. 'It's unlikely, but as he's so busy ruling the country, he might be distracted enough to hand the child over.'

'I doubt it. Remember the words you spoke ten seconds ago about him not letting go. How is Conradus?'

'Neglected, but the servants at Caius's villa do at least feed him. But he runs wild and there is no one to love him. Last time I could get in, the little chap sobbed in my arms and they had to prise him off me when I left.' His fists balled. 'He's such a sensitive child. I just hope he's not been ruined for life.'

'Are you safe, Quintus?'

'So far. Mostly, Caius ignores me. I ignore him. I refuse to be afraid of him. I still hold my deputy *praetor* job, but how long that'll last, I don't know. Let me tell you, being Caius's brother is no sinecure; few speak to me in the department now and those who do are either toadies wanting an introduction or true friends. The *praetor urbanus*, my chief, doesn't know whether to be frosty or friendly. The office is half empty as the women magistrates and managerial staff have all been dismissed. Two young men, who know as much law as Cato's cat, have appeared to fill two of their places. At present, we're all very civilised and polite, pretending nothing's happened.'

'What's it like in the city? I mean, how are people taking it?'

'People were confused at first, but quite a number are pleased things have settled down. There's the odd shuttered up shop here and there, and I've noticed women go around in groups on the streets, rather than in ones and twos. I was surprised when my clerk asked if her job was safe this morning. She hesitated, then asked if there was any possibility of taking her sister on – she's just been chucked out of the *vigiles*. What I'm going to do with a former police shift leader, I don't know.' He sighed. 'I have a horrible feeling this is just the beginning. It all seems normal out there despite the curfew and these bloody toga toughs. Mars, but they're rude, shoving people off the street as if they own the place.'

'I think they think they do. Caius's sidekick, Phobius, struts around like a pompous ostrich, but he's a vindictive little sod.'

Quintus uncrossed his arms and walked over to the filing cabinets, turned and leant back against them. 'It's intolerable the way he's treating you. If I weren't here for Conradus, I'd demand he release you. You know you'd be welcome at my house.'

'Thank you, Quintus. You have no idea what a relief it is to talk to a rational human being. Caius is taking revenge and using me to manipulate others. Until now, I've complied because he threatened to execute my comrades-in-arms and send the Mitelae to his new work camps. He's supposed to have released the two Praetorians across the border this morning.'

'I'd have thought you'd be planning your escape.'

'That's moved to the top of the agenda today. It's just a question of whether I can organise it before Caius snaps and finishes me. But then what happens to my cousins and household?'

He took my hand. 'You know I'll help if I can, but—'

'No, you must concentrate on protecting the child.'

The tag buzzed and flashed.

'My cue. You might as well come with me, Quintus.'

Caius was sitting on the sofa in a group of easy chairs by the tall windows. A large manila envelope and a number of small colour photos were scattered on the low table in the middle of the group of chairs. He looked up as we came through the doors and frowned when he saw Quintus.

'What are you doing here?'

'I've come to ask you a favour, brother to brother.'

'Really?' Caius snapped back. 'Bad luck. I've exhausted my count of favours for today.'

Quintus looked at me. I shook my head.

'In that case, I'll call another day,' Quintus said, 'if, of course, it's not too inconvenient.' The irony seeped out of every word.

'Make an appointment,' Caius retorted. He glanced up at Quintus and shifted in his chair. Just for a moment, a fleeting moment, I felt sorry for Caius. Beside the hard-working and career-minded Quintus, who was universally described as 'sound', Caius looked shallow and undeveloped.

Quintus didn't have a tenth of Caius's undoubted charm and although he'd had a good education, he'd grown up in circumstances in their father's house far more modest than the privileged and undisciplined Tella household headed by their redoubtable grandmother where Caius had been granted every expensive whim.

Rumour had it that the brothers, never close, had had a major falling out a few months ago and Quintus had beaten Caius unconscious. Neither had confirmed or denied it. Perhaps if Caius had had more discipline and less privilege, he might have trodden a straighter path and the brothers might have enjoyed a completely different relationship. Perhaps.

'I will leave you to your, er, business,' Quintus said. He took my hand, raised it and kissed the back of my fingers. 'Look after yourself, Aurelia. It was a pleasure to see you, even in such difficult circumstances.' He looked at Caius. 'I'm sure my brother will ensure your welfare, won't you, Caius?'

'See yourself out, Quintus, and don't meddle in my affairs.'

I swallowed hard as I watched Quintus leave; it was like the tide going out, leaving me high and dry on the beach.

31

'Fetch me a whisky and then sit down, Aurelia. And have the courtesy not to gather wool over my tiresome brother while I'm talking to you.'

I poured a double measure over ice and placed the tumbler on the table. Damn, I had obeyed him like a good servant without thinking about it. Had I been so well 'trained' in the past few days, then?

He sat up, gathered the photographs together and half threw them at me. They were a series of the instant self-developing type, washed-out colour, but I could clearly see Calavia and Atrius. In the first one, they were sitting in a train carriage and looking out of the window at the New Austrian border post. The next, they were walking up to the customs office and then they were through the border. The last showed them getting into a Vienna registered taxi on the New Austrian side.

'Convinced?'

'Thank you.' Now I could relax a little and possibly claw back some of my dignity. 'I've done as you've asked, Caius, and you've honoured our agreement. But now things must change. You have no right to treat me like a household skivvy at your beck and call. You've destroyed my reputation with my peers and colleagues and falsely increased your own. Most of the palace staff think I'm sleeping with you. This stops here. Put me on trial or let me go.'

'Dear me, quite the little rebel speech. You've been very useful to me these past few days, Aurelia. The answer is no.' He looked me up and down, then brought his gaze back to my face and half closed his eyes. 'Sleeping with me? Now there's a thought.'

'No.'

'You wouldn't be disappointed, Aurelia. And when was the last time you had sex? You must miss it without your gypsy to service you.'

'You're revolting.'

'Merely stating the obvious.'

'You can't force me. I refuse.'

'We'll see. In the meantime, we continue as we are.'

'No, I will not cooperate any longer.'

'Let me show you some more photos that might help you change your mind.'

Oh gods, what did he have now? I couldn't save everybody. The only way to do that was to get rid of Caius. And after his off-colour suggestion, that was a more attractive course of action than merely escaping. But he was almost always guarded.

He passed me the manila envelope. My hands trembled as I drew out three black and white photographs. Taken from a distance, so probably surveillance, my analytical mind told me. When I turned them the right way up, there was no mistaking the young woman's identity. Marina. She was huddled up against William Brown and they were coming out of a hospital. Even though the image was blurred, she looked as though she was crying her heart out.

'Read the letters,' he said.

I tipped out two envelopes with EUS stamps and New Hampshire postmarks. The sender's name was 'M. Brown'. How strange that looked. They were addressed to me at Domus Mitelarum and had been opened.

'How did you get hold of these?'

'Really, Aurelia, don't be so naive.'

'Now you're intercepting private post – how is that a sign of "fair" rule?'

'Be careful. Just read your letters.'

Marina chattered on in her usual style, mostly about her new house and going shopping for curtains and clothes, and towards the end, she wrote, *…oh, I'm going to have a baby.*

I nearly dropped the letter. 'Oh, that's wonderful news. I must phone at once to congratulate— ' I caught Caius's eyes watching me. 'No, I suppose it won't be possible.'

'Read the second one.'

I took it out of its envelope. The paper was curled as if it had been damp, then dried out. Inside were two pages of sadness, rage and tears. She'd lost the baby. Gods, I needed to be with my daughter now. When I'd miscarried my unborn child thirteen years ago due to this brutal man opposite me, I'd nearly died inside. The injury had closed off any hope of conceiving another. He knew nothing of the devastation, nor could he even imagine it. And nor would he care if he could.

'Caius, please let me go to her.'

'That's not possible.'

'I will promise to stay in the EUS and not come back to Europe. Please.'

'No.'

'You're a complete bastard.'

He said nothing, but lit a cigarette and took a sip of his drink. After a few minutes, he said, 'You can telephone her, but I will listen. And the second you say anything I don't like, I will cut the call. Understood?'

I stood at his desk while he pushed the zero key for the palace switchboard and instructed the operator. He didn't ask me for the Browns' ex-directory number; he already knew it. That was unnerving. And why had he allowed me to make the call? I couldn't follow his thought processes. When it rang back, he stretched his arm out with the handset, which I grabbed. He pressed the loudspeaker button.

'Hello?' All I heard was a ring tone, then clicks just before the call was answered. Somebody was listening in and recording this.

'William? It's Aurelia.'

'Thank God. We've left several messages on the answerphone. Are you all right?'

'I've just received Marina's latest letter. I'm so, so sorry.'

'Speak to Marina herself, why don't you?'

'Hello, darling.'

'Oh, Mama,' she sobbed down the phone.

'I know, truly, I do. You'll feel better in a few weeks' time. You're young, so another baby will come along. Try not to fret.'

More sobbing. Caius raised an eyebrow and looked at his watch. I glowered at him. 'I only have another minute. Give yourself time to recover and eat properly. You have all my love. You know that, Marina. Now put William on again, please.'

'Make her rest,' I said. 'Please don't worry about us here. We're… we're fine,' I lied.

'You expect me to believe that?' William replied.

'Not really, but all will be well. Eventually.'

Then Caius jabbed the hook and cut the call.

I stared at the handset I was gripping, then looked up at his face. He was frowning and his faced flushed dark pink with anger.

'That's the last phone call you'll make.' He slammed the flat of his hand on his desk.

'What did you expect me to say? I kept it as neutral as I could.'

'Not enough.'

'You can't make things happen exactly as you want *all* the time, Caius. That's how life works.' My poor child, distraught after losing her own child, was breaking apart while this stupid man was having a tantrum about a few words that nobody would believe anyway.

His face calmed after a minute.

'Now this charming interlude is over, we'll return to the real world. You've heard how upset your daughter is. She's such a delicate thing, if I remember correctly. My friend, Mr White from the EUS, took those photographs for me. He passes on his regards, by the way.'

'White? Who's he?'

'You met him in Berlin.'

It came back to me; White was the EUS government spook who'd pumped me for information about Severina and whether her government was stable while supplying me with constant martinis.

'He's keeping an eye on Marina as part of his study of William Brown. You see, his government is very interested in Brown Industries. Unfortunately, your daughter's husband seems completely uninterested in them. Perhaps I should suggest they try to cultivate Marina and exert pressure through her?'

'No! Leave her alone. She's an innocent.'

'Well, that would be entirely in your hands.'

'You can't mean that.' I heard my voice shaking. I started trembling. A noise filled my ears and rushed through my head. I lost my balance. The blackness rushed up. Gone.

32

———

Cool and wet, lavender. Somebody was dabbing my forehead. I looked up. Drusilla.

'Welcome back, *domina*.'

'What happened?'

'You fainted. Well, that's what the first consul said.' Her face carried a disapproving look.

I grabbed her wrist. 'Where is he?'

'In the atrium.'

I released my breath then looked around. High ceiling and rich blue curtains, and a bed with soft cotton sheets. This wasn't the under-housekeeper's room. 'Where in Hades am I?'

'In one of the first floor guestrooms.' She looked away. 'He brought you here, then called me. I have to tell him when you're awake, but first you must eat.' She handed me a plate of fresh sandwiches and salad.

'I'm not hungry.'

'You've been living on coffee and tension. And very little sleep. You must keep your strength up if you're to survive.' She watched me as I ate. When I'd finished, she pressed my hand, then left.

I pulled myself up onto my elbows. My head spun. The penalty of not eating properly for days. Drusilla had left a glass of fruit drink. I devoured it in two swallows. I pulled the covers back and swung my legs down so I could sit on the edge of the bed. I took a deep breath and stood up. Wobbly, but not falling, I made my way to the door, turned the handle and pulled. Locked. The Furies scourge him and his to a long and painful death.

I tottered back to the bed, lay down, wept then slept.

The door was still locked next morning. If I'd had my old lock pick set, I would have been through it in moments. I washed in the bathroom, then sat down at the small table and waited. In a funny way I felt energised, and clearer in my mind. Probably the result of a full night's sleep.

After an hour, the door opened to show a guard and admit one of the kitchen staff with a tray of coffee, olives, rolls and honey. I thanked her, but she said nothing and left. What was going on? Why was I in this room?

After my breakfast, I went to the window and discovered I was on the first floor to the right of the entrance portico. Unlike the domestic hall which was at semi-basement level in the heart of the house, with nats guards and troopers everywhere, I was on the outside wall. I knew about the handholds built down the concealed vertical recess at the side of the portico. They were for maintenance; I'd climbed them several times for fun when I was younger. I could get out of the palace. I could escape from Caius. My heart thudded. But I needed my walking clothes and boots if I was going to go cross-country in October to the border and through the mountain passes.

I had to ensure I kept this room, whatever it took. Then I would start acquiring my supplies. Drusilla would know what happened to my clothes on that first night.

Caius must have been bluffing yesterday about the threats to Marina, my logical mind told me. He couldn't possibly have such a reach. Besides, William would ensure she was protected. Caius had mentioned White, stationed at the Berlin EUS embassy when I was investigating the silver smuggling nearly fifteen years ago. Had Caius met him in Washington when he'd been there just before the night of the fires? I hadn't heard any American accents here. But then I'd hardly seen anybody apart from at that humiliating reception, and they were all Roma Novans.

After I'd searched the room for listening bugs, I rifled through the drawers and built-in wardrobes. Their white surfaces and raised gold decorations looked so serene and elegant but they yielded nothing except blankets, pillows and towels. But in the bureau by the window I found writing paper and a fountain pen that worked.

My darling Marina,

I was devastated to read you had lost your baby. I am so sorry. My dearest wish is to take you in my arms and comfort you.

Many years ago, this happened to me. I was consumed by rage and grief, but foremost by a sense of failure. The child had been conceived in love, a deep love. I wanted to turn my face to the wall and go into the shades. But your grandmother's friend, Justina, pulled me out of it. Nature is a harsh mistress and sometimes she intervenes for no good reason we can think of at the time.

You are young and will carry another, and a healthy, baby to term. But now you must rest and not allow yourself to give way to depression, or indeed obsession. Be kind to yourself, spoil yourself, indulge.

Life is not always as it should be, but William must, and I'm sure will, protect you from the harshness and sometimes danger that surrounds us.

You will never forget that lost little life that never was, but catch your breath and look forward to the time when a new child comes into your and William's lives.

My fondest love,

Mama

I slipped the letter into an envelope, addressed it and tucked it into my waist pouch. Perhaps I could persuade Drusilla to smuggle it out. No doubt the post was subject to strict censorship now, but I hoped my warning would get through. I could see Marina reading it, puzzled at my penultimate sentence and wrinkling her nose, then passing my letter to her husband. William Brown was no fool and would take appropriate action to increase protection around her.

More food arrived, chicken and vegetables, and a large jug of water. Looking towards the satiny ball of the sun behind the clouds, I calculated it must have been between one and two. With nothing to do afterwards, and no summons, I took a nap.

A tingle spread across the skin of my face, into my neck and down through my body. Fingers brushed my cheekbone, my jaw and chin touching every pleasure nerve on the way. When the fingertips caressed the hollow of my throat and skimmed the rise of my breast, the nerves exploded and I moaned. A wonderful dream. Pure sensation. I caught my breath. Miklós, you are with me even in this hell.

I fought against waking up. Lips were nuzzling my neck. I was nearly overwhelmed by a cloud of jasmine and citrus and the scent of a warm, masculine body. Jasmine? Miklós would never wear that. My mind was confused. I snapped my eyes open and found Caius on top of me.

'What are you doing? Get off,' I shrieked.

He grasped each of my wrists. 'No, you're enjoying it too much.'

I wrenched my head from side to side and bucked my body to try to push him off. His grip on my wrists so hard my fingers couldn't move. He was so heavy I couldn't even bring my knee up.

'Stop fighting it, Aurelia. Just for once in your life, give in.'

'No, you will not do this to me.'

'I will do what I want.'

I spat in his face, but he just laughed and drove into my body. I forced myself to relax as he thrust. He moaned in some kind of perverted pleasure. I lay back and waited for it to be over.

I couldn't feel my body. I didn't want to; it no longer belonged to me.

He sat at the delicate bureau and was staring through the gauze that shielded the window. He wore a patterned silk dressing gown with gold lapels and was sipping a glass of whisky, his face expressionless. From the side, and highlighted by the outside light, the scar from the punch when I'd floored him that time stood out, distorting his mouth. His mouth. Oh, gods.

I buried myself under the sheets, anything to blot out what had happened last night. I trembled with rage. At this exact moment, I wanted to kill Caius, to beat and slash him until he was a bloody heap at my feet. But Phobius would take over and exact an excruciating revenge. I wanted to escape and live. I had to calm down.

The sheets were pulled back and he sat down on the bed.

'What a passionate creature you are, Aurelia.' He stroked my hairline. I jerked away from his hand, repelled that this creature had touched me so intimately. 'Not only in your loyalty and love for Roma Nova and your daughter, but as a bed partner you are outstanding.'

'Shut up! Shut up!'

'That's no way to greet your lover.'

'You are not my lover.'

He laughed. 'You don't know yourself very well, do you?'

'What do you want, Caius?'

'Something I've been refused all my life.'

'What?'

He looked away, as if stretching back into his memory.

'You.' He looked back at me, his eyes shining, not with hate, but like a child anticipating a great treat. 'Oh, not the wilful hoyden dressed up in a military uniform, nor the stroppy madam in the Families Council, but the true woman underneath. A strong one who would be a proper companion for an ambitious man, who would stand with him, supporting him.'

'You wanted to kill me in Berlin.'

'You were blocking my plans. I realised afterwards that I couldn't crush you. You were made of stronger steel than I thought. So I had to catch you, then bend you. You would see then what we could achieve together.'

He was mad.

He stroked the side of my neck, as a lover would. I steeled myself not to flinch, but failed. He stopped, his fingers just on my carotid, and brought his thumb round to my throat. I stayed completely still. One hard press from those strong fingers and I'd be gone.

'But at present, you are far too impulsive and prone to meddle in affairs. You need to learn boundaries and proper behaviour if you are to be part of Roma Nova in the future. So your training continues.'

'You used my comrades' lives to coerce me and now you are threatening my daughter.'

'Your comrades have gone into exile, and you have learned a lesson in humility.'

'Humiliation, you mean.'

He didn't reply.

'You do not love me or even like me. Why are you doing this to me?'

'I possess you. That is enough.'

I waited until he had left. I scrubbed myself mercilessly, despising the body that had been violated. I hated that it had been the instrument of my worst humiliation.

When I was red raw enough, I reached for yesterday's tunics and dressed quickly. I tried the bedroom door. Not locked. I tugged the door open. No guard in the corridor. I went to see Drusilla, ostensibly to collect my change of clothes from the under-housekeeper's room, but in fact to question her about my outdoor wear.

I was relieved Caius wasn't in the atrium. My cheeks burned and I shuddered as I remembered the night. I couldn't face him. To my surprise, the guard by the doors opened one for me. I stalked along the corridor then down the service stairs to the domestic hall. Two girls counting cutlery on a service table stopped chattering, handfuls of knives and forks silenced mid-air. They pressed themselves against the wall. I glanced back. They were watching me as I walked on down the corridor. I knocked on Drusilla's room door and entered. She glanced up then stood immediately.

'*Domina*.' Then she bowed her head. She had never done that before, not even in Severina's time.

'Drusilla?'

'What service can I do for you, *domina*?'

'For a start, you can stop calling me *domina* with every sentence you speak.'

'As you wish.'

What was wrong with her? She moved and talked like an automaton.

'Are you well?' I tried.

'Yes, thank you. How can I help you?'

I sensed an edge behind the formality. And tension. She glanced towards the open door. I turned and shut it. Now we were alone, I glanced round. Was she nervous because concealed microphones had been installed? Unlikely in the housekeeper's room, but I'd put nothing beyond Caius. Nothing had changed position on the shelves or on her desk, nor had any new 'ornaments' appeared since I'd last been here.

'Now, sit down and tell me what's going on.'

She twisted her hands together and looked down at her housekeeper's record book. When she raised her eyes again they searched my face, as if trying to reach a decision.

I tore a piece of paper off a memo pad and scribbled, *Are they listening in?* She stared at the message, then shook her head.

'Drusilla, whatever it is worrying you, you can speak in confidence. You are my friend and friends don't blab on each other.'

'It's about you,' she blurted out. 'Can I really trust you not to go running to the first consul?'

'Juno save me! He's the last person on this earth I would tell anything useful or confidential. All he's done since they caught me and brought me here is humiliate and abuse me. My dearest wish is to escape. That's why I'm here. I need walking clothes and boots. Can you get hold of any for me?'

'But—' Her eyes narrowed, pulling her face into a frown. 'You don't know about this morning's orders, do you?'

A sense of dread crept over me. What had he done now?

'The whole staff is to treat you with utmost respect as the first consul's official companion. You are to be addressed as *domina* at all times. Any infringement is to be reported to Representative Phobius who will discipline as appropriate,' she said in a flat voice.

'Why have you done this?' I flung the notice down on his desk. 'I'm not your "companion", whatever the Hades that is.'

'Be calm,' he said.

'I will not.'

He turned a photo frame towards me. It contained one of the black and white pictures of Marina he'd showed me yesterday. I could see her tears despite the blurred outlines. 'This may help you,' he said.

I took a deep breath. 'I am sure you mean it as some kind of honour,' I winced at my hypocritical words. 'But I do not wish my title and status returned to me on your orders.'

'I am returning nothing to you. Your status and authority only come through me.'

'No wonder they looked at me with such terror this morning.'

'Terror, perhaps. Respect, certainly. That is all I require. And you should remember that.' His eyes seemed to take on a greener tint chasing out the amber. 'You pleased me last night, more than I thought possible. Perhaps you are starting to adapt.' He touched the notice. 'This is a small reward.'

How dared he treat me like some paid sex worker? I wanted to rip his tongue out. No, I wanted to kill him. One chop to the bridge of his nose then a hard blow to his temple. He'd be finished. But so would I. But should I ignore what would happen to me and do it for Roma Nova?

As I raged inside, he smiled at me as if he could read what I was feeling. He was relentless. Granting me this new status, he had eroded my public image and isolated me even further from those who could be my allies. Like Drusilla, they would worry about trusting me and play safe.

'You will prove yourself useful by running this house,' he continued. 'Its organisation is lamentable.'

I suspected that apart from the cook, the reduced household staff was exerting wilful insolence and non-cooperation. In Justina's time and even in Severina's, the palace domestic system had run ultra efficiently.

He reached for his diary. 'Next, the day after tomorrow, you will be at my side at the reception for the foreign diplomatic corps. You will wear formal dress – *palla* and *stola*. You will not give any opinions, merely be polite and deferential to our guests.'

'That's ridiculous. I've worked with most of them first-hand on complex and delicate matters and know many on first-name terms. I am still the legally appointed foreign minister. You can't expect me to suddenly become a stuffed doll you parade for your political ends.'

'A simplistic way of putting it, but that's exactly what I mean. You would do well to be less proud. And you are no longer foreign minister.'

I turned my back on him and stalked towards the door.

'Aurelia.' His voice vibrated with menace. I stopped. 'I have not dismissed you,' he said. What a child, but a lethal one. And one determined to control me. I had to comply for the moment as I worked out the details of my escape plan, but in my heart, my hatred for him grew. With his personal strength and intelligence, he could have given so much to Roma Nova. Now he was destroying everything precious in it, spreading the canker through others. I had to remove myself from the tyranny of being his creature whether I was ready or not or I would go mad.

33

I heard the shouting from the top of the stairs leading down to the domestic hall; Drusilla protesting, and the bullying tones of the cook.

'… and if you can't keep those bloody girls in order, I'll whip them myself. They won't forget that in a hurry.'

'They spilt one jug of water and chipped a glass. A nuisance, to be sure, but not enough for a punishment. And that would be the responsibility of housekeeping. That is not in your remit.'

'Remit? I spit on your remit.' And I heard the sound of him hawking. 'Now clear that up.'

'I will not. It's a kitchen matter. Call one of your stewards, or do it yourself.'

Then the sound of a slap and Drusilla's cry of shock.

'Do as I tell you, woman.'

I strode through to the kitchen.

'What in Hades are you doing?' I said to the cook. 'How dare you assault the housekeeper? You will be fined and lose pay for this. First, apologise to her.'

'Who are you to tell— Oh.' He flushed and looked down at the floor.

I crossed my arms. 'I'm waiting.'

He mumbled an apology to Drusilla.

'Now you can clear up that disgusting mess and disinfect the floor. Yourself.'

I eased Drusilla onto a chair and fetched her ice and a towel, then watched the cook until he had finished. I took Drusilla back into her office.

'He should leave you alone now.' I shrugged. 'At least I've done something positive with my borrowed authority.'

'Thank you, *domina*. He is an atrocious man. Like many of these people.' She gave me half a smile. 'And I have something for you.' She stood and went over to a small cupboard. Behind a stack of files was a pair of boots. Mine.

'My daughter wore the selfsame pattern.' Drusilla looked into the distance. 'She was killed in that border post massacre a month ago.' She gave a huge sob and hugged the boots to her.

'I'm so sorry, Drusilla, so sorry. A very loyal colleague who lost his life on the night of the fires led the enquiry, but they couldn't find an obvious cause or any clue to the attackers' identity.'

'Yes, but we know who was behind it, don't we?'

'We can't prove it in a court of law, if there still are such things, but yes, more than a strong suspicion.'

'I will help you in any possible way, but you must promise to get these bastards.'

'I will, Drusilla, for your daughter, mine and all the other daughters, and sons.'

Caius invited me to eat in the dining room at midday with his cronies; the idea made me feel sick and I pleaded a headache. He seemed to accept it which, after his previous controlling behaviour, unnerved me. One of the kitchen assistants brought my lunch to my room with a message that Drusilla would like to consult me about domestic matters if I was well enough. When she struggled in with armfuls of formal clothing an hour later, I was intrigued. She threw the lot down on my bed.

'I'm so pleased I never became a dresser. These weigh a ton.' She shook her arms. 'The first consul said you should have your choice for the reception and ordered me to bring you some of Imperatrix Severina's clothes.'

I turned them over one by one; the white tunic with a broad stripe for Senate ceremonies, the dark purple silk *stola* she had worn as a guest to the last Families' formal gathering, the shot gold *palla* to complement it. I fingered a fine dark red wool *stola* with gold embroidery. She'd worn it at the formal Saturnalia party for the foreign press corps last year. Oh, Severina, you were weak much of the time, but you didn't deserve to die so young and have an interloper wear your clothes. Then I noticed some dark, less fine clothes at the bottom of the pile. My walking trousers, shirt, socks and waterproof field jacket.

'Drusilla, thank you.' I hugged her, much to her surprise, and mine. I stuffed them in the shoe drawer at the back of the wardrobe, then beckoned her into the bathroom and shut the door.

I flushed the lavatory and while it filled, whispered, 'I swept the room, but there may still be bugs. I don't know when I'll try to go, but it'll be soon.' I fished in my waist pouch and gave Drusilla my letter to Marina. 'If you can post this, I'd be very grateful. But please don't take any silly risks. Thinking about it, take it to Quintus Tellus. He might get it out via one of the foreign legations.' I was planning to escape, but so much could go wrong. At least I would have told Marina how much I loved her. Drusilla looked at the envelope and nodded.

I ran both basin taps and made a lot of splashing noise washing my hands.

'I'll leave a water carrier in my cupboard and refill it every day,' she whispered back. 'Take what you need from the kitchen. Here, this is the cool cupboard combination for the next week.'

I lay in bed that night, waiting. I was afraid, but not sure exactly what I was afraid of. If I fought him, he'd hand me over to Phobius. If I complied, I would be betraying myself at every level. When the luminous hands of the clock showed past one in the morning and Caius hadn't appeared, I trembled with relief.

The next morning, I managed to get hold of the *Acta Diurna*, the official gazette. I hadn't seen any printed news since the day before the night of the fires nearly three weeks ago. The columns were set out in the same way and with the same headings, but instead of Senate meetings, government committees, news of trials and enquiries and the personal notices, it was bursting with Caius's speeches, edicts 'from the office of the first consul', sycophantic distorted accounts of the night of the fires, libellous and totally fabricated stories about the 'enemies of the state', and more importantly, notice of an increased reward for the sighting of Silvia Apulia, whom the first consul wished to protect from 'criminal elements'.

Last night, it reported, Caius had attended a rally in his honour. The photo of him, arm raised, saluting the torchlight procession of thousands of nats made me want to be sick. Then in the forthcoming events column, I was horrified to see my name beside Caius's. The diplomatic reception tomorrow evening. That was why Drusilla had brought me Severina's clothes. Anybody who read that would draw only one conclusion.

Pouring a few drinks as a servant in front of ex-colleagues wasn't anywhere near as significant as standing by Caius's side in luxurious clothes as his so-called companion. I would be completely damned not only in the eyes of everybody who knew me, but the world would think that as a patrician and former foreign minister, I was underwriting Caius's brutal regime.

I had betrayed my country enough.

I had to go tonight.

I went down to see Drusilla, as if to discuss a household matter, and gave her a message for Quintus. Whether it would reach him was debatable.

The minute the sun went down, I changed into my walking clothes. As I buttoned up the shirt and zipped the trousers, I felt more natural than I had for days. Dusk crept in agonisingly slowly; it would be another twenty minutes before the dying sunlight was dim enough to mask me, but not so dark that the exterior lighting would pinpoint me. I tested the window again; it slid open noiselessly. I'd lubricated it with some olive oil I'd stolen from the kitchen. I had no bag, but I'd stuffed my pockets with first aid kit, a notebook, torch, a penknife I'd filched from a study and some food I'd taken from the kitchen along with Drusilla's water bottle. Pathetic, but it was the best I could do. My gloves were, miraculously, still in the lower pocket and my thermal hat in the opposite one. At least my hands and ears wouldn't freeze off when I crossed the mountains.

A knock at the door.

A pang of fear ran through me. I swallowed hard. Surely nobody knew what I was about to do?

Again.

'Yes?' I tried to keep my voice even.

'A package from the first consul.'

Merda.

'I'm in the bathroom. Please leave it on the table.'

I grabbed my boots and scuttled into the bathroom where I ran the taps and tore off my outer jacket, trousers and shirt. Humming a little tune, I locked the door shut, but held on to the handle. My room door clicked open, a rustle as something was deposited on a surface, presumably the table, then I heard the door open and close and the latch click. I counted a good minute. It was the oldest trick in the book – pretend to leave, and wait for your quarry to emerge. I unlocked the bathroom door and poked my head around it.

'Hello?'

No answer. I waited another minute, then turned off the taps and came into the room, wearing the dressing gown from the back of the bathroom door. There was a small box on the table. Inside was one of Severina's small tiaras, with a note, *Wear this tomorrow evening.* I picked up the gold piece. It was small, quite old, set with cabochon rubies and sapphires. How dared he? It belonged to Silvia by rights, certainly not me. Well, I'd take it for her. I scooped it out of the box, folded it along the two hinges and stuffed it in the inside zipped map pocket of my jacket.

Back in the bathroom, I scrambled into my clothes and boots. I lifted the edge of the curtain just enough to see down to the courtyard. The sun had fled below the horizon, leaving red and orange streaks. I slid the sash window up. Five minutes to get to the ground before the floodlights came on.

On the outside sill, I pulled the window closed behind me. The ledge to the top of the portico was about twenty centimetres wide, plenty of width for me to shuffle along, if I was careful. But I hadn't climbed the face of a building for years, so I went a few centimetres at a time. Agonisingly slowly. I sweated at every step.

Half a metre from the portico, the floodlights burst into vibrant orange life. If anybody looked up, they'd see my figure outlined against the pale stone. If I moved, it would catch a guard's eye. If I didn't, I'd be prey caught in cross hairs and picked off instantly. Very slowly, I crouched down, stretched out my hand, grabbed the edge of the parapet and rolled over the top.

Lying there, the sweat poured off me. It wasn't the effort on a cool night; it was fear. I took several deep breaths to slow my heart down again. Gods, I was too old for this. After a couple of minutes, I pulled myself together and shuffled across the portico roof, using my elbows to propel me until I reached the far side. I slid my hand over the back edge and found the top of the vertical recess. A quick silent prayer of thanks to Mercury, then I turned over onto my stomach and slithered over the edge of the recess feet first. My right foot found the highest foothold. Then my left foot the next. I was on the ground within moments, my back pressed against the wall, my heart thudding against my ribs with fear, relief and this time, excitement.

I was out.

My fallback plan was to dodge through the car park at the side of the palace using the cars as cover then a dash for the side gate that led to the wooded slope down to the city park. After that, I would take it as I found it. Perhaps the gate Calavia and I had used to get through the old city wall would still be unlocked. If not, there were other ways. Then it was the eighty-kilometre hike to the mountains. I would have to lie low in the daytime and steal food, then march at night. Cars would have no petrol now, but maybe I could steal a horse from some stables or one of the farms. But whatever I did, I'd have to run the first few hours until the damn tag was out of range. And keep moving. If they used portable base units they'd find me as soon as I came within range. But any risk was better than the existence I had at the moment.

I peeped round the corner of the recess. Nobody. Then I heard a car approaching. I snapped back. It stopped at the portico. I heard a challenge from the nats guards, only metres away from me, but separated by thick sandstone. I couldn't hear the words or distinguish the voices. The car passed through and drove round my side of the portico. The engine cut, then I heard footsteps going in the direction of the back entrance. Some functionary or other, or one of those nats bastards.

After a couple of minutes to let the guards relax, I eased my way out of the protective recess and prepared to launch myself towards the parked cars. I had ten metres to cross in the open. The next second I was thrust back against the wall. A hand clamped across my mouth.

'Quiet!' a voice hissed.

My heart hammering, I brought my hand up to attack my assailant.

'Stop, Aurelia. It's me.'

Quintus.

'Jupiter's balls! What the hell?'

'Listen.' I could hear his breaths coming in short gasps. Had he been running or was it fear? 'I've brought my car to get you out.'

'You *did* get my message? How—'

'I'll explain more later. Wait here. I'll draw up and get out as if to check something in the boot. You jump in the back, in the seat well, and cover yourself in the blanket. Got it?'

I nodded. He sidled off towards the back entrance. A minute later, I spotted him walking with a file briefcase towards his car. He threw it in the boot, got in and started his car. He stopped with the car's rear door exactly by the back of the portico. He got out, opened the rear door, bent inside as if looking for something, left the door open, then opened up the boot lid. He looked for all the world like a man who was sure he had something, but couldn't remember where he'd left it. I crept forward, then jumped in, stretched out behind the front seats and pulled the dark plaid blanket over me. The boot lid slammed down, the back door thumped home and we were moving.

Quintus slowed down at the palace gates.

'Evening, sir,' a voice came, presumably from the guard.

I didn't hear a reply from Quintus, just the sound of the engine accelerating. I tried to keep track of where we were as Quintus drove through the town, but I was so elated by escaping that I lost my concentration for a few moments.

'Just going through the city gate,' Quintus said as if he was talking about the games results. We stopped. I held my breath. Then the bloody tag on my wristband flashed red and buzzed. I thrust my hand down the front of my jacket, praying the engine noise would drown it. Quintus coughed loudly.

'Going far, sir?'

'Just to an old friend's for the evening.'

'Don't forget the curfew's at nine.'

'So my brother keeps reminding me,' Quintus replied, sharply.

'Yes, of course, sir. Have a safe trip.'

Quintus didn't reply. A barrier squeaked, and the car moved forward.

I let my breath out in a sob.

'Steady, Aurelia. Stay where you are.'

'The tag's alarmed.'

'Damn, I never thought to bring anything to cut those things off.'

'You won't. They're forged steel, heat sealed.' I snorted. 'Don't think I haven't tried.'

'Hold on, then,' he said, 'I'm going to go a little faster.'

I was bumped up and down and thrown around corners as if I were a sack of cabbages on the way to market as Quintus drove like a maniac. Thirty minutes later, the red light had petered out.

'Right, I've driven west on the Aquae Caesaris road. That should confuse the issue. Now we have to get across to the road north. You know yourself how narrow these lanes are and how windy they get as we get near the foothills. I suggest you hitch yourself up onto the back seat and try to rest.'

'Quintus, how did you know I would be just by the portico?'

'The palace housekeeper phoned my steward with a strange message about a girl called Cloelia who could meet her lover tonight after all. My steward thought she was raving and remarked that it must be getting very difficult at the palace if the housekeeper was losing it that much. I knew instantly it was you and exactly where you'd be from that stupid game we played as children.'

I allowed myself a little smile. When I'd given Drusilla that message to convey to Quintus, I'd prayed it would get through. I'd never expected him to turn up with a car.

34

I woke with a jolt. The vehicle had stopped.

'What?' I rubbed my stiff neck. Quintus's car wasn't very big and I'd been lying awkwardly. I blinked and sat up. The only light came from the dashboard backlights. Quintus had turned the headlights off.

'We're nearly at Driscia. I'm sorry, but I'm going to have to drop you off here if I'm going to get back to the city before the curfew.'

Driscia. The last real settlement before the mountain passes.

'Quintus, that's marvellous. I'm so grateful.' I grabbed his hand and pressed it hard.

'Steady.' But I could see the smile, even in the dim light. He handed me a walking stick and rucksack with a sleeping bag rolled up and strapped on at the base. 'There's a survival pack inside and more water. It's going to be an uncomfortable journey, but you should make it.' He turned and looked me full in the face. 'You must get across the border, Aurelia, and rally the opposition. You have all the contacts and possibly the resources. And you must not let yourself be taken again. I'll do my best here and as long as Caius doesn't sling me in prison, I should be able to help. Go with Juno.' He leant over and kissed my cheek.

On the track skirting Driscia in the chill of the night, I comforted myself with the thought that in eight hours I would be over the frontier. And that was allowing for climbing up through the mountains and taking rest periods. I had freed myself from Caius, at least physically. As I marched along a field boundary on the north side of the town, I understood what the expression 'with a song in my heart' meant.

I walked on for nearly three hours; only the occasional wild animal calls, owls hooting and my boots on the track broke the silence of the night. My breath plumed, but that was the only sign of my presence as I climbed steadily in this beautiful alpine upland. I paused for a five-minute break. Frost had formed on the meadows and the moonlight transformed them into silver carpets. Soon, I would be scrambling through the pine trees up through the scree line, then higher into the mountains and the pure sharp air towards freedom.

Then the bloody tag buzzed. A feeble sound, more like a creak than a hard buzz. The red light glimmered and faltered. I tried bashing the unit against a rock, the sound echoing mercilessly, but all I did was rip the skin on my wrist. Pluto take it and hurl it to the depth of Tartarus. I couldn't fail now. I leapt up and ran along the track and aimed for the woods. Only distance was my friend. Crouching behind an old stone wall, I stopped for a few breaths. The tag glimmered again, then burst into bright red like some devil's eye and emitted a harsh tone.

They were near, within metres, with a portable tracker.

I could see no one. Fear stabbed my stomach. And I began to shake. They couldn't take me back. I'd rather die. And those who had helped me would suffer as well. I crouched where I was and buried my wrist under my armpit, praying it was a fault in the unit.

Nothing, I could hear nothing; no vehicle, no footsteps, but no wildlife either. Where in Hades were they? If I stayed here, they'd be sure to pinpoint me. If I ran for the trees, that would confuse them. I stood, took a last look round. I drew a long breath and sprinted full pelt for the treeline, zigzagging across the empty space. The dark space of the pine trees engulfed me and, sure I was invisible from the edge, I stopped. I rested against the rough trunk of a pine, the flat of my hands on the broken bark bracing my weight. I gasped at the freezing air as my lungs dragged it in and bent over, coughing it out. My heart hammered against my ribcage. After a few moments, I stood upright.

A chorus of clicks as weapons were cocked. Numb with shock as black figures surrounded me, rifles aimed at my head.

'Stay completely still.'

I knew that voice. It couldn't be. He stepped forward from the mass of the figures. Callixtus, my former security chief who had betrayed me at the Castra Lucilla farm, whom I'd thrown out, who was a Roman Nationalist. He took a step forward, but stayed out of reach of my hands.

'Our orders are to take you alive, but we're authorised to terminate you if necessary. I know what you are and what you can do, so I'm fully prepared to do that.' His voice was hard, but his face harder, more lined than before, ridged almost in the harsh light of the torches. He stood rock still. The only sounds were an owl call and feet shuffling. I stared at him, pleading with my eyes. For just a few moments, his face softened and I saw that grave, gentle face that I'd known for years. Then he blinked and the hard lines returned. He stretched out his hands, clicked his fingers and one of his group handed him a set of handcuffs. Oh gods, not again. I brought my hands to my sides, and flexed my feet ready to make a run. Two of the group lurched toward me. Gods, they were keyed up, over nervous. Not regular troops.

'Stop,' he shouted. We all froze. 'You two, back.' They snapped back into their circle immediately. 'You.' He stabbed his finger at me. 'I won't tell you again. Now hold out your wrists.'

I swallowed hard. Surely I couldn't give in this meekly? There were five of them plus Callixtus. Three I might manage, but the other three would shoot me before I got five metres. But better dead than back at Caius's mercy.

The pine trees behind them were black, dense. Perhaps there were reinforcements. I took a slow breath in through my teeth, keeping my shoulders relaxed. I shrugged and rotated my arms backwards as if readying myself for the inevitable. As Callixtus relaxed slightly, I spun round the back of the tree and launched myself into the darkness.

Shouts followed me, whistle shrieks and curses. My rucksack thumped into my back with every step. I couldn't abandon it – I'd never make it through the mountains without it. I wove in and out of the trees, leaping over roots, dodging shrubs. No sounds of pursuit. Then the tag buzzed and glinted. Hades. With that bloody thing, I was sunk. I pushed myself harder. Panting short breaths as I pounded along. Cold searing my throat as I dragged air in. The tag light flickered and went out. Mercury, my friend. On, on up to the scree bank, into the gap to the pass to the border.

My legs started wobbling, sweat ran down my neck and between my breasts, but I had to keep going. I reached the edge of the treeline, just below the track through the scree. I glanced up. It was a hell of a climb. Any false step and I could rick or break my ankle. And I'd be exposed to Callixtus's thugs, even on this dark night. I took a deep breath and, almost reluctantly, took the first step out of the shelter of the upper treeline.

I cried out as the bolt of white heat seared my face. Stumbled and crumpled onto the rocks. Tears ran down my face from the shock and I gasped for breath. I pinched my lips together and fumbled for my handkerchief to press on my face. I shook it open after a moment and tied it round my jaw like a field bandage. Within moments it started throbbing. Pain was too simple a word. But I had to get up. I rolled onto my hands and knees, panned around, but I couldn't see anybody. Those bastards were hiding in the trees, but I had no option.

I tucked my feet under and sprang up and to the left in one movement. Another shot, right of me. Every twenty steps I seized a small rock and lobbed it in a different direction from the previous one. I strained to go faster, but I couldn't make my legs work any harder. Sour fumes rose from my throat and I felt dizzy. I bent my head and forced myself on.

When I looked up five minutes later, Callixtus stood there alone, breathing hard, but blocking the path.

'Give up. You are never going to make it through those mountains losing blood like that.'

'I'll take my chances. I'd rather die than go back.'

'Don't be ridiculous. You need medical help now. I have to arrest you and you'll be imprisoned for a while, but if you submit, you'll be allowed to live.'

I laughed. Was it hysteria or laughing at him for his naivety? My head and neck were aching now and I swayed, then staggered to one side. I just held my balance.

'Callixtus, for pity's sake,' I gasped. 'Please don't give me up to him.' My voice was scarcely a croak. This man who had assured my family's security for many years, yet betrayed me, was about to hand me over to my enemy who never forgave.

'I must,' he said. 'It's a different world now and you have become a terrorist threatening it. You have to be stopped.'

He strode towards me, the handcuffs in his left hand, and grabbed my right wrist. I had no energy left to pull away. My sleeve fell back. The steel bracelet and mesh tag band reflected moonlight.

'What's that?' he asked.

'What do you mean? It's your bloody tag. You know, the thing that's trapped me here barely two kilometres from my freedom.'

'I know perfectly well what a tag looks like. No, that steel bracelet.' He frowned at me, and looked puzzled.

'You really don't know? That's my slave ring that marks me as Caius Tellus's property.'

'You're lying.'

'Look inside the ring. You'll find his name. Didn't you know your wonderful first consul is forcibly contracting free citizens?' I looked at him, willing him to look directly at me, but he couldn't meet my eyes. 'His thugs are abusing and flogging our people.'

'Now you *are* lying.'

'Did you ever know me do that when you worked for me?'

He didn't answer.

'And don't think being a fellow patrician is any protection,' I said. 'He raped me, Callixtus.' I choked at the memory. My heart thudded while Callixtus hesitated. After five seconds, I began to hope I'd won. After ten, that hope grew. I straightened up, ready to take a first step away from him.

A whistle blast tore the air.

'You're a criminal and my job is to detain you,' he said in a mechanical voice.

Cold despair washed through me. I struggled in his grip, but I was too exhausted to break away. He snapped the handcuffs on. He pushed me in front of him back through the trees. My cheek was so painful, my eye watered and I couldn't see properly, so I stumbled several times. In the end, he grasped my arm and half dragged me back to the lower edge of the treeline.

His men were there, grouped in a circle, talking and smoking. They stopped one by one as they saw us. Callixtus dumped me on my bottom by the base of a tree and ordered one of them to tie me to it. He crouched down and removed my makeshift bandage none too gently and I felt warm blood dribble down my cheek. He pressed a freezing cold pad against my skin, which made me gasp, but it numbed the pain.

As he stood up, I heard the sound of a helicopter. Were they so anxious to transport me back to the city that quickly? The throbbing mechanical roar intensified and then cut. I presumed it had landed. Five minutes later, Caius strode into the clearing.

35

Dressed in black belted jacket and trousers, polished riding boots, revolver at his waist and a red armband on his left upper arm with the Nationalists' symbolic *fasces* and a mailed fist, he looked every inch the dark power he was. Flanked by two assistants dressed in the same way, he strolled over to Callixtus.

'My congratulations, Section Leader, for a job well done. You must feel satisfaction in reversing the fortune of one who treated you so badly.'

'Sir. I was happy to carry out my duty.'

Caius patted him on his shoulder and gave him one of his dazzling smiles. 'A very proper answer.' Then he looked down at me. 'Get her up.'

One of Callixtus's men untied me from the tree and another one pulled me to my feet. Caius stared at me with hard eyes. I looked straight back at him. He flicked his fingers backwards and his henchmen, Callixtus and his men melted into the background.

'What is this?' He ran his fingertip just under the wound on my cheek. I winced.

'One of your men took a shot at me.'

'And missed? How careless of him.'

I shrugged. My stomach was turning into knots, but I'd be damned to Tartarus if I showed how frightened I was. Then he struck my wounded cheek hard with the flat of his hand. An instant of numbness. I couldn't breathe, then I choked against the pain flooding my face. I bent over and staggered with the shock. But I kept my balance. I brought my manacled hands up to wipe away the tears, blood and snot. When I looked at him, his face was impassive.

'You bastard.'

'A tiny taste of what is coming. You've disappointed me, Aurelia. I know you are wayward, rebellious even, but I mistakenly thought you were learning to adapt.' He sighed. 'I should have thrown you in Truscium at the beginning.'

Gods, the maximum security prison in the mountains for the most vicious hardened criminals. If you survived the prison system, working in the silver mines behind it would kill you.

'I gave in to my weakness for you,' he said. 'Even the exceptional privileges I granted you couldn't soften your stubbornness. Evidently, I was expecting too much.'

'Privileges? Running around as your menial, humiliated before my peers and forced to sleep with you?' I looked down, full of shame. 'You kept me as your slave.'

'I gave you my protection and the chance to find a life in the new Roma Nova. I would have loved you, you know.'

His face softened and his eyes shone. He actually believed that.

'But you wanted to dominate me – that's not love.'

'You needed to be controlled first.'

'No, love is given freely, and unreservedly.'

'Sentimental nonsense.' He glanced away, then back, fire in his eyes. 'You've thrown everything I offered back in my face.'

'Can't you see that living like that would be a sham? I would be a collaborator in my own and everybody else's eyes.'

'You exaggerate. You are supposed to be intelligent, but like all women, you allow emotion to cloud your judgement.'

'Caius, I—'

'Enough.' The neutral expression returned. 'You are not worthy of any further effort on my part. I don't wish to hear any excuses or explanations. You've rejected me for the last time. You are outside now, Aurelia. You will disappear into one of the new work colonies for recalcitrants. The regime is strict, but at least you will contribute in some way before you die.'

'I would rather you killed me now and got it over with.'

'Undoubtedly, but that's a privilege I'm not inclined to grant you.'

Work colonies – slave camps, he meant. I'd read the reports from the Russian gulags eons ago when I'd been foreign minister. Had he brought such monstrous things to Roma Nova? People condemned to a desperate, feral life with exhaustion and a starving death?

I had to break his shell and enrage him so he'd kill me quickly.

'You know I'll stir up rebellion there. There'll be plenty of people prepared to join me. I'll fight you with every cell in my body.'

'You may think differently when you are whipped back into your hut every night or one of your tentmates is taken out and hanged every time you blink in an insubordinate way.'

I shivered inside.

'Oh, I forgot,' I countered, 'you use the coward's way, bullying people by attacking the weak. How pathetic.'

His face tightened, his mouth becoming a straight, grim line.

'You raped me but you never touched me, not the real me. You never possessed me, nor will you in any way you like to think of.'

He took a step forward, his hand raised.

'Yes, go on, hit me again. I can't defend myself. Hitting women is one of your new regime's rules, is it?'

'You really are a first-class bitch.'

'No, I'm a strong woman, Caius, and you can't stand that, can you?'

His eyes narrowed and his face tensed in anger. I thought he was going to explode. A crackle from one of his sidekicks' radios broke the silence. The assistant murmured into the handset, then advanced to Caius and whispered something into his ear. Caius frowned, then nodded.

'Section Leader,' Caius called, and Callixtus emerged from the shadows and brought himself to attention at Caius's side. 'You and a driver are seconded for special duty. Dismiss your other men and bring your vehicle here.'

Callixtus returned within a minute, just as the helicopter engine started. I could hear the whump-whump of the blades turning.

'I don't have time to deal with this, Aurelia, so I've changed my plans for you. I'm going to grant your dearest wish.' He waved his fingers at Callixtus. 'This man is going to take you across the border and drop you there. But you'll be dead. Goodbye.'

He raised his revolver. His hand seemed to tremble, but perhaps it was the poor light. I blinked ready for the blow. He fired three shots at point-blank range. The bullets slammed into my chest and leg. I dropped like a stone.

No breath.

Black.

Pain. Tight. Water on my lips. Give me more.

'*Domina.*' A hiss in my ear.

Fire in my chest and leg. Sore face. Tightness.

'Don't speak or make any noise.'

Cold cloth on my face.

'Don't move,' the voice hissed. 'You're supposed to be dead.'

Jolting. We were travelling in a vehicle.

'I'm covering you with a blanket. Play dead.'

We stopped.

'Delivery for a colleague in Vienna,' a voice in the front of the vehicle said. 'For the legation.'

'Are you carrying any weapons?' A New Austrian-accented voice.

'Of course not, Officer.'

'We'll have to look in the back.'

'No, sorry, sealed diplomatic baggage. Here's my authorisation.'

'Humph, I'll have to check with my captain.'

Footsteps. Come back. Save me. I tried to move, but pain shot through my chest and rippled through my body. Something, somebody pushed me back and I passed out.

I was jolted awake. I nearly screamed with the pain, but my mouth was taped shut. Pitch black, hot, something covering my face.

'Lie still,' the same voice whispered. 'I hope you can hear me. You were shot. The first consul said to leave you to bleed to death or finish you off if you were still alive by the time we got here. We're supposed to dump you in the public park in Vienna. I've stopped the bleeding, but I can't do any more or my driver will get suspicious.'

Callixtus.

'He was wrong to treat you like that. I… I didn't know about the slave thing. I'll get you to safety. Hang on, if you can.' He pressed my hand. I heard clambering noises, then his voice came from the front.

'Stop at this garage, Sergius. I want some ciggies.'

'Cheaper, eh?'

'This near the border, they should still take *solidi*. In Vienna, no chance. Better get petrolled up as well.'

I closed my eyes and tried to breathe slowly and quietly; not easy through a blocked nose. But without the engine noise masking my snuffling, it would be lethal if Callixtus's man heard me. He opened the vehicle passenger door and I heard the clatter of a petrol pump nozzle against the side of the van. I breathed out heavily against the hum of the pump filling the tank.

'Here,' Callixtus's voice at the front, 'I got us some drinks as well and some tabs for my headache.'

'Headache?'

'Chasing that silly bitch at full speed after a few beers with the lads. Not recommended.'

The driver laughed.

'Think I'll lie down in the back for a kip,' Callixtus said. 'Wake me up when we get near.'

He peeled back the tape across my mouth and gave me water. I couldn't drink enough, but he only let me take small sips at a time. He pressed something on my tongue. Ugh. Bitter.

'Painkillers.' He tilted my head up, and slopped more water into my mouth. I had to swallow or drown. But I tensed against the pain that would follow such a muscle movement. Callixtus grabbed my jaw and pulled my chin up as if I were a reluctant cat. I swallowed, and he let out a loud yawn to cover my sob as pain spasmed through my diaphragm. My reward was more water.

. . .

Next time we stopped, I was awake. The van doors opened with a crash. I took a deep breath just in time before the blanket was pulled off me. Faint daylight seeped in through my eyelids, so it was early morning. Hands on my ankles. Then they heaved my body. Juno knows how I stayed quiet against the agony that shot through me.

'Half a tick,' the driver said, 'let's have those handcuffs off. They're official issue. Some shiny arse will deduct the cost off our wages if we don't take them back.'

Callixtus laughed. 'Good thinking. You're brighter than you look, Sergius.' As the metal slid off my wrists, I let my arms flop away. From the sound level of their banter, they must have then turned away from the van doors. I opened my eyelids a millimetre and could see thick green bushes and trees. Sergius pushed into them.

Callixtus sat on the back edge of the van floor and lit up one of his newly acquired cigarettes. He blew out a cloud of smoke, stood up and looked in the direction Sergius had gone.

'We're dumping you here,' he muttered. 'For Mars' sake, don't make a sound. Act dead.'

'Who you talking to, Callixtus?' Sergius's voice. Just by the van. How?

'Gods, Sergius, don't bloody creep up on me like that, you stupid sod,' Callixtus said. 'You'll get yourself killed. And I wasn't talking to anybody.'

'Yeah? Well, it sounded like it to me.'

'Let's get on with it so we can get back home.'

'Squeamish?'

'Not one of my favourite jobs.'

''Spect there'll be more like it.'

'I'm taller,' Callixtus said. 'Help me heave her onto my shoulder and make sure nobody's nosing around.'

'At half-six in the morning? You're kidding.'

'Do it.'

'Keep your hair on.'

Sergius heaved on my legs and next second, I was upside down on Callixtus's shoulder, trying to hang like a rag doll. My head swam as I swung to and fro while Callixtus walked into the wood. He dropped me down on the earth none too gently and nudged me onto my side with his foot. I was in such agony, it became numbness.

'Let's go,' Callixtus said. 'We don't want any dog-walkers finding us.'

I watched them retreat, then Sergius suddenly turned and sprinted back. He thrust his hand under my jacket and swore. He stared at me, horror in his eyes.

'She's still warm.'

Still crouching over me, he pulled his handgun out and leapt up. I groaned as loudly as I could to warn Callixtus. But he had already pulled his own pistol out, complete with suppressor, and was aiming it at Sergius's face.

'You knew she was still alive,' Sergius shrieked at Callixtus. 'What's your game? She your tart or something?'

'You wouldn't understand if I tried to explain,' Callixtus said. His voice sounded tired as well as impatient.

'Well, I'll finish the job if you won't.' Sergius spun round towards me and stood over me, his pistol a metre away. His face was distorted, full of hate. I couldn't move. Had I finally come to my end in a damp New Austrian park? The next second, he grunted and fell across my legs. Callixtus kicked him off me. And dropped to his knees.

'Are you all right?'

'Wonderful,' I croaked. I searched his face. 'Why, Callixtus?' I gasped. 'You gave me to Caius. Going to get a reward. Gods. Hot.'

'Keep still. Help is on the way. I called an ambulance from the garage we stopped at.'

'Why? Tell me.'

'When the first consul thumped you on the face, on your wound, I thought that was harsh, but possibly justified. But I didn't know he'd made you a household slave. Is that really happening in the city?'

He pleaded with me for it not to be true. I nodded my head.

'Then he mentioned work camps. That sounded like those hell-holes in Russia. He or his commanders never said anything to us in briefings or speeches. We were all going to have jobs, good ones, and respect.'

He looked away.

'I know you think I let you down,' he continued in a subdued voice. 'But I thought he made a lot of sense.'

I tried to stretch my hand out to him but my muscles wouldn't work.

'I'll stay here and give myself up to the New Austrians for killing Sergius.'

'Self-defence,' I mumbled. 'I'll testify. That turd – not worth it.' I glanced over at Sergius's body. It was moving. His hand grasped his pistol and raised it at Callixtus's back.

'C'llixtus! Behind you,' I cried. I heard the shot, then passed out.

36

———

The smell told me I was in a hospital. Elysium, or even Tartarus, wouldn't smell so antiseptic, crisp and sour. Humming and beeping. I was half-propped up on pillows. I moved my head, which made my chest hurt, so I panned around with my eyes. A notice in Germanic about washing hands, the white melamine top of a bed table reaching across the white coverlet, a folded screen. In an easy chair in the corner, dozing, was Numerus, former Senior Centurion Numerus, my comrade-in-arms. Now I knew I was safe. The tears rolled down my face in sheer relief. Ah, my cheek stung.

I watched him for a few minutes. The bruising I'd seen on his face had disappeared; his mouth was slightly open as he leaned against the back of the chair. The door opened and a nursing sister bustled in. Numerus jerked awake. I smiled at him.

'*Salve*, Numerus,' I said. It came out more as a whisper. He stared at me, then leapt up and grabbed my hand. The nurse tutted, but neither he nor I cared.

'Ten minutes only,' the nurse said and left us.

Numerus's eyes shone and then dimmed. He let my hand drop.

'Welcome back,' he said, formally.

'Back? Hardly arrived here last time before I went. Silvia, Volusenia – are they safe? Here?'

'Yes, four days after you all left to find them. They had a hell of a time, but made it in one piece.'

I closed my eyes for a few moments.

'Calavia, Atrius? Base party at Castra Lucilla?'

'Yes, all here.'

'Thank the gods.'

'We thought you were all dead, then Atrius and Lieutenant Calavia turned up and confirmed you were alive, but—' He stopped and looked away.

I took some shallow breaths and waited. He looked down at the floor and said nothing. What was wrong? We were all safe back. Despite the grim circumstances, surely it was something to celebrate?

'What day is it?' I said to break the silence.

'The twenty-third of October. You were in a bad way when they brought you in, so they put you under for a week. The New Austrian police want to question you – three bodies in a public park, one of them female and raving in Latin, is a bit much for them.'

'Did the men with me survive?'

He shook his head.

'One of them wanted to finish me off. The other saved my life.'

'Finish you off? Who shot you, then?'

'Caius Tellus. The bastard. He told them to let me bleed to death.' I turned my head away.

'He shot you? But everybody says you were under his protection.'

'What in Hades do you mean?'

Now he brought his eyes up and searched my face.

'Calavia and Atrius said you were physically intimate with Tellus, his lover.'

'No!' I shrieked, then coughed. Pure agony.

'That's what they say it looked like. Tellus told them you'd decided to stay in Roma Nova and rule with him.'

'Gods, how can they believe that?

'*I* know what a manipulative bastard he is and I know you. But one of the palace staff has escaped and confirmed you were sleeping with him.' He stared at me, his grey eyes like granite, and waited.

I was so shocked, I couldn't speak.

'I've known you a long time, Aurelia Mitela,' he spoke at last. 'I trust your word and know you would never willingly have sex with Tellus or even let him touch you. But the exiles are hurting. They've lost their homes, contact with their families, their property. They're destitute, most of them. Atrius has recovered physically, but inside he's raging. He holds you personally responsible for his ill-treatment.'

'Caius Tellus didn't beat me physically, except for a few slaps, but he humiliated and assaulted me mentally and emotionally in every way he could.' I looked away, attempting to keep a lid on the anger burning inside me.

'So did you give in to him?' His voice was hard, implacable.

'He raped me, Numerus,' I whispered.

'Did you fight him as hard as you could?'

'He threatened Calavia, Atrius, even Marina far away in the EUS if I didn't comply.' The warmth rose up my neck and into my face. I looked away. What else could I say? My head was swimming and tears ready to escape.

Numerus stood abruptly. He threw me a look of deep contempt, turned his back and marched out.

The nurse found me crouched in bed like an unborn child. I was pain. I felt her hand touch my forehead and heard several clicks of the drip switch before a sensation of heaviness pushed me into unconsciousness.

When I woke next, my head was foggy inside and it took a few moments to remember where I was. The face of a nurse with a starched cap perched on a head of grey-blond curls hovered over me.

'That's the last Roma Novan that comes and visits you if that's what they do to you.' Her face was hard, set like concrete.

'No, you don't understand,' I said. 'It was just a disagreement.'

She raised an eyebrow. 'He left these for you.'

Two letters with EUS stamps. From Marina and William. I tore the envelopes open and devoured the contents; they'd been so worried, but Numerus had written them care of William's company with news of my survival.

The New Austrian police came to take my statement. They were courteous, but extremely curious. I told them I was a refugee and the first consul's political troops had shot me trying to escape the repressive new regime. I asked for asylum and was surprised to receive forms to complete within days. Perhaps giving my cousin David Soane, who ran Soanes Bank in Vienna, and the New Austrian foreign minister, whom I knew on first-name terms, as referees helped.

I stayed in the hospital for two weeks and was then transferred to a convalescent home. When I asked who was paying for it, they wouldn't say; just an anonymous donor, the administrator said. I was too tired to argue with him. Mercifully, the bullets had missed anything vital, and Callixtus's first aid had stopped me bleeding to death. The tiara I'd stuffed in my top jacket pocket for Silvia was ruined, but it had saved my life. One of the ancient stones was smashed along with the hinges, but folded into three, it had deflected the fatal bullet. When he came to visit me, I asked David Soane to have it scrapped for the gold and remaining gemstones and send the proceeds to the exiles. He admitted on his second visit that he was funding my healthcare.

But I was frustrated by how slowly my recovery was going. I tried hard not to think about everything that had happened to me in Roma Nova, especially about my surrender to Caius, and the accusations in Numerus's eyes, but when I woke up every morning weeping, the doctor insisted I talked to a therapist.

'You are not progressing, Frau Gräfin Mitela. Unless you resolve what is in your head, your body will not heal itself.'

Just because Vienna was the headquarters of the famous Freud Centre, every doctor here thought he was a psychologist. But I couldn't voice how much I despised myself. Perhaps the other Roma Novans here felt the same about me, which was why none of them had visited me, not even Quirinia, one of my oldest friends. I wrote to Silvia, but received no reply. I was wrapping myself in a cocoon of boredom and despair and I couldn't decide whether I was happy or unhappy about it. In reality, I didn't care.

I was returning from a gruelling physiotherapy session in the third week and was almost asleep as a porter rolled my wheelchair back to my room. The sound of arguing voices roused me and as we came round the corner into my corridor, I recognised the tall figure leaning over the ward sister. He was gesticulating, swinging a set of car keys from his index finger. He wasn't using any of his charm, but was angry and frustrated.

'Miklós! Oh, gods, Miklós!'

He spun round, stared for an instant, then ran to me. He threw himself on his knees, grabbed my hands and laid his head in my lap.

'Aurelia.'

I stroked the beautiful curls on his head. I leant back and let out a deep sigh. After a minute, he looked up and wiped my tears away with his thumbs. He stood and took the wheelchair handles, edging the porter aside. He wheeled me to my room and closed the door. He sat close and I held his sinewy tanned hand and searched his face. The same strong cheekbones, the generous mouth, but now an angry expression.

'They wouldn't tell me where you were. That Calavia woman had me thrown out of the house the day she returned. She looked at me with such scorn in her eyes. She said you weren't coming back, you'd settled in Roma Nova with Tellus. I didn't believe her and after she had me escorted off the premises, I hammered on the door, but nobody answered. I went back the next day, but they wouldn't let me in to talk to anybody. In the end, I waited until the old centurion, Numerus, came out and collared him.'

'Numerus said nothing when he visited me in hospital. None of the others has come near me. Are they waiting for me to recover?'

He shrugged. 'You're better off without them. Old Numerus was polite, but wouldn't say anything, even when I bought him drink after drink.'

'He always had hollow legs.' I smiled.

'I went back to Roma Nova in the end.'

I dropped his hand and grasped my throat.

'Oh, gods, no! I told you not to!'

'I'm sorry I broke my promise, but did you expect me to sit in Vienna and do nothing?'

'How? Did you go over the mountains?'

He laughed – that rich, deep, incredibly sexy laugh. 'You don't expect me to tell you my trade secrets.'

I flicked my fingers at him and he caught them and kissed the back of my hand. A soft electric tingle flowed out of my hand up my arm. He looked up at me through his long eyelashes and I caught my breath. If ever there was a reason to live it was here in front of me.

'I stayed with one of my trading associates—'

'Your smuggling friends, you mean!'

'No, she's just a middlewoman.' He looked down, his face serious now. 'She's always had to work under the radar. She'll just have to be even more careful than usual.'

He said nothing for a few moments.

'I saw the *Acta Diurna* where you were named as Tellus's companion. I knew it couldn't be true. I just knew.' He pressed my hand, then almost squashed it in his.

'I was trying to protect Calavia and Atrius and get them released. Then he threatened Marina. I had to comply, I—'

'Stop. You have nothing to apologise for.'

'Miklós, I surrendered to him.'

'No, you survived.' He looked away, then back. 'Sometimes, we have to do undignified or even dishonourable things for the best reasons. We can only make the choices available to us at the time.' He stroked my cheek just below my eye. 'I see the real Aurelia in there. A little bruised, perhaps, hurt and angry, but it's still you.'

I held my arms out and he bent down and gently circled my body with his.

'Thank you,' I whispered. 'Thank you for believing in me.'

I left the convalescent home a week later. Miklós drove me through the wet streets to a suburban house, whitewashed walls and grey slate roof surrounded by overgrown shrubs and trees. Black metal gates with pointed finials guarded the front entrance. He switched off the engine and we sat in the car waiting for the rain shower to finish.

'I've bought this house with my share from my father's farm,' he said, looking straight ahead through the windscreen covered in breaking rivulets of rain. 'It needs some work, but nothing I can't do. I know you'll want to think about Roma Nova again one day. It's in your blood. But for now it's a home we can share.'

'Everything I've known and loved has gone, except you,' I said. 'I love my country and its people, and I will never stop being a Roma Novan in my heart and soul. But now I need to heal.'

He folded me in his arms and I knew I was home.

The story continues in RETALIO…

WOULD YOU LEAVE A REVIEW?

I hope you enjoyed INSURRECTIO, the danger, adventures and passions.

If you did, I'd really appreciate it if you would write a few words of review on the site where you purchased this book.

Reviews will really help INSURRECTIO to feature more prominently on retailer sites and let more people into the world of Roma Nova.

Very many thanks!

HISTORICAL NOTE

What if Julius Caesar had taken notice of the warning that assassins wanted to murder him on the ides of March? Suppose Elizabeth I had married and had children? If plague hadn't rampaged through Europe in the fourteenth century? Or if Christianity had remained a Middle Eastern minor cult, or Napoleon had won at Waterloo? If we dive into an alternative timeline where history took a different turn, who knows what might have happened?

INSURRECTIO goes back to the early 1980s in an alternative Europe where the small but tough country of Roma Nova has survived since the break-up of the Roman Empire. But the early 1980s are the dark days of the beginning of the Great Rebellion when the very existence of Roma Nova is threatened by a charismatic tyrant.

While the whole idea of a society with Roman values surviving fifteen centuries is intriguing, I have dropped background history about Roma Nova into the novel only where it impacts on the story. Nobody likes a straight history lesson in the middle of a thriller! But if you are interested in finding out more about the mysterious Roma Nova, read on...

What happened in our timeline

Of course, our timeline may turn out to be somebody else's alternative one as shown in Philip K. Dick's *The Grasshopper Lies Heavy*, the story within the story in *The Man in the High Castle*. Nothing is fixed. But for the sake of convenience I will take ours as the default.

The Western Roman Empire didn't 'fall' in a cataclysmic event as often portrayed in film and television; it localised and eventually dissolved like chain mail fragmenting into separate links, giving way to rump provinces, local city states and petty kingdoms. The Eastern Roman Empire survived until the Fall of Constantinople in 1453 to the Muslim Ottoman Empire.

Some scholars think that Christianity fatally weakened the traditional Roman way of life and was a significant factor in the collapse. Emperor Constantine's personal conversion to Christianity in AD 313 was a turning point for the new religion. By late AD 394, his several times successor, Theodosius, had banned all traditional Roman religious practice, closed and destroyed temples and dismissed all priests. The sacred flame that had burned for over a thousand years in the College of Vestals was extinguished and the Vestal Virgins expelled. The Altar of Victory, said to guard the fortune of Rome, was hauled away from the Senate building and disappeared from history. The Roman senatorial families pleaded for religious tolerance, but Theodosius made any pagan practice, even dropping a pinch of incense on a family altar in a private home, into a capital offence. And his 'religious police', driven by the austere and ambitious bishop Ambrosius of Milan, became increasingly active in pursuing pagans.

The alternate Roma Nova timeline

In AD 395, three months after Theodosius's final decree banning all pagan religious activity, four hundred Romans loyal to the old gods, and so in danger of execution, trekked north out of Italy to a semi-mountainous area similar in character to modern Slovenia. Led by Senator Apulius at the head of twelve prominent families, they established a colony based initially on land owned by Apulius's Celtic father-in-law. By purchase, alliance and conquest, this grew into Roma Nova.

Norman Davies in *Vanished Kingdoms: The History of Half-Forgotten Europe* reminds us that:

> …in order to survive, newborn states need to possess a set of viable internal organs, including a functioning executive, a defence force, a revenue system and a diplomatic force. If they possess none of these things, they lack the means to sustain an autonomous existence and they perish before they can breathe and flourish.

I would add history, willpower and adaptability as essential factors. Roma Nova survived by changing its social structure; as men constantly fought to defend the new colony, women took over the social, political and economic roles, weaving new power and influence networks based on family structures. Given the unstable, dangerous times in Roma Nova's first few hundred years, daughters as well as sons put on armour and carried weapons to defend their homeland and their way of life. Fighting danger side by side with brothers and fathers changed women's roles and status forever.

The Roma Novans never allowed the incursion of monotheistic, paternalistic religions. Service to the state was valued higher than personal advantage, echoing Roman Republican virtues, and the women heading the families guarded and enhanced these values to provide a core philosophy throughout the centuries. Inheritance passed from these powerful women to their daughters and granddaughters.

Roma Nova's continued existence has been favoured by three factors: the discovery and exploitation of high-grade silver in their mountains, their efficient technology, and their robust response to any threat. Remembering their Eastern (Byzantine) cousins' defeat in the Fall of Constantinople, Roma Novan troops assisted the western nations at the Battle of Vienna in 1683 to halt the Ottoman advance into Europe. Nearly two hundred years later, they used their diplomatic skills to help forge an alliance to push Napoleon IV back across the Rhine as he attempted to expand his grandfather's empire.

Prioritising survival, Roma Nova remained neutral in the Great War of the twentieth century which lasted from 1925 to 1935. The Greater German Empire was broken up afterwards into its former small kingdoms, duchies and counties; some became republics.

Despite the legal reforms in the mid 1700s, there was little fundamental change in Roma Nova's governance. Until the late 1970s, tough female rulers drawing on centuries of experience had generally provided active, solid if traditional leadership. But a weak imperatrix without vision or desire for change in the modern age opened up the opportunity for a power hungry, amoral and charismatic leader and his populist, brutal nationalist movement in the early 1980s. *INSURRECTIO* is the story of that crisis and the parts played by Aurelia Mitela and her nemesis, Caius Tellus.

THE ROMA NOVA THRILLER SERIES

The Carina Mitela adventures

INCEPTIO

Early 21st century. Terrified after a kidnap attempt, New Yorker Karen Brown, has a harsh choice – being terminated by government enforcer Renschman or fleeing to Roma Nova, her dead mother's homeland in Europe. Founded sixteen hundred years ago by Roman exiles and ruled by women, it gives Karen safety – at a price. But Renschman follows and sets a trap she has no option but to enter.

CARINA – *A novella*

Carina Mitela is a new officer in the Praetorian Guard Special Forces. Disgraced for a disciplinary offence, she is sent out of everybody's way to bring back a traitor from the Republic of Quebec. But the conspiracy reaches into the highest levels of Roma Nova…

PERFIDITAS

Falsely accused of conspiracy, 21st century Praetorian Carina Mitela flees into the criminal underworld. Hunted by both security services and traitors she struggles to save her beloved Roma Nova as well as her own life. Who is her ally and who her enemy? But the ultimate betrayal is waiting for her.

SUCCESSIO

21st century Praetorian Carina Mitela's attempt to resolve a past family indiscretion is spiralling into a nightmare of blackmail and terror. Convinced her beloved husband has deserted her and her children, and with her enemy holding a gun to the imperial heir's head, Carina has to make the hardest decision of her life.

The Aurelia Mitela adventures

AURELIA

Late 1960s. Sent to Berlin to investigate silver smuggling, former Praetorian Aurelia Mitela barely escapes a near-lethal trap. Her old enemy is at the heart of all her troubles and she pursues him back home to Roma Nova but he strikes at her most vulnerable point – her young daughter.

NEXUS – A novella

Mid 1970s. Aurelia Mitela is serving as ambassador in London. Helping a British colleague to find his missing son, Aurelia is sure he'll turn up.

But a spate of high-level killings pulls Aurelia away into a pan-European investigation and the killers threaten to terminate her life companion.

But Aurelia is a Roma Novan – they never give up…

INSURRECTIO

Early 1980s. Caius Tellus, the charismatic leader of a rising nationalist movement, threatens to destroy Roma Nova.

Aurelia Mitela, ex-Praetorian and imperial councillor, attempts to counter the growing fear and instability. But it may be too late to save Roma Nova from meltdown and herself from destruction by her lifelong enemy….

RETALIO

1980s Vienna. Aurelia Mitela chafes at enforced exile. She barely escaped from her nemesis, Caius Tellus, who grabbed power in Roma Nova.

Aurelia is determined to liberate her homeland. But Caius's manipulations have ensured that she is ostracised by her fellow exiles.

Powerless and vulnerable, she fears she will never see Roma Nova again.

————

ROMA NOVA EXTRA

A collection of short stories

Four historical and four present day and a little beyond

A young tribune is sent to a backwater in 370 AD for practising the wrong religion – his lonely sixty-fifth descendant labours in the 1980s to reconstruct her country. A Roma Novan imperial councillor attempting to stop the Norman invasion of England in 1066 – her 21st century Praetorian descendant flounders as she searches for her own happiness.

Some are love stories, some lessons learned, some resolve tensions or unrealistic visions, some are adventures. Above all, they tell of people with dilemmas and in conflict, and of their courage and effort to resolve them.